D1562242

STORIES OF THE SOUTH
OLD AND NEW

STORIES *of the* SOUTH

OLD AND NEW

EDITED BY

ADDISON HIBBARD

WITH AN INTRODUCTION, BIOGRAPHICAL NOTES, AND BIBLIOGRAPHY BY THE EDITOR

CHAPEL HILL

THE UNIVERSITY OF NORTH CAROLINA PRESS

MANUFACTURED IN THE UNITED STATES OF AMERICA

To the story writers who made possible this collection and to the many others who have written faithfully of the South

CONTENTS

INTRODUCTION

THESE stories of the old and the new South are brought together here with just one purpose: to offer in something like a logical arrangement a picture of the South, past and present, as that region has been portrayed by writers of short fiction.

In such a plan, stories of local color naturally play a large part. But the twenty-seven stories reprinted are more than local color stories. It is true that we have here the familiar mountains of North Carolina and Kentucky, the lowlands of South Carolina and Georgia, the tidewater region of Virginia, and the delta country of Louisiana; but over and above this it is believed that the stories offer some conception of the different peoples which inhabit the South, of the varying periods of history through which the section has passed, of the different attitudes of mind of these people at different epochs and in varying localities, and, finally, that the more recent stories somehow hint at a new spirit which is developing in the region. The editor is conscious of no special pleading; he has tried simply to let the story-tellers themselves unfold the picture, with its high lights and its shadows, for him. His intent has been to include stories for two reasons only: their excellence as stories and their success in speaking for one phase or another of life in the South.

Readers naturally will quibble with the editor for his inclusion of this story and his exclusion of that. So much I freely concede. In preparation for this volume I have read carefully some eleven hundred stories and scanned four or five hundred more. (The bibliographies at the close of the book will testify to some of this reading.) I freely grant that another collection, another half-dozen collections, might be brought together from this mass of material with as much success as this book can hope to attain. But the critic who condemns because certain of his favorite writers are excluded will not get my attention. This book is not designed to represent the work of the authors of the South—that sort of thing has been done before; it is planned to represent the South itself.

I regret as much as anyone the omission of certain authors. The names of James Lane Allen, Roark Bradford, James Branch Cabell, Harry Stillwell Edwards, John Fox, Jr., Joseph Hergesheimer, Mary Johnston, Edgar Valentine Smith, and Stark Young would of themselves add distinction to any volume. And there are easily thirty others who might reasonably be accorded representation here were the intent to focus on the story-tellers rather than on the region of which they have written. My objective, however, has precluded my representing the same situation, the same theme, the same class of people too many times. Too readily these stories of the South group themselves about certain set conventions; many good stories are omitted simply because they represent one or another of these conventions already illustrated by another story. The book after all can offer only a limited number of stories about the plantation gentleman, the loyal Negro slave, the mountaineer. Indeed those who object to my inclusions and exclusions are, in all sincerity, cordially invited to partake in a pleasant and profitable pastime—that of making similar anthologies of their own. My living with these stories for a year leaves me with but one regret—that I am not editing a five-foot shelf instead of a single volume. If others pick flowers for their anthologies from this same field they are more than welcome. The fences are down. The sport is pleasant.

A word should be said, too, about the sequence in

which the stories are arranged. The plan is a simple one. Loosely it is that of the chronology of the periods covered by the stories themselves. It might have been interesting to begin with Captain John Smith and the Pocahontas episode, to follow through the early travelers in the South representing each with an incident. It has seemed better, however, to await the actual beginning of the short story in America, say 1840, to pick up the thread of the South's story. Poe is excluded because Poe wrote usually of a light that was not on land or sea, in the South or elsewhere.

Stories of the South, then, opens with the work of Richard Malcolm Johnston, Augustus Baldwin Longstreet, and William Gilmore Simms, who speak of backwoods and frontier life in the middle South. Next, we drop down to Louisiana, still concerned with the pre-war settings. Then follow stories of the mountaineer, often actually contemporary in time, but dealing with a people who so frequently seem timeless that chronology itself becomes insignificant. From the mountaineer we pass to the plantation tradition—the relations between the white and black—as sketched for us by Thomas Nelson Page, Paul Laurence Dunbar, Charles W. Chesnutt, and the rest. One story only—that by Joel Chandler Harris—represents the struggle between North and South. This phase of the book brings us up sharp against the Negro himself as he was according to tradition and as he is beginning to be thought of now that the glitter of this tradition is somewhat dulled by actuality. George Madden Martin speaks out in meeting on the question of lynching. Benjamin Brawley writes briefly and simply of the tragedy confronting his race in its effort to climb out of its traditional place. Julia Peterkin drops all propaganda and looks at the black as a subject for objective artistry. The last four stories must somehow be left to speak for the modern South. Emily Clark gently satirizes a tradition; Barry Benefield frankly romanticizes an old type in a new manner; Wilbur Daniel Steele brings into sharp contrast the spirit of commercialism dominating the North and the genteel tradition of the Charleston family. And, in Paul Green's *A Tempered Fellow* we come out boldly into the cold air of realism as it is related to one little-represented aspect of life in the South—that of the white tenant farmer.

One who has recently read widely in a restricted field of literature may, perhaps, be pardoned for pointing out certain conventions. Looking back over the stories read or reread this past year I am tempted to generalize and say that ninety out of every hundred conventionalized one of three types: the Negro, the mountaineer, the planter. A reader who deliberately elbows to one side most imaginative literature and searches out that which is essentially indigenous must not, I realize, be surprised to find that certain subjects recur more frequently than others. But frequency of theme is not my objection. What cannot but strike one as weak is the similarity of treatment. The Negro, the mountaineer, the planter—these are not so often individuals, personalities, as clichés.

Take, for instance, the Negro. He perhaps is most frequently abused in short story writing. He is the butt of a few constantly recurring motivations. He is, first of all, superstitious. His religion is "conjur" (that word in itself is almost enough to convince a Northern editor that he must buy the story); when superstition fails there is always the reliable second quality—loyalty and faithfulness of a former slave to his "marster's fam'bly." And there is a third attitude,—the slapstick comedy. Recently, it is true, I think, that a few writers have dropped these set forms and looked more objectively, more carefully at individual Negroes. But they are few among hundreds. The mould is still serviceable.

How does all this traditional treatment of the black impress such an intelligent member of the Negro race as Benjamin Brawley, author of various books, student of Negro culture and art, and a professor of literature in a Southern University for Negroes? I quote from a recent statement he made to me:

> For some years about the turn of the century the Negro in American fiction was chiefly represented by the former slaves of the novels of Thomas Nelson Page and, in a more exaggerated vein by the criminals in the books of Thomas Dixon. More recently, however, and especially since the World War, there has been some shifting of ground and in a certain degree the Negro may even be said to have been the fashion. The more we look beneath the surface, however, the more do we have to wonder if portrayal has been really more faithful. All seem to have been done according to a preconceived theory or pattern, and again there has been the note of fatalism or abandon. On the one hand there have been the stories of Octavus Roy Cohen, with such a type of the flashlight Negro as Florian Slappey; and on the other *Black April* and *Scarlet Sister Mary* by Julia Peterkin, and *Rainbow Round my Shoulder* and *Wings on My Feet* by Howard W. Odum. From the sale of such books it would appear that thousands of Americans like to read of black roustabouts and dope-fiends and prostitutes. We have to suggest, however, that this side of the picture has already received more than enough attention, and that, with all of his shortcomings, the Negro is advancing in education, in the ownership of homes, and in respect for himself and for others. Would it not be in the interest of simple truth for Southern writers, who profess so well to "Know the Negro," to vary the theme, to look into the subject more deeply, and to see the infinite tragedy as well as comedy at its heart?

The same sort of conventionalized treatment is too often accorded the mountaineer. It's a different mould from that used for the Negro, but it is no less binding. A few adjectives are all that is needed; he is "rangy," "shiftless," "improvident," "proud." He resents change. He is suspicious of all strangers. He always "totes" a rifle in the crook of an arm. And safely concealed in a laurel thicket there is always the still. No one is a fit character for a mountain story who has not shot at least one "revenoor" and does not hate the neighboring McCoys with the hate of a deadly feud. The prescription for this sort of story runs: "Take one proud mountaineer, grant him a lovely and buxom daughter of thirteen, stir up the events by a feud with the McCoys, lock the father in jail, marry off the girl to the proud scion of the McCoy's, and than have young McCoy release the old man from the county jail. Curtain." As an antidote for the sort of indigestion which springs from too much of this fiction I suggest to the reader one book, not fiction, by Horace Kephart: *Our Southern Highlanders*. Obviously sincere, too, are the volumes of Olive Tilford Dargan and Lucy Furman—two authors represented in this collection.

There are grateful signs that the third convention—plantation life—is disappearing. Edgar Valentine Smith still writes of this gentility, and writes graciously, but as a rule one thinks of the older authors when honeysuckle and hoopskirts, moonlit Negro quarters, the thrum of a banjo occur in a story of the South. Thomas Nelson Page, Harry Stillwell Edwards, Marion Harland—these are the people who taught readers to think of the South as one huge cotton plantation populated by goateed "colonels" living in the "big house" and loyal "uncles" and "aunts" longing for the old days of slavery when "Chris'mus *was* Chris'mus." Dancing, fox-hunts, and the code-duello were the very stuff of which such stories were made. The scale of life, of hospitality, was elaborated. Small farms were remembered as great establishments.

All gentlemen were perfect in grace and courtly manner. Everyone rode to the chase; fair ladies who danced in the evening shot wickedly in the hunt on the morrow. Swords leaped readily from scabbards to avenge injustice and slight. By the eighteen-eighties the movement was in full swing; the grand gesture was complete. Domestic sentimentalism had gone to its extreme. Until James Boyd wrote *Drums* and *Marching On* a small-landholder, a farmer, who actually tilled his soil without slaves was almost unknown to Southern romantic fiction. Romance was the manner and the plantation the setting for the great bulk of Southern stories.

Just how long these conventions are to dominate literature from the South is pretty largely speculation. There are signs, however, that they are breaking down before a new spirit. In the novel they have been already pretty well shattered. Ellen Glasgow has written of a farm and neglected, in her later work, the plantation tradition. She has even ventured to satirize the very type which Thomas Nelson Page, of her own state, held so dear. As long ago as O. Henry the gaily-colored and over-esteemed bubble of "Southern Literature" was pricked in a story called *The Rose o' Dixie*. Frances Newman evinced a manner new to the South when she satirized so sacred an institution as the Atlanta Driving Club. The mountaineer has been treated more realistically than ever before in certain dramas of the day. The Negro is being looked at anew by a group of Negro writers and by some few native born Southerners as well. Clement Wood, George Madden Martin, T. S. Stribling, Julia Peterkin, Dubose Heyward, Paul Green, Howard W. Odum—these surely present a different Negro from the type fixed by Edwards and Page. Most of these writers make little issue of the "race question" as such; they pay the Negro an even higher compliment than defending him. They isolate him from argument. They throw over the slapstick tradition. They scorn the easy manner of caricature and vaudeville. They elevate him by the honest admission that he is a human being with natural emotions and natural feelings. As Benjamin Brawley has charged, they often pick an extreme social outcast for this treatment, but isn't it—for white or black alike—the tendency for writers to select extremes as the subjects for their stories? If these writers are all a little self-conscious in their portraying of the Negro some allowance must be made. The old tradition was firmly rooted; a new harvest can hardly spring up without some tares from the old growing along with the new. The interesting fact is that there is new seed in the ground.

The picture of the South presented in these stories is, in one respect, quite inadequate. Here are, it is true, the various regional interests—the mountains, the lowlands, the plains. Here, too, are the various peoples—pioneers and frontiersmen, Creoles, plantation whites and blacks, the aristocratic planter and the poor white, the tenant farmer and the new Negro. Here are stories of the various epochs in the development of the South, stories of the pioneer and the plantation period, of the Civil War. But where are the stories of the new industrial life in the South? What is there to show the realistic life in the cotton field, the tobacco barn, the factory? What story-writer has adopted for his milieu the textile town and the labor in the cotton mill? Who has really made capital of the church and such fundamentalism as has been displayed in Tennessee and Arkansas? What inside stories of politics and the new growth of capitalism have we had?

Whatever opinion one may have concerning the industrialization of the South, the organization of labor in the region, the advance of modern knowledge, one must admit that these are among the most real problems in the South of to-day. Why, then, if literature, as people have been telling us for hundreds of years, is at its highest an interpretation of life, are not our contemporary writers manifesting a more deliberate consciousness of these shifting attitudes? Here, I believe, is the challenge which must be taken up by the young story writers of the next decade.

Addison Hibbard

Chapel Hill
North Carolina
August 1, 1930

STORIES OF THE SOUTH

OLD AND NEW

KING WILLIAM AND HIS ARMIES*

By RICHARD MALCOLM JOHNSTON

"And thus it is to reign."

I THINK it well to announce, right in the beginning of this story, that Miles Bunkly is not properly its hero, though some preliminary things must be told concerning him. Although Miles had loved Miss Caroline Thigpen long before Mr. Bill Williams courted her, yet he never had told her so in set words, until—well, you may say it was too late. Yet everybody was surprised. Miles was a most excellent young man, industrious, sober, thrifty, fond of laying up, and had a right good deal laid up already. Then he was quite passable as to looks. Mr. Bill could not have been said, even by Miss Thigpen, to have any advantage of Miles as to looks. As for the rest, all except Miss Thigpen and his own mother considered him the inferior. Yet Dukesborough manners, or something else, put him in the lead on his first entry upon the field. It was then, and not till then, that Miles Bunkly made one, and but one, avowed effort, and, failing, gave up the contest, and resigned himself to what he called *moloncholly*.

He had never been—at least he had never seemed to be—a cheerful-minded person anyway. His courtship even had been a rather solemn piece of business, and the final declaration sounded somewhat as if he had invited Miss Thigpen to go with him to the graveyard instead of taking charge of his domestic affairs. The lady, after gently declining his suit, and claiming the privilege of regarding him as a friend—nay, a brother—announced her

* Reprinted from *Dukesborough Tales* by Richard Malcolm Johnston through arrangement with the publishers, D. Appleton & Company.

intention of ever keeping his proposal a secret, and requested him to do the same.

"No, ma'am," said Miles; "no, Miss Karline. I shall *not* deny it, nor I *shall* not deny it. I'm much obliged to you, and I shall be a friend to you and to yourn. The waound is in my heart, and it'll stay thar, and it'll be obleeged to stay thar, but I'll be a friend to you and yourn."

On his way home he called to his neighbor and friend Abram Grice, who was standing in his door:

"Mawnin'? Abom."

"Mawnin', Miles. 'Light and come in."

Step out here a minute, Abom, ef you please."

Mr. Grice came out to the gate.

"Kicked, Abom."

"Kicked, Miles? Who?"

"Me."

"Kicked bad, Miles?"

"Powerful."

"Your horse, Miles, or a mule, or a steer?"

"Nary one. It's here, Abom."

Then he laid his hands broadly on his breast.

"In the stomach, Miles? Bad place to git kicked. What in the thunder kicked you 'way up thar? Git down; come in and take a drink, and tell me about it afterward."

"It's not my stomach, Abom; it's my bres. The waound's inside—'*way* inside. Sperrits wouldn't do it no good; they wouldn't retch it."

"My goodness gracious! Miles Bunkly, what in the dickens *is* the matter with you?"

"I've been yonder, Abom," and he pointed mournfully toward the Thigpens', "and my desires is to tell no lies. I got it from a human person over thar, and that not of the sect of a man person."

"Who?—Miss Karline?"

"Ef I was to name the name, Abom, that were the name I should name."

Mr. Grice shouted with laughter.

"Miles Bunkly, you skeered me out of a year's growth. I thought you been kicked by a whole team o' mules, or at least a yoke o' steers. Well, look here, you ain't a-goin' to stand it?"

"It's done done, Abom."

"Yes, but I've knowed sich as that *on*done. Why, Sarann kicked me three times han' runnin'; but I told her every time she done it that sich talk as that didn't *phaze* me. That's women, Miles. Them's their ways. They ain't a-goin' to let a fellow know, not at the first offstart, that they goin' to have him. I don't know what it's for, 'ithout it's jest natchelly to try to git the whip-hand of him at the start. It's the natchel instinc' of the woman sect. You go back to Karline Thigpen, and don't let on that you 'member anything about her kickin' of you, and that you ain't even phazed by it. You're sorter slow, old fellow—that is, in sich notions—but Karline Thigpen got too much sense to give up sich a chance."

" 'Nother person, Abom," replied Miles, most mournfully—" 'nother person, of the male sect."

"Who's he?"

"William Williams."

"Who? Bill Williams?" exclaimed Mr. Grice, in astonishment and disgust.

"That's the name of the name, Abom."

"Well, Miles Bunkly, ef you can't whip out Bill Williams, even *with* his Dukesborough ways he got by livin' in town six months, all I got to say is you *ought* to git kicked by a yoke o' steers, and run over by the keart in the bargain."

Such and similar remonstrances were ineffectual to make Mr. Bunkly continue the contest. He retired at once, leaving the field to his rival. At the wedding, though he did not join in the dance, nor even in the plays, yet he partook sufficiently, it was thought, of meats, cakes, and syllabub. Mr. Bill and Miss Karline, her brother Allen and his young bride Betsan, were specially attentive to his wants. He yielded with profound sadness to their persistent offerings of good things, and the more syllabub he took, the mournfuller grew his deportment. To several persons, mainly elderly, he said during the evening that it was the moloncholiest of all days to him.

"Yit, furthersomemore," he would add, with touching unselfishness, "ef her who is now Missis Karline Williams, and who *were* Miss Karline Thigpen, be it her or be it hern, ef her or them might ever want for anything which it might be her and their good rights, or their desires, and ef then I'm a-livin'—providin', you understand, I'm a-livin'—they shall have it, ef it's in my retch."

* * *

Some four years passed. Mr. Bunkly, though plunged in his dear melancholy, yet attended punctually to his business in a gloomy, slow, sure way, made good crops, sold at good times, added to his land and plantation stock, and, claiming to despise wealth, heaped it up more and more, as if to show, evidently, how vain are earthly goods for the happiness of a man in whose breast is an incurable wound.

Mr. Bill Williams was getting along, too, better than had been expected and prophesied. Much of the exuberant vivacity contracted by several months' residence in town had subsided in these four years of living with a wife (a settled 'oman, he styled her) who was probably the most industrious in the neighborhood. He well knew that everybody believed Miss Thigpen to have made a mistake in preferring himself to Miles Bunkly, and he had said at the beginning of his conjugal career that he should take it upon himself to convince the world that it was mistaken. When his twin sons, Romerlus and Remerlus, were born and named, he felt that he was making reasonable headway on that ambitious road. Then he too had added somewhat to his estate, and his wife had picked up many a dollar by her extra work. They did not rise as rapidly as Miles, but Miles remained but one, while Mr. Bill, so to speak, had been two, and now he was four. People cannot ignore figures in such calculations, especially when they represent mouths. Never mind, thought Mr. Bill—never mind. Thus the contemplation of a former rival, with whom, however, he was on the friendliest of terms, spurred a nature that otherwise might have been wanting in the energy becoming the head of a family.

Only one thing interfered with the happiness of that rising family, and that was becoming serious. It would sting the wife painfully sometimes when she would hear of the practical jokes put upon her husband, who had become rather liable thereto by what was considered in the neighborhood his too great forwardness of speech and other deportment. Too great a talker, as from the very first she had told him he was, she would tell him further that a man who got into scrapes ought to get out of them. In these four years he had sobered much under that benign influence. Yet when a man has once been the butt of neighborhood ridicule, it requires time to release him even when he has ceased to deserve it. Sometimes it seems that the only way to obtain such release is to fight for it. That exigency, in the opinion of Mrs. Williams, had now arrived.

One night, when the children had been put to bed, she said, "William, you've got to whip somebody."

She spoke pointedly.

Mr. Bill looked behind him at the trundle-bed, and asked himself, "Is it Rom, or is it Reme?"

"Nary one," was the audible answer. "It's somebody bigger'n them, harder to whip, and a more deservin' of it."

Then Mr. Bill peered through the window into the outer darkness, and speculated if there were insubordination among his little lot of negroes.

"Nor them neither. It's white folks; it's MOSE GRICE, that's who it is, and it's nobody else—that is, to *start* with."

Mr. Bill was startled. Colonel Grice had, indeed, been extremely rough with Mr. Bill on several occasions, and especially since the day of the circus repeatedly ridiculed the father of the twins. Yet he was a man of means, a considerable fighter, and colonel of the regiment. So Mr. Bill was obliged to be startled, and he looked at his wife.

"You've been joked by Mose Grice, William, and poked fun at, and made game of by him, until *I* don't feel like standin' of it no longer, nor I don't think Rom and Reme would feel like standin' of it, not if they were big enough and had sense enough to understan' his impudence."

"Why, Karline—" remonstrated Mr. Bill.

"Oh, you needn't be a-Karlinin' o' me!" she said. And never before had Mrs. Williams addressed her husband in precisely that language. But her feelings had been hurt, and allowance ought to be made. She cried somewhat, but tears did not serve at once to produce the softening influence that is their legitimate result.

"There's brother Allen," she continued, "and which

Betsan told me herself that Allen told her that the fact of the business was, if you didn't make Mose Grice keep his mouth shet, 'specially about Rom and Reme, *he would;* and then there's Miles Bunkly—"

"Oh, Lordie!" exclaimed Mr. Bill.

"There's Miles Bunkly, and which Betsan say is about as mad as brother, and which, ef he *ain't* any fighter, yit, when Mose Grice was one day a-makin' game of him about his moloncholy, Miles told him that his moloncholy was his business and not his'n, and that if he kept on meddlin' with it, he mout ketch the disease, and Mose Grice let Miles Bunkly's moloncholy alone, he did."

"And then," Mr. Bill said afterward, "Karline sot up a cry, she did, and it woke up Rom and Reme, and they sot up a howl apiece, and I says to myself, I'll stan' a whippin' from Mose Grice rather'n run agin sich as this."

* * *

After that night Mrs. Williams did not again allude to its matter of conversation, and was as affectionate to her husband as always. Mr. Bill gloried in the possession of her, and he had good reason. He brooded and brooded. The allusion to Miles Bunkly stung him deeply, usually imperturbable as his temper was, tho not a jot of jealousy was in the pang. He would have known himself to be the greatest of fools to feel that. Yet, easy-going, self-satisfied as he was, he knew that other people, including his brother-in-law, still regarded his wife less fortunate than she might have been. The more Mr. Bill brooded, the more serious appeared to him the relation of his case to that of several others, especially Colonel Grice.

Superadded to a general disposition to impose upon whomsoever would endure him, Colonel Grice had a spite against Mr. Bill on account of the friendship that, since the intermarriage with Miss Thigpen, had grown up between him and Abram Grice, the colonel's younger brother, whose relations with himself were not only not fraternal, but hostile. The colonel was a fighter, and had managed somehow always to come victorious out of combat; for he was a man of powerful build, and of great vigor and activity. Some, indeed, had often said that he knew whom to encounter and whom not. His position of head of the regiment had been obtained at a time when military ardor, after a long peace, had subsided, and leading citizens cared not for the éclat of the office. He had sought it eagerly, and obtained it because there was no strong competitor, and especially because his election was expected and intended to ridicule and discourage regimental parades. He was greatly exalted by his election, and became yet more overbearing whenever he could do so with safety.

"That's Mose," said his brother Abram one day to Miles Bunkly—"that's jest him. He'll impose on anybody that'll let him, and he'll try it with anybody that he thinks likes me. He's been so from a boy. He imposed on me till I got big enough to whip him, which I done a time or two, and then he quit it. But he took his revenge on me by cheatin' me out of part o' the prop'ty, and he done that the quicker because he knowed I, bein' of his brother, wouldn't prosecute him for it. That's Mose—that's jest him."

"I hate the case, Abom," answered Miles, "because I has that respects of Karline Williams that it mortify me, and make me, so to speak, git moloncholier than what I natchelly am, to see a man that's her husband, and the father, as it were, o' them two far pinks of boys, runned over in the kind o' style that Mose run over him, nigh and in and about every time he come up along of William Williams. I never keered no great deal about *him*, with them town ways o' his'n, untell he were married to Miss Karline, and then I knowed that there was obleeged to be that in William Williams which people in general never supposened."

"Ah, Miles, old fellow," said Abram, "you ought to took that prize, and you'd a done it ef you'd a listened to me, and been peerter in your motions, and hilt on longer."

"No, no, Abom," answered Miles, his arm giving a mournful deprecatory wave. "It were not my lot. I tried, and I tried honest and far. I were not worth of Miss Karline, Abom. I didn't know it, but she did. And yit I could see it hurt her to put the waound where she knowed it were obleeged to stay. I wasn't a-supposenen, though, as to that, that William were worth of Miss Karline neither. But Karline Thigpen—I ain't a-speakin' o' your wife now. Abom, and a-leavin' of her out o' the case—Karline Thigpen, but which she is now Missis Karline Williams, is the smartest woman, and got the best jedgment, *I* ever saw. And sence she have choosed William Williams, I been certain in my mind that there were that in William Williams that the balance of us never supposened, and which'll show itself some day if William can ever git farly fotch to a right pint."

Thus that nature, upright, unselfish, simple, fond to persuade itself that it was unhappy, took its chief solace in contemplating and magnifying its own disappointments, and in sympathizing with those who had been their chief occasion.

* * *

IT WAS MUSTER-DAY for the battalion. Colonel Grice always felt it his duty to be at these occasions, preparatory to the great regimental parade. The exercises, after many hours, were coming to an end, as the companies marched, with short intervals between, down the one street of the village, preparatory to disbandment. Alternately had the colonel been complimentary and censorious, as he rode, sometimes in a walk, other times at full gallop, up and down the lines.

"Peerter, peerter, major," he remonstrated with Major Pounds, respectfully indeed, but with a warmth that seemed difficult to repress—"peerter; make them captains peerten up them lines. My blood and thunder! my Juberter and Julus Caesar! if the enemy was to come upon us with fixed bannets—Oh, you've done your part ad*mar*rably, major. It's them captains."

It was just before the final halt that the colonel addressed Captain Collins, whose company was in the center, and then immediately in front of Bland's store. "Ah, Cap'n Collins, look to your rar. It's so fur behind that it look like two companies 'stid o' one. That sergeant o' yourn you'll have to talk to and drill in private. He's arfter makin' *twins* out o' your company. Sergeant Williams is a great man for twins, you know, cap'n. But you better tell him to make 'em keep his cubs at home. We want solid columes when we come to the field of battle."

The warrior enjoyed his jest, that had been heard by all in the company, and others besides. But he did not allow himself even to smile when at the head of the military forces of his country, in order to keep himself ever on the alert against sudden attacks of her enemies. His gloomy brow indicated indignation at the thought that a petty subaltern, from some vain notion of making his own domestic status the model of the nation's principal means of defense, sought to demoralize it, and actually invite invasion.

"My Lord!" said Allen Thigpen, when they told him, "if Bill don't fight him for that, I will! To think that

Sister Karline's feelin's is to be hurt by hearin' of sich as that!"

"I don't think, Abom," said Miles (who overheard the remark), "that it can be put off any longer. Ef there's that in William Williams which I been a-supposen is obleeged to be thar, he'll fetch it out now. Now you go right on home, Abom."

Miles said, afterward, "My respects of Abom was that as he wouldn't stand up *to* his brother, it wouldn't look right to be agin' him."

When the battalion was dismissed, Allen walked rapidly to Mr. Bill. The latter was wiping the tears from his eyes with his handkerchief. Having finished this operation, he went with a resolute step toward Bland's piazza, whither Colonel Grice, after dismounting and giving his horse to a servant to hold, had repaired.

"Ah, Mr. Bland," said the colonel, about to light a cigar, "you peaceful men, you who follow in the peaceable ways—departiments, I might ruther say—of dry-goods, and hardwar', and molasses, and blankets, and trace-chains, and other sich departiments, so to call all o' the warious warieties of a sto'-keeper's business—you don't know—I may say you don't dream—Mr. Bland, of the responsuability of a military man whose country's enemies may be at the very gates—"

"Colonel Grice!" said Mr. Bill Williams, in a tone nobody had ever heard from him before. The colonel turned to see who called. Mr. Bill was standing on the ground, Allen Thigpen and Miles Bunkly by his side.

"Hello, Bill!" said the colonel, with careless cordiality. "What'll you have, my dear fellow?"

"I'll have satisfaction, sir. I'm not a fightin' man, and I know I have sometimes been keerless in my talk, yit

I never went to hurt people's feelings a-purpose, and I always helt myself more of a gentleman than to insult women and little children, and which you can't say for yourself without tellin' a lie, and a fightin' lie at that."

Those words operated the greatest surprise that ever befell Colonel Mose Grice. Partly in astonishment, partly in wrath, and partly in deprecation, he exclaimed:

"What in this wide omnipotent world! Is the Colonel of the Fourteenth Regiment got to study his langwidges—"

"Come, Mose," said Miles, slowly but distinctly, "the muster's over now, and William Williams is your ekal, and he is liable to have his satisfaction, onlest you apologizes for your langwidges."

"I don't *want* his apologies," said Mr. Bill. "I won't *have* his apologies. He's got to fight, 'ithout he gits on his horse and runs away."

"I can't stand that," said the colonel. Throwing off his coat, he came rapidly down the steps to where Mr. Bill, similarly stripped, awaited him.

* * *

WHOEVER HAS NOT SEEN a combat between two powerful, irate men, with no weapons other than those supplied by nature, has missed the sight, though he may not regret it, of a thrilling scene. The blows, the grapplings, the struggles of every kind are as if each combatant had staked every dear thing upon the result, and set in to save it or die. The advantages on this occasion, except the right, were with the colonel. Taller by an inch, though perhaps not heavier, agile, practiced, and in the full maturity of his physical powers, he had, besides, a contempt for his adversary, and expected to prevail speedily. Mr. Bill himself rather counted upon this result; but he had made up his mind that such was preferable to what he would endure without an attempt to punish this persistent insulting raillery. He had never been a participant in a fight of any sort; but he had labored habitually at the heaviest work upon his farm, and he had broken, unassisted, many a colt, horse, and mule of his famous Molly Sparks—the most willful and indocile of dams. He had now the special disadvantage of having been upon his feet during several hours of tiresome exercises.

"He'll try to ride you, Bill," said Allen hastily, "but you keep him off. He can fling you, I expect; but you can outlast him in licks. Don't let him ride you."

As the colonel advanced, Mr. Bill—

But alas! I am not an epic bard, nor even a Pindaric, nor is there one whom I can command to duly celebrate this combat. Mr. Bowden, the village postmaster, was a person somewhat addicted to poetry (reading it, I mean), and he was heard to say several times afterward that it reminded him, he thought, more than any fight he had ever witnessed, of the famous one between Diomede and Mars on the plain of Troy. But the schoolmaster, who was a Homeric scholar, rather intimated to some of the advanced pupils that Mr. Bowden did not seem quite clear in his mind which was Mars and which Diomede. For a first fight, and that with an experienced antagonist, Mr. Bill conducted himself with surprising dexterity in the giving and evasion of blows, and, when evasion was not successful, with becoming fortitude. It was, however, a tiresome business. He showed that, and once, after putting in one of his best, when he was attempting to withdraw himself from the return, he had the misfortune to tread upon a corn-cob that happened to be lying in his rear. This turning beneath him, he lost his balance, and the colonel rushing upon him, he fell to the ground upon his left side.

"There, now!" said Miles Bunkly. "Hadn't been for that confounded corn-cob—"

Unable to finish what he would have said, he raised his hands on high, and clasped them in intense grief. Whispering to Allen a few words, he took out his handkerchief and covered his eyes for several moments.

"Bill," said Allen, "Miles says, hold on as long as you can. If you git too badly used up, he'll help you take care o' Rom and Reme."

Then Mr. Bill Williams was worth seeing, though prostrate on the field. These words fell upon his ear with a force irresistible. But for Mr. Bowden's incertitude as to the impersonation of those combatants of the heroic age, he might have compared these words of Miles to those of the goddess, when

> "Raged Tydides, boundless in his ire:
> 'Pallas commands, and Pallas lends thee force.'"

As it was, Mr. Bill pronounced the names "Rom" and "Reme" once, then he gave a groan that sounded less a groan than a roar. And then, in spite of the superincumbent weight, he suddenly reached his arm around the colonel's neck, and drew his head to the ground.

It was said of Miles Bunkly by people of veracity, and those who had known him longest and most intimately, that this was the only occasion during life whereon he was known to shout. Then, with the mildness yet the solemnity of an experienced good man whose admonitions thereto have gone unheeded, he remarked to the colonel, as the latter's body was slowly but inevitably following his head beneath Mr. Bill, like the stag in the anaconda's mouth, "You see how it is, Mose; I told you, if you didn't mind, you'd ketch the moloncholy yourself some day."

The colonel, apparently concluding that the time had come, said, as distinctly as he could, "Stop it, Bill; I give it up."

"Let him up, Bill," said Allen; you got his word."

"No, sir, not till he's 'poligized. He's jest acknowledged hisself whipped; he ain't 'poligized."

"I'm sorry, Bill, for havin' hurted your feelin's and your wife's," said the colonel.

"So fur so good," answered Mr. Bill, leisurely stretching himself at ease on his foe, as if he would repose after his fatigue—"so fur so good; but what about Romerlus Williams and Remerlus Williams?" He never called the full names of his boys except on impressive occasions.

"Come, Bill," said Allen, taking him by the arm, "enough's enough."

Mr. Bill rose with the reluctant air of a man roused from a luxurious couch whereon he had been indulging, though not to the full, in sweet sleep and sweeter dreams. The colonel arose, and, unpitied of all, slunk limping away. Miles Bunkly, the tears in his eyes, laid his hands on Mr. Bill's shoulders, and said:

"I knowed it were obleeged to be in you, William, ef it could be fotch out; and my respects of a certain person was that, that I knowed she'd fetch it out in time. It's done fotch out, and from this time forrards you and yourn may go 'long your gayly way down the hill o' life, and all I got to say to you and them, William, is, GO IT! And now go wash your face and hands, and go 'long home to happiness and bliss. I don't say you never deserved 'em before, but I do say you deserve 'em now."

* * *

"MY!" SAID MR. BILL, when he had washed, and was feeling the knots and bruises on his face, and trying to open his eyes—"my! but ain't it tiresome? I ruther maul rails all day 'ithout my dinner, or break two o' old Molly's colts, mules at that, than to have to go through sich as that agin. Thanky, Miles, and come and see a fellow." He bade all adieu, and went on home, where something in the bosom of his family awaited him that is worth relating. The news having preceded him, his wife, a pious woman, was a little troubled in her mind at first for having given to her husband the spur to a feeling that was not entirely consistent with duty; yet when they had told her the whole story, she rose, laid aside her work, went to her chest, got out her very best frock, and every thread of her children's Sunday clothes, including many a ribbon that had survived its ancient use, and arrayed herself and them to greet the hero upon his return. The whicker of old Molly at the foot of the lane, and the answer of the colt in the lot, announced the joyous moment. Dismounting at his gate, Mr. Bill would fain have indulged his eyes with that goodly sight; but one of them was entirely and the other partially closed. He became aware of the rushing into his arms of a person of about the size of his wife, and justly guessed to be her, and the cries of two children which he rather thought were familiar to his ears. For the boys, when they saw their father all battered and bruised, set up a yelling, and retreated.

"You Rom! you Reme!" cried the indignant mother, laughing the while, "if you don't stop that crying and making out like you don't know your father, I'll skin you both alive! Come back here, and if you as much as whimper, I'll pull off them ribbons, strip you to your shirts, and put you to bed without a mouthful for your supper!"

They came back, did those boys.

"Look at him, sirs. Don't tell me you don't know him. Who is it?"

"Pappy," said Rom, on a venture, followed by Reme.

"And ain't he the grandest man that's a-livin'?"

"Eth'm," said Rom.

"Eth'm," said Reme.

"Now git behind thar, and let's all march in."

"And we did march in," said Mr. Bill, afterward—"me, and Karline, and Rom, and Reme; and as we was a-marchin' along, I felt—blamed if I didn't—like King William at the head of his armies."

* * *

Miles Bunkly had become too fond of his "moloncholy" to let it depart entirely; but its severest pains subsided in spite of him, now that the rival who had been preferred to him had justified the preference.

"My respects of William Williams," he would often say, "is that, that it riconcile me and do my moloncholy good that he's the husband and the protector, as it were, of—well, ef I should name the name, it would be Karline Thigpen that were."

For some weeks immediately following the day of the fight he had been observed, from time to time, in the intervals of other business, engaged with a work seeming to require much painstaking, the result of which will immediately appear. One morning Mr. Bill, standing in his door, called to his wife:

"Come here, Karline, quick! Who and what can them be yonder a-comin' up to the gate? Somebody, 'pear like, a-leadin' of a par o' dogs hitched to a little waggin."

Mrs. Williams, looking intently at the comers, cried:

"It's brother, leading of a par o' calves yoked to a little cart."

She was right.

"Good gracious, brother—"

But Allen paid not the slightest attention to his sister, not even saying good-morning.

"Here, Rom; here, Reme" (his business being with them), "here's a present for you from Miles Bunkly; and he in particklar charge me to tell you, and which ef you weren't old enough yit to have sense enough, 'twouldn't be long before you would be to understan' sich langwidges, that his respects of your father was that, that he sent you the follerin' keart with his own hands, the paintin' and all, and likewise broke the steers, and which they're jest six months old to-day, which you moutn't believe it, but they are twin calves, them steers is, of his old cow Speckle-face, and which he say is the best and walliblest cow he ever possessioned, and which them was the very words he said."

Then, turning to his sister and brother-in-law, he said, "Mawnin', sister Karline; mawnin', Bill."

Mr. Bill roared with laughter; Mrs. Bill shed tears in silence, both in their abounding gratitude.

"And twins at that!" said Mr. Bill, "jes like Rom and Reme!" An idea struck him as with the suddenness of inspiration.

"Allen," he asked vaguely, "does you know the names o' them steers?"

"No, Bill; Miles didn't—"

"Makes no odds ef he did. *I* names them steers; and you see they're adzactly alike, exceptin' that that one in the lead got the roundest—a leetly the roundest—blaze in the forrard." "Going slowly to the latter, and laying his hand upon his head, he said, "This here steer here is name Mierlus." Then walking slowly down around the cart and up to the other, he laid his hand upon his head, saying, "This here steer here is name Bunkerlus." He took his boys, lifted them into the cart, contemplated all with a satisfaction that had no bottom to it, then waved his hand in preparation for a harangue that few other things could have prevented than that which presently transpired. Miles Bunkly himself appeared at the gate, and walked in, his face wreathed in melancholy smiles.

"Why, Miles, you blessed everlastin' old fellow!" exclaimed Mr. Bill.

They were people too honest and plain to feel any embarrassment. The generous donor at once took the lines into his hands, and led the procession several times about the yard and the lot, as innocent, and in many respects as much a child, as those on whom he had bestowed his gift. The ardor of Mr. Bill could not be subdued as he looked upon the scene. Tears like those in his wife's eyes came into his own, and he said, softly, to her and to Allen:

"I never spected to live to see sich a skene and sich a ewent. Thar they goes, Romerlus Williams, and Remerlus Williams, and Mierlus—ahem!—Williams, and Bunkerlus Williams, and Miles Bunkly hisself, *and* the keart and all; and I'll channelge, I don't say this county, but I'll channelge this whole State o' Georgy, to pejuce a skene and pejuce a ewent as lovely as the present skene and the present ewent on this lovely mawnin' like. It do look like, Allen—it do look like the families is united and jinded together." Mr. Bill's throat choked up with just enough space left to allow of breathing, but of not another word.

"Allen," said Miles, when, the visit being over, they were on their way home, "to think of William a-couplin' of my name along with them lovely boys! Well, I never expects to git intirely over my moloncholy, but I tell you, Allen, I were never as nigh of bein' of riconciled to it."

THE TURN OUT*

By AUGUSTUS BALDWIN LONGSTREET

IN THE good old days of *fescues*, *abisselfas*, and *anpersants*,† terms which used to be familiar in this country during the Revolutionary war, and which lingered in some of our county schools for a few years afterward, I visited my friend Captain Griffin, who resided about seven miles to the eastward of Wrightsborough, then in Richmond, but now in Columbia county. I reached the captain's hospitable home on Easter, and was received by him and his good lady with a *Georgia welcome* of 1790. It was warm from the heart, and taught me in a moment that the obligations of the visit were upon their side, not mine. Such receptions were not peculiar, at that time, to the captain and his family; they were common throughout the state. Where are they now! and where the generous hospitalities which invariably follow them! I see them occasionally at the contented farmer's door and at his festive board, but when they shall have taken leave of these, Georgia will know them no more.

The day was consumed in the interchange of news between the captain and myself (though, I confess, it might have been better employed), and the night found us seated round a temporary fire, which the captain's sons had kin-

* Reprinted from *Georgia Scenes* by Augustus Baldwin Longstreet with the courteous permission of the publishers, Harper and Brothers.

† The *fescue* was a sharpened wire or other instrument used by the preceptor to point out the letters to the children.

Abisselfa is a contraction of the words "a by itself, a." It was usual, when either of the vowels constituted a syllable of a word, to pronounce it, and denote its independent character by the words just mentioned, thus: "a by itself, *a*-c-o-r-n corn, *acorn*," "e by itself, *e*-v-i-l, *evil*," &c.

The character which stands for the word *"and"* (&) was probably pronounced by the same accompaniment, but in terms borrowed from the Latin language, thus: "& *per se*" (by itself) & Hence, "anpersant."

dled up for the purpose of dyeing eggs. It was a common custom of those days with boys to dye and peck eggs on Easter Sunday and for a few days afterward. They were coloured according to the fancy of the dyer; some yellow, some green, some purple, and some with a variety of colours, borrowed from a piece of calico. They were not unfrequently beautified with a taste and skill which would have extorted a compliment from Hezekiah Niles, if he had seen them a year ago, in the hands of the "*young operatives*," in some of the northern manufactories. No sooner was the work of dyeing finished, than our "young operatives" sallied forth to stake the whole proceeds of their "*domestic industry*" upon a peck. Egg was struck against egg, point to point, and the egg that was broken was given up as lost to the owner of the one which came whole from the shock.

While the boys were busily employed in the manner just mentioned, the captain's youngest son, George, gave us an anecdote highly descriptive of the Yankee and Georgia character, even in their buddings, and at this early date. "What you think, pa," said he, "Zeph Pettibone went and got his Uncle Zach to turn him a wooden egg; and he won a whole hatful o' eggs from all us boys 'fore we found it out; but, when we found it out, maybe John Brown didn't smoke him for it, and took away all his eggs and give 'em back to us boys; and you think he didn't go then and git a guinea-egg, and win most as many more, and John Brown would o' give it to him agin if all we boys hadn't said we thought it was fair. I never see such a boy as that Zeph Pettibone in all my life. He don't mind whipping no more 'an nothing at all, if he can win eggs."

This anecdote, however, only fell in by accident, for there was an all-absorbing subject which occupied the minds of the boys during the whole evening, of which I could occasionally catch distant hints, in undertones and whispers, but of which I could make nothing, until they were afterward explained by the captain himself. Such as "I'll be bound Pete Jones and Bill Smith stretches him." "By Jockey, soon as they seize him, you'll see me down upon him like a duck upon a June-bug." "By the time he touches the ground, he'll think he's got into a hornet's nest," &c.

"The boys," said the captain, as they retired, "are going to turn out the schoolmaster to-morrow, and you can perceive they think of nothing else. We must go over to the schoolhouse and witness the contest, in order to prevent injury to preceptor or pupils; for, though the master is always, upon such occasions, glad to be turned out, and only struggles long enough to present his patrons a fair apology for giving the children a holyday, which he desires as much as they do, the boys always conceive a holyday gained by a "turn out" as the sole achievement of their valour; and, in their zeal to distinguish themselves upon such memorable occasions, they sometimes become too rough, provoke the master to wrath, and a very serious conflict ensues. To prevent these consequences, to bear witness that the master was *forced* to yield before he would withhold a day of his promised labour from his employers, and to act as a mediator between him and the boys in settling the articles of peace, I always attend; and you must accompany me to-morrow." I cheerfully promised to do so.

The captain and I rose before the sun, but the boys had risen and were off to the schoolhouse before the dawn. After an early breakfast, hurried by Mrs. G. for our accommodation, my host and myself took up our line of march towards the schoolhouse. We reached it about half an hour before the master arrived, but not before the boys had completed its fortifications. It was a simple log-pen, about twenty feet square, with a doorway cut out of the logs, to which was fitted a rude door, made of clapboards, and swung on wooden hinges. The roof was covered with clapboards also, and retained in their places by heavy logs placed on them. The chimney was built of logs, diminishing in size from the ground to the top, and overspread inside and out with red clay mortar. The classic hut occupied a lovely spot, overshadowed by majestic hickorys, towering poplars, and strong-armed oaks. The little plain on which it stood was terminated, at the distance of about fifty paces from its door, by the brow of a hill, which descended rather abruptly to a noble spring, that gushed joyously forth from among the roots of a stately beech at its foot. The stream from this fountain scarcely burst into view, before it hid itself beneath the dark shade of a field of cane, which overspread the dale through which it flowed, and marked its windings, until it turned from the sight among vine-covered hills, at a distance far beyond that to which the eye could have traced it without the help of its evergreen belt. A remark of the captain's, as we viewed the lovely country around us, will give the reader my apology for the minuteness of the foregoing description. "These lands," said he, "will never wear out. Where they lie level, they will be as good fifty years hence as they are now." Forty-two years afterward I visited the spot on which he stood when he made the remark. The sun poured his whole strength upon the bald hill which once supported the sequestered schoolhouse; many a deep-washed gully met at a sickly bog where gushed the limpid fountain; a dying willow rose from the soil which nourished the venerable beech; flocks wandered among the dwarf pines, and cropped a scanty meal from the vale where the rich cane bowed and rustled to every breeze, and all around was barren, dreary, and cheerless. But to return.

As I before remarked, the boys had strongly fortified the schoolhouse, of which they had taken possession. The door was barricaded with logs, which I should have supposed would have defied the combined powers of the whole school. The chimney, too, was nearly filled with logs of goodly size; and these were the only passways to the interior. I concluded, if a *turn out* was all that was necessary to decide the contest in favor of the boys, they had already gained the victory. They had, however, not as much confidence in their outworks as I had, and, therefore, had armed themselves with long sticks; not for the purpose of using them upon the master if the battle should come to close quarters, for this was considered unlawful warfare; but for the purpose of guarding their *works* from his approaches, which it was considered perfectly lawful to protect by all manner of jabs and punches through the cracks. From the early assembling of the girls, it was very obvious that they had been let into the conspiracy, though they took no part in the active operations. They would, however, occasionally drop a word of encouragement to the boys, such as "I wouldn't turn out the master but if I did turn him out, I'd die before I'd give up." These remarks doubtless had an imboldening effect upon "*the young freeborns,*" as Mrs. Trollope would call them; for I never knew the Georgian of any age who was indifferent to the smiles and praises of the ladies—before his marriage.

At length Mr. Michael St. John, the schoolmaster, made his appearance. Though some of the girls had met him a quarter of a mile from the schoolhouse, and told him all that had happened, he gave signs of sudden astonishment and indignation when he advanced to the door, and was assailed by a whole platoon of sticks from the cracks: "Why, what does all this mean?" said he, as he approached the captain and myself, with a countenance of two or three varying expressions.

"Why," said the captain, "the boys have turned you out, because you have refused to give them an Easter holyday."

"Oh," returned Michael, "that's it, is it? Well, I'll see whether their parents are to pay me for letting their children play when they please." So saying, he advanced to the schoolhouse, and demanded, in a lofty tone, of its inmates, an unconditional surrender.

"Well, give us holyday then," said twenty little urchins within, "and we'll let you in."

"Open the door of the *Academy*"—(Michael would allow nobody to call it a schoolhouse)—"Open the door of the academy this instant," said Michael, "or I'll break it down."

"Break it down," said Pete Jones and Bill Smith, "and we'll break you down."

During this colloquy I took a peep into the fortress, to see how the garrison were affected by the parley. The little ones were obviously panic-struck at the first words of the command; but their fears were all chased away by the bold, determined reply of Pete Jones and Bill Smith, and they raised a whoop of defiance.

Michael now walked around the academy three times, examining all its weak points with great care. He then paused, reflected for a moment, and wheeled off suddenly towards the woods, as though a bright thought had just struck him. He passed twenty things which I supposed he might be in quest of, such as huge stones, fence-rails, portable logs, and the like, without bestowing the least attention upon them. He went to one old log, searched it thoroughly, then to another, then to a hollow stump, peeped into it with great care, then to a hollow log, into which he looked with equal caution, and so on.

"What is he after ?" inquired I.

"I'm sure I don't know," said the captain, "but the boys do. Don't you notice the breathless silence which prevails in the schoolhouse, and the intense anxiety with which they are eying him through the cracks?"

At this moment Michael had reached a little excavation at the root of a dogwood, and was in the act of putting his hand into it, when a voice from the garrison exclaimed, with most touching pathos, "Lo'd o' messy, he's found my eggs! boys, let's give up."

"I won't give up," was the reply from many voices at once.

"Rot your cowardly skin, Zeph Pettibone, you wouldn't give a wooden egg for all the holydays in the world."

If these replies did not reconcile Zephaniah to his apprehended loss, it at least silenced his complaints. In the mean time Michael was employed in relieving Zeph's storehouse of its provisions; and, truly, its contents told well for Zeph's skill in egg-pecking. However, Michael took out the eggs with great care, and brought them within a few paces of the schoolhouse, and laid them down with equal care in full view of the besieged. He revisited the places which he had searched, and to which he seemed to have been led by intuition; for from nearly all of them did he draw eggs, in greater or less numbers. These he treated as he had done Zeph's, keeping each pile separate. Having arranged the eggs in double files before the door, he marched between them with an air of triumph, and once more demanded a surrender, under pain of an entire destruction of the garrison's provisions.

"Break 'em just as quick as you please," said George Griffin; "our mothers'll give us a plenty more, won't they, pa?"

"I can answer for yours, my son," said the captain; "she would rather give up every egg upon the farm, than see you play the coward or traitor to save your property."

Michael, finding that he could make no impression upon the fears or the avarice of the boys, determined to carry their fortifications by storm. Accordingly, he produced a heavy fence-rail, and commenced the assault upon the door. It soon came to pieces, and the upper logs fell out, leaving a space of about three feet at the top. Michael boldly entered the breach, when, by the articles of war, sticks were thrown aside as no longer lawful weapons. He was resolutely met on the half-demolished rampart by Peter Jones and William Smith, supported by James Griffin. These were the three largest boys in the school; the first about sixteen years of age, the second about fifteen, and the third just eleven. Twice was Michael repulsed by these young champions; but the third effort carried him fairly into the fortress. Hostilities now ceased for a while, and the captain and I, having levelled the remaining logs at the door, followed Michael into the house. A large three inch plank (if it deserves that name, for it was wrought from the half of a tree's trunk entirely with the axe), attached to the logs by means of wooden pins, served the whole school for a writing desk. At a convenient distance below it, and on a line with it, stretched a smooth log, resting upon the logs of the house, which answered for the writers' seat. Michael took his seat upon the desk, placed his feet on the seat, and was sitting very composedly, when, with a simultaneous movement, Pete and Bill seized each a leg, and marched off with it in quick time. The consequence is obvious; Michael's head first took the desk, then the seat, and finally the ground (for the house was not floored), with three sonorous thumps of most doleful portent. No sooner did he touch the ground than he was completely buried with boys. The three elder laid themselves across his head, neck, and breast, the rest arranging themselves *ad libitum*. Michael's equanimity was considerably disturbed by the first thump, became restive with the second, and took flight with the third. His first effort was to disengage his legs, for without them he could not rise, and to lie in his present position was extremely inconvenient and undignified. Accordingly, he drew up his right, and kicked at random. This movement laid out about six in various directions upon the floor. Two rose crying: "Ding his old red-headed skin," said one of them, "to go and kick me right in my sore belly, where I fell down and raked it, running after that fellow that cried 'school-butter.' "‡

"Drot his old snaggle-tooth picture," said the other, "to go and hurt my sore toe, where I knocked the nail off going to the spring to fetch a gourd of *warter* for him, and not for myself n'other."

"Hut!" said Captain Griffin, "young Washingtons mind these trifles! At him again."

The name of Washington cured their wounds and dried up their tears in an instant, and they legged him *de novo*. The left leg treated six more as unceremoniously as the right had those just mentioned; but the talismanic

‡ I have never been able to satisfy myself clearly as to the literal meaning of these terms. They were considered an unpardonable insult to a country school, and always justified an attack by the whole fraternity upon the person who used them in their hearing. I have known the scholars pursue a traveller two miles to be revenged of the insult. Probably they are a corruption of "The school's better." "*Better*" was the term commonly used of old to denote a *superior*, as it sometimes is in our day: "Wait till your betters are served," for example. I conjecture, therefore, the expression just alluded to was one of challenge, contempt, and defiance by which the person who used it avowed himself the *superior* in all respects of the whole school, from the preceptor down. If anyone can give a better account of it, I shall be pleased to receive it.

name had just fallen upon their ears before the kick, so they were invulnerable. They therefore returned to the attack without loss of time. The struggle seemed to wax hotter and hotter for a short time after Michael came to the ground, and he threw the children about in all directions and postures, giving some of them thumps which would have placed the *ruffle-shirted* little darlings of the present day under the discipline of paregoric and opodeldoc for a week; but these hardy sons of the forest seemed not to feel them. As Michael's head grew easy, his limbs, by a natural sympathy, became more quiet, and he offered one day's holyday as the price. The boys demanded a week; but here the captain interposed, and, after the common but often unjust custom of arbitrators, split the difference. In this instance the terms were equitable enough, and were immediately acceded to by both parties. Michael rose in a good humour, and the boys were, of course. Loud was their talking of their deeds of valour as they retired. One little fellow about seven years old, and about three feet and a half high, jumped up, cracked his feet together, and exclaimed, "By Jingo, Pete Jones, Bill Smith, and *me* can hold any *Sinjin* that ever trod Georgy grit." By-the-way, the name of *St. John* was always pronounced "*Sinjin*" by the common people of that day; and so it must have been by Lord Bolingbroke himself, else his friend Pope would never have addressed him in a line so unmusical as

> "Awake, my St. John, leave all meaner things."

Nor would Swift, the friend and companion of both have written

> "What *St. John's* skill in state affairs,
> What Ormond's valour, Oxford's cares."
>
> * * * *
>
> "Where folly, pride, and faction sway,
> Remote from *St. John*, Pope, and Gray.

HALL.

HOW SHARP SNAFFLES GOT HIS CAPITAL AND WIFE*

By WILLIAM GILMORE SIMMS

THE DAY'S work was done, and a good day's work it was. We had bagged a couple of fine bucks and a fat doe; and now we lay camped at the foot of the "Balsam Range" of mountains in North Carolina, preparing for our supper. We were a right merry group of seven; four professional hunters, and three amateurs—myself among the latter. There was Jim Fisher, Aleck Wood, Sam or Sharp Snaffles, *alias* "Yaou," and Nathan Langford, *alias* the "Pious."

These were our *professional* hunters. Our *amateurs* may well continue nameless, as their achievements do not call for any present record. Enough that we had gotten up the "camp hunt," and provided all the creature comforts except the fresh meat. For this we were to look to the mountain ranges and the skill of our hunters.

These were all famous fellows with the rifle—moving at a trot along the hill-sides, and with noses quite as keen of scent as those of their hounds in rousing deer and bear from their deep recesses among the mountain laurels.

A week had passed with us among these mountain ranges, some sixty miles beyond what the conceited world calls "civilization."

Saturday night had come; and, this Saturday night closing a week of exciting labors, we were to carouse.

We were prepared for it. There stood our tent pitched at the foot of the mountains, with a beautiful cascade leap-

* Reprinted from *Harper's Magazine* with the courteous permission of the publishers and of Judge Charles Carroll Simms.

ing headlong toward us, and subsiding into a mountain runnel, and finally into a little lakelet, the waters of which, edged with perpetual foam, were as clear as crystal.

Our baggage wagon, which had been sent round to meet us by trail routes through the gorges, stood near the tent, which was of stout army canvas.

That baggage wagon held a variety of luxuries. There was a barrel of the best bolted wheat flour. There were a dozen choice hams, a sack of coffee, a keg of sugar, a few thousand of cigars, and last, not least, a corpulent barrel of Western usquebaugh,* vulgarly, "whisky"; to say nothing of a pair of demijohns of equal dimensions, one containing peach brandy of mountain manufacture, the other the luscious honey from the mountain hives.

Well, we had reached Saturday night. We had hunted day by day from the preceding Monday with considerable success—bagging some game daily, and camping nightly at the foot of the mountains. The season was a fine one. It was early winter, October, and the long ascent to the top of the mountains was through vast fields of green, the bushes still hanging heavy with their huckleberries.

From the summits we had looked over into Tennessee, Virginia, Georgia, North and South Carolina. In brief, to use the language of Natty Bumpo, we beheld "Creation." We had crossed the "Blue Ridge"; and the descending water-courses, no longer seeking the Atlantic, were now gushing headlong down the western slopes, and hurrying to lose themselves in the Gulf Stream and the Mississippi.

From the eyes of fountains within a few feet of each other we had blended our *eau de vie* with limpid waters

* "Uisquebaugh," or the "water of life," is Irish. From the word we have dropped the last syllable. Hence we have "uisque," or, as it is commonly written, "whisky"—a very able-bodied man-servant, but terrible as a mistress or housekeeper.

which were about to part company forever—the one leaping to the rising, the other to the setting of the sun.

And buoyant, full of fun, with hearts of ease, limbs of health and strength, plenty of venison, and a wagon full of good things, we welcomed the coming of Saturday night as a season not simply of rest, but of a royal carouse. We were decreed to make a night of it.

But first let us see after our venison.

The deer, once slain, is, as soon after as possible, clapped upon the fire. All the professional hunters are good butchers and admirable cooks—of bear and deer meat at least. I doubt if they could spread a table to satisfy Delmonico; but even Delmonico might take some lessons from them in the preparation for the table of the peculiar game which they pursue, and the meats on which they feed. We, at least, rejoice at the supper prospect before us. Great collops hiss in the frying-pan, and finely cut steaks redden beautifully upon the flaming coals. Other portions of the meat are subdued to the stew, and make a very delightful dish. The head of the deer, including the brains, is put upon a flat rock in place of gridiron, and thus baked before the fire—being carefully watched and turned until every portion has duly imbibed the necessary heat, and assumed the essential hue which it should take to satisfy the eye of appetite. This portion of the deer is greatly esteemed by the hunters themselves; and the epicure of genuine stomach for the *haut gout* takes to it as an eagle to a fat mutton, and a hawk to a young turkey.

The rest of the deer—such portions of it as are not presently consumed or needed for immediate use—is cured for future sale or consumption; being smoked upon a scaffolding raised about four feet above the ground, under which, for ten or twelve hours, a moderate fire will be kept up.

Meanwhile the hounds are sniffing and snuffing around, or crouched in groups, with noses pointed at the roast and broil and bake; while their great liquid eyes dilate momently while watching for the huge gobbets which they expect to be thrown to them from time to time from the hands of the hunters.

Supper over, and it is Saturday night. It is the night dedicated among the professional hunters to what is called "The Lying Camp!"

"The Lying Camp!" quoth Columbus Mills, one of our party, a wealthy mountaineer, of large estates, of whom I have been for some time the guest.

"What do you mean by the 'Lying Camp,' Columbus?"

The explanation soon followed.

Saturday night is devoted by the mountaineers engaged in a camp hunt, which sometimes contemplates a course of several weeks, to stories of their adventures—"long yarns"—chiefly relating to the objects of their chase, and the wild experiences of their professional life. The hunter who actually inclines to exaggeration is, at such a period, privileged to deal in all the extravagancies of invention; nay, he is *required* to do so! To be literal, or confine himself to the bald and naked truth, is not only discreditable, but a *finable* offense! He is, in such a case, made to swallow a long, strong, and difficult potation! He can not be too extravagant in his incidents; but he is also required to exhibit a certain degree of *art*, in their use; and he thus frequently rises into a certain realm of fiction, the ingenuities of which are made to compensate for the exaggerations, as they do in the "Arabian Nights," and other Oriental romances.

This will suffice for explanation.

Nearly all our professional hunters assembled on the

present occasion were tolerable *raconteurs*. They complimented Jim Fisher, by throwing the raw deer-skin over his shoulders; tying the antlers of the buck with a red handkerchief over his forehead; seating him on the biggest boulder which lay at hand; and, sprinkling him with a stoup of whisky, they christened him "The Big Lie," for the occasion. And in this character he complacently presided during the rest of the evening, till the company prepared for sleep, which was not till midnight. He was king of the feast.

It was the duty of the "Big Lie" to regulate proceedings, keep order, appoint the *raconteurs* severally, and admonish them when he found them foregoing their privileges, and narrating bald, naked, and uninteresting truth. They must deal in fiction.

Jim Fisher was seventy years old, and a veteran hunter, the most famous in all the country. He *looked* authority, and promptly began to assert it, which he did in a single word:

"Yaou!"

* * *

"YAOU" WAS the *nom de nique* of one of the hunters, whose proper name was Sam Snaffles, but who, from his special smartness, had obtained the farther sobriquet of "*Sharp* Snaffles."

Columbus Mills whispered me that he was called "Yaou" from his frequent use of that word, which, in the Choctaw dialect, simply means "Yes." Snaffles had rambled considerably among the Choctaws, and picked up a variety of their words, which he was fond of using in preference to the vulgar English; and his common use of "*Yaou*," for the affirmative, had prompted the substitution of it for his own name. He answered to the name.

"Ay—yee, Yaou," was the response of Sam. "I was

afeard, 'Big Lie,' that you'd be hitching me up the very first in your team."

"And what was you afeard of? You knows as well how to take up a crooked trail as the very best man among us; so you go ahead and spin your thread a'ter the best fashion."

"What shill it be?" asked Snaffles, as he mixed a calabash full of peach and honey, preparing evidently for a long yarn.

"Give 's the history of how you got your capital, Yaou!" was the cry from two or more.

"O Lawd! I've tell'd that so often, fellows, that I'm afeard you'll sleep on it; and then again, I've tell'd it so often I've clean forgot how it goes. Somehow it changes a leetle every time I tells it."

"Never you mind! The Jedge never haird it, I reckon, for one; and I'm not sure that Columbus Mills ever did."

So the "Big Lie."

The "Jedge" was the *nom de guerre* which the hunters had conferred upon me; looking, no doubt, to my venerable aspect—for I had traveled considerably beyond my teens—and the general dignity of my bearing.

"Yaou," like other bashful beauties in oratory and singing, was disposed to hem and haw, and affect modesty and indifference, when he was brought up suddenly by the stern command of the "Big Lie," who cried out:

"Don't make yourself an etarnal fool, Sam Snaffles, by twisting your mouth out of shape, making all sorts of redickilous ixcuses. Open upon the trail at onst and give tongue, or, dern your digestion, but I'll fine you to hafe a gallon at a single swallow!"

Nearly equivalent to what Hamlet says to the conceited player:

"Leave off your damnable faces and begin."

Thus adjured with a threat, Sam Snaffles swallowed his peach and honey at a gulp, hemmed thrice lustily, put himself into an attitude, and began as follows. I shall adopt his language as closely as possible; but it is not possible, in any degree, to convey any adequate idea of his *manner*, which was admirably appropriate to the subject matter. Indeed, the fellow was a born actor.

* * *

"You see, Jedge," addressing me especially as the distinguished stranger, "I'm a telling this hyar history of mine jest to please *you*, and I'll try to please you ef I kin. These fellows hyar have hearn it so often that they knows all about it jest as well as I do my own self; and they knows the truth of it all, and would swear to it afore any hunters' court in all the county, ef so be the affidavy was to be tooken in camp and on a Saturday night.

"You see then, Jedge, it's about a dozen or fourteen years ago, when I was a young fellow without much beard on my chin, though I was full grown as I am now—strong as a horse, ef not quite so big as a buffalo. I was then jest a-beginning my 'prenticeship to the hunting business, and looking to sich persons as the 'Big Lie' thar to show me how to take the track of b'ar, buck, and painther.

"But I confess I weren't a-doing much. I hed a great deal to l'arn, and I reckon I miss'd many more bucks than I ever hit—that is, jest up to that time—"

"Look you, Yaou," said "Big Lie," interrupting him, "you're gitting too close upon the etarnal stupid truth! All you've been a-saying is jest nothing but the naked truth as I knows it. Jest crook your trail!"

"And how's a man to lie decently onless you lets him hev a bit of truth to go upon? The truth's nothing but a peg in the wall that I hangs the lie upon. A'ter a while I promise that you shan't see the peg."

"Worm along, Yaou!"

"Well, Jedge, I warn't a-doing much among the *bucks* yit—jest for the reason that I was quite too eager in the scent a'ter a sartin *doe!* Now, Jedge, you never seed my wife—my Merry Ann, as I calls her; and ef you was to see her *now*—though she's prime grit yit—you would never believe that, of all the womankind in all these mountains, she was the very yaller flower of the forest; with the reddest rose cheeks you ever did see, and sich a mouth, and sich bright curly hair, and so tall, and so slender, and so all over beautiful! O Lawd! when I thinks of it and them times, I don't see how 'twas possible to think of buck-hunting when thar was sich a doe, with sich eyes shining me on!

"Well, Jedge, Merry Ann was the only da'ter of Jeff Hopson and Keziah Hopson, his wife, who was the da'ter of Squire Claypole, whose wife was Margery Clough, that lived down upon Pacolet River—"

"Look you, Yaou, ain't you gitting into them derned facts again, eh?"

"I reckon I em, 'Big Lie!' Scuse me: I'll kiver the pegs *direct-lie*, one a'ter t'other. Whar was I? Ah! Oh! Well, Jedge, poor hunter and poor man—jest, you see, a squatter on the side of a leetle bit of a mountain close on to Columbus Mills, at Mount Tryon, I was all the time on a hot trail a'ter Merry Ann Hopson. I went thar to see her a'most every night; and sometimes I carried a buck for the old people, and sometimes a doe-skin for the gal, and I do think, bad hunter as I then was, I pretty much kept the fambly in deer meat through the whole winter."

"Good for you, Yaou! You're a-coming to it! That's the only fair trail of a lie that you've struck yit!"

So the "Big Lie," from the chair.

"Glad to hyar you say so," was the answer. "I'll git on in time! Well, Jedge, though Jeff Hopson was glad enough to git my meat always, he didn't affection me, as I did his da'ter. He was a sharp, close, money-loving old fellow, who was always considerate of the main chaince; and the old lady, his wife, who hairdly dare say her soul was her own, she jest looked both ways, as I may say, for Sunday, never giving a fair look to me or my chainces, when his eyes were sot on *her*. But 'twa'n't so with my Merry Ann. She hed the eyes for me from the beginning, and soon she hed the feelings; and, you see, Jedge, we sometimes did git a chaince, when old Jeff was gone from home, to come to a sort of onderstanding about our feelings; and the long and the short of it was that Merry Ann confessed to me that she'd like nothing better than to be my wife. She liked no other man but me. Now, Jedge, a'ter that, what was a young fellow to do? That, I say, was the proper kind of incouragement. So I said, 'I'll ax your daddy.' Then she got scary, and said, 'Oh, don't; for somehow, Sam, I'm a-thinking daddy don't like you enough *yit*. Jest hold on a bit, and come often, and bring him venison, and try to make him laugh, which you kin do, you know, and a'ter a time you kin try him.' And so I did—or rether I didn't. I put off the axing. I come constant. I brought venison all the time, and b'ar meat a plenty, a'most three days in every week."

"That's it, Yaou. You're on trail. That's as derned a lie as you've tell'd yit; for all your hunting, in them days, didn't git more meat than you could eat your one self."

"Thank you, 'Big Lie.' I hopes I'll come up in time to the right measure of the camp.

"Well, Jedge, this went on for a long time, a'most the

whole winter, and spring, and summer, till the winter begun to come in agin. I carried 'em the venison, and Merry Ann meets me in the woods, and we hes sich a pleasant time when we meets on them little odd chainces that I gits hot as thunder to bring the business to a sweet honey finish.

"But Merry Ann keeps on scary, and she puts me off; ontil, one day, one a'ternoon, 'bout sundown, she meets me in the woods, and she's all in a flusteration. And she ups and tells me how old John Grimstead, the old bachelor (a fellow about forty years old, and the dear gal not yet twenty), how he's a'ter her, and bekaise he's got a good farm, and mules and horses, how her daddy's giving him the open mouth incouragement.

"Then I says to Merry Ann:

" 'You sees, I kain't put off no longer. I must out with it, and ax your daddy at onst.' And then her scary fit come on again, and she begs me not to—not *jist yit.* But I swears by all the Hokies that I won't put off another day; and so, as I haird the old man was in the house that very hour, I left Merry Ann in the woods, all in a trimbling, and I jist went ahead, detarmined to have the figure made straight, whether odd or even.

"And Merry Ann, poor gal, she wrings her hainds, and cries a smart bit, and she wouldn't go to the house, but said she'd wait for me out thar. So I gin her a kiss into her very mouth—and did it over more than onst—and I left her, and pushed headlong for the house.

"I was jubous; I was mighty oncertain, and a leetle bit scary myself; for, you see, old Jeff was a fellow of tough grit, and with big grinders; but I was so oneasy, and so tired out waiting, and so desperate, and so fearsome that old bachelor Grimstead would get the start on me, that nothing could stop me now, and I jist bolted into the house, as free and easy and bold as ef I was the very best customer that the old man wanted to see."

Here Yaou paused to renew his draught of peach and honey.

* * *

"WELL, JEDGE, as I tell you, I put a bold face on the business, though my hairt was gitting up into my throat, and I was almost a-gasping for my breath, when I was fairly in the big room, and standing up before the old Squaire. He was a-setting in his big squar hide-bottom'd arm-chair, looking like a jedge upon the bench, jist about to send a poor fellow to the gallows. As he seed me come in, looking queer enough, I reckon, his mouth put on a sort of grin, which showed all his grinders, and he looked for all the world as ef he guessed the business I come about. But he said, good-natured enough:

" 'Well, Sam Snaffles, how goes it?'

"Says I:

" 'Pretty squar, considerin'. The winter's comin on fast, and I reckon the mountains will be full of meat before long.'

"Then says he, with another ugly grin, 'Ef 'twas your smoke-house that had it all, Sam Snaffles, 'stead of the mountains, 'twould be better for you, I reckon.'

" 'I 'grees with you,' says I. 'But I rether reckon I'll git my full shar' of it afore the spring of the leaf agin'

" 'Well, Sam,' says he, 'I hopes, for your sake, 'twill be a big shar', Sam Snaffles. Seems to me you're too easy satisfied with a small shar'; sich as the fence-squarrel carries onder his two airms, calkilating only on a small corn-crib in the chestnut-tree.'

" 'Don't you be afeard, Squaire. I'll come out right. My cabin sha'n't want for nothing that a strong man with a stout hairt kin git, with good working—enough and more for himself, and perhaps another pusson.'

" 'What other pusson?' says he, with another of his great grins, and showing of his grinders.

" 'Well,' says I, 'Squaire Hopson, that's jest what I come to talk to you about this blessed Friday night.'

"You see 'twas Friday!

" 'Well,' says he, 'go ahead, Sam Snaffles, and empty your brain-basket as soon as you kin, and I'll light my pipe while I'm a-hearin you.'

"So he lighted his pipe, and laid himself back in his chair, shet his eyes, and begin to puff like blazes.

"By this time my blood was beginning to bile in all my veins, for I seed that he was jest in the humor to tread on all my toes, and then ax a'ter my feelings. I said to myself:

" 'It's jest as well to git the worst at onst, and then thar'll be an eend of the oneasiness.' So I up and told him, in pretty soft, smooth sort of speechifying, as how I was mighty fond of Merry Ann, and she, I was a-thinking, of me; and that I jest come to ax ef I might hev Merry Ann for my wife.

"Then he opened his eyes wide, as ef he never ixpected to hear sich a proposal from me.

" 'What!' says he. 'You?'

" 'Jest so, Squaire,' says I. 'Ef it pleases you to believe me, and to consider it reasonable, the axing.'

"He sot quiet for a minit or more, then he gits up, knocks all the fire out of his pipe on the chimney, fills it, and lights it agin, and then comes straight up to me, where I was a-setting on the chair in front of him, and without a word he takes the collar of my coat betwixt the thumb and forefinger of his left hand, and he says:

" 'Git up, Sam Snaffles. Git up, ef you please.'

"Well, I gits up, and he says:

" 'Hyar! Come! Hyar!'

"And with that he leads me right across the room to a big looking-glass that hung agin the partition wall, and thar he stops before the glass, facing it and holding me by the collar all the time.

"Now that looking-glass, Jedge, was about the biggest I ever did see! It was a'most three feet high, and a'most two feet wide, and it had a bright, broad frame, shiny like gold, with a heap of leetle figgers worked all round it. I reckon thar's no sich glass now in all the mountain country. I 'member when first that glass come home. It was a great thing, and the old Squaire was mighty proud of it. He bought it at the sale of some rich man's furniter, down at Greenville, and he was jest as fond of looking into it as a young gal, and whenever he lighted his pipe, he'd walk up and down the room, seeing himself in the glass.

"Well, thar he hed me up, both on us standing in front of this glass, whar he could a'most see the whole of our figgers, from head to foot.

"And when we hed stood thar for a minit or so, he says, quite solemn like:

" 'Look in the glass, Sam Snaffles.'

"So I looked.

" 'Well,' says I. 'I sees you, Squaire Hopson, and myself, Sam Snaffles.'

" 'Look good,' says he, '*obzarve* well.'

" 'Well,' says I, 'I'm a-looking with all my eyes. I only sees what I tells you.'

" 'But you don't *obzarve*,' says he. 'Looking and seeing's one thing,' says he, 'but obzarving's another. Now *obzarve*.'

"By this time, Jedge, I was getting sort o' riled, for

I could see that somehow he was jest a-trying to make me feel redickilous. So I says:

" 'Look you, Squaire Hopson, ef you thinks I never seed myself in a glass afore this, you're mighty mistaken. I've got my own glass at home, and though it's but a leetle sort of a small, mean consarn, it shows me as much of my own face and figger as I cares to see at any time. I never cares to look in it 'cept when I'm brushing, and combing, and clipping off the straggling beard when it's too long for my eating.'

" 'Very well,' says he; 'now obzarve! You sees your own figger, and your face, and you air obzarving as well as you know how. Now Mr. Sam Snafflles—now that you've hed a fair look at yourself—jest now answer me, from your honest conscience, a'ter all you've seed, ef you honestly thinks you're the sort of pusson to hev *my* da'ter!'

"And with that he gin me a twist, and when I wheeled round he hed wheeled round too, and thar we stood, full facing one another.

"Lawd! how I was riled! But I answered quick:

" 'And why not, I'd like to know, Squaire Hopson? I ain't the handsomest man in the world, but I'm not the ugliest; and folks don't generally consider me at all among the uglies. I'm as tall a man as you, and as stout and strong, and as good a man o' my inches as ever stepped in shoe-leather. And it's enough to tell you, Squaire, whatever *you* may think, that Merry Ann believes in me, and she's a way of thinking that I'm jest about the very pusson that ought to hev her.'

" 'Merry Ann's thinking,' says he, 'don't run all fours with her faything's thinking. I axed you, Sam Snaffles, to *obzarve* yourself in the glass. I telled you that seeing warn't edzactly obzarving. You seed only the inches; you seed that you hed eyes and mouth and nose and the airms and legs of the man. But eyes and mouth and legs and airms don't make a man!'

" 'Oh, they don't!' says I.

" 'No, indeed,' says he. 'I seed that you hed all them; but then I seed thar was one thing thet you hedn't got.'

" 'Jimini!' says I, mighty conflustered. 'What thing's a-wanting to me to make me a man?'

" '*Capital!*' says he, and he lifted himself up and looked mighty grand.

" 'Capital!' says I; 'and what's that?'

" 'Thar air many kinds of capital,' says he. 'Money's capital, for it kin buy every thing. House and lands is capital; cattle and horses and sheep—when thar's enough on 'em—is capital. And as I obzarved you in the glass, Sam Snaffles, I seed that *capital* was the very thing that you wanted to make a man of you! Now I don't mean that any da'ter of mine shall marry a pusson that's not a *parfect* man. I obzarved you long ago, and seed whar you was wanting. I axed about you. I axed your horse.'

" 'Axed my horse!' says I, pretty nigh dumfoundered.

" 'Yes; I axed your horse, and he said to me: "Look at me! I hain't got an ounce of spar' flesh on my bones. You kin count all my ribs. You kin lay the whole length of your airm betwixt any two on 'em, and it 'll lie thar as snug as a black snake betwixt two poles of a log-house." Says he, "Sam's got *no capital*! He ain't got, any time, five bushels of corn in his crib; and he's such a monstrous feeder himself that he'll eat out four bushels, and think it mighty hard upon him to give *me* the other one." Thar, now, was your horse's testimony, Sam, agin you. Then I axed about your cabin, and your way of living. I was curious, and went to see you one day when I knowed you waur at home. You hed but one chair, which you gin me to set on, and you sot on the eend of a barrel for yourself.

You gin me a rasher of bacon what hedn't a streak of fat in it. You hed a poor quarter of a poor doe hanging from the rafters—a poor beast that somebody hed disabled—'

" 'I shot it myself,' says I.

" 'Well, it was a-dying when you shot it; and all the hunters say you was a poor shooter at any thing. You cooked our dinner yourself, and the hoe-cake was all dough, not hafe done, and the meat was all done as tough as ef you had dried it for a month of Sundays in a Fluriday sun! Your cabin hed but one room, and that you slept in and ate in; and the floor was six inches deep in dirt! Then, when I looked into your garden, I found seven stalks of long collards only, every one seven foot high, with all the leaves stript off it, as ef you wanted 'em for broth; till thar waur only three top leaves left on every stalk. You hedn't a stalk of corn growing, and when I scratched at your turnip-bed I found nothing bigger than a chestnut. Then, Sam, I begun to ask about your fairm, and I found that you was nothing but a squatter on land of Columbus Mills, who let you have an old nigger pole-house, and an acre or two of land. Says I to myself, says I, "This poor fellow's got *no capital*; and he hasn't the head to git *capital*;" and from that moment, Sam Snaffles, the more I obzarved you, the more sartin 'twas that you never could be a man, ef you waur to live a thousand years. You may think, in your vanity, that you air a man; but you ain't, and never will be, onless you kin find a way to git *capital*; and I loves my gal child too much to let her marry any pusson whom I don't altogether consider a man!'

"A'ter that long speechifying, Jedge, you might ha' ground me up in a mill, biled me down in a pot, and scattered me over a manure heap, and I wouldn't ha' been able to say a word!

"I cotched up my hat, and was a-gwine, when he said to me, with his derned infernal big grin:

" 'Take another look in the glass, Sam Snaffles, and obzarve well, and you'll see jest whar it is I thinks that you're wanting.'

"I didn't stop for any more. I jest bolted, like a hot shot out of a shovel, and didn't know my own self, or whatever steps I tuk, tell I got into the thick and met Merry Ann coming towards me.

"I must liquor now!"

* * *

"WELL, JEDGE, it was a hard meeting betwixt me and Merry Ann. The poor gal come to me in a sort of run, and hairdly drawing her breath, she cried out:

" 'Oh, Sam! What does he say?'

" What could I say? How tell her? I jest wrapped her up in my airms, and I cries out, making some violent remarks about the old Squaire.

"Then she screamed, and I hed to squeeze her up, more close than ever, and kiss her, I reckon, more than a dozen times, jest to keep her from gwine into historical fits. I telled her all, from beginning to eend.

"I telled her that thar waur some truth in what the old man said: that I hedn't been keerful to do the thing as I ought; that the house *was* mean and dirty; that the horse was mean and poor; that I hed been thinking too much about her own self to think about other things; but that I would do better, would see to things, put things right, git corn in the crib, git 'capital,' ef I could, and make a good, comfortable home for *her*.

" 'Look at me,' says I, 'Merry Ann. Does I look like a man?'

" 'You're all the man I wants,' says she.

" 'That's enough,' says I. 'You shall see what I kin do, and what I *will* do! That's ef you air true to me.'

" 'I'll be true to you, Sam,' says she.

" 'And you won't think of nobody else?'

" 'Never,' says she.

" 'Well, you'll see what I kin do, and what I *will* do. You'll see that I *em* a man; and ef thar's capital to be got in all the country, by working and hunting, and fighting, ef that's needful, we shill hev it. Only you be true to me, Merry Ann.'

"And she throwed herself upon my buzzom, and cried out:

" 'I'll be true to you, Sam. I loves nobody in all the world so much as I loves you.'

" 'And you won't marry any other man, Merry Ann, no matter what your daddy says?'

" 'Never,' she says.

" 'And you won't listen to this old bachelor fellow, Grimstead, that's got the "capital" already, no matter how they spurs you?'

" 'Never!' she says.

" 'Sw'ar it!' says I—'sw'ar it, Merry Ann—that you will be my wife, and never marry Grimstead!'

" 'I sw'ars it,' she says, kissing *me*, bekaize we had no book.

" 'Now,' says I, 'Merry Ann, that's not enough. Cuss him for my sake, and to make it sartin. Cuss that fellow Grimstead.'

" 'Oh, Sam, I kain't cuss,' says she; 'that's wicked.'

" 'Cuss him on my account,' says I—'to my credit.'

" 'Oh,' says she, 'don't ax me. I kain't do that.'

"Says I, 'Merry Ann, if you don't cuss that fellow, some way, I do believe you'll go over to him a'ter all.

Jest you cuss him, now. Any small cuss will do, ef you're in airnest.

" 'Well,' says she, 'ef that's your idee, then I says, "*Drot his skin*,* and drot *my* skin, too, ef I ever marries any body but Sam Snaffles.' "

" 'That'll do, Merry Ann,' says I. 'And now I'm easy in my soul and conscience. And now, Merry Ann, I'm gwine off to try my best, and git the "capital." Ef it's the "capital" that's needful to make a man of me, I'll git it, by all the Holy Hokies, if I kin.'

"And so, after a million of squeezes and kisses, we parted; and she slipt along through the woods, the back way to the house, and I mounted my horse to go to my cabin. But, afore I mounted the beast, I gin him a dozen kicks in his ribs, jest for bearing his testimony agin me, and telling the old Squaire that I hedn't 'capital' enough for a corn crib."

* * *

"I WAS MIGHTILY LET DOWN, as you may think, by old Squaire Hopson; but I was mightily lifted up by Merry Ann.

"But when I got to my cabin, and seed how mean every thing was there, and thought how true it was, all that old Squaire Hopson had said, I felt overkim, and I said to myself, 'It's all true! How can I bring that beautiful yaller flower of the forest to live in sich a mean cabin, and with sich poor accommydations? She that had every thing comforting and nice about her.'

* "Drot," or "Drat," has been called an American vulgarism, but it is genuine old English, as ancient as the days of Ben Jonson. Originally the oath was, "God rot it"; but Puritanism, which was unwilling to take the name of God in vain, was yet not prepared to abandon the oath, so the pious preserved it in an abridged form, omitting the G from God, and using, "Od rot it." It reached its final contraction, "Drot," before it came to America. "Drot it" "Drat it," "Drot your eyes," or "Drot his skin," are so many modes of using it among the uneducated classes.

"Then I considered all about 'capital'; and it growed on me, ontil I begin to see that a man might hev good legs and arms and thighs, and a good face of his own, and yit not be a parfect and proper man a'ter all! I hed lived, you see, Jedge, to be twenty-three years of age, and was living no better than a three-old-year b'ar, in a sort of cave, sleeping on shuck and straw, and never looking after to-morrow.

"I couldn't sleep all that night for the thinking, and obzarvations. That impudent talking of old Hopson put me on a new track. I couldn't give up hunting. I knowed no other business, and I didn't hafe know that.

"I thought to myself, 'I must l'arn my business so as to work like a master.'

"But then, when I considered how hard it was, how slow I was to git the deers and the b'ar, and what a small chaince of money it brought me, I said to myself:

" 'Whar's the "capital" to come from?'

"Lawd save us! I ate up the meat pretty much as fast as I got it!

"Well, Jedge, as I said, I had a most miserable night of consideration and observation and concatenation accordingly. I felt all over mean, 'cept now and then, when I thought of dear Merry Ann, and her felicities and cordialities and fidelities; and then, the cuss which she gin, onder the kiver of 'Drot,' to that dried up old bachelor Grimstead. But I got to sleep at last. And I hed a dream. And I thought I seed the prettiest woman critter in the world, next to Merry Ann, standing close by my bedside; and, at first, I thought 'twas Merry Ann, and I was gwine to kiss her agin; but she drawed back and said:

" 'Scuse me! I'm not Merry Ann; but I'm her friend and your friend; so don't you be down in the mouth, but keep a good hairt, and you'll hev help, and git the "capital" whar you don't look for it now. It's only needful that you be detarmined on good works and making a man of yourself.'

"A'ter that dream I slept like a top, woke at day-peep, took my rifle, called up my dog, mounted my horse, and put out for the laurel hollows.

"Well, I hunted all day, made several *starts*, but got nothing; my dog ran off, the rascally pup, and, I reckon, ef Squaire Hopson had met him he'd ha' said 'twas bekaise I starved him! Fact is, we hedn't any of us much to eat that day, and the old mar's ribs stood out bigger than ever.

"All day I rode and followed the track and got nothing.

"Well, jest about sunset I come to a hollow of the hills that I hed never seed before; and in the middle of it was a great pond of water, what you call a lake; and it showed like so much purple glass in the sunset, and 'twas jest as smooth as the big looking-glass of Squaire Hopson's. Thar wa'n't a breath of wind stirring.

"I was mighty tired, so I eased down from the mar', tied up the bridle and check, and let her pick about, and laid myself down onder a tree, jest about twenty yards from the lake, and thought to rest myself ontil the moon riz, which I knowed would be about seven o'clock.

"I didn't mean to fall asleep, but I did it; and I reckon I must ha' slept a good hour, for when I woke the dark hed set in, and I could only see one or two bright stars hyar and thar, shooting out from the dark of the heavens. But, ef I seed nothing, I haird; and jest sich a sound and noise as I hed never haird before.

"Thar was a rushing and a roaring and a screaming and a plashing, in the air and in the water, as made you think the univarsal world was coming to an eend!

"All that set me up. I was waked up out of sleep and

dreams, and my eyes opened to every thing that eye could see; and sich another sight I never seed before! I tell you, Jedge, ef there was one wild-goose settling down in that lake, thar was one hundred thousand of 'em! I couldn't see the eend of 'em. They come every minit, swarm a'ter swarm, in tens and twenties and fifties and hundreds; and sich a fuss as they did make! sich a gabbling, sich a splashing, sich a confusion, that I was fairly conflusterated; and I jest lay whar I was, a-watching 'em.

"You never seed beasts so happy! How they flapped their wings; how they gabbled to one another; how they swam hyar and thar, to the very middle of the lake and to the very edge of it, jest a fifty yards from whar I lay squat, never moving leg or arm! It was wonderful to see! I wondered how they could find room, for I reckon thar waur forty thousand on 'em, all scuffling in that leetle lake together!

"Well, as I watched 'em, I said to myself:

" 'Now, if a fellow could only captivate all them wild-geese—fresh from Canniday, I reckon—what would they bring in the market at Spartanburg and Greenville? Walker, I knowed, would buy 'em up quick at fifty cents a head. Thar war "capital!" '

"I could ha' fired in among 'em with my rifle, never taking aim, and killed a dozen or more, at a single shot; but what was a poor dozen geese, when thar waur forty thousand to captivate?

"What a haul 'twould be, ef a man could only get 'em all in one net! Kiver 'em all at a fling!

"The idee worked like so much fire in my brain.

"How kin it be done?

"That was the question!

" 'Kin it be done?' I axed myself.

" 'It kin,' I said to myself; 'and I'm the very man

to do it!' Then I begun to work away in the thinking. I thought over all the traps and nets and snares that I hed ever seen or haird of; and the leetle eends of the idee begun to come together in my head; and, watching all the time how the geese flopped and splashed and played and swum, I said to myself:

" 'Oh! most beautiful critters; ef I don't make some "capital" out of you, then I'm not dezarving sich a beautiful yāller flower of the forest as my Merry Ann!'

"Well, I watched a long time, ontil dark night, and the stars begun to peep down upon me over the high hill-tops. Then I got up and tuk to my horse and rode home.

"And thar, when I hed swallowed my bit of hoe-cake and bacon and a good strong cup of coffee, and got into bed, I couldn't sleep for a long time, thinking how I was to git them geese.

"But I kept nearing the right idee every minit, and when I was fast asleep it come to me in my dream.

"I seed the same beautifulest young woman agin that hed given me the incouragement before to go ahead, and she helped me out with the idee.

"So, in the morning, I went to work. I rode off to Spartanburg, and bought all the twine and cord and hafe the plow-lines in town; and I got a lot of great fishhooks, all to help make the tanglement parfect; and I got lead for sinkers, and I got cork-wood for floaters; and I pushed for home as fast as my poor mar' could streak it.

"I was at work day and night for nigh on to a week, making my net; and when 'twas done I borrowed a mule and cart from Columbus Mills, thar;—he'll tell you all about it—he kin make his affidavy to the truth of it.

"Well, off I driv with my great net, and got to the lake about noonday. I knowed 'twould take me some hours to make my fixings parfect, and git the net fairly stretched across the lake, and jest deep enough to do the tangling of every leg of the birds in the very midst of their swimming and snorting and splashing and cavorting! When I hed fixed it all fine, and jest as I wanted it, I brought the eends of my plow-lines up to where I was gwine to hide myself. This was onder a strong sapling, and my calkilation was when I hed got the beasts all hooked, forty thousand, more or less—and I could tell how that was from feeling on the line—why, then, I'd whip the line round the sapling, hitch it fast, and draw in my birds at my own ease, without axing much about their comfort.

"'Twas a most beautiful and parfect plan, and all would ha' worked beautiful well but for one leetle over-sight of mine. But I won't tell you about that part of the business yit, the more pretickilarly as it all turned out for the very best, as you'll see in the eend.

"I hedn't long finished my fixings when the sun suddenly tumbled down the heights, and the dark begun to creep in upon me, and a pretty cold dark it waur! I remember it well! My teeth began to chatter in my head, though I was boiling over with inward heat, all jest coming out of my hot eagerness to be captivating the birds.

"Well, Jedge, I hedn't to wait overlong. Soon I haird them coming, screaming fur away, and then I seed them pouring, jest like so many white clouds, straight down, I reckon, from the snow mountains off in Canniday.

"Down they come, millions upon millions, till I was sartin thar waur already pretty nigh on to forty thousand in the lake. It waur always a nice calkilation of mine that the lake could hold fully forty thousand, though onst, when I went round to measure it, stepping it off, I was jubous whether it could hold over thirty-nine thousand; but, as I tuk the measure in hot weather and in a dry spell,

I concluded that some of the water along the edges hed dried up, and 'twa'n't so full as when I made my first calkilation. So I hev stuck to that first calkilation ever since.

"Well, thar they waur, forty thousand, we'll say, with, it mout be, a few millions and hundreds over. And Lawd! how they played and splashed and screamed and dived! I calkilated on hooking a good many of them divers, in pretickilar, and so I watched and waited, ontil I thought I'd feel of my lines; and I begun, leetle by leetle, to haul in, when Lawd love you, Jedge, sich a ripping and raging, and bouncing and flouncing, and flopping and splashing, and kicking and screaming, you never did hear in all your born days!

"By this I knowed that I hed captivated the captains of the host, and a pretty smart chaince, I reckoned, of the rigilar army, ef 'twa'n't edzactly forty thousand; for I calkilated that some few would git away—run off, just as the cowards always does in the army, jest when the shooting and confusion begins; still, I reasonably calkilated on the main body of the rigiments; and so, gitting more and more hot and eager, and pulling and hauling, I made one big mistake, and, instid of wrapping the eends of my lines around the sapling that was standing jest behind me, what does I do but wraps 'em round my own thigh—the right thigh, you see—and some of the loops waur hitched round my left arm at the same time!

"All this come of my hurry and ixcitement, for it was burning like a hot fever in my brain, and I didn't know when or how I hed tied myself up, ontil suddently, with an all-fired scream, all together, them forty thousand geese rose like a great black cloud in the air, all tied up, tangled up—hooked about the legs, hooked about the gills, hooked and fast in some way in the beautiful leetle twistings of my net!

"Yes, Jedge, as I'm a living hunter to-night, hyar a-talking to you, they riz up all together, as ef they hed consulted upon it, like a mighty thunder-cloud, and off they went, screaming and flouncing, meaning, I reckon, to take the back track to Canniday, in spite of the freezing weather.

"Before I knowed whar I was, Jedge, I was twenty feet in the air, my right thigh up and my left arm, and the other thigh and arm a-dangling useless, and feeling every minit as ef they was gwine to drop off.

"You may be sure I pulled with all my might, but that waur mighty leetle in the fix I was in, and I jest hed to hold on, and see whar the infernal beasts would carry me. I couldn't loose myself, and ef I could I was by this time quite too fur up in the air, and darsn't do so, onless I was willing to hev my brains dashed out, and my whole body mashed to a mammock!

"Oh, Jedge, jest consider my sitivation! It's sich a ricollection, Jedge, that I must rest and liquor, in order to rekiver the necessary strength to tell you what happened next."

* * *

"Yes, Jedge," said Yaou, resuming his narrative, "jest stop whar you air, and consider my sitivation!

"Thar I was dangling, like a dead weight, at the tail of that all-fired cloud of wild-geese, head downward, and gwine, the Lawd knows whar! to Canniday, or Jericho, or some other heathen territory beyond the Massissipp, and it mout be, over the great etarnal ocean!

"When I thought of *that*, and thought of the plow-lines giving way, and that on a suddent I should come down plump into the big sea, jest in a middle of a great gathering of shirks and whales, to be dewoured and tore to bits by their bloody grinders, I was ready to die of skeer outright. I thought over all my sinnings in a moment, and I thought of my poor dear Merry Ann, and I called out her name, loud as I could, jest as ef the poor gal could hyar me or help me.

"And jest then I could see we waur a drawing nigh a great thunder-cloud. I could see the red tongues running out of its black jaws; and 'Lawd!' says I, 'ef these all-fired infarnal wild beasts of birds should carry me into that cloud to be burned to a coal, fried, and roasted, and biled alive by them tongues of red fire!'

"But the geese fought shy of the cloud, though we passed mighty nigh on to it, and I could see one red streak of lightning run out of the cloud and give us chase for a full hafe a mile; but we waur too fast for it, and, in a tearing passion bekaise it couldn't ketch us, the red streak struck its horns into a great tree jest behind us, that we hed passed over, and tore it into flinders, in the twink of a musquito.

"But by this time I was beginning to feel quite stupid. I knowed that I waur fast gitting onsensible, and it did seem to me as ef my hour waur come, and I was gwine to die—and die by rope, and dangling in the air, a thousand miles from the airth!

"But jest then I was roused up. I felt something brush agin me; then my face was scratched; and, on a suddent, thar was a stop put to my travels by that conveyance. The geese had stopped flying, and waur in a mighty great conflusteration, flopping their wings, as well as they could, and screaming with all the tongues in their jaws. It was clar to me now that we hed run agin something that brought us all up with a short hitch.

"I was shook roughly agin the obstruction, and I put out my right arm and cotched a hold of a long arm of an almighty big tree; then my legs waur cotched betwixt two other branches, and I rekivered myself, so as to set up a leetle and rest. The geese was a tumbling and flopping among the branches. The net was hooked hyar and thar; and the birds waur all about me, swinging and splurging, but onable to break loose and git away.

"By leetle and leetle I come to my clar senses, and begun to feel my sitivation. The stiffness was passing out of my limbs. I could draw up my legs, and, after some hard work, I managed to onwrap the plow-lines from my right thigh and my left arm, and I hed the sense this time to tie the eends pretty tight to a great branch of the tree which stretched clar across and about a foot over my head.

"Then I begun to consider my sitivation. I hed hed a hard riding, that was sartin; and I felt sore enough. And I hed hed a horrid bad skear, enough to make a man's wool turn white afore the night was over. But now I felt easy, bekaise I considered myself safe. With day-peep I calkilated to let myself down from the tree by my plow-lines, and thar, below, tied fast, warn't thar my forty thousand captivated geese?

" 'Hurrah!' I sings out. 'Hurrah, Merry Ann; we'll hev the "capital" now, I reckon!'

"And singing out, I drawed up my legs and shifted my body so as to find an easier seat in the crutch of the tree, which was an almighty big chestnut oak, when, O Lawd! on a suddent the stump I hed been a-setting on give way onder me. 'Twas a rotten jint of the tree. It give way, Jedge, as I tell you, and down I went, my legs first and then my whole body—slipping down not on the outside, but into a great hollow of the tree, all the hairt of it being eat out by the rot; and afore I knowed whar I waur, I waur some twenty foot down, I reckon; and by the time I touched bottom, I was up to my neck in honey!

"It was an almighty big honey-tree, full of the sweet treacle; and the bees all gone and left it, I reckon, for a hundred years. And I in it up to my neck.

"I could smell it strong. I could taste it sweet. But I could see nothing.

"Lawd! Lawd! From bad to worse; buried alive in a hollow tree with never a chaince to git out! I would then ha' given all the world ef I was only sailing away with them bloody wild-geese to Canniday, and Jericho, even across the sea, with all its shirks and whales dewouring me.

"Buried alive! O Lawd! O Lawd! 'Lawd save me and help me!' I cried out from the depths. And 'Oh, my Merry Ann,' I cried, 'shill we never meet agin no more!' Scuse my weeping, Jedge, but I feels all over the sinsation, fresh as ever, of being buried alive in a bee-hive tree and presarved in honey. I must liquor, Jedge."

* * *

YAOU, AFTER a great swallow of peach and honey, and a formidible groan after it, resumed his narrative as follows:

"Only think of me, Jedge, in my sitivation! Buried alive in the hollow of a mountain chestnut oak! Up to my neck in honey, with never no more an appetite to eat than ef it waur the very gall of bitterness that we reads of in the Holy Scripters!

"All dark, all silent as the grave; 'cept for the gabbling and the cackling of the wild-geese outside, that every now and then would make a great splurging and cavorting, trying to break away from their hitch, which was jist as fast fixed as my own.

"Who would git them geese that hed cost me so much to captivate? Who would inherit my 'capital'? and who would hev Merry Ann? and what will become of the mule and cart of Mills fastened in the woods by the leetle lake?

"I cussed the leetle lake, and the geese, and all the 'capital.'

"I cussed. I couldn't help it. I cussed from the bottom of my hairt, when I ought to ha' bin saying my prayers. And thar was my poor mar' in the stable with never a morsel of feed. She had told tales upon me to Squaire Hopson, it's true, but I forgin her, and thought of her feed, and nobody to give her none. Thar waur corn in the crib and fodder, but it warn't in the stable; and onless Columbus Mills should come looking a'ter me at the cabin, thar waur no hope for me or the mar.'

"Oh, Jedge, you couldn't jedge of my sitivation in that deep hollow, that cave, I may say, of mountain oak! My head waur jest above the honey, and ef I backed it to look up, my long ha'r at the back of the neck a'most stuck fast, so thick was the honey.

"But I couldn't help looking up. The hollow was a wide one at the top, and I could see when a star was passing over. Thar they shined, bright and beautiful, as ef they waur the very eyes of the angels; and, as I seed them come and go, looking smiling in upon me as they come, I cried out to 'em, one by one:

" 'Oh, sweet sperrits, blessed angels! ef so be thar's an angel sperrit, as they say, living in all them stars, come down and extricate me from this fix; for, so fur as I kin see, I've got no chaince of help from mortal man or woman. Hardly onst a year does a human come this way; and ef they did come, how would they know I'm hyar? How could I make them hyar me? O Lawd! O blessed, beautiful angels in them stars! O give me help! Help me out!' I knowed I prayed like a heathen sinner, but I prayed as well as I knowed how; and thar warn't a star passing over me that I didn't pray to, soon as I seed them shining over the opening of the hollow; and I prayed fast and faster as I seed them passing away and gitting out of sight.

"Well, Jedge, suddently, in the midst of my praying, and jest after one bright, big star hed gone over me without seeing my sitivation, I hed a fresh skeer.

"Suddent I haird a monstrous fluttering among my geese—my 'capital.' Then I haird a great scraping and scratching on the outside of the tree, and suddent, as I looked up, the mouth of the hollow was shet up.

"All was dark. The stars and sky waur all gone. Something black kivered the hollow, and, in a minit a'ter, I haird something slipping down into the hollow right upon me.

"I could hairdly draw my breath. I begun to fear that I was to be siffocated alive; and as I haird the strange critter slipping down, I shoved out my hands and felt ha'r—coarse wool—and with one hand I cotched hold of the ha'ry leg of a beast, and with t'other hand I cotched hold of his tail.

"'Twas a great ba'r, one of the biggest, come to git his honey. He knowed the tree, Jedge, you see, and ef any beast in the world loves honey, 'tis a b'ar beast. He'll go his death on honey, though the hounds are tearing at his very haunches.

"You may be sure, when I onst knowed what he was, and onst got a good gripe on his hindquarters, I warn't gwine to let go in a hurry. I knowed that was my only chaince for gitting out of the hollow, and I do believe them blessed angels in the stars sent the beast, jest at the right time, to give me human help and assistance.

"Now, yer see, Jedge, thar was no chaince for him turning round upon me. He pretty much filled up the hollow. He knowed his way, and slipped down, eend foremost—the latter eend, you know. He could stand up on his hind-legs and eat all he wanted. Then, with his great sharp claws and his mighty muscle, he could work up, holding on to the sides of the tree, and git out a'most as easy as when he come down.

"Now, you see, ef he weighed five hundred pounds, and could climb like a cat, he could easy carry up a young fellow that hed no flesh to spar', and only weighed a hundred and twenty-five. So I laid my weight on him, eased him off as well as I could, but held on to tail and leg as ef all life and etarnity depended upon it.

"Now I reckon, Jedge, that b'ar was pretty much more skeered than I was. He couldn't turn in his shoes, and with something fastened to his ankles, and, as he thought, I reckon some strange beast fastened to his tail, you never seed beast more eager to git away, and git upwards. He knowed the way, and stuck his claws in the rough sides of the hollow, hand over hand, jest as a sailor pulls a rope, and up we went. We hed, howsomdever, more than one slip back; but, Lawd bless you! I never let go. Up we went, I say, at last, and I stuck jest as close to his haunches as death sticks to a dead nigger. Up we went. I felt myself moving. My neck was out of the honey. My airms were free. I could feel the sticky thing slipping off from me, and a'ter a good quarter of an hour the b'ar was on the great mouth of the hollow; and as I felt that I let go his tail, still keeping fast hold of his leg, and with one hand I cotched hold of the outside rim of the hollow; I found it fast, held on to it; and jest then the b'ar sat squat on the very edge of the hollow, taking a sort of rest a'ter his labor.

"I don't know what 'twas, Jedge, that made me do it. I warn't a-thinking at all. I was only feeling and drawing a long breath. Jest then the b'ar sort o' looked round, as ef to see what varmint it was a-troubling him, when I gin him a mighty push, strong as I could, and he lost his balance and went over outside down cl'ar to the airth, and I could hyar his neck crack, almost as loud as a pistol.

"I drawed a long breath a'ter that, and prayed a short prayer; and feeling my way all the time, so as to be sure agin rotten branches, I got a safe seat among the limbs of the tree, and sot myself down, detarmined to wait tell broad daylight before I tuk another step in the business."

* * *

"AND THERE I SOT. So fur as I could see, Jedge, I was safe. I hed got out of the tie of the flying geese, and thar they all waur, spread before me, flopping now and then and trying to ixtricate themselves; but they couldn't come it! Thar they waur, captivated, and so much 'capital' for Sam Snaffles.

"And I hed got out of the lion's den; that is, I hed got out of the honey-tree, and warn't in no present danger of being buried alive agin. Thanks to the b'ar, and to the blessed beautiful angel sperrits in the stars, that hed sent him thar seeking honey, to be my deliverance from my captivation!

"And thar he lay, jest as quiet as ef he waur a-sleeping, though I knowed his neck was broke. And that b'ar, too, was so much 'capital.'

"And I sot in the tree making my calkilations. I could see now the meaning of that beautiful young critter that come to me in my dreams. I was to hev the 'capital,' but I was to git it through troubles and tribulations, and a mighty bad skeer for life. I never knowed the valley of 'capital' till now, and I seed the sense in all that Squaire Hopson told me, though he did tell it in a mighty spiteful sperrit.

"Well, I calkilated.

"It was cold weather, freezing, and though I had good warm clothes on, I felt monstrous like sleeping, from the cold only, though perhaps the tire and the skeer together hed something to do with it. But I was afeard to sleep. I didn't know what would happen, and a man has never his right courage ontil daylight. I fou't agin sleep by keeping on my calkilation.

"Forty thousand wild geese!

"Thar wa'n't forty thousand, edzactly—very far from it—but thar they waur, pretty thick; and for every goose I could git from forty to sixty cents in all the villages in South Carolina.

"Thar was 'capital!'

"Then thar waur the b'ar.

"Jedging from his strength in pulling me up, and from his size and fat in filling up that great hollow in the tree, I calkilated that he couldn't weigh less than five hundred pounds. His hide, I knowed, was worth twenty dollars. Then thar was the fat and tallow, and the biled marrow out of his bones, what they makes b'ars grease out of, to make chicken whiskers grow big enough for game-cocks. Then thar waur the meat, skinned, cleaned, and all; thar couldn't be much onder four hundred and fifty pounds, and whether I sold him as fresh meat or cured, he'd bring me ten cents a pound at the least.

"Says I, 'Thar's capital!'

" 'Then,' says I, 'thar's my honey-tree! I reckon thar's a matter of ten thousand gallons in this hyar same honey-tree; and if I kain't git fifty to seventy cents a gallon for it thar's no alligators in Flurriday!'

"And so I calkilated through the night, fighting agin

sleep, and thinking of my 'capital' and Merry Ann together.

"By morning I had calkilated all I hed to do and all I hed to make.

"Soon as I got a peep of day I was bright on the lookout.

"Thar all around me were the captivated geese critters. The b'ar laid down parfectly easy and waiting for the knife; and the geese, I reckon they waur much more tired than me, for they didn't seem to hev the hairt for a single flutter, even when they seed me swing down from the tree among 'em, holding on to my plow-lines and letting myself down easy.

"But first I must tell you, Jedge, when I seed the first signs of daylight and looked around me, Lawd bless me, what should I see but old Tryon Mountain, with his great head lifting itself up in the ast! And beyant I could see the house and fairm of Columbus Mills; and as I turned to look a leetle south of that, thar was my own poor leetle log-cabin standing quiet, but with never a smoke streaming out from the chimbley.

" 'God bless them good angel sperrits,' I said, 'I ain't two miles from home!' Before I come down from the tree I knowed edzactly whar I waur. 'Twas only four miles off from the lake and whar I hitched the mule of Columbus Mills close by the cart. Thar, too, I hed left my rifle. Yit in my miserable fix, carried through the air by them wild-geese, I did think I hed gone a'most a thousand miles towards Canniday.

"Soon as I got down from the tree I pushed off at a trot to git the mule and cart. I was pretty sure of my b'ar and geese when I come back. The cart stood quiet enough. But the mule, having nothing to eat, was sharping her teeth upon a boulder, thinking she'd hev a bite or so before long.

"I hitched her up, brought her to my bee-tree, tumbled the b'ar into the cart, wrung the necks of all the geese that waur thar—many hed got away—and counted some twenty-seven hundred that I piled away atop of the b'ar."

"Twenty-seven hundred!" cried the "Big Lie" and all the hunters at a breath. "Twenty-seven hundred! Why, Yaou, whenever you telled of this thing before you always counted them at 3150!"

"Well, ef I did, I reckon I was right. I was sartainly right then, it being all fresh in my 'membrance; and I'm not the man to go back agin his own words. No, fellows, I sticks to first words and first principles. I scorns to eat my own words. Ef I said 3150, then 3150 it waur, never a goose less. But you'll see how to 'count for all. I reckon 'twas only 2700 I fotched to market. Thar was 200 I gin to Columbus Mills. Then thar was 200 more I carried to Merry Ann; and then thar waur 50 at least, I reckon, I kep for myself. Jest you count up, Jedge, and you'll see how to squar' it on all sides. When I said 2700 I only counted what I sold in the villages, every head of 'em at fifty cents a head; and a'ter putting the money in my pocket I felt all over that I hed the 'capital.'

"Well, Jedge, next about the b'ar. Sold the hide and tallow for a fine market-price; sold the meat, got ten cents a pound for it fresh—'twas most beautiful meat; biled down the bones for the marrow; melted down the grease; sold fourteen pounds of it to the barbers and apothecaries; got a dollar a pound for that; sold the hide for twenty dollars; and got the cash for everything.

"Thar warn't a fambly in all Greenville and Spartanburg and Asheville that didn't git fresh, green wild-geese from me that season, at fifty cents a head, and glad to git, too; the cheapest fresh meat they could buy; and, I reckon, the finest. And all the people of them villages, ef they hed gone to heaven that week, in the flesh, would have carried nothing better than goose-flesh for the risurrection! Every body ate goose for a month, I reckon, as the weather was freezing cold all the time, and the beasts kept week after week, ontil they waur eaten. From the b'ar only I made a matter of full one hundred dollars. First, thar waur the hide, $20; then 450 pounds of meat, at 10 cents, was $45; then the grease, 14 pounds, $14; and the tallow, some $6 more; and the biled marrow, $11.

"Well, count up, Jedge; 2700 wild-geese, at 50 cents, you sees, must be more than $1350. I kin only say, that a'ter all the selling—and I driv at it day and night, with Columbus Mills's mule and cart, and went to every house in every street in all them villages. I hed a'most fifteen hundred dollars, safe stowed away onder the pillows of my bed, all in gould and silver.

"But I warn't done! Thar was my bee-tree. Don't you think I waur gwine to lose that honey! No, my darlint! I didn't beat the drum about nothing. I didn't let on to a soul what I was a-doing. They axed me about the wild-geese, but I sent 'em on a wild-goose chase; and 'twa'n't till I hed sold off all the b'ar meat and all the geese that I made ready to git at that honey. I reckon them bees must ha' been making that honey for a hundred years, and was then driv out by the b'ars.

"Columbus Mills will tell you; he axed me all about it; but, though he was always my good friend, I never even telled it to him. But he lent me his mule and cart, good fellow as he is, and never said nothing more; and, quiet enough, without beat of drum, I bought up all the tight-bound barrels that ever brought whisky to Spartanburg and Greenville, whar they hes the taste for that article strong; and day by day I went off carrying as many barrels as the cart could hold and the mule could draw. I tapped the old tree—which was one of the oldest and biggest chestnut oaks I ever did see close to the bottom, and drawed off the beautiful treacle. I was more than sixteen days about it, and got something over two thousand gallons of the purest, sweetest, yellowest honey you ever did see. I could hairdly git barrels and jimmyjohns enough to hold it; and I sold it out at seventy cents a gallon, which was mighty cheap. So I got from the honey a matter of fourteen hundred dollars.

"Now, Jedge, all this time, though it went very much agin the grain, I kept away from Merry Ann and the old Squaire, her daddy. I sent him two hundred head of geese—some fresh, say one hundred, and another hundred that I hed cleaned and put in salt—and I sent him three jimmyjohns of honey, five gallons each. But I kept away and said nothing, beat no drum, and hed never a thinking but how to git in the 'capital.' And I did git it in!

"When I carried the mule and cart home to Columbus Mills I axed him about a sartin farm of one hundred and sixty acres that he hed to sell. It hed a good house on it. He selled it to me cheap. I paid him down, and put the titles in my pocket. 'Thar's capital!' says I.

"*That* waur a fixed thing for ever and ever. And when I hed moved every thing from the old cabin to the new farm, Columbus let me hev a fine milch cow that gin eleven quarts a day, with a beautiful young caif. Jest about that time thar was a great sale of the furniter of the Ashmore family down at Spartanburg, and I remembered I hed no decent bedstead, or anything rightly sarving for a young woman's chamber; so I went to the sale, and bought a fine strong mahogany bedstead, a dozen chairs, a chist of drawers, and some other things that ain't quite mentionable, Jedge, but all proper for a lady's chamber; and I soon hed the house fixed up ready for anything. And up to this time I never let on to any body what I was a-thinking about or what I was a-doing, ontil I could stand up in my own doorway and look about me, and say to myself—this is my 'capital,' I reckon; and when I hed got all that I thought a needcessity to git, I took 'count of every thing.

"I spread the title-deeds of my fairm out on the table. I read 'em over three times to see ef 'twaur all right. Thar was my name several times in big letters, 'to hev and to hold.'

"Then I fixed the furniter. Then I brought out into the stable-yard the old mar'—you couldn't count her ribs *now*, and she was spry as ef she hed got a new conceit of herself.

"Then thar was my beautiful cow and caif, sealing fat, both on 'em, and sleek as a doe in autumn.

"Then thar waur a fine young mule that I bought in Spartanburg; my cart, and a strong second-hand buggy, that could carry two pussons convenient of two different sexes. And I felt big, like a man of consekence and capital.

"That warn't all.

"I had the shiners, Jedge, besides—all in gould and silver—none of your dirty rags and blotty spotty paper. That was the time of Old Hickory—General Jackson, you know—when he kicked over Nick Biddle's consarn, and gin us the beautiful Benton Mint Drops, in place of rotten paper. You could git the gould and silver jest for the axing, in them days, you know.

"I hed a grand count of my money, Jedge. I hed it in a dozen or twenty little bags of leather—the gould—

and the silver I hed in shot-bags. It took me a whole morning to count it up and git the figgers right. Then I stuffed it in my pockets, hyar and thar, every whar—wharever I could stow a bag; and the silver I stuffed away in my saddle-bags, and clapped it on the mar'.

"Then I mounted myself, and sot the mar's nose straight in a bee-line for the fairm of Squaire Hopson.

"I was a-gwine, you see, to surprise him with my 'capital'; but, fust, I meant to give him a mighty grand skeer.

"You see, when I was a-trading with Columbus Mills about the fairm and cattle and other things, I ups and tells him about my courting of Merry Ann; and when I telled him about Squaire Hopson's talk about 'capital,' he says:

" 'The old skunk! What right hes he to be talking big so, when he kain't pay his own debts. He's been owing me three hundred and fifty dollars now gwine on three years, and I kain't git even the *intrust* out of him. I've got a mortgage on his fairm for the whole, and ef he won't let you hev his da'ter, jest you come to me, and I'll clap the screws to him in short order.'

"Says I, 'Columbus, won't you sell me that mortgage?'

" 'You shall hev it for the face of the debt,' says he, 'not considerin' the intrust.'

" 'It's a bargain,' says I; and I paid him down the money, and he signed the mortgage over to me for a vallyable consideration.

"I hed that beautiful paper in my breast pocket, and felt strong to face the Squaire in his own house, knowing how I could turn him out of it! And I mustn't forget to tell you how I got myself a new rig of clothing, with a mighty fine over-coat, and a new fur cap; and as I looked in the glass I felt my consekence all over at every for'a'd step I tuk; and I felt my inches growing with every pace of the mar' on the high-road to Merry Ann and her beautiful daddy!"

* * *

"WELL, JEDGE, before I quite got to the Squaire's farm, who should come out to meet me in the road but Merry Ann, her own self! She hed spied me, I reckon, as I crossed the bald ridge a quarter of a mile away. I do reckon the dear gal hed been looking out for me every day the whole eleven days in the week, counting in all the Sundays. In the mountains, you know, Jedge, that the weeks sometimes run to twelve, and even fourteen days, specially when we're on a long camp-hunt!

"Well, Merry Ann cried and laughed together, she was so tarnation glad to see me agin. Says she:

" 'Oh, Sam! I'm so glad to see you! I was afeard you had clean gin me up. And thar's that fusty old bachelor Grimstead, he's a-coming here a'most every day; and daddy, he sw'ars that I shill marry him, and nobody else; and mammy, she's at me too, all the time, telling me how fine a fairm he's got, and what a nice carriage, and all that; and mammy says as how daddy'll be sure to beat me ef I don't hev him. But I kain't bear to look at him, the old griesly!'

" 'Cuss him!' says I. 'Cuss him, Merry Ann!'

"And she did, but onder her breath—the old cuss.

" 'Drot him!' says she; and she said louder, 'and drot me, too, Sam, ef I ever marries any body but you.'

"By this time I hed got down and gin her a long strong hug, and a'most twenty or a dozen kisses, and I says:

" 'You sha'n't marry nobody but me, Merry Ann; and we'll hev the marriage this very night, ef you says so!'

" 'Oh! psho, Sam! How you does talk!'

" 'Ef I don't marry you tonight, Merry Ann, I'm a holy mortar, and a sinner not to be saved by any salting, though you puts the petre with the sale. I'm come for that very thing. Don't you see my new clothes?'

" 'Well, you hev got a beautiful coat, Sam; all so blue, and with sich shiny buttons.'

" 'Look at my waistcoat, Merry Ann! What do you think of that?'

" 'Why, it's a most beautiful blue welvet!'

" 'That's the very article,' says I. 'And see the breeches, Merry Ann; and the boots!'

" 'Well,' says she, 'I'm fair astonished, Sam! Why whar, Sam, did you find all the money for these fine things?'

" 'A beautiful young woman, a'most as beautiful as you, Merry Ann, come to me the very night of that day when your daddy driv me off with a flea in my ear. She come to me to my bed at midnight—'

" 'Oh, Sam! *ain't* you ashamed!'

" ''Twas in a dream, Merry Ann; and she tells me something to incourage me to go for'a'd, and I went for'a'd, bright and airly next morning, and I picked up three sarvants that hev been working for me ever sence.'

" 'What sarvants?' says she.

" 'One was a goose, one was a b'ar, and t'other was a bee!'

" 'Now you're a-fooling me, Sam.'

" 'You'll see! Only you git yourself ready, for, by the eternal Hokies, I marries you this very night, and takes you home to *my* fairm bright and airly to-morrow morning.'

" 'I do think, Sam, you must be downright crazy.'

" 'You'll see and believe! Do you go home and git yourself fixed up for the wedding. Old Parson Stovall lives only two miles from your daddy, and I'll hev him hyar by sundown. You'll see!'

" 'But ef I waur to b'lieve you, Sam—'

" 'I've got on my wedding-clothes, o'purpose, Merry Ann.'

" 'But *I* hain't got no clothes fit for a gal to be married in,' says she.

" 'I'll marry you this very night, Merry Ann,' says I, 'though you hedn't a stitch of clothing at all!'

" 'Git out you sassy Sam,' says she, slapping my face. Then I kissed her in her very mouth, and a'ter that we walked on together, I leading the mar'.

"Says she, as we neared the house, 'Sam, let me go before, or stay hyar in the thick, and you go in by yourself. Daddy's in the hall, smoking his pipe and reading the newspapers.'

" 'We'll walk in together,' says I, quite consekential.

"Says she, 'I'm so afeard.'

" 'Don't you be afeard, Merry Ann,' says I; 'you'll see that all will come out jest as I tells you. We'll be hitched to-night, ef Parson Stovall, or any other parson, can be got to tie us up!'

"Says she, suddently, 'Sam, you're a-walking lame, I'm a-thinking. What's the matter? Hev you hurt yourself anyway?'

"Says I, 'It's only owing to my not balancing my accounts even in my pockets. You see I feel so much like flying in the air with the idee of marrying you to-night that I filled my pockets with rocks, jest to keep me down.'

" 'I do think, Sam, you're a leetle cracked in the upper story.'

" 'Well,' says I, 'ef so, the crack has let in a blessed chaince of the beautifulest sunlight! You'll see! Cracked, indeed! Ha, ha, ha! Wait till I've done with your daddy! I'm gwine to square accounts with *him*, and, I reckon, when I'm done with him, you'll guess that the crack's in *his* skull, and not in mine.'

"'What! you wouldn't knock my father, Sam!' says she, drawing off from me and looking skeary.

"'Don't be afeard; but it's very sartin, ef our heads don't come together, Merry Ann, you won't hev me for your husband to-night. And that's what I've swore upon. Hyar we air!'

"When we got to the yard I led in the mar', and Merry Ann she ran away from me and dodged round the house. I hitched the mar' to the post, took off the saddle-bags, which was mighty heavy, and walked into the house stiff enough I tell you, though the gould in my pockets pretty much weighed me down as I walked.

"Well, in I walked, and thar sat the old Squaire smoking his pipe and reading the newspaper. He looked at me through his spects over the newspaper, and when he seed who 'twas his mouth put on that same conceited sort of grin and smile that he ginerally hed when he spoke to me.

"'Well,' says he, gruffly enough, 'it's you, Sam Snaffles, is it?' Then he seems to diskiver my new clothes and boots, and he sings out, 'Heigh! you're tip-toe fine to-day! What fool of a shop-keeper in Spartanburg have you tuk in this time, Sam?'

"Says I, cool enough, 'I'll answer all them iligant questions a'ter a while, Squaire; but would prefar to see to business fust.'

"'Business!' says he; 'and what business kin you hev with me, I wants to know?'

"'You shill know, Squaire, soon enough; and I only hopes it will be to your liking a'ter you l'arn it.'

"So I laid my saddle-bags down at my feet and tuk

a chair quite at my ease; and I could see that he was all astare in wonderment at what he thought my sassiness. As I felt I had my hook in his gills, though he didn't know it yit, I felt in the humor to tickle him and play him as we does a trout.

"Says I, 'Squaire Hopson, you owes a sartin amount of money, say $350, with intrust on it for now three years, to Dr. Columbus Mills.'

"At this he squares round, looks me full in the face, and says:

"'What the old Harry's that to you?'

"Says I, gwine on cool and straight, 'you gin him a mortgage on this fairm for security.'

"'What's that to you?' says he.

"'The mortgage is over-due by two years, Squaire,' says I.

"'What the old Harry's all that to you, I say?' he fairly roared out.

"'Well, nothing much, I reckon. The $350, with three years' intrust at seven per cent., making it now—I've calkelated it all without compounding—something over $425—well, Squaire, that's not much to *you*, I reckon, with your large capital. But it's something to me.'

"'But I ask you again, Sir,' he says, 'what is all this to you?'

"'Jist about what I tells you—say $425; and I've come hyar this morning, bright and airly, in hope you'll be able to square up and satisfy the mortgage. Hyar's the dockyment.'

"And I drawed the paper from my breast pocket.

"'And you tell me that Dr. Mills sent you hyar,' says he, 'to collect this money?'

"'No; I come myself on my own hook.'

"'Well,' says he, 'you shill hev your answer at onst.

Take that paper back to Dr. Mills and tell him that I'll take an airly opportunity to call and arrange the business with him. You hev your answer, Sir,' he says, quite grand, 'and the sooner you makes yourself scarce the better.'

" 'Much obleeged to you, Squaire, for your ceveelity,' says I; 'but I ain't quite satisfied with that answer. I've come for the money due on this paper, and must hev it, Squaire, or thar will be what the lawyers call *four closures* upon it!'

" 'Enough! Tell Dr. Mills I will answer his demand in person.'

" 'You needn't trouble yourself, Squaire; for ef you'll jest look at the back of that paper, and read the 'signmeant, you'll see that you've got to settle with Sam Snaffles, and not with Columbus Mills!'

"Then he snatches up the dockyment, turns it over, and reads the rigilar 'signmeant, writ in Columbus Mills's own handwrite.

"Then the Squaire looks at me with a great stare, and he says, to himself like:

" 'It's a *bonny fodder* 'signmeant.'

" 'Yes,' says I, 'it's *bonny fodder*—rigilar in law—and the titles all made out complete to me, Sam Snaffles; signed, sealed, and delivered, as the lawyers says it.'

" 'And how the old Harry come you by this paper?' says he.

"I was getting riled, and I was detarmined, this time, to gin my hook a pretty sharp jerk in his gills; so I says:

" 'What the old Harry's that to *you*, Squaire? Thar's but one question 'twixt us two—air you ready to pay that money down on the hub, at onst, to me, Sam Snaffles?'

" 'No, Sir, I am not.'

" 'How long a time will you ax from me, by way of marciful indulgence?'

" 'It must be some time yit,' says he, quite sulky; and then he goes on agin:

" 'I'd like to know how you come by that 'signmeant, Mr. Snaffles.'

"Mr. Snaffles! Ah! ha!

" 'I don't see any neecessity,' says I, 'for answering any questions. Thar's the dockyment to speak for itself. You see that Columbus Mills 'signs to me for full *con*sideration. That means I paid him!'

" 'And why did you buy this mortgage?'

" 'You might as well ax me how I come by the money to buy any thing,' says I.

" 'Well, I do ax you,' says he.

" 'And I answers you,' says I, 'in the very words from your own mouth, What the old Harry's that to you?'

" 'This is hardly 'spectful, Mr. Snaffles,' says he.

"Says I, ''Spectful gits only what 'spectful gives! Ef any man but you, Squaire, hed been so onrespectful in his talk to me as you hev been I'd ha' mashed his muzzle! But I don't wish to be onrespectful. All I axes is the civil answer. I wants to know when you kin pay this money?'

" 'I kain't say, Sir.'

" 'Well, you see, I thought as how you couldn't pay, spite of all your "capital," as you hedn't paid even the *intrust* on it for three years; and, to tell you the truth, I was in hopes you couldn't pay, as I hed a liking for this fairm always; and as I am jest about to git married, you see'—

" 'Who the old Harry air you gwine to marry?' says he.

" 'What the old Harry's that to you?' says I, giving him as good as he sent. But I went on:

" 'You may be sure it's one of the woman kind. I don't hanker a'ter a wife with a beard; and I expects—

God willing, weather permitting, and the parson being sober—to be married this very night!'

"'To-night!' says he, not knowing well what to say.

"'Yes; you see I've got my wedding-breeches on. I'm to be married to-night, and I wants to take my wife to her own fairm as soon as I kin. Now, you see, Squaire, I all along set my hairt on this fairm of yourn, and I detarmined, ef ever I could git the "capital," to git hold of it; and that was the idee I hed when I bought the 'signmeant of the mortgage from Columbus Mills. So, you see, ef you kain't pay a'ter three years, you never kin pay, I reckon; and ef I don't git my money this day, why—I kain't help it—the lawyers will hev to see to the *four closures* to-morrow!'

"'Great God, Sir!' says he, rising out of his chair, and crossing the room up and down, 'do you coolly propose to turn me and my family headlong out of my house?'

"'Well, now,' says I, 'Squaire, that's not edzactly the way to put it. As I reads this dockyment'—and I tuk up and put the mortgage in my pocket—'the house and fairm are *mine* by law. They onst was yourn; but it wants nothing now but the *four closures* to make 'em mine.'

"'And would you force the sale of property worth \$2000 and more for a miserable \$400?'

"'It must sell for what it'll bring, Squaire; and I stands ready to buy it for my wife, you see, ef it costs me twice as much as the mortgage.'

"'Your wife!' says he; 'who the old Harry is she? You once pertended to have an affection for my da'ter.'

"'So I hed; but you hedn't the proper affection for your da'ter that I hed. You prefar'd money to her affections, and you driv me off to git "capital!" Well, I tuk your advice, and I've got the capital.'

"'And whar the old Harry,' said he, 'did you git it?'

" 'Well, I made good tairms with the old devil for a hundred years, and he found me in the money.'

" 'It must hev been so,' said he. 'You waur not the man to git capital in any other way.'

"Then he goes on: 'But what becomes of your pertended affection for my da'ter?'

" ''Twa'n't pertended; but you throwed yourself betwixt us with all your force, and broke the gal's hairt, and broke mine, so far as you could; and as I couldn't live without company, I hed to look out for myself and find a wife as I could. I tell you, as I'm to be married to-night, and I've sworn a most etarnal oath to hev this fairm, you'll hev to raise the wind to-day, and square off with me, or the lawyers will be at you with the *four closures* to-morrow, bright and airly.'

" 'Dod dern you!' he cries out. 'Does you want to drive me mad!'

" 'By no manner of means,' says I, jest about as cool and quiet as a cowcumber.

"But he was at biling heat. He was all over in a stew and a fever. He filled his pipe and lighted it, and then smashed it over the chimbly. Then he crammed the newspaper in the fire, and crushed it into the blaze with his boot. Then he turned to me, suddent, and said:

" 'Yes, you pertended to love my da'ter, and now you are pushing her father to desperation. Now ef you ever did love Merry Ann, honestly, raally, truly, and *bonny fodder*, you couldn't help loving her yit. And yit, hyar you're gwine to marry another woman, that, prehaps, you don't affection at all.'

" 'It's quite a sensible view you takes of the subject,' says I; 'the only pity is that you didn't take the same squint at it long ago, when I axed you to let me hev Merry Ann. *Then* you didn't valley her affections or mine. You hed no thought of nothing but the "capital" then, and the affections might all go to Jericho, for what you keered! I'd ha' married Merry Ann, and she me, and we'd ha' got on for a spell in a log-cabin, for, though I was poor, I hed the genwine grit of a man, and would come to something, and we'd ha' got on; and yit, without any "capital" your own self, and kivered up with debt as with a winter over-coat, hyar, you waur positive that I shouldn't hev your da'ter, and you waur a-preparing to sell her hyar to an old sour-tempered bachelor, more than double her age. Dern the capital! A man's the best capital for any woman, ef so be he *is* a man. Bekaise, ef he be a man, he'll work out cl'ar, though he may hev a long straining for it through the sieve. Dern the capital! You've as good as sold that gal child to old Grimstead, jest from your love of money!'

" 'But she won't hev him,' says he.

" 'The wiser gal child,' says I. 'Ef you only hed onderstood me and that poor child, I hed it in me to make the "capital"—dern the capital!—and now you've ruined her, and yourself, and me, and all; and dern my buttons but I must be married to-night, and jest as soon a'ter as the lawyers kin fix it I must hev this fairm for my wife. My hairt's set on it, and I've swore it a dozen o' times on the Holy Hokies!'

"The poor old Squaire fairly sweated; but he couldn't say much. He'd come up to me and say:

" 'Ef you only did love Merry Ann!'

" 'Oh,' says I, 'what's the use of your talking that? Ef you only hed ha' loved your own da'ter!'

"Then the old chap begun to cry, and as I seed that I jest kicked over my saddle-bags lying at my feet, and the silver Mexicans rolled out—a bushel on 'em, I reckon

—and O Lawd! how the old fellow jumped, staring with all his eyes at me and the dollars!

" 'It's money!' says he.

" 'Yes,' says I, 'jest a few hundreds of thousands of *my* "capital." ' I didn't stop at the figgers, you see.

"Then he turns to me and says, 'Sam Snaffles, you're a most wonderful man. You're a mystery to me. Whar, in the name of God, hev you been? and what hev you been doing? and whar did you git all this power of capital?'

"I jest laughed, and went to the door and called Merry Ann. She come mighty quick. I reckon she was watching and waiting.

"Says I, 'Merry Ann, that's money. Pick it up and put it back in the saddle-bags, ef you please.'

"Then says I, turning to the old man, 'Thar's that whole bushel of Mexicans, I reckon. Thar monstrous heavy. My old mar'—ax her about her ribs now!—she fairly squelched onder the weight of me and that money. And I'm pretty heavy loaded myself. I must lighten; with your leave, Squaire.'

"And I pulled out a leetle doeskin bag of gould half eagles from my right-hand pocket and poured them out upon the table; then I emptied my left-hand pocket, then the side pockets of the coat, then the skairt pockets, and jist spread the shiners out upon the table.

"Merry Ann was fairly frightened, and run out of the room; then the old woman she come in, and as the old Squaire seed her, he tuk her by the shoulder and said:

" 'Jest you look at that thar.'

"And when she looked and seed, the poor old hypercritical scamp sinner turned round to me and flung her airms round my neck, and said:

" 'I always said you waur the only right man for Merry Ann.'

"The old spooney!

"Well, when I hed let 'em look enough, and wonder enough, I jest turned Merry Ann and her mother out of the room.

"The old Squaire, he waur a-setting down agin in his airm-chair, not edzactly knowing what to say or what to do, but watching all my motions, jest as sharp as a cat watches a mouse when she is hafe hungry.

"Thar was all the Mexicans put back in the saddle-bags, but he hed seen 'em, and thar was all the leetle bags of gould spread upon the table; the gould—hafe and quarter eagles—jest lying out of the mouths of the leetle bags as ef wanting to creep back agin.

"And thar sot the old Squaire, looking at 'em as greedy as a fish-hawk down upon a pairch in the river. And, betwixt a whine and a cry and a talk, he says:

" 'Ah, Sam Snaffles, ef you ever did love my leetle Merry Ann, you would never marry any other woman.'

"Then you ought to ha' seed me. I felt myself sixteen feet high, and jest as solid as a chestnut oak. I walked up to the old man, and I tuk him quiet by the collar of his coat, with my thumb and forefinger, and I said:

" 'Git up, Squaire, for a bit.'

"And up he got.

"Then I marched him to the big glass agin the wall, and I said to him: 'Look, ef you please.'

"And he said, 'I'm looking.'

"And I said, 'What does you see?'

"He answered, 'I sees you and me.'

"I says, 'Look agin, and tell me what you *obzarves.*'

" 'Well,' says he, 'I obzarves.'

"And says I, 'What does your *obzarving* amount to? That's the how.'

"And says he, 'I sees a man alongside of me, as good-looking and handsome a young man as ever I seed in all my life.'

" 'Well,' says I, 'that's a correct obzarvation. But,' says I, 'what does you see of *your own self?*'

" 'Well, I kain't edzactly say.'

" 'Look good!' says I. 'Obzarve.'

"Says he, 'Don't ax me.'

" 'Now,' says I, 'that won't edzactly do. I tell you now, look good, and ax yourself ef you're the sawt of looking man that hes any right to be a feyther-in-law to a fine, young, handsome-looking fellow like me, what's got the "capital?" '

"Then he laughed out at the humor of the sitivation; and he says, 'Well, Sam Snaffles, you've got me dead this time. You're a different man from what I thought you. But, Sam, you'll confess, I reckon, that ef I hedn't sent you off with a flea in your ear when I hed you up afore the looking-glass, you'd never ha' gone to work to git in the "capital." '

" 'I don't know *that*, Squaire,' says I. 'Sarcumstances sarve to make a man take one road when he mout take another; but when you meets a man what has the hairt to love a woman strong as a lion, and to fight an inimy as big as a buffalo, he's got the raal grit in him. You knowed I was young, and I was poor, and you knowed the business of a hunter is a mighty poor business ef the man ain't born to it. Well, I didn't do much at it jest bekaise my hairt was so full of Merry Ann; and you should ha' made a calkilation and allowed for *that*. But you poked your fun at me and riled me consumedly; but I was detarmined that you shouldn't break *my* hairt, or the hairt of Merry Ann. Well, you hed your humors, and I've tried to take the change out of you. And now, ef you raally thinks, a'ter that obzarvation in the glass, that you kin make a respectable feyther-in-law to sich a fine-looking fellow as me, what's got the "capital," jest say the word, and we'll call Merry Ann in to bind the bargin. And you must talk out quick, for the wedding's to take place this very night. I've swore it by the etarnal Hokies.'

"'To-night!' says he.

"'Look at the "capital,"' says I; and I pinted to the gould on the table and the silver in the saddle-bags.

"'But, Lawd love you, Sam,' says he, 'it's so suddent, and we kain't make the preparations in time.'

"'Says I, 'look at the "capital," Squaire, and dern the preparations!'

"'But,' says he, 'we hain't time to ax the company.'

"'Dern the company!' says I; 'I don't believe in company the very night a man gits married. His new wife's company enough for him ef he's sensible!'

"'But, Sam,' says he, 'it's not possible to git up a supper by to-night.'

"Says I, 'Look you, Squaire, the very last thing a man wants on his wedding night is supper.'

"Then he said something about the old woman, his wife.

"Says I, 'Jest you call her in and show her the "capital."'

"So he called in the old woman, and then in come Merry Ann, and thar was great hemmings and hawings; and the old woman she said:

"'I've only got the one da'ter, Sam, and we *must* hev a big wedding! We must spread ourselves. We've got a smart chaince of friends and acquaintances, you see, and 'twon't be decent onless we axes them, and they won't like it! We *must* make a big show for the honor and 'spect-ability of the family.'

"Says I, 'Look you, old lady! I've swore a most tremendous oath, by the Holy Hokies, that Merry Ann and me air to be married this very night, and I kain't break sich an oath as that! Merry Ann,' says I, 'you wouldn't hev me break sich a tremendous oath as that?'

"And, all in a trimble, she says, 'Never, Sam! No!'

" 'You hyar that, old lady!' says I. ' We marries to-night, by the Holy Hokies! and we'll hev no company but old Parson Stovall, to make the hitch; and Merry Ann and me go off by sunrise to-morrow morning—you hyar?—to my own fairm, whar thar's a great deal of furniter fixing for her to do. A'ter that you kin advartise the whole county to come in, ef you please, and eat all the supper you kin spread! Now hurry up,' says I, 'and git as ready as you kin, for I'm gwine to ride over to Parson Stovall's this minit. I'll be back to dinner in hafe an hour. Merry Ann, you gether up that gould and silver, and lock it up. It's *our* "capital!" As for you, Squaire, thar's the mortgage on your fairm, which Merry Ann shill give you, to do as you please with it, as soon as the parson has done the hitch, and I kin call Merry Ann, Mrs. Snaffles—Madam Merry Ann Snaffles, and so forth, and aforesaid.'

"I laid down the law that time for all parties, and showed the old Squaire sich a picter of himself, and me standing aside him, looking seven foot high, at the least, that I jest worked the business 'cording to my own pleasure. When neither the daddy nor the mammy hed any thing more to say, I jumped on my mar' and rode over to old Parson Stovall.

"Says I, 'Parson, thar's to be a hitch to-night, and you're to see a'ter the right knot. You knows what I means. I want you over at Squaire Hopson's. Me and Merry Ann, his da'ter, mean to hop the twig to-night, and you're to see that we hop squar', and that all's even, 'cording to the law, Moses, and the profits! I stand treat, Parson, and you won't be the worse for your riding. I pays in gould!'

"So he promised to come by dusk; and come he did. The old lady hed got some supper, and tried her best to do what she could at sich short notice. The venison ham was mighty fine, I reckon, for Parson Stovall played a great stick at it; and ef they hedn't cooked up four of my wild-geese, then the devil's an angel of light, and Sam Snaffles no better than a sinner! And thar was any quantity of jimmyjohns, peach and honey considered. Parson Stovall was a great feeder, and I begun to think he never would be done. But at last he wiped his mouth, swallowed his fifth cup of coffee, washed it down with a stiff dram of peach and honey, wiped his mouth agin, and pulled out his prayer-book, psalmody, and Holy Scrip—three volumes in all—and he hemmed three times, and begun to look out for the marriage text, but begun with giving out the 100th Psalm.

" 'With one consent, let's all unite—'

" 'No,' says I, 'Parson; not all! It's only Merry Ann and me what's to unite to-night!'

"Jest then, afore he could answer, who should pop in but old bachelor Grimstead! and he looked round 'bout him, specially upon me and the parson, as ef to say:

" 'What the old Harry's they doing hyar!'

"And I could see that the old Squaire was oneasy. But the blessed old Parson Stovall, he gin 'em no time for ixplanation or palaver; but he gits up, stands up squar', looks solemn as a meat-ax, and he says:

"'Let the parties which I'm to bind together in the holy bonds of wedlock stand up before me!'

"And Lawd bless you, as he says the words, what should that old skunk of a bachelor do, but he gits up, stately as an old buck in spring time, and he marches over to my Merry Ann! But I was too much and too spry for him. I puts in betwixt 'em, and I takes the old bachelor by his coat-collar, 'twixt my thumb and forefinger, and afore he knows whar he is, I marches him up to the big looking-glass, and I says:

"'Look!'

"'Well,' says he, 'what?'

"'Look good,' says I.

"'I'm looking,' says he. 'But what do you mean, Sir?'

"Says I, 'Obzarve! Do you see yourself? Obzarve!'

"'I reckon I do,' says he.

"'Then,' says I, 'ax yourself the question, ef you're the sawt of looking man to marry my Merry Ann.'

"Then the old Squaire burst out a-laughing. He couldn't help it.

"'Capital!' says he.

"'It's capital,' says I. 'But hyar we air, Parson. Put on the hitch, jest as quick as you kin clinch it; for thar's no telling how many slips thar may be 'twixt the cup and the lips when these hungry old bachelors air about.'

"'Who gives away this young woman?' axes the parson; and the Squaire stands up and does the thing needful. I hed the ring ready, and before the parson had quite got through, old Grimstead vamoosed.

"He waur a leetle slow in onderstanding that he warn't wanted, and warn't, nohow, any party to the business. But he and the Squaire hed a mighty quarrel a'terwards, and ef 't hedn't been for me, he'd ha' licked the

Squaire. He was able to do it; but I jest cocked my cap at him one day, and, says I, in the Injin language:

"'Yaou!' And he didn't know what I meant; but I looked tomahawks at him, so he gin ground; and he's getting old so fast that you kin see him growing downwards all the time.

"All that, Jedge, is jest thirteen years ago; and me and Merry Ann git on famously, and thar's no eend to the capital! Gould breeds like the cows, and it's only needful to squeeze the bags now and then to make Merry Ann happy as a tomtit. Thirteen years of married life, and look at me! You see for yourself, Jedge, that I'm not much the worse for wear; and I kin answer for Merry Ann, too, though, Jedge, we hev hed thirty-six children.

"What!" says I, "thirty-six children in thirteen years!"

The "Big Lie" roared aloud.

"Hurrah, Sharp! Go it! You're making it spread. That last shot will make the Jedge know that you're a right truthful sinner, of a Saturday night, and in the 'Lying Camp.'"

"To be sure! You see, Merry Ann keeps on. But you've only got to do the ciphering for yourself. Here, now, Jedge, look at it. Count for yourself. First we had *three* gal children, you see. Very well! Put down three. Then we had *six* boys, one every year for four years; and then, the fifth year, Merry Ann throwed deuce. Now put down the six boys a'ter the three gals, and ef that don't make thirty-six, thar's no snakes in all Flurriday!

"Now, men," says Sam, "let's liquor all round, and drink the health of Mrs. Merry Ann Snaffles and the thirty-six children, all alive and kicking; and glad to see you, Jedge, and the rest of the company. We're doing right well; but I hes, every now and then, to put my thumb and forefinger on the Squaire's collar, and show him his face in the big glass, and call on him for an *obzarvation*—for he's mighty fond *of going shar's* in my 'capital.' "

JEAN-AH POQUELIN*

By GEORGE WASHINGTON CABLE

IN THE first decade of the present century, when the newly established American Government was the most hateful thing in Louisiana—when the Creoles were still kicking at such vile innovations as the trial by jury, American dances, anti-smuggling laws, and the printing of the Governor's proclamation in English—when the Anglo-American flood that was presently to burst in a crevasse of immigration upon the delta had thus far been felt only as slippery seepage which made the Creole tremble for his footing—there stood, a short distance above what is now Canal Street, and considerably back from the line of villas which fringed the river-bank on Tchoupitoulas Road, an old colonial plantation-house half in ruin.

It stood aloof from civilization, the tracts that had once been its indigo fields given over to their first noxious wilderness, and grown up into one of the horridest marshes within a circuit of fifty miles.

The house was of heavy cypress, lifted up on pillars, grim, solid, and spiritless, its massive build a strong reminder of days still earlier, when every man had been his own peace officer and the insurrection of the blacks a daily contingency. Its dark, weather-beaten roof and sides were hoisted up above the jungly plain in a distracted way, like a gigantic ammunition-wagon stuck in the mud and abandoned by some retreating army. Around it was a dense growth of low water willows, with half a hundred sorts of thorny or fetid bushes, savage strangers alike to the "language of flowers" and to the botanist's

* Reprinted from *Old Creole Days* by George Washington Cable through arrangement with the holders of the copyright, Charles Scribner's Sons.

Greek. They were hung with countless strands of discolored and prickly smilax, and the impassable mud below bristled with *chevaux de frise* of the dwarf palmetto. Two lone forest-trees, dead cypresses, stood in the centre of the marsh, dotted with roosting vultures. The shallow strips of water were hid by myriads of aquatic plants, under whose coarse and spiritless flowers, could one have seen it, was a harbor of reptiles, great and small, to make one shudder to the end of his days.

The house was on a slightly raised spot, the levee of a draining canal. The waters of this canal did not run; they crawled, and were full of big, ravening fish and alligators, that held it against all comers.

Such was the home of old Jean Marie Poquelin, once an opulent indigo planter, standing high in the esteem of his small, proud circle of exclusively male acquaintances in the old city; now a hermit, alike shunned by and shunning all who had ever known him. "The last of his line," said the gossips. His father lies under the floor of the St. Louis Cathedral, with the wife of his youth on one side, and the wife of his old age on the other. Old Jean visits the spot daily. His half-brother—alas! there was a mystery; no one knew what had become of the gentle, young half-brother, more than thirty years his junior, whom once he seemed so fondly to love, but who, seven years ago, had disappeared suddenly, once for all, and left no clew of his fate.

They had seemed to live so happily in each other's love. No father, mother, wife to either, no kindred upon earth. The elder a bold, frank, impetuous, chivalric adventurer; the younger a gentle, studious, book-loving recluse; they lived upon the ancestral estate like mated birds, one always on the wing, the other always in the nest.

There was no trait in Jean Marie Poquelin, said the old gossips, for which he was so well known among his few friends as his apparent fondness for his "little brother." "Jacques said this," and "Jacques said that"; he "would leave this or that, or any thing to Jacques," for Jacques was a scholar, and "Jacques was good," or "wise," or "just," or "far-sighted," as the nature of the case required; and "he should ask Jacques as soon as he got home," since Jacques was never elsewhere to be seen.

It was between the roving character of the one brother, and the bookishness of the other, that the estate fell into decay. Jean Marie, generous gentleman, gambled the slaves away one by one, until none was left, man or woman, but one old African mute.

The indigo-fields and vats of Louisiana had been generally abandoned as unremunerative. Certain enterprising men had substituted the culture of sugar; but while the recluse was too apathetic to take so active a course, the other saw larger, and, at that time, equally respectable profits, first in smuggling, and later in the African slave-trade. What harm could he see in it? The whole people said it was vitally necessary, and to minister to a vital public necessity,—good enough, certainly, and so he laid up many a doubloon, that made him none the worse in the public regard.

One day old Jean Marie was about to start upon a voyage that was to be longer, much longer, than any that he had yet made. Jacques had begged him hard for many days not to go, but he laughed him off, and finally said, kissing him:

"Audieu, 'tit frère."

"No," said Jacques, "I shall go with you."

They left the old hulk of a house in the sole care of

the African mute, and went away to the Guinea coast together.

Two years after, old Poquelin came home without his vessel. He must have arrived at his house by night. No one saw him come. No one saw "his little brother"; rumor whispered that he, too, had returned, but he had never been seen again.

A dark suspicion fell upon the old slave-trader. No matter that the few kept the many reminded of the tenderness that had ever marked his bearing to the missing man. The many shook their heads. "You know he has a quick and fearful temper"; and "why does he cover his loss with mystery?" "Grief would out with the truth."

"But," said the charitable few, "look in his face; see that expression of true humanity." The many did look in his face, and, as he looked in theirs, he read the silent question: "Where is thy brother Abel?" The few were silenced, his former friends died off, and the name of Jean Marie Poquelin became a symbol of witchery, devilish crime, and hideous nursery fictions.

The man and his house were alike shunned. The snipe and duck hunters forsook the marsh, and the woodcutters abandoned the canal. Sometimes the hardier boys who ventured out there snake-shooting heard a low thumping of oar-locks on the canal. They would look at each other for a moment half in consternation, half in glee, then rush from their sport in wanton haste to assail with their gibes the unoffending, withered old man who, in rusty attire, sat in the stern of a skiff, rowed homeward by his white-headed African mute.

"O Jean-ah Poquelin! O Jean-ah! Jean-ah Poquelin!"

It was not necessary to utter more than that. No hint of wickedness, deformity, or any physical or moral demerit; merely the name and tone of mockery: "Oh, Jean-ah Poquelin!" and while they tumbled one over another in their needless haste to fly, he would rise carefully from his seat, while the aged mute, with downcast face, went on rowing, and rolling up his brown fist and extending it toward the urchins, would pour forth such an unholy broadside of French imprecation and invective as would all but craze them with delight.

Among both blacks and whites the house was the object of a thousand superstitions. Every midnight, they affirmed, the *feu follet* came out of the marsh and ran in and out of the rooms, flashing from window to window. The story of some lads, whose word in ordinary statements was worthless, was generally credited, that the night they camped in the woods, rather than pass the place after dark, they saw, about sunset, every window blood-red, and on each of the four chimneys an owl sitting, which turned his head three times round, and moaned and laughed with a human voice. There was a bottomless well, everybody professed to know, beneath the sill of the big front door under the rotten veranda; whoever set his foot upon that threshold disappeared forever in the depth below.

What wonder the marsh grew as wild as Africa! Take all the Faubourg Ste. Marie, and half the ancient city, you would not find one graceless dare-devil reckless enough to pass within a hundred yards of the house after nightfall.

The alien races pouring into old New Orleans began to find the few streets named for the Bourbon princes too strait for them. The wheel of fortune, beginning to whirl, threw them off beyond the ancient corporation lines, and sowed civilization and even trade upon the lands of the Graviers and Girods. Fields became roads, roads streets. Everywhere the leveller was peering through his glass, rodsmen were whacking their way through willow-brakes and rose-hedges, and the sweating Irishmen tossed the blue clay up with their long-handled shovels.

"Ha! that is all very well," quoth the Jean-Baptistes, feeling the reproach of an enterprise that asked neither coöperation nor advice of them, "but wait till they come yonder to Jean Poquelin's marsh; ha! ha! ha!" The supposed predicament so delighted them, that they put on a mock terror and whirled about in an assumed stampede, then caught their clasped hands between their knees in excess of mirth, and laughed till the tears ran; for whether the street-makers mired in the marsh, or contrived to cut through old "Jean-ah's" property, either event would be joyful. Meantime a line of tiny rods, with bits of white paper in their split tops, gradually extended its way straight through the haunted ground, and across the canal diagonally.

"We shall fill that ditch," said the men in mud-boots, and brushed close along the chained and padlocked gate of the haunted mansion. Ah, Jean-ah Poquelin, those were not Creole boys, to be stampeded with a little hard swearing.

He went to the Governor. That official scanned the odd figure with no slight interest. Jean Poquelin was of short, broad frame, with a bronzed leonine face. His brow was ample and deeply furrowed. His eye, large and black, was bold and open like that of a war-horse, and his jaws shut together with the firmness of iron. He was dressed in a suit of Attakapas cottonade, and his shirt unbuttoned and thrown back from the throat and bosom, sailor-wise, showed a herculean breast, hard and grizzled. There was no fierceness or defiance in his look, no harsh ungentleness, no symptom of his unlawful life or violent temper; but rather a peaceful and peaceable fearlessness. Across the whole face, not marked in one or another feature, but as if it were laid softly upon the countenance like an almost imperceptible veil, was the imprint of some great grief. A careless eye might easily overlook it, but, once seen, there it hung—faint, but unmistakable.

The Governor bowed.

"*Parlez-vous français?*" asked the figure.

"I would rather talk English, if you can do so," said the Governor.

"My name, Jean Poquelin."

"How can I serve you, Mr. Poquelin?"

"My 'ouse is yond'; *dans le marais la-bas.*"

The Governor bowed.

"Dat marais billong to me."

"Yes, sir."

"To me, Jean Poquelin; I hown 'im meself."

"Well, sir?"

"He don't billong to you; I get him from me father."

"That is perfectly true, Mr. Poquelin, as far as I am aware."

"You want to make strit pass yond'?"

"I do not know, sir; it is quite probable; but the city will indemnify you for any loss you may suffer—you will get paid, you understand."

"Strit can't pass dare."

"You will have to see the municipal authorities about that, Mr. Poquelin."

A bitter smile came upon the old man's face.

"*Pardon, Monsieur*, you is not *le Gouverneur?*"

"Yes."

"*Mais*, yes. You har *le Gouverneur*—yes. Veh-well. I come to you. I tell you, strit can't pass at me 'ouse."

"But you will have to see"—

"I come to you. You is *le Gouverneur*. I know not the new laws. I ham a Fr-r-rench-aman! Fr-rencha-a man have something *aller au contraire*—he come at his *Gouverneur*. I come at you. If me not had been bought from me king like *bossals* in the hold time, *ze* king gof-France would-a-show *Monsieur le Gouverneur* to take care his men to make strit in right places. *Mais*, I know; we billong to *Monsieur le President*. I want you do some-sin for me, eh?"

"What is it?" asked the patient Governor.

"I want you tell *Monsieur le President*, strit - can't - pass - at - me - 'ouse."

"Have a chair, Mr. Poquelin"; but the old man did not stir. The Governor took a quill and wrote a line to a city official, introducing Mr. Poquelin, and asking for him every possible courtesy. He handed it to him, instructing him where to present it.

"Mr. Poquelin," he said, with a conciliatory smile, "tell me, is it your house that our Creole citizens tell such odd stories about?"

The old man glared sternly upon the speaker, and with immovable features said:

"You don't see me trade some Guinea nigga'?"

"Oh, no."

"You don't see me make some smugglin'?"

"No, sir; not at all."

"But, I am Jean Marie Poquelin. I mine me own bizniss. Dat all right? Adieu."

He put his hat on and withdrew. By and by he stood, letter in hand, before the person to whom it was addressed. This person employed an interpreter.

"He says," said the interpreter to the officer, 'he come to make you the fair warning how you muz not make the street pas' at his 'ouse.' "

The officer remarked that "such impudence was refreshing"; but the experienced interpreter translated freely.

"He says: 'Why you don't want?'" said the interpreter.

The old slave-trader answered at some length.

"He says," said the interpreter, again turning to the officer, "the marass is a too unhealth' for peopl' to live."

"But we expect to drain his old marsh; it's not going to be a marsh."

"*Il dit*"—The interpreter explained in French.

The old man answered tersely.

"He says the canal is a private," said the interpreter.

"Oh! *that* old ditch; that's to be filled up. Tell the old man we're going to fix him up nicely."

Translation being duly made, the man in power was amused to see a thunder-cloud gathering on the old man's face.

"Tell him," he added, "by the time we finish, there'll not be a ghost left in his shanty."

The interpreter began to translate, but—

"*J' comprends, J' comprends,*" said the old man, with an impatient gesture, and burst forth, pouring curses upon the United States, the President, the Territory of Orleans, Congress, the Governor and all his subordinates, striding out of the apartment as he cursed, while the object of his maledictions roared with merriment and rammed the floor with his foot.

"Why, it will make his old place worth ten dollars to one," said the official to the interpreter.

"'Tis not for de worse of de property," said the interpreter.

"I should guess not," said the other, whittling his chair,—"seems to me as if some of these old Creoles would liever live in a crawfish hole than to have a neighbor."

"You know what make old Jean Poquelin make like that? I will tell you. You know"—

The interpreter was rolling a cigarette, and paused to light his tinder; then, as the smoke poured in a thick double stream from his nostrils, he said, in a solemn whisper:

"He is a witch."

"Ho, ho, ho!" laughed the other.

"You don't believe it? What you want to bet?" cried the interpreter, jerking himself half up and thrusting out one arm while he bared it of its coat-sleeve with the hand of the other. "What you want to bet?"

"How do you know?" asked the official.

"Dass what I goin' to tell you. You know, one evening I was shooting some *grosbec*. I killed three; but I had trouble to find them, it was becoming so dark. When I have them I start' to come home; then I got to pas' at Jean Poquelin's house."

"Ho, ho, ho!" laughed the other, throwing his leg over the arm of his chair.

"Wait," said the interpreter. "I come along slow, not making some noises; still, still"—

"And scared," said the smiling one.

"*Mais,* wait. I get all pas' the 'ouse. 'Ah!' I say; 'all right!' Then I see two thing' before! Hah! I get as cold and humide, and shake like a leaf. You think it was nothing? There I see, so plain as can be (though it was making nearly dark), I see Jean—Marie—Poquelin walkin' right in front, and right there beside of him was something like a man—but not a man—white like paint!—I dropp' on the grass from scared—they pass'; so sure as I live 'twas the ghos' of Jacques Poquelin, his brother!"

"Pooh!" said the listener.

"I'll put my han' in the fire," said the interpreter.

"But did you never think," asked the other, "that that might be Jack Poquelin, as you call him, alive and well, and for some cause hid away by his brother?"

"But thar har'no cause!" said the other, and the entrance of third parties changed the subject.

Some months passed and the street was opened. A canal was first dug through the marsh, the small one which passed so close to Jean Poquelin's house was filled, and the street, or rather a sunny road, just touched a corner of the old mansion's dooryard. The morass ran dry. Its venomous denizens slipped away through the bulrushes; the cattle roaming freely upon its hardened surface trampled the superabundant undergrowth. The bellowing frogs croaked to westward. Lilies and the flower-de-luce sprang up in the place of reeds; smilax and poison-oak gave way to the purple-plumed iron-weed and pink spiderwort; the bind-weeds ran everywhere blooming as they ran, and on one of the dead cypresses a giant creeper hung its green burden of foliage and lifted its scarlet trumpets. Sparrows and red-birds flitted through the bushes, and dewberries grew ripe beneath. Over all these came a sweet, dry smell of salubrity which the place had not known since the sediments of the Mississippi first lifted it from the sea.

But its owner did not build. Over the willowbrakes, and down the vista of the open street, bright new houses, some singly, some by ranks, were prying in upon the old man's privacy. They even settled down toward his southern side. First a wood-cutter's hut or two, then a market gardener's shanty, then a painted cottage, and all at once the faubourg had flanked and half surrounded him and his dried-up marsh.

Ah! then the common people began to hate him. "The old tyrant!" "You don't mean an old *tyrant?*" "Well, then, why don't he build when the public need demands it? What does he live in that unneighborly way for?" "The old pirate!" "The old kidnapper!" How easily even the most ultra Louisianians put on the imported virtues of the North when they could be brought to bear against the hermit. "There he goes, with the boys after him! Ah! ha! ha! Jean-ah Poquelin! Ah! Jean-ah! Aha! aha! Jean-ah Marie! Jean-ah Poquelin! The old villain!" How merrily the swarming Américains echo the spirit of persecution! "The old fraud," they say—"pretends to live in a haunted house, does he? We'll tar and feather him some day. Guess we can fix him."

He cannot be rowed home along the old canal now; he walks. He has broken sadly of late, and the street urchins are ever at his heels. It is like the days when they cried: "Go up, thou bald-head," and the old man now and then turns and delivers ineffectual curses.

To the Creoles—to the incoming lower class of superstitious Germans, Irish, Sicilians, and others—he became an omen and embodiment of public and private ill-fortune. Upon him all the vagaries of their superstitions gathered and grew. If a house caught fire, it was imputed to his machinations. Did a woman go off in a fit, he had bewitched her. Did a child stray off for an hour, the mother shivered with the apprehension that Jean Poquelin had offered him to strange gods. The house was the subject of every bad boy's invention who loved to contrive ghostly lies. "As long as that house stands we shall have bad luck. Do you not see our pease and beans dying, our cabbages and lettuce going to seed and our gardens turning to dust, while every day you can see it raining in the woods? The rain will never pass old Poquelin's house. He keeps a fetich. He has conjured the whole Faubourg St. Marie. And why, the old wretch? Simply because our playful and innocent children call after him as he passes."

A "Building and Improvement Company," which had not yet got its charter, "but was going to," and which had not, indeed, any tangible capital yet, "but was going to have some," joined the "Jean-ah Poquelin" war. The haunted property would be such a capital site for a market-house! They sent a deputation to the old mansion to ask its occupant to sell. The deputation never got beyond the chained gate and a very barren interview with the African mute. The President of the Board was then empowered (for he had studied French in Pennsylvania and was considered qualified) to call and persuade M. Poquelin to subscribe to the company's stock; but—

"Fact is, gentlemen," he said at the next meeting, "it would take us at least twelve months to make Mr. Pokaleen understand the rather original features of our system, and he wouldn't subscribe when we'd done; besides, the only way to see him is to stop him on the street."

There was a great laugh from the Board; they couldn't help it. "Better meet a bear robbed of her whelps," said one.

"You're mistaken as to that," said the President. "I did meet him, and stopped him, and found him quite polite. But I could get no satisfaction from him; the fellow wouldn't talk in French, and when I spoke in English he hoisted his old shoulders up, and gave the same answer to everything I said."

"And that was—?" asked one or two, impatient of the pause.

"That it 'don't worse w'ile?' "

One of the Board said: "Mr. President, this market-house project, as I take it, is not altogether a selfish one; the community is to be benefited by it. We may feel that we are working in the public interest (the Board smiled knowingly), if we employ all possible means to oust this old nuisance from among us. You may know that at the time the street was cut through, this old Poquelin did all he could to prevent it. It was owing to a certain connection which I had with that affair that I heard a ghost story (smiles, followed by a sudden dignified check)—ghost story, which, of course, I am not going to relate; but I *may* say that my profound conviction, arising from a prolonged study of that story, is, that this old villain, John Poquelann, has his brother locked up in that old house. Now, if this is so, and we can fix it on him, I merely *suggest* that we can make the matter highly useful. I don't know," he added, beginning to sit down, "but that it is an action we owe to the community—hem!"

"How do you propose to handle the subject?" asked the President.

"I was thinking," said the speaker, "that, as a Board of Directors, it would be unadvisable for us to authorize any action involving trespass; but if you, for instance, Mr. President, should, as it were, for mere curiosity, *request* some one, as, for instance, our excellent Secretary, simply as a personal favor, to look into the matter—this is merely a suggestion."

The Secretary smiled sufficiently to be understood that, while he certainly did not consider such preposterous service a part of his duties as secretary, he might, notwithstanding, accede to the President's request; and the Board adjourned.

Little White, as the Secretary was called, was a mild,

kind-hearted little man, who, nevertheless, had no fear of anything, unless it was the fear of being unkind.

"I tell you frankly," he privately said to the President, "I go into this purely for reasons of my own."

The next day, a little after nightfall, one might have descried this little man slipping along the rear fence of the Poquelin place, preparatory to vaulting over into the rank, grass-grown yard, and bearing himself altogether more after the manner of a collector of rare chickens than according to the usage of secretaries.

The picture presented to his eye was not calculated to enliven his mind. The old mansion stood out against the western sky, black and silent. One long, lurid pencil-stroke along a sky of slate was all that was left of daylight. No sign of life was apparent; no light at any window, unless it might have been on the side of the house hidden from view. No owls were on the chimneys, no dogs were in the yard.

He entered the place, and ventured up behind a small cabin which stood apart from the house. Through one of its many crannies he easily detected the African mute crouched before a flickering pine-knot, his head on his knees, fast asleep.

He concluded to enter the mansion, and, with that view, stood and scanned it. The broad rear steps of the veranda would not serve him; he might meet some one midway. He was measuring, with his eye, the proportions of one of the pillars which supported it, and estimating the practicability of climbing it, when he heard a footstep. Some one dragged a chair out toward the railing, then seemed to change his mind and began to pace the veranda, his footfalls resounding on the dry boards with singular loudness. Little White drew a step backward, got the figure between himself and the sky, and at once recognized the short, broad-shouldered form of old Jean Poquelin.

He sat down upon a billet of wood, and, to escape the stings of a whining cloud of mosquitoes, shrouded his face and neck in his handkerchief, leaving his eyes uncovered.

He had sat there but a moment when he noticed a strange, sickening odor, faint, as if coming from a distance, but loathsome and horrid.

Whence could it come? Not from the cabin; not from the marsh, for it was as dry as powder. It was not in the air; it seemed to come from the ground.

Rising up, he noticed, for the first time, a few steps before him a narrow footpath leading toward the house. He glanced down it—ha! right there was some one coming—ghostly white!

Quick as thought, and as noiselessly, he lay down at full length against the cabin. It was bold strategy, and yet, there was no denying it, little White felt that he was frightened. "It is not a ghost," he said to himself. "I *know* it cannot be a ghost"; but the perspiration burst out at every pore, and the air seemed to thicken with heat. "It is a living man," he said in his thoughts. "I hear his footstep, and I hear old Poquelin's footsteps, too, separately, over on the veranda. I am not discovered; the thing has passed; there is that odor again; what a smell of death! Is it coming back? Yes. It stops at the door of the cabin. Is it peering in at the sleeping mute? It moves away. It is in the path again. Now it is gone." He shuddered. "Now, if I dare venture, the mystery is solved." He rose cautiously, close against the cabin, and peered along the path.

The figure of a man, a presence if not a body—but whether clad in some white stuff or naked, the darkness would not allow him to determine—had turned, and now, with a seeming painful gait, moved slowly from him. "Great Heaven! can it be that the dead do walk?" He withdrew again the hands which had gone to his eyes. The dreadful object passed between two pillars and under the house. He listened. There was a faint sound as of feet upon a staircase; then all was still except the measured tread of Jean Poquelin walking on the veranda, and the heavy respirations of the mute slumbering in the cabin.

The little Secretary was about to retreat; but as he looked once more toward the haunted house a dim light appeared in the crack of a closed window, and presently old Jean Poquelin came, dragging his chair, and sat down close against the shining cranny. He spoke in a low, tender tone in the French tongue, making some inquiry. An answer came from within. Was it the voice of a human? So unnatural was it—so hollow, so discordant, so unearthly—that the stealthy listener shuddered again from head to foot; and when something stirred in some bushes near by—though it may have been nothing more than a rat—and came scuttling through the grass, the little Secretary actually turned and fled. As he left the enclosure he moved with bolder leisure through the bushes; yet now and then he spoke aloud: "Oh, oh! I see, I understand!" and shut his eyes in his hands.

How strange that henceforth little White was the champion of Jean Poquelin! In season and out of season—wherever a word was uttered against him—the Secretary, with a quiet, aggressive force that instantly arrested gossip, demanded upon what authority the statement or conjecture was made; but as he did not condescend to explain his own remarkable attitude, it was not long before the disrelish and suspicion which had followed Jean Poquelin so many years fell also upon him.

It was only the next evening but one after his adventure that he made himself a source of sullen amazement to one hundred and fifty boys, by ordering them to desist from their wanton hallooing. Old Jean Poquelin, standing and shaking his cane, rolling out his long-drawn maledictions, paused and stared, then gave the Secretary a courteous bow and started on. The boys, save one, from pure astonishment, ceased; but a ruffianly little Irish lad, more daring than any had yet been, threw a big hurtling clod, that struck old Poquelin between the shoulders and burst like a shell. The enraged old man wheeled with uplifted staff to give chase to the scampering vagabond; and—he may have tripped, or he may not, but he fell full length. Little White hastened to help him up, but he waved him off with a fierce imprecation and staggering to his feet resumed his way homeward. His lips were reddened with blood.

Little White was on his way to the meeting of the Board. He would have given all he dared spend to have staid away, for he felt both too fierce and too tremulous to brook the criticisms that were likely to be made.

"I can't help it, gentlemen; I can't help you to make a case against the old man, and I'm not going to."

"We did not expect this disappointment, Mr. White."

"I can't help that, sir. No, sir; you had better not appoint any more investigations. Somebody'll investigate himself into trouble. No, sir; it isn't a threat, it is only my advice, but I warn you that whoever takes the task in hand will rue it to his dying day—which may be hastened, too."

The President expressed himself surprised.

"I don't care a rush," answered little White, wildly

and foolishly. "I don't care a rush if you are, sir. No, my nerves are not disordered; my head's as clear as a bell. No, I'm *not* excited."

A Director remarked that the Secretary looked as though he had waked from a nightmare.

"Well, sir, if you want to know the fact, I have; and if you choose to cultivate old Poquelin's society you can have one, too."

"White," called a facetious member, but White did not notice. "White," he called again.

"What?" demanded White, with a scowl.

"Did you see the ghost?"

"Yes, sir; I did," cried White, hitting the table, and handing the President a paper which brought the Board to other business.

The story got among the gossips that somebody (they were afraid to say little White) had been to the Poquelin mansion by night and beheld something appalling. The rumor was but a shadow of the truth, magnified and distorted as is the manner of shadows. He had seen skeletons walking, and had barely escaped the clutches of one by making the sign of the cross.

Some madcap boys with an appetite for the horrible plucked up courage to venture through the dried marsh by the cattle-path, and come before the house at a spectral hour when the air was full of bats. Something which they but half saw—half a sight was enough—sent them tearing back through the willow-brakes and acacia bushes to their homes, where they fairly dropped down, and cried:

"Was it white?" "No—yes—nearly so—we can't tell—but we saw it." And one could hardly doubt, to look at their ashen faces, that they had, whatever it was.

"If that old rascal lived in the country we come from,"

said certain Américains, "he'd have been tarred and feathered before now, wouldn't he, Sanders?"

"Well, now he just would."

"And we'd have rid him on a rail, wouldn't we?"

"That's what I allow."

"Tell you what you *could* do." They were talking to some rollicking Creoles who had assumed an absolute necessity for doing *something*. "What is it you call this thing where an old man marries a young girl, and you come out with horns and"—

"*Charivari?*" asked the Creoles.

"Yes, that's it. Why don't you shivaree him?" Felicitous suggestion.

Little White, with his wife beside him, was sitting on their doorsteps on the sidewalk, as Creole custom had taught them, looking toward the sunset. They had moved into the lately-opened street. The view was not attractive on the score of beauty. The houses were small and scattered, and across the flat commons, spite of the lofty tangle of weeds and bushes, and spite of the thickets of acacia, they needs must see the dismal old Poquelin mansion, tilted awry and shutting out the declining sun. The moon, white and slender, was hanging the tip of its horn over one of the chimneys.

"And you say," said the Secretary, "the old black man has been going by here alone? Patty, suppose old Poquelin should be concocting some mischief; he don't lack provocation; the way that clod hit him the other day was enough to have killed him. Why, Patty, he dropped as quick as *that!* No wonder you haven't seen him. I wonder if they haven't heard something about him up at the drug-store. Suppose I go and see."

"Do," said his wife.

She sat alone for half an hour, watching that sudden going out of the day peculiar to the latitude.

"That moon is ghost enough for one house," she said, as her husband returned. "It has gone right down the chimney."

"Patty," said little White, "the drug-clerk says the boys are going to shivaree old Poquelin to-night. I'm going to try to stop it."

"Why, White," said his wife, "You'd better not. You'll get hurt."

"No, I'll not."

"Yes, you will."

"I'm going to sit out here until they come along. They're compelled to pass right by here."

"Why, White, it may be midnight before they start; you're not going to sit out here till then."

"Yes, I am."

"Well, you're very foolish," said Mrs. White in an undertone, looking anxious, and tapping one of the steps with her foot.

They sat a very long time talking over little family matters.

"What's that?" at last said Mrs. White.

"That's the nine-o'clock gun," said White, and they relapsed into a long-sustained, drowsy silence.

"Patty, you'd better go in and go to bed," said he at last.

"I'm not sleepy."

"Well, you're very foolish," quietly remarked little White, and again silence fell upon them.

"Patty, suppose I walk out to the old house and see if I can find out any thing."

"Suppose," said she, "you don't do any such—listen!"

Down the street arose a great hubbub. Dogs and boys

were howling and barking; men were laughing, shouting, groaning, and blowing horns, whooping, and clanking cow-bells, whinnying, and howling, and rattling pots and pans.

"They're coming this way," said little White. "You had better go into the house, Patty."

"So had you."

"No. I'm going to see if I can't stop them."

"Why, White!"

"I'll be back in a minute," said White, and went toward the noise.

In a few moments the little Secretary met the mob. The pen hesitates on the word, for there is a respectable difference, measurable only on the scale of the half century between a mob and a *charivari*. Little White lifted his ineffectual voice. He faced the head of the disorderly column, and cast himself about as if he were made of wood and moved by the jerk of a string. He rushed to one who seemed, from the size and clatter of his tin pan, to be a leader, "*Stop these fellows, Bienvenu, stop them just a minute, till I tell them something.*" Bienvenu turned and brandished his instruments of discord in an imploring way to the crowd. They slackened their pace, two or three hushed their horns and joined the prayer of little White and Bienvenu for silence. The throng halted. The hush was delicious.

"Bienvenu," said little White, "don't shivaree old Poquelin to-night; he's—"

"My fwang," said the swaying Bienvenu, "who tail you I goin' to chahivahi somebody, eh? You sink bickause I make a little playfool wiz zis tin pan zat I am *dhonk?*"

"Oh, no, Bienvenu, old fellow, you're all right. I was afraid you might not know that old Poquelin was sick, you know, but you're not going there, are you?"

"My fwang, I vay soy to tail you zat you ah dhonk as de dev'. I am *shem* of you. I ham ze servan' of ze *publique.* Zese *citoyens* goin' to wickwest Jean Poquelin to give to the Ursuline' two hondred fifty dolla'—"

"*Hé quoi!*" cried a listener, "*Cinq cent piastres, oui!*

"*Oui!*" said Bienvenu, "and if he wiffuse we make him some lit' *musiqui;* ta-ra-ta!" He hoisted a merry hand and foot, then frowning, added: "Old Poquelin got no bizniz dhink s'much w'isky."

"But, gentlemen," said little White, around whom a circle had gathered, "the old man is very sick."

"My faith!" cried a tiny Creole, "we did not make him to be sick. W'en we have say we going make *le charivari,* do you want that we hall tell a lie? My faith! 'sfools!"

"But you can shivaree somebody else," said desperate little White.

"*Oui!*" cried Bienvenu, "*et chahivahi* Jean-ah Poquelin tomo'w!"

"Let us go to Madame Schneider!" cried two or three, and amid huzzas and confused cries, among which was heard a stentorian Celtic call for drinks, the crowd again began to move.

"*Cent piastres pour l'hôpital de charité!*"

"Hurrah!"

"Whang!" went a tin pan, the crowd yelled, and Pandemonium gaped again. They were off at a right angle.

Nodding, Mrs. White looked at the mantle-clock.

"Well, if it isn't away after midnight."

The hideous noise down street was passing beyond earshot. She raised a sash and listened. For a moment there was silence. Some one came to the door.

"Is that you, White?"

"Yes." He entered. "I succeeded, Patty."

"Did you?" said Patty joyfully.

"Yes. They've gone down to shivaree the old Dutch-woman who married her step-daughter's sweetheart. They say she has got to pay a hundred dollars to the hospital before they stop."

The couple retired, and Mrs. White slumbered. She was awakened by her husband snapping the lid of his watch.

"What time?" she asked.

"Half-past three. Patty, I haven't slept a wink. Those fellows are out yet. Don't you hear them?"

"Why, White, they're coming this way!"

"I know they are," said White, sliding out of bed and drawing on his clothes, "and they're coming fast. You'd better go away from that window, Patty! My! what a clatter!"

"Here they are," said Mrs. White, but her husband was gone. Two or three hundred men and boys pass the place at a rapid walk straight down the broad, new street, toward the hated house of ghosts. The din was terrific. She saw little White at the head of the rabble brandishing his arms and trying in vain to make himself heard; but they only shook their heads, laughing and hooting the louder, and so passed, bearing him on before them.

Swiftly they pass out from among the houses, away from the dim oil lamps of the street, out into the broad starlit commons, and enter the willowy jungles of the haunted ground. Some hearts fail and the owners lag behind and turn back, suddenly remembering how near morning it is. But the most part push on, tearing the air with their clamor.

Down ahead of them in the long, thicket-darkened way there is—singularly enough—a faint, dancing light. It must be very near the old house; it is. It has stopped now. It is a lantern, and is under a well-known sapling which has grown up on the wayside since the canal was filled. Now it swings mysteriously to and fro. A goodly number of the more ghost-fearing give up the sport; but a full hundred move forward at a run, doubling their devilish howling and banging.

"Yes; it is a lantern, and there are two persons under the tree. The crowd draws near—drops into a walk; one of the two is the old African mute; he lifts the lantern up so that it shines on the other; the crowd recoils; there is a hush of all clangor, and all at once, with a cry of mingled fright and horror from every throat, the whole throng rushes back, dropping everything, sweeping past little White and hurrying on, never stopping until the jungle is left behind, and then to find that not one in ten has seen the cause of the stampede, and not one of the tenth is certain what it was.

There is one huge fellow among them who looks capable of any villainy. He finds something to mount on, and, in the Creole *patois*, calls a general halt. Bienvenu sinks down, and, vainly trying to recline gracefully, resigns the leadership. The herd gather round the speaker; he assures them that they have been outraged. Their right peaceably to traverse the public streets has been trampled upon. Shall such encroachments be endured? It is now daybreak. Let them go now by the open light of day and force a free passage of the public highway!

A scattering consent was the response, and the crowd, thinned now and drowsy, straggled quietly down toward the old house. Some drifted ahead, others sauntered behind, but every one, as he again neared the tree, came to a stand-still. Little White sat upon a bank of turf on the opposite side of the way looking very stern and sad. To each newcomer he put the same question:

"Did you come here to go to old Poquelin's?"

"Yes."

"He's dead." And if the shocked hearer started away he would say: "Don't go away."

"Why not?"

"I want you to go to the funeral presently."

If some Louisianian, too loyal to dear France or Spain to understand English, looked bewildered, some one would interpret for him; and presently they went. Little White led the van, the crowd trooping after him down the middle of the way. The gate, that had never been seen before unchained, was open. Stern little White stopped a short distance from it; the rabble stopped behind him. Something was moving out from under the veranda. The many whisperers stretched upward to see. The African mute came very slowly toward the gate, leading by a cord in the nose a small brown bull, which was harnessed to a rude cart. On the flat body of the cart, under a black cloth, were seen the outlines of a long box.

"Hats off, gentlemen," said little White, as the box came in view, and the crowd silently uncovered.

"Gentlemen," said little White, "here comes the last remains of Jean Marie Poquelin, a better man, I'm afraid, with all his sins,—yes, a better—a kinder man to his blood—a man of more self-forgetful goodness—than all of you put together will ever dare to be."

There was a profound hush as the vehicle came creaking through the gate; but when it turned away from them toward the forest, those in front started suddenly. There was a backward rush, then all stood still again staring one way; for there, behind the bier, with eyes cast down and labored step, walked the living remains—

all that was left—of little Jacques Poquelin, the long hidden brother—a leper, as white as snow.

Dumb with horror, the cringing crowd gazed upon the walking death. They watched, in silent awe, the slow *cortège* creep down the long, straight road and lessen on the view, until by and by it stopped where a wild, unfrequented path branched off into the undergrowth toward the rear of the ancient city.

"They are going to the *Terre aux Lépreux*," said one in the crowd. The rest watched them in silence.

The little bull was set free; the mute, with the strength of an ape, lifted the long box to his shoulder. For a moment more the mute and the leper stood in sight, while the former adjusted his heavy burden; then, without one backward glance upon the unkind human world, turning their faces toward the ridge in the depths of the swamp known as the Leper's Land, they stepped into the jungle, disappeared, and were never seen again.

A DRAMA OF THREE*

By GRACE KING

IT WAS a regular dramatic performance every first of the month in the little cottage of the old General and Madame B———.

It began with the waking up of the General by his wife, standing at the bedside with a cup of black coffee.

"Hé! Ah! Oh, Honorine! Yes; the first of the month, and affairs—affairs to be transacted."

On those mornings when affairs were to be transacted there was not much leisure for the household; and it was Honorine who constituted the household. Not the old dressing-gown and slippers, the old, old trousers, and the antediluvian neck-foulard of other days! Far from it. It was a case of warm water (with even a fling of cologne in it), of the trimming of beard and mustache by Honorine, and the black broadcloth suit, and the brown satin stock, and that *je ne sais quoi de dégagé* which no one could possess or assume like the old General. Whether he possessed or assumed it is an uncertainty which hung over the fine manners of all the gentlemen of his day, who were kept through their youth in Paris to cultivate *bon ton* and an education.

It was also something of a gala-day for Madame la Générale too, as it must be a gala-day for all old wives to see their husbands pranked in the manners and graces that had conquered their maidenhood, and exhaling once more that ambrosial fragrance which once so well incensed their compelling presence.

Ah, to the end a woman loves to celebrate her con-

* Reprinted from *Balcony Stories* by Grace King through arrangement with the publishers, The Macmillan Company.

quest! It is the last touch of misfortune with her to lose in the old, the ugly, and the commonplace her youthful lord and master. If one could look under the gray hairs and wrinkles with which time thatches old women, one would be surprised to see the flutterings, the quiverings, the thrills, the emotions, the coals of the heart-fires which death alone extinguishes, when he commands the tenant to vacate.

Honorine's hands chilled with the ice of sixteen as she approached scissors to the white mustache and beard. When her finger-tips brushed those lips, still well formed and roseate, she felt it, strange to say, on her lips. When she asperged the warm water with cologne,—it was her secret delight and greatest effort of economy to buy this cologne,—she always had one little moment of what she called faintness—that faintness which had veiled her eyes, and chained her hands, and stilled her throbbing bosom, when as a bride she came from the church with him. It was then she noticed the faint fragrance of the cologne bath. Her lips would open as they did then, and she would stand for a moment and think thoughts to which, it must be confessed, she looked forward from month to month. What a man he had been! In truth he belonged to a period that would accept nothing less from Nature than physical beauty; and Nature is ever subservient to the period. If it is to-day all small men, and to-morrow gnomes and dwarfs, we may know that the period is demanding them from Nature.

When the General had completed—let it be called no less than the ceremony of—his toilet, he took his chocolate and his *pain de Paris*. Honorine could not imagine him breakfasting on anything but *pain de Paris*. Then he sat himself in his large arm-chair before his escritoire, and began transacting his affairs with the usual—

"But where is that idiot, that dolt, that sluggard, that snail, with my mail?"

Honorine, busy in the breakfast-room:

"In a moment, husband. In a moment."

"But he should be here now. It is the first of the month, it is nine o'clock, I am ready; he should be here."

"It is not yet nine o'clock, husband."

"Not yet nine! Not yet nine! Am I not up? Am I not dressed? Have I not breakfasted before nine?"

Honorine's voice, prompt in cheerful acquiescence, came from the next room, where she was washing his cup, saucer, and spoon.

"It is getting worse and worse every day. I tell you, Honorine, Pompey must be discharged. He is worthless. He is trifling. Discharge him! Discharge him! Do not have him about! Chase him out of the yard! Chase him out as soon as he makes his appearance! Do you hear, Honorine?"

"You must have a little patience, husband."

It was perhaps the only reproach one could make to Madame Honorine, that she never learned by experience.

"Patience! Patience! Patience is the invention of dullards and sluggards. In a well-regulated world there should be no need of such a thing as patience. Patience should be punished as a crime, or at least as a breach of of the peace. Wherever patience is found police investigation should be made as for smallpox. Patience! Patience! I never heard the word—I assure you, I never heard the word in Paris. What do you think would be said there to the messenger who craved patience of you? Oh, they know too well in Paris—a rataplan from the walking-stick on his back, that would be the answer; and a, 'My good fellow, we are not hiring professors of patience, but legs.' "

"But, husband, you must remember we do not hire

Pompey. He only does it to oblige us, out of his kindness."

"Oblige us! Oblige me! Kindness! A negro oblige me! Kind to me! That is it; that is it. That is the way to talk under the new régime. It is favor, and oblige, and education, and monsieur, and madame, now. What child's play to call this a country—a government! I would not be surprised"—jumping to his next position on this ever-recurring first of the month theme—"I would not be surprised if Pompey has failed to find the letter in the box. How do I know that the mail has not been tampered with? From day to day I expect to hear it. What is to prevent? Who is to interpose? The honesty of the officials? Honesty of the officials—that is good! What a farce—honesty of officials! That is evidently what has happened. The thought has not occurred to me in vain. Pompey has gone. He has not found the letter, and—well; that is the end."

But the General had still another theory to account for the delay in the appearance of his mail which he always posed abruptly after the exhaustion of the arraignment of the post-office.

"And why not Journel?" Journel was their landlord, a fellow of means, but no extraction, and a favorite aversion of the old gentleman's. "Journel himself? You think he is above it, hé? You think Journel would not do such a thing? Ha! your simplicity, Honorine—your simplicity is incredible. It is miraculous. I tell you, I have known the Journels, from father to son, for—yes, for seventy-five years. Was not his grandfather the overseer on my father's plantation? I was not five years old when I began to know the Journels. And this fellow, I know him better than he knows himself. I know him as well as God knows him. I have made up my mind.

I have made it up carefully that the first time that letter fails on the first of the month I shall have Journel arrested as a thief. I shall land him in the penitentiary. What! You think I shall submit to have my mail tampered with by a Journel? Their contents appropriated? What! You think there was no coincidence in Journel's offering me his post-office box just the month—just the month, before those letters began to arrive? You think he did not have some inkling of them? Mark my words, Honorine, he did—by some of his subterranean methods. And all these five years he has been arranging his plans—that is all. He was arranging theft, which no doubt has been consummated to-day. Oh, I have regretted it—I assure you I have regretted it, that I did not promptly reject his proposition, that, in fact, I ever had anything to do with the fellow."

It was almost invariably, so regularly do events run in this world,—it was almost invariably that the negro messenger made his appearance at this point. For five years the General had perhaps not been interrupted as many times, either above or below the last sentence. The mail, or rather the letter, was opened, and the usual amount—three ten-dollar bills—was carefully extracted and counted. And as if he scented the bills, even as the General said he did, within ten minutes after their delivery, Journel made his appearance to collect the rent.

It could only have been in Paris, among that old retired nobility, who counted their names back, as they expressed it, "au de çá du déluge," that could have been acquired the proper manner of treating a "roturier" landlord: to measure him with the eyes from head to foot; to hand the rent—the ten-dollar bill—with the tips of the fingers; to scorn a look at the humbly tendered receipt; to say: "The cistern needs repairing, the roof leaks; I must warn you that unless such notifications meet with more prompt attention than in the past, you must look for another tenant," etc., in the monotonous tone of supremacy, and in the French, not of Journel's dictionary, nor of the dictionary of any such as he, but in the French of Racine and Corneille; in the French of the above suggested circle, which inclosed the General's memory, if it had not inclosed—as he never tired of recounting—his star-like personality.

A sheet of paper always infolded the bank-notes. It always bore, in fine but sexless tracery, "From one who owes you much."

There, that was it, that sentence, which like a locomotive, bore the General and his wife far on these firsts of the month to two opposite points of the horizon, in fact, one from the other—"From one who owes you much."

The old gentleman would toss the paper aside with the bill receipt. In the man to whom the bright New Orleans itself almost owed its brightness, it was a paltry act to search and pick for a debtor. Friends had betrayed and deserted him; relatives had forgotten him; merchants had failed with his money; bank presidents had stooped to deceive him; for he was an old man, and had about run the gamut of human disappointments—a gamut that had begun with a C major of trust, hope, happiness, and money.

His political party had thrown him aside. Neither for ambassador, plenipotentiary, senator, congressman, not even for a clerkship, could he be nominated by it. Certes! "From one who owed him much." He had fitted the cap to a new head, the first of every month, for five years, and still the list was not exhausted. Indeed, it would have been hard for the General to look anywhere and not see some one whose obligation to him far exceeded this thirty dollars a month. Could he avoid being happy with such eyes?

But poor Madame Honorine! She who always gathered up the receipts, and the "From one who owes you much"; who could at an instant's warning produce the particular ones for any month of the past half-decade. She kept them filed, not only in her armoire, but the scrawled papers—skewered, as it were, somewhere else—where women from time immemorial have skewered such unsigned papers. She was not original in her thoughts—no more, for the matter of that, than the General was. Tapped at any time on the first of the month, when she would pause in her drudgery to reimpale her heart by a sight of the written characters on the scrap of paper, her thoughts would have been found flowing thus, "One can give everything, and yet be sure of nothing."

When Madame Honorine said "everything," she did not, as women in such cases often do, exaggerate. When she married the General, she in reality gave the youth of sixteen, the beauty (ah, do not trust the denial of those wrinkles, the thin hair, the faded eyes!) of an angel, the dot of an heiress. Alas! It was too little at the time. Had she in her own person united all the youth, all the beauty, all the wealth, sprinkled parsimoniously so far and wide over all the women in this land, would she at that time have done aught else with this than immolate it on the burning pyre of the General's affection? "And yet be sure of nothing."

It is not necessary, perhaps, to explain that last clause. It is very little consolation for wives that their husbands have forgotten, when some one else remembers. Some one else! Ah! there could be so many some one elses in the General's life, for in truth he had been irresistible to excess. But this was one particular some one else who had been faithful for five years. Which one?

When Madame Honorine solves that enigma she has made up her mind how to act.

As for Journel, it amused him more and more. He would go away from the little cottage rubbing his hands with pleasure (he never saw Madame Honorine, by the way, only the General). He would have given far more than thirty dollars a month for this drama; for he was not only rich, but a great *farceur*.

OVER ON THE T'OTHER MOUNTING*

By CHARLES EGBERT CRADDOCK

STRETCHING out laterally from a long oblique line of the Southern Alleghanies are two parallel ranges, following the same course through several leagues, and separated by a narrow strip of valley hardly half a mile in width. As they fare along arm in arm, so to speak, sundry differences between the close companions are distinctly apparent. One is much the higher, and leads the way; it strikes out all the bold curves and angles of the course, meekly attended by the lesser ridge; its shadowy coves and sharp ravines are repeated in miniature as its comrade falls into the line of march; it seems to have its companion in charge, and to conduct it away from the majestic procession of mountains that traverses the State.

But, despite its more imposing appearance, all the tangible advantages are possessed by its humble neighbor. When Old Rocky-Top, as the lower range is called, is fresh and green with the tender verdure of spring, the snow still lies on the summit of the T'other Mounting, and drifts deep into treacherous rifts and chasms, and muffles the voice of the singing pines; and all the crags are hung with gigantic glittering icicles, and the woods are gloomy and bleak. When the sun shines bright on Old Rocky-Top, clouds often hover about the loftier mountain, and storms brew in that higher atmosphere; the all-pervading winter winds surge wildly among the groaning forests, and wrench the limbs from the trees, and dash huge fragments of cliffs down deep gorges, and spend their fury before they reach the sheltered

* Reprinted from *In the Tennessee Mountains* by Charles Egbert Craddock with the permission of and by arrangement with Houghton Mifflin Company.

lower spur. When the kindly shades of evening slip softly down on drowsy Rocky-Top, and the work is laid by in the rough little houses, and the simple homefolks draw around the hearth, day still lingers in a weird, paralytic life among the tree-tops of the T'other Mounting; and the only remnant of the world visible is that stark black line of its summit, stiff and hard against the faint green and saffron tints of the sky. Before the birds are well awake on Old Rocky-Top, and while the shadows are still thick, the T'other Mounting has been called up to a new day. Lonely dawns these: the pale gleam strikes along the October woods, bringing first into uncertain twilight the dead yellow and red of the foliage, presently heightened into royal gold and crimson by the first ray of sunshine; it rouses the timid wild-fowl; it drives home the plundering fox; it meets, perhaps, some lumbering bear or skulking mountain wolf; it flecks with light and shade the deer, all gray and antlered; it falls upon no human habitation, for the few settlers of the region have a persistent predilection for Old Rocky-Top. Somehow, the T'other Mounting is vaguely in ill repute among its neighbors,—it has a bad name.

"It's the onluckiest place ennywhar nigh about," said Nathan White, as he sat one afternoon upon the porch of his log-cabin, on the summit of Old Rocky-Top, and gazed up at the heights of the T'other Mounting across the narrow valley. "I hev hearn tell all my days ez how, ef ye go up thar on the T'other Mounting, suthin' will happen ter ye afore ye kin git away. An' I knows myself ez how—'t war ten year ago an' better—I went up thar, one Jan'ry day, a-lookin' fur my cow, ez hed strayed off through not hevin' enny calf ter our house; an' I fund the cow, but jes' tuk an' slipped on a icy rock, an' bruck my ankle-bone. 'Twar sech a job a-gittin' off'n that thar T'other Mounting an' back over hyar, it hev l'arned me ter stay away from thar."

"Thar war a man," piped out a shrill, quavering voice from within the door,—the voice of Nathan White's father, the oldest inhabitant of Rocky-Top,—"thar war a man hyar, nigh on ter fifty year ago,—he war mightily gin ter thievin' horses; an' one time, while he war a-running away with Pete Dilks's dapple-gray mare,—Pete, he war a-ridin' a-hint him on his old sorrel mare,—*her* name 't war Jane, an'—the Jeemes boys, they war a-ridin' arter the horse-thief too. Thar, now! I clar forgits what horses them Jeemes boys war a-ridin' of." He paused for an instant in anxious reflection. "Waal, sir! it do beat all that I can't remember them Jeemes boys' horses! Anyways, they got ter that thar tricky ford through Wild-Duck River, thar on the side o' the T'other Mounting, an' the horse-thief war ahead, an' he hed ter take it fust. An' that thar river,—it rises yander in them pines, nigh about," pointing with a shaking fore-finger,—"an' that thar river jes' spun him out 'n the saddle like a top, an' he war n't seen no more till he hed floated nigh ter Colbury, ez dead ez a door-nail, nor Pete's dapple-gray mare nuther; she bruk her knees agin them high stone banks. But he war a good swimmer, an' he war drowned. He war witched with the place, ez sure ez ye air born."

A long silence ensued. Then Nathan White raised his pondering eyes with a look of slow curiosity. "What did Tony Britt say he war a-doin' of, when ye kem on him suddint in the woods on the T'other Mounting?" he asked, addressing his son, a stalwart youth, who was sitting upon the step, his hat on the back of his head, and his hands in the pockets of his jeans trousers.

"He said he war a-huntin', but he hed n't hed no sort 'n luck. It 'pears ter me ez all the game thar is witched somehow, an' ye can't git no good shot at nuthin'. Tony tole me to-day that he got up three deer, an' hed toler'ble aim; an' he missed two, an' the t'other jes' trotted off with a rifle-ball in his flank, ez onconsarned ez ef he hed hit him with an acorn."

"I hev always hearn ez everything that belongs on that thar T'other Mounting air witched, an' ef ye brings away so much ez a leaf, or a stone, or a stick, ye fotches a curse with it," chimed in the old man, "'kase thar hev been sech a many folks killed on the T'other Mounting."

"I tole Tony Britt that thar word," said the young fellow, "an' 'lowed ter him ez how he hed tuk a mighty bad spot ter go a-huntin'."

"What did he say?" demanded Nathan White.

"He say he never knowed ez thar war murders commit on T'other Mounting, an' ef thar war he 'spects 't war nuthin' but Injuns, long time ago. But he 'lowed the place war powerful onlucky, an' he believed the mounting war witched."

"Ef Tony Britt's arter enny harm," said the octogenarian, "he'll never come off'n that thar T'other Mounting. It's a mighty place fur bad folks ter make thar eend. Thar 's that thar horse thief I war a-tellin' 'bout, an' that dapple-gray mare,—her name 't war Luce. An' folks ez is a-runnin' from the sheriff jes' takes ter the T'other Mounting ez nateral ez ef it war home; an' ef they don't git cotched, they is never hearn on no more." He paused impressively. "The rocks falls on 'em, an' kills 'em; an' I'll tell ye jes' how I knows," he resumed, oracularly. "'T war sixty year ago, nigh about, an' me an' them Jeemes boys war a-burnin' of lime tergether over on the T'other Mounting. We hed a lime-kiln over thar, jes' under Piney Notch, an' never hed no luck, but jes' stuck ter it like fools, till Hiram Jeemes got one of his eyes put out. So we quit burnin' of lime on the T'other Mounting, 'count of the place bein' witched, an' kem over hyar ter Old Rocky-Top, an' got along toler'ble well, cornsiderin'. But one day, whilst we war a-workin' on the T'other Mounting, what d' ye think I fund in the rock? The print of a bare foot in the solid stone, ez plain an' ez nateral ez ef the track hed been lef' in the clay yestiddy. Waal, I knowed it war the track o' Jeremiah Stubbs, what shot his step-brother, an' gin the sheriff the slip, an' war las' seen on the T'other Mounting, 'kase his old shoe jes' fit the track, fur we tried it. An' a good while arterward I fund on that same T'other Mounting —in the solid stone, mind ye—a fish, what he had done br'iled fur supper, jes' turned ter a stone."

"So thar's the Bible made true," said an elderly woman, who had come to the door to hear this reminiscence, and stood mechanically stirring a hoe-cake batter in a shallow wooden bowl. "Ax fur a fish, an' ye'll git a stone."

The secret history of the hills among which they lived was indeed as a sealed book to these simple mountaineers.

"The las' time I war ter Colbury," said Nathan White, "I hearn the sheriff a-talkin' 'bout how them evil-doers an' sech runs fur the T'other Mounting fust thing; though he 'lowed ez it war powerful foxy in 'em ter try ter hide thar, 'kase he said, ef they wunst reaches it, he mought ez well look fur a needle in a hay-stack. He 'lowed ef he hed a posse a thousand men strong he could n't git 'em out."

"He can't find 'em, 'kase the rocks falls on 'em, or swallers 'em in," said the old man. "Ef Tony Britt is up ter mischief he'll never come back no more. He'll git into worser trouble than ever he see afore."

"He hev done seen a powerful lot of trouble, fust

one way an' another, 'thout foolin' round the T'other Mounting," said Nathan White. "They tells me ez he got hisself indicted, I believes they calls it, or suthin', down yander ter the court at Colbury,—that war year afore las',—an' he hed ter pay twenty dollars fine; 'kase when he war overseer of the road he jes' war constant in lettin' his friends, an' folks ginerally, off 'thout hevin' 'em fined, when they did n't come an' work on the road,—though that air the way ez the overseers hev always done, without nobody a-tellin' on 'em an' sech. But them ez war n't Tony Britt's friends seen a mighty differ. He war dead sure ter fine Caleb Hoxie seventy-five cents, 'cordin' ter the law, fur every day that he war summonsed ter work an' never come; 'kase Tony and Caleb hed some sort'n grudge agin one another 'count of a spavined horse what Caleb sold ter Tony, makin' him out to be a sound critter,—though Caleb swears he never knowed the horse war spavined when he sold him ter Tony, no more 'n nuthin'. Caleb war mightily worked up 'bout this hyar finin' business, an' him an' Tony hed a tussle 'bout it every time they kem tergether. But Caleb war always sure ter git the worst of it, 'kase Tony, though he air tol-er'ble spindling sort o' build, he air somehow or other sorter stringy an' tough, an' makes a right smart show in a reg'lar knock-down an' drag-out fight. So Caleb he war beat every time, an' fined too. An' he tried wunst ter shoot Tony Britt, but he missed his aim. An' when he war a-layin' off how ter fix Tony, fur treatin' him that way, he war a-stoppin', one day, at Jacob Green's black-smith shop, yander, a mile down the valley, an' he war a-talkin' 'bout it ter a passel o' folks thar. An' Lawyer Rood from Colbury war thar, an' Jacob war a-shoein' of his mare; an' he hearn the tale, an' axed Caleb why n't he report Tony ter the court, an' git him fined fur neglect of his duty, bein' overseer of the road. An' Caleb never knowed before that it war the law that everybody what war summonsed an' did n't come must be fined, or the overseer must be fined hisself; but he knowed that Tony hed been a-lettin' of his friends off, an' folks ginerally, an' he jes' 'greed fur Lawyer Rood ter stir up trouble fur Tony. An' he done it. An' the court fined Tony twenty dollars fur them ways o' his'n. An' it kept him so busy a-scufflin' ter raise the twenty dollars that he never hed a chance ter give Caleb Hoxie more'n one or two beatin's the whole time he war a-scrapin' up the money."

This story was by no means unknown to the little circle, nor did its narrator labor under the delusion that he was telling a new thing. It was merely a verbal act of recollection, and an attentive silence reigned as he related the familiar facts. To people who live in lonely regions this habit of retrospection (especially noticeable in them) and an enduring interest in the past may be something of a compensation for the scanty happenings of the present. When the recital was concluded, the hush for a time was unbroken, save by the rush of the winds, bringing upon their breath the fragrant woodland odors of balsams and pungent herbs, and a fresh and exhilarating suggestion of sweeping over a volume of falling water. They stirred the fringed shadow of a great pine that stood, like a sentinel, before Nathan White's door and threw its colorless simulacrum, a boastful lie twice its size, far down the sunset road. Now and then the faint clangor of a cow-bell came from out the tangled woods about the little hut, and the low of homeward-bound cattle sounded upon the air, mellowed and softened by the distance. The haze that rested above the long, narrow valley was hardly visible, save in the illusive beauty with which it invested the scene,—the tender azure of the far-away ranges; the exquisite tones of the gray and purple shadows that hovered about the darkening coves and along the deep lines marking the gorges; the burnished brilliance of the sunlight, which, despite its splendor, seemed lonely enough, lying motionless upon the lonely landscape and on the still figures clustered about the porch. Their eyes were turned toward the opposite steeps, gorgeous with scarlet oak and sumac, all in autumnal array, and their thoughts were busy with the hunter on the T'other Mounting and vague speculations concerning his evil intent.

"It 'pears ter me powerful strange ez Tony goes a-foolin' round that thar T'other Mounting, cornsiderin' what happened yander in its shadow," said the woman, coming again to the door, and leaning idly against the frame; the bread was baking over the coals. "That thar wife o' his'n, afore she died, war always frettin' 'kase way down thar on the backbone, whar her house war, the shadow o' the T'other Mounting laid on it fur an hour an' better every day of the worl'. She 'lowed ez it always put her in mind o' the shadow o' death. An' I thought 'bout that thar sayin' o' hern the day when I see her a-lyin' stiff an' cold on the bed, an' the shadow of the T'other Mounting drapping in at the open door, an' a-creepin' an' a-creepin' over her face. An' I war plumb glad when they got that woman under ground, whar, ef the sunshine can't git ter her, neither kin the shadow. Ef ever thar war a murdered woman, she war one. Arter all that hed come an' gone with Caleb Hoxie, fur Tony Britt ter go arter him, 'kase he war a yerb-doctor, ter git him ter physic his wife, who war nigh about dead with the lung fever, an' gin up by old Dr. Marsh!—it looks ter me like he war plumb crazy,—though him an' Caleb hed sorter made friends 'bout the spavined horse an' sech afore then. Jes' ez soon ez she drunk the stuff that Caleb fixed fur her she laid her head back an' shet her eyes, an' never opened 'em no more in this worl'. She war a murdered woman, an' Caleb Hoxie done it through the yerbs he fixed fur her."

A subtile amethystine mist had gradually overlaid the slopes of the T'other Mounting, mellowing the brilliant tints of the variegated foliage to a delicious hazy sheen of mosaics; but about the base the air seemed dun-colored, though transparent; seen through it, even the red of the crowded trees was but a sombre sort of magnificence, and the great masses of gray rocks, jutting out among them here and there, wore a darkly frowning aspect. Along the summit there was a blaze of scarlet and gold in the full glory of the sunshine; the topmost cliffs caught its rays, and gave them back in unexpected gleams of green or grayish-yellow, as of mosses, or vines, or huckleberry bushes, nourished in the heart of the deep fissures.

"Waal," said Nathan White, "I never did believe ez Caleb gin her ennythink ter hurt,—though I knows thar is them ez does. Caleb is the bes' yerb-doctor I ever see. The rheumatiz would nigh on ter hev killed me, ef it war n't fur him, that spell I hed las' winter. An' Dr. Marsh, what they hed up afore the gran' jury, swore that the yerbs what Caleb gin her war nuthin' ter hurt; *he* said, though, they could n't holp nor hender. An' but fur Dr. Marsh they would hev jailed Caleb ter stand his trial, like Tony wanted 'em ter do. But Dr. Marsh said she died with the consumption, jes' the same, an' Caleb's yerbs war wholesome, though they war n't no 'count at all."

"I knows I ain't a-goin' never ter tech nuthin' he fixes fur me no more," said his wife, "an' I'll be bound nobody else in these hyar mountings will, nuther."

"Waal," drawled her son, "I knows fur true ez he air tendin' now on old Gideon Croft, what lives over yander in the valley on the t'other side of the T'other Mounting, an' is down with the fever. He went over thar yestiddy evening, late; I met him when he war goin' an' he tole me."

"He hed better look out how he comes across Tony Britt," said Nathan White; "fur I hearn, the las' time I war ter the Settlemint, how Tony hev swore ter kill him the nex' time he see him, fur a-givin' of pizenous yerbs ter his wife. Tony air mightily outdone 'kase the gran' jury let him off. Caleb hed better be sorter keerful how he goes a-foolin' round these hyar dark woods."

The sun had sunk, and the night, long held in abeyance, was coming fast. The glooms gathered in the valley; a soft gray shadow hung over the landscape, making familiar things strange. The T'other Mounting was all a dusky, sad purple under the faintly pulsating stars, save that high along the horizontal line of its summit gleamed the strange red radiance of the dead and gone sunset. The outline of the foliage was clearly drawn against the pure lapis lazuli tint of the sky behind it; here and there the uncanny light streamed through the bare limbs of an early leafless tree, which looked in the distance like some bony hand beckoning, or warning, or raised in horror.

"*Anythink* mought happen thar!" said the woman, as she stood on night-wrapped Rocky-Top and gazed up at the alien light, so red in the midst of the dark landscape. When she turned back to the door of the little hut, the meagre comforts within seemed almost luxury, in their cordial contrast to the desolate, dreary mountain yonder and the thought of the forlorn, wandering hunter. A genial glow from the hearth diffused itself over the puncheon floor; the savory odor of broiling venison filled the room as a tall, slim girl knelt before the fire and placed the meat upon the gridiron, her pale cheeks flushing with the heat; there was a happy suggestion of peace and unity when the four generations trooped in to their supper, grandfather on his grandson's arm, and a sedate two-year-old bringing up the rear. Nathan White's wife paused behind the others to bar the door, and once more, as she looked up at the T'other Mounting, the thought of the lonely wanderer smote her heart. The red sunset light had died out at last, but a golden aureola heralded the moon-rise, and a gleaming thread edged the masses of foliage; there was no faint suggestion now of mist in the valley, and myriads of stars filled a cloudless sky. "He hev done gone home by this time," she said to her daughter-in-law, as she closed the door, "an' ef he ain't, he'll hev a moon ter light him."

"Air ye a-studyin' 'bout Tony Britt yit?" asked Nathan White. "He hev done gone home a good hour by sun, I'll be bound. Jes' ketch Tony Britt a-huntin' till sundown, will ye! He air a mighty pore hand ter work. 'Stonishes me ter hear he air even a-huntin' on the T'other Mounting."

"I don't believe he 's up ter enny harm," said the woman; "he hev jes' tuk ter the woods with grief."

"'Pears ter me," said the daughter-in-law, rising from her kneeling posture before the fire, and glancing reproachfully at her husband,—"'pears ter me ez ye mought hev brought him hyar ter eat his supper along of we-uns, stiddier a-leavin' him a-grievin' over his dead wife in them witched woods on the T'other Mounting."

The young fellow looked a trifle abashed at this suggestion. "I never wunst thought of it," he said. "Tony never stopped ter talk more'n a minit, nohow."

The evening wore away; the octogenarian and the sedate two-year-old fell asleep in their chairs shortly after supper; Nathan White and his son smoked their cob-pipes, and talked fitfully of the few incidents of the day; the women sat in the firelight with their knitting, silent and absorbed, except that now and then the elder, breaking from her reverie, declared, "I can't git Tony Britt out'n my head nohow in the worl'."

The moon had come grandly up over the T'other Mounting, casting long silver lights and deep black shadows through all the tangled recesses and yawning chasms of the woods and rocks. In the vast wilderness the bright rays met only one human creature, the belated hunter making his way homeward through the dense forest with an experienced woodman's craft. For no evil intent had brought Tony Britt to the T'other Mounting; he had spent the day in hunting, urged by that strong necessity without which the mountaineer seldom makes any exertion. Dr. Marsh's unavailing skill had cost him dear; his only cow was sold to make up the twenty dollars fine which his revenge on Caleb Hoxie had entailed upon him; without even so much as a spavined horse tillage was impossible, and the bounteous harvest left him empty-handed, for he had no crops to gather. The hardships of extreme poverty had reinforced the sorrows that came upon him in battalions, and had driven him far through long aisles of the woods, where the night fell upon him unaware. The foliage was all embossed with exquisite silver designs that seemed to stand out some little distance from the dark masses of leaves; now and then there came to his eyes that emerald gleam never seen upon verdure in the day-time,—only shown by some artificial light, or the moon's sweet uncertainty. The wind was strong and fresh, but not cold; here and there was a glimmer of dew. Once, and once only, he thought of the wild traditions which peopled the T'other Mounting with evil spirits. He paused with a sudden chill; he glanced nervously over his shoulder down the illimitable avenues of the lonely woods. The grape-vines, hanging in festoons from tree to tree, were slowly swinging back and forth, stirred by the wind. There was a dizzy dance of shadows whirling on every open space where the light lay on the ground. The roar and fret of Wild-Duck River, hidden there somewhere in the pines, came on the breeze like a strange, weird, fitful voice, crying out amid the haunted solitudes of the T'other Mounting. He turned abruptly, with his gun on his shoulder, and pursued his way through the trackless desert in the direction of his home. He had been absorbed in his quest and his gloomy thoughts, and did not realize the distance he had traversed until it lay before him to be retraced; but his superstitious terror urged him to renewed exertions. "Ef ever I gits off'n this hyar witched mounting," he said to himself, as he tore away the vines and brambles that beset his course, "I'll never come back agin while I lives." He grew calmer when he paused on a huge projecting crag, and looked across the narrow valley at the great black mass opposite, which he knew was Old Rocky-Top; its very presence gave him a sense of companionship and blunted his fear, and he sat down to rest for a few minutes, gazing at the outline of the range he knew so well, so unfamiliar from a new standpoint. How low it seemed from the heights of the T'other Mounting! Could that faint gleam be the light in Nathan White's house? Tony Britt glanced further down the indistinct slope, where he knew his own desolate, deserted hut was crouched. "Jes' whar the shadow o' the T'other Mounting can reach it," he thought, with a new infusion of bitterness. He averted his eyes; he would look no longer; he threw himself at full length among the ragged clumps of grass and fragments of rock, and turned his face to the stars. It all came back to him then. Sometimes, in his sordid cares and struggles for his scanty existence, his past troubles were dwarfed by the present. But here on the lonely cliff, with the infinite spaces above him and the boundless forest below, he felt anew his isolation. No light on earth save the far gleam from another man's home, and in heaven only the drowning face of the moon, drifting slowly through the blue floods of the skies. He was only twenty-five; he had youth and health and strength, but he felt that he had lived his life; it seemed long, marked as it was by cares and privation and persistent failure. Little as he knew of life, he knew how hard his had been, even meted by those of the poverty-stricken wretches among whom his lot was cast. "An' sech luck!" he said, as his sad eyes followed the drifting dead face of the moon. "Along o' that thar step-mother o' mine till I war growed; an' then when I war married, an' we hed got the house put up, an' war beginnin' ter git along like other folks kin, an' Car'line's mother gin her that thar calf what growed ter a cow, an' through pinchin' an' savin' we made out ter buy that thar horse from Caleb Hoxie, jes' as we war a-startin' ter work a crap he lays down an' dies; an' that cussed twenty dollars ez I hed ter pay ter the court; an' Car'line jes' a-gittin' sick, an' a-wastin' an' a-wastin' away, till I, like a fool, brung Caleb thar, an' he pizens her with his yerbs—God A'mighty! ef I could jes' lay my hands wunst on that scoundrel I wouldn't leave a mite of him, ef he war pertected by a hundred lyin', thievin' gran' juries! But he can't stay a-hidin' forevermo'. He's got ter 'count ter me, ef he ain't ter the law; an' he'll see a mighty differ atwixt us. I swear he'll never draw another breath!"

He rose with a set, stern face, and struck a huge bowlder beside him with his hard clenched hand as he spoke. He had not even an ignorant idea of an impressive dramatic pose; but if the great gaunt cliff had been the stage of a theatre his attitude and manner at that instant would have won him applause. He was all alone with his poverty and his anguished memories, as men with such burdens are apt to be.

The bowlder on which, in his rude fashion, he had registered his oath was harder than his hard hand, and the vehemence of the blow brought blood; but he had scarcely time to think of it. His absorbed reverie was broken by a rustling other than that of the eddying wind. He raised his head and looked about him, half expecting to see the antlers of a deer. Then there came to his ears the echo of the tread of man. His eyes mechanically followed the sound. Forty feet down the face of the crag a broad ledge jutted out, and upon it ran a narrow path, made by stray cattle, or the feet of their searching owners; it was visible from the summit for a distance of a hundred yards or so, and the white glamour of the moonbeams fell full upon it. Before a speculation had suggested itself, a man walked slowly into view along the path, and with starting eyes the hunter recognized his dearest foe. Britt's hand lay upon the bowlder; his oath was in his mind; his unconscious enemy had come within his power. Swifter than a flash the temptation was presented. He remembered the warnings of his lawyer at Colbury last week, when the grand jury had failed to find a true bill against Caleb Hoxie,—that he was an innocent man, and must go unscathed, that any revenge for fancied wrongs would be dearly rued; he remembered, too, the mountain traditions of the falling rocks burying evil-doers in the heart of the hills. Here was his opportunity. He would have a life for a life, and there would be one more legend of the very stones conspiring to punish malefactors escaped from men added to the terrible "sayin's" of the T'other Mounting. A strong belief in the supernatural influences of the place was rife within him; he knew nothing of Gideon Croft's fever and the errand that had brought the herb-doctor through the "witched mounting"; had he not been transported thither by some invisible agency, that the rocks might fall upon him and crush him?

The temptation and the resolve were simultaneous. With his hand upon the bowlder, his hot heart beating fast, his distended eyes burning upon the approaching figure, he waited for the moment to come. There lay the long, low, black mountain opposite, with only the moonbeams upon it, for the lights in Nathan White's house were extinguished; there was the deep, dark gulf of the valley; there, forty feet below him, was the narrow, moon-flooded path on the ledge, and the man advancing carelessly. The bowlder fell with a frightful crash, the echoes rang with a scream of terror, and the two men—one fleeing from the dreadful danger he had barely escaped, the other from the hideous deed he thought he had done—ran wildly in opposite directions through the tangled autumnal woods.

Was every leaf of the forest endowed with a woeful voice, that the echo of that shriek might never die from Tony Britt's ears? Did the storied, retributive rocks still vibrate with this new victim's frenzied cry? And what was this horror in his heart! Now,—so late,—was coming a terrible conviction of his enemy's innocence, and with it a fathomless remorse.

All through the interminable night he fled frantically along the mountain's summit, scarcely knowing whither, and caring for nothing except to multiply the miles between him and the frightful object that he believed lay under the bowlder which he had dashed down the precipice. The moon sank beneath the horizon; the fantastic shadows were merged in the darkest hour of the night; the winds died, and there was no voice in all the woods, save the wail of Wild-Duck River and the forever-resounding screams in the flying wretch's ears. Sometimes he answered them in a wild, hoarse, inarticulate cry; sometimes he flung his hands above his head and wrung them in agony; never once did he pause in his flight. Panting, breathless, exhausted, he eagerly sped through the darkness; tearing his face upon the brambles; plunging now and then into gullies and unseen quagmires; sometimes falling heavily, but recovering himself in an instant, and once more struggling on; striving to elude the pursuing voices, and to distance forever his conscience and his memory.

And then came that terrible early daylight that was wont to dawn upon the T'other Mounting when all the world besides was lost in slumber; the wan, melancholy light showed dimly the solemn trees and dense undergrowth; the precarious pitfalls about his path; the long deep gorges; the great crags and chasms; the cascades, steely gray, and white; the huge mass, all hung about with shadows, which he knew was Old Rocky-Top, rising from the impenetrably dark valley below. It seemed wonderful to him, somehow, that a new day should break at all. If, in a revulsion of nature, that utter blackness had continued forever and ever it would not have been strange, after what had happened. He could have borne it better than the sight of the familiar world gradually growing into day, all unconscious of his secret. He had begun the descent of the T'other Mounting, and he seemed to carry that pale dawn with him; day was breaking when he reached the foot of Old Rocky-Top, and as he climbed up to his own deserted, empty little shanty, it too stood plainly defined in the morning light. He dragged himself to the door, and impelled by some morbid fascination he glanced over his shoulder at the T'other Mounting. There it was, unchanged, with the golden largess of a gracious season blazing upon every autumnal leaf. He shuddered, and went into the fireless, comfortless house. And then he made an appalling discovery. As he mechanically divested himself of his shot-pouch and powder-horn he was stricken by a sudden consciousness that he did not have his gun! One doubtful moment, and he remembered that he had laid it upon the crag when he had thrown himself down to rest. Beyond question, it was there yet. His conscience was still now,—his remorse had fled. It was only a matter of time when his crime would be known. He recollected his meeting with young White while he was hunting, and then Britt cursed the gun which he had left on the cliff. The discovery of the weapon there would be strong evidence against him, taken in connection with all the other circumstances. True, he could even yet go back and recover it, but he was mastered by the fear of meeting some one on the unfrequented road, or even in the loneliness of the T'other Mounting, and strengthening the chain of evidence against him by the fact of being once more seen in the fateful neighborhood. He resolved that he would wait until nightfall, and then he would retrace his way, secure his gun, and all might yet be well with him. As to the bowlder,—were men never before buried under the falling rocks of the T'other Mounting?

Without food, without rest, without sleep, his limbs rigid with the strong tension of his nerves, his eyes bloodshot, haggard, and eager, his brain on fire, he sat through the long morning hours absently gazing across the narrow valley at the solemn, majestic mountain opposite, and that sinister jutting crag with the indistinctly defined ledges of its rugged surface.

After a time, the scene began to grow dim; the sun was still shining, but through a haze becoming momently more dense. The brilliantly tinted foliage upon the T'other Mounting was fading; the cliffs showed strangely distorted faces through the semi-transparent blue vapor, and presently they seemed to recede altogether; the valley disappeared, and all the country was filled with the smoke of distant burning woods. He was gasping when he first became sensible of the smoke-laden haze, for he had seen nothing of the changing aspect of the landscape. Before his vision was the changeless picture of a night of mingled moonlight and shadow, the ill-defined black mass where Old Rocky-Top rose into the air, the impenetrable gloom of the valley, the ledge of the crag, and the unconscious figure slowly coming within the power of his murderous hand. His eyes would look on no other scene, no other face, so long as he should live.

He had a momentary sensation of stifling, and then a great weight was lifted. For he had begun to doubt whether the unlucky locality would account satisfactorily for the fall of that bowlder and the horrible object beneath it; a more reasonable conclusion might be deduced from the fact that he had been seen in the neighborhood, and the circumstance of the deadly feud. But what wonder would there be if the dry leaves on the T'other Mounting should be ignited and the woods burned! What explanations might not such a catastrophe suggest!—a frantic flight from the flames toward the cliff and an accidental fall. And so he waited throughout the long day, that was hardly day at all, but an opaque twilight, through which could be discerned only the stony path leading down the slope from his door, only the blurred outlines of the bushes close at hand, only the great gaunt limbs of a lightning-scathed tree, seeming entirely severed from the unseen trunk, and swinging in the air sixty feet above the earth.

Toward night-fall the wind rose and the smoke-curtain lifted, once more revealing to the settlers upon Old Rocky-Top the sombre T'other Mounting, with the belated evening light still lurid upon the trees,—only a strange, faint resemblance of the sunset radiance, rather the ghost of a dead day. And presently this apparition was gone, and the deep purple line of the witched mountain's summit grew darker against the opaline skies, till it was merged in a dusky black, and the shades of the night fell thick on the landscape.

The scenic effects of the drama, that serve to widen the mental vision and cultivate the imagination of even the poor in cities, were denied these primitive, simple people; but that magnificent pageant of the four seasons, wherein was forever presented the imposing splendor of the T'other Mounting in an ever-changing grandeur of aspect, was a gracious recompense for the spectacular privileges of civilization. And this evening the humble family party on Nathan White's porch beheld a scene of unique impressiveness.

The moon had not yet risen; the winds were awhirl; the darkness draped the earth as with a pall. Out from the impenetrable gloom of the woods on the T'other Mounting there started, suddenly, a scarlet globe of fire; one long moment it was motionless, but near it the spectral outline of a hand appeared beckoning, or warning, or raised in horror,—only a leafless tree, catching in the distance a semblance of humanity. Then from the still ball of fire there streamed upward a long, slender plume of golden light, waving back and forth against the pale horizon. Across the dark slope of the mountain below, flashes of lightning were shooting in zig-zag lines, and wherever they gleamed were seen those frantic skeleton hands raised and wrung in anguish. It was cruel sport for the cruel winds; they maddened over gorge and cliff and along the wooded steeps, carrying far upon their wings the sparks of desolation. From the summit, myriads of jets of flame reached up to the placid stars; about the base of the mountain lurked a lake of liquid fire, with wreaths of blue smoke hovering over it; ever and anon, athwart the slope darted the sudden lightning, widening into sheets of flame as it conquered new ground.

The astonishment on the faces grouped about Nathan White's door was succeeded by a startled anxiety. After the first incoherent exclamations of surprise came the pertinent inquiry from his wife, "Ef Old Rocky-Top war ter ketch too, whar would we-uns run ter?"

Nathan White's countenance had in its expression more of astounded excitement than of bodily fear. "Why, bless my soul!" he said at length, "the woods away over yander, what hev been burnin' all day, ain't nigh enough ter the T'other Mounting ter ketch it,—nuthin' like it."

"The T'other Mounting would burn, though, ef fire war put ter it," said his son. The two men exchanged a glance of deep significance.

"Do ye mean ter say," exclaimed Mrs. White, her fire-lit face agitated by a sudden superstitious terror, "that that thar T'other Mounting is fired by witches an' sech?"

"Don't talk so loud, Matildy," said her husband. "Them knows best es done it."

"Thar 's one thing sure," quavered the old man: "that thar fire will never tech a leaf on Old Rocky-Top. Thar 's a church on this hyar mounting,—bless the Lord fur it!—an' we lives in the fear o' God."

There was a pause, all watching with distended eyes the progress of the flames.

"It looks like it mought hev been kindled in torment," said the young daughter-in-law.

"It looks down thar," said her husband, pointing to the lake of fire, "like the pit itself."

The apathetic inhabitants of Old Rocky-Top were stirred into an activity very incongruous with their habits and the hour. During the conflagration they traversed long distances to reach each other's houses and confer concerning the danger and the questions of supernatural agency provoked by the mysterious firing of the woods. Nathan White had few neighbors, but above the crackling of the timber and the roar of the flames there rose the quick beat of running footsteps; the undergrowth of the forest near at hand was in strange commotion; and at last, the figure of a man burst forth, the light of the fire showing the startling pallor of his face as he staggered to the little porch and sank, exhausted, into a chair.

"Waal, Caleb Hoxie!" exclaimed Nathan White, in good-natured raillery; "ye're skeered, fur true! What ails ye, ter think Old Rocky-Top air a-goin' ter ketch too? 'T ain't nigh dry enough, I'm a-thinkin'."

"Fire kindled that thar way can't tech a leaf on Old Rocky-Top," sleepily piped out the old man, nodding in his chair, the glare of the flames which rioted over the T'other Mounting gilding his long white hair and peaceful, slumberous face. "Thar's a church on Old Rocky-

Top,—bless the"— The sentence drifted away with his dreams.

"Does ye believe—them—them" Caleb Hoxie's trembling lips could not frame the word—"them—done it?"

"Like ez not," said Nathan White. "But that ain't a-troublin' of ye an' me. I ain't never hearn o' them witches a-tormentin' of honest folks what ain't done nuthin' hurtful ter nobody," he added, in cordial reassurance.

His son was half hidden behind one of the rough cedar posts, that his mirth at the guest's display of cowardice might not be observed. But the women, always quick to suspect, glanced meaningly at each other with widening eyes, as they stood together in the door-way.

"I dunno,—I dunno," Caleb Hoxie declared huskily. "I ain't never done nuthin' ter nobody, and what do ye s'pose them witches an' sech done ter me las' night, on that T'other Mounting? I war a-goin' over yander to Gideon Croft's fur ter physic him, ez he air mortal low with the fever; an' ez I war a-comin' alongside o' that thar high bluff"—it was very distinct, with the flames wreathing fantastically about its gray, rigid features—"they throwed a bowlder ez big es this hyar porch down on ter me. It jes' grazed me, an' knocked me down, an' kivered me with dirt. An' I run home a-hollerin'; an' it seemed ter me ter-day ez I war a-goin' ter screech an' screech all my life, like some onsettled crazy critter. It 'peared like 't would take a bar'l o' hop tea ter git me quiet. An' now look yander!" and he pointed tremulously to the blazing mountain.

There was an expression of conviction on the women's faces. All their lives afterward it was there whenever Caleb Hoxie's name was mentioned; no more to be moved or changed than the stern, set faces of the crags among the fiery woods.

"Thar 's a church on this hyar mounting," said the old man feebly, waking for a moment, and falling asleep the next.

Nathan White was perplexed and doubtful, and a superstitious awe had checked the laughing youngster behind the cedar post.

A great cloud of flame came rolling through the sky toward them, golden, pellucid, spangled through and through with fiery red stars; poising itself for one moment high above the valley, then breaking into myriads of sparks, and showering down upon the dark abysses below.

"Look-a-hyar!" said the elder woman in a frightened under-tone to her daughter-in-law; "this hyar wicked critter air too onlucky ter be a-sittin' 'longside of us; we 'll all be burnt up afore he gits hisself away from hyar. An' who is that a-comin' yander?" For from the encompassing woods another dark figure had emerged, and was slowly approaching the porch. The wary eyes near Caleb Hoxie saw that he fell to trembling, and that he clutched at a post for support. But the hand pointing at him was shaken as with a palsy, and the voice hardly seemed Tony Britt's as it cried out, in an agony of terror, "What air ye a-doin' hyar, a-sittin' 'longside o' livin' folks? Yer bones air under a bowlder on the T'other Mounting, an' ye air a dead man!"

* * *

THEY SAID EVER AFTERWARD that Tony Britt had lost his mind "through goin' a-huntin' jes' one time on the T'other Mounting. His spirit air all broke, an' he's a mighty tame critter nowadays." Through his persistent endeavor he and Caleb Hoxie became quite friendly, and he was even reported to "'low that he war sati'fied that Caleb never gin his wife nuthin' ter hurt." "Though," said the gossips of old Rocky-Top, "them women up ter White's will hev it no other way but that Caleb pizened her, an' they would n't take no yerbs from him no more 'n he war a rattlesnake. But Caleb always 'pears sorter skittish when he an' Tony air tergether, like he did n't know when Tony war a-goin' to fotch him a lick. But law! Tony air that changed that ye can't make him mad 'thout ye mind him o' the time he called Caleb a ghost."

A dark, gloomy, deserted place was the charred T'other Mounting through all the long winter. And when spring came, and Old Rocky-Top was green with delicate fresh verdure, and melodious with singing birds and chorusing breezes, and bedecked as for some great festival with violets and azaleas and laurel-blooms, the T'other Mounting was stark and wintry and black with its desolate, leafless trees. But after a while the spring came for it, too: the buds swelled and burst; flowering vines festooned the grim gray crags; and the dainty freshness of the vernal season reigned upon its summit, while all the world below was growing into heat and dust. The circuit-rider said it reminded him of a tardy change in a sinner's heart: though it come at the eleventh hour, the glorious summer is before it, and a full fruition; though it work but an hour in the Lord's vineyard, it receives the same reward as those who labored through all the day.

"An' it always did 'pear ter me ez thar war mighty little jestice in that," was Mrs. White's comment.

But at the meeting when that sermon was preached Tony Britt told his "experience." It seemed a confession, for according to the gossips he "'lowed that he hed flung that bowlder down on Caleb Hoxie,—what the witches flung, ye know,—'kase he believed than that Caleb hed killed his wife with pizenous yerbs; an' went back the nex' night an' fired the woods, ter make folks think when they fund Caleb's bones that he war a-runnin' from the blaze an' fell off'n the bluff." And everybody on Old Rocky-Top said incredulously, "Pore Tony Britt! He hev los' his mind through goin' a-huntin' jes' one time on the T'other Mounting."

UNCLE TUTT'S TYPHOIDS*

By LUCY FURMAN

IT WAS three days before the opening of the women's school in mid-August that Susanna Reeves, their visitor from the Blue Grass, rode off behind Uncle Tutt Logan as volunteer nurse for the family of five, renters on his place, down with typhoid. Uncle Tutt was an old man who lived by himself about two miles up Troublesome. He had been, as he expressed it, of a "rambling natur' " in his youth, had somewhere acquired a taste for reading, and now came down frequently to get books from the women's library.

When Susanna stepped into the door of the tumble-down cabin up the hollow from Uncle Tutt's house, the five sick persons, a man and a little boy in one bed, a woman and two little girls in the other, lay in their soiled day-clothing among the dingy quilts—there were no sheets. A boy of seven sat on the floor, trying to pacify two dirty, wailing babies. A piece of fat meat dripped over a meal-barrel in one corner, and flies swarmed everywhere.

"Hit's beyand a man-person," said Uncle Tutt, with a gesture of despair. "I never knowed where to begin at. A woman is called for."

Susanna's heart was in her shoes, but she made no sign. "The first thing," she said, "is to fill the wash-kettle there in the yard and build a fire under it. While you do that, I must try to find a place where these babies can be taken care of. Is there no woman in the neighborhood?"

"Milly Graham is the most nighest," he replied. "She

* Reprinted from *The Glass Window* by Lucy Furman, copyright by Little, Brown & Company.

lives about two-whoops-and-a-holler up Troublesome, and is as clever-turned a woman as ever I seed, with not more 'n nine or ten of her own."

Susanna quickly washed some of the dirt off the faces, hands, and feet of the babies, one of whom was two years old, the other less than one, sought in vain for clean things to put on them, and then, with the help of the small boy, George, took them up the creek.

Milly Graham, who was lifting clothes out of a steaming kettle by the water's edge and battling them on a smooth stump, laid down her battling stick and came forward, bare-footed and kind-faced, followed by a train of towheads.

"Sartain I'll take 'em in, pore leetle scraps," she said, when Susanna had explained the situation, "Two more hain't nothing to me, nohow, with sech a mess of my own." Gathering both babies in her arms, she sat down on the battling-stump, opened her dress, and offered a generous breast to each. "I allow the biggest hain't beyand taking the teat," she said. It was not indeed—both sucked as if they were starved.

"I heared about Uncle Tutt's typhoids," continued Milly, "and I would have went right down; but that-air next-to-least-one of mine is croupy and chokes so bad I'm afeard to leave hit a minute, and all is jest a-getting over measles. Onliest time I been off the place in a year was to the quare women's Working, the Fourth of July. I mustered the whole biling and tuck 'em down-along, and seed as fine a time as ever I seed. But that was where they all kotched them measles. I mind you a-being there that day—I allus remembered you from them pretty black eyes and that lavish of black hair.

"Next thing I heared, you women was all holping with the typhoid down at The Forks—'pears like hit strikes 'em reg'lar as summer. Hit was right sensible for Uncle Tutt to go down atter one of you women. Pore old widder—what could he do? A lone man's the most helplessest creatur on top of the earth. What possesses him to live that a-way, cooking and washing and even milking for hisself, the Lord only knows; no wonder he's a leetle turned. Hit's a pyore pity, and flying right in the face of Scripter, too. Not that Uncle Tutt keers for that—he's a master hand to rail at the Scripter and the preachers and the Lord—Eh, law! if he did n't cuss God Almighty Hisself when a big wind blowed down the most of his corn a year gone! Said there wa'n't no dependence to be put in Him nohow!

"Them renters of his'n I hain't never got acquainted with; they hain't belongers here—jest blowed in one day about corn-planting time in Aprile. I seed 'em go down one morning about sunup, the man big and stout, with a poke on his back and a babe on one arm, the woman pore and puny and all drug-out from packing tother baby. Most people in these parts don't confidence strangers and furriners, but Uncle Tutt, though he's hard on the Lord, allus was saft-hearted to folks; and he tuck pity-sake on 'em and allowed they could stay and crap for him, and give 'em 'steads and kivers and cheers and sech-like gear. They allowed their name was Johnson, and they come from Magoffin. Hit's quare, folks being that fur from home; hit's quare, too, they don't never put foot off'n the place. But maybe hit's right. I'll lay the woman's right anyways—she's as good-countenanced as ever I seed."

Returning to the cabin with the little boy, who seemed old and quiet beyond his years, Susanna found the water boiling in the big kettle, and in the teeth of Uncle Tutt's solemn warnings and dire prophecies,—"Hit'll sartain kill 'em to wash 'em when they're sick; I never in all my life and travels heared of sech doings,"—and with his very reluctant assistance, bathed the five patients and got them into the nightgowns the women had sent, then cleared away the soiled covers and put the women's sheets on the lumpy shuck mattresses. Then, after meat and meal-barrel had been removed to Uncle Tutt's, the joists and walls were washed down with strong suds, and the floor scrubbed, first with a broom, then with the scrub-brush Susanna had brought.

Uncle Tutt went home to get dinner for himself, Susanna, and little George, and to bring milk for the sick ones, and he was then sent back to The Forks after mosquito netting—which the women had had brought in at the beginning of the typhoid—and the doctor; for a Forks boy, Doctor Benoni Swope, had just come back from medical school to be the first physician in his community.

When at last the day was almost over, and Uncle Tutt was leaving the cabin to get supper, he said, looking back through the net-curtained doorway to the two white beds, "Looks pine-blank like a passel of corps laid out yander. If I was to wake up and find one of them shrouds on me and a burying-sheet drawed over, I'd give hit up I was everly dead and gone!"

Susanna sat down on the porch and dashed off the following letter:—

Dear Robert,

This will reach you about the time I had expected to start for home. I was only waiting for the opening of school on Monday. I hope you'll feel *dreadfully* disappointed when I don't come—Aunt Ailsie to the contrary notwithstanding! I am staying to nurse a family of five, down with typhoid, about two miles up Troublesome. Now don't scoff; of course I know nothing about nursing, except what little I have learned this summer, but anyhow I'm a human being, with a pair of hands and a strong body and a willing mind; and the motto here is "Learn by Doing."

If you could have stepped with me into this cabin this morning you'd have had the shock of your life; but if you came now, I flatter myself that, finicky surgeon as you are, even you would be pleased. The five patients are in nightgowns, the first they ever wore; the beds are in sheets, the first *they* ever wore; walls, ceiling, and floor are scrubbed,—you should have been your idle, useless Susanna down on her wet knees!—and the mosquito netting over doors, fireplace, and all cracks will soon do away with the flies.

One thing only disturbs me; while the father and three children look as if they could stand anything, the mother is terribly weak and sick to begin with, and Dr. Benoni says we can hardly expect to pull her through.

Now don't be foolish about me—I am splendidly fit. I boil all the water; Uncle Tutt brings me food from his house; and both he and Dr. Benoni have offered to "spell" me at night so that I may sleep on my cot on the porch. Best of all, it's so wonderful to feel that I am at last of some actual use in the world, that I am thrilled beyond words—it beats dancing, cards, even the races—can I say more?

Call up Sister and swage her down all you can. And take time from your "cyarving" to miss me *real hard* occasionally during the next four or five weeks!

Devotedly,

SUSANNA

Next morning the sick woman, who the day before had said nothing save to assure herself the babies were in safe hands, lying all day with dull, suffering eyes fixed on the doorway, said weakly to Susanna, while the latter was gently washing her face, "You look gooder to me than ary angel."

Susanna laid a hand on the drawn, troubled brow. "I'm so very glad to be here," she said; "and everything will be all right now—you must just stop worrying, and rest, and get well."

Two slow tears trickled from beneath the closed lids. A little later, when Susanna had washed the worn hands and was about to turn away, the fingers closed spasmodically upon her own. "You don't aim to go away, do you?" asked the frightened voice.

"Not at all," replied Susanna. "Not once until you are all well again."

The patient sighed deeply—a sigh that carried an utmost burden of care and sorrow—and then, as if in apology, said quickly, "'Pears like I'm all werried-out, hit's been so long!"

"Yes, I know it has seemed long since you got down, though it is really only a few days."

The woman shook her head weakly. "Not that," she said in a low tone, "not that!" Then she opened her eyes as if frightened at her words. "My wits they must be a-wandering," she explained.

The rest of the day she lay quiet, with eyes, as usual, on the doorway. Her husband, a strong, well-built young man, who appeared to be at least a dozen years younger than his wife, also lay always silent, one hand under his pillow, inscrutable eyes on the door.

"She looks to me as if she had some dreadful trouble on her mind," said Susanna to Uncle Tutt that evening, as she ate her supper of corn bread, milk, and honey under the apple tree in the yard. "What do you suppose it is?"

"Hit's been that way ever sence they come—Bill allus

silent and surly, Cory narvious as a skairt rabbit."

"Is he unkind or cruel to her?"

"I never seed him beat her none, or handle her rough."

"He looks much younger than she does."

"He's got a reason for it, by grab—That-air Bill is the triflingest sluggardly do-nothing ever I come acrost! Strikes about one lick with a hoe to her three, and allus leaves her take the bottom row. That's the kind of a cuss he is! But he's a fine-pretty feller to look at, and she worships his tracks in the mud, and works herself pine-blank to a shadder for him and his offsprings—works, and worries too." He stopped and pulled a stem of grass and began to chew on it, then said, in a confidential tone:—

"You mind that-air weepon he keeps under his pillow, with his thumb allus nigh the trigger, and would n't no-wise have took away?"

"Yes."

"And that-air new growth of beard all over his face?"

"Yes."

"And how he keeps his eyes, like she keeps hern, everly fixed on the door?"

"Yes."

"Well, the way I riddle hit out, he's maybe a mean man that has got into a leetle trouble somewheres—kilt somebody, say, and is hiding out here. I never tuck the leastest stock in their being from up Magoffin way; I'd sooner believe hit was ary other p'int of the compass—or their name being Johnson, either. No, the very minute I laid eyes on 'em I suspicioned they was hunting a hole to hide in. But I knowed too, from the woman's face, she was a right woman, and I allowed here with me was as safe a place for 'em to hide out as anywheres. If he had kilt ten men, or was the very old Devil hisself, I would n't give him up and break pore Cory's heart. My sympathies allus was with the women-folks anyhow—'pears like the universe is again' 'em, and God and man confederates to keep 'em down-trod. In all my travels I have seed hit, and hit's been the same old story ever sence Eve et the apple. I gonnies! ef I'd 'a had the ordering of things then, I'd a predestyned the female sect to better things. If replenishing the earth was to be their job, I would n't have laid on 'em the extry burden of being everly subject to some mis-begotten, hell-borned man-brute! Yes, dad burn my looks, when I see a puny creetur like Cory there, not only childbearing every year reg'lar, but likewise yearning the family bread by the sweat of her brow, hit fairly makes my blood bile, and eends my patience with the ways of the Lord. Yes, taking Him up one side and down tother, God Almighty sartain does as much harm as He does good, if not a leetle more. His doings is allus a myxtery, and sometimes a scandal!"

Doctor Benoni, after his visit the following morning, shook his head ominously when Susanna followed him to the porch. "A very sick woman," he said; "vitality all gone to begin with. She'll not pull through typhoid."

"The little girls are so restless—might n't it help if Cory had a bed to herself?" asked Susanna.

"It's worth trying," he said.

Uncle Tutt, appealed to, said yes, by Ned! Cory should have his last remaining 'stead—a pallet was good enough for him,—and the two men went at once for it, bringing also Uncle Tutt's own feather bed to put on it, "her bones being so nigh through," said the old man. Susanna made up the bed, and poor Cory was carefully lifted into it. Uncle Tutt had his reward when she sighed gratefully, "These feathers feels so saft to my bones!" A little later she said, wonderingly, "Hit's quare to have so much room to lay in. I never was in a bed to myself afore."

In mid-afternoon, while Susanna was giving her the second temperature-bath of the day, for her fever ran very high, she said deprecatingly, "I hate for you to do so much nasty work for me. I allow you have sot on a silk piller all your days!"

"I suppose I have," replied Susanna, in a startled and contrite tone, "but I'm very much ashamed of it now, and want to make up for it by being of some use."

"You so good to look at I can't hardly keep my hands off'n you. I allus did love pretty people. Your hair—I wisht I could feel hit!"

Susanna bent her head and laid one of the feeble hands on the thick waves of her hair.

"Now hain't hit pretty and saft! I follered having saft hair myself when I was young, but gee-oh! that's been so long I can't hardly ricollect hit!"

"Why, you're not that old," said Susanna. "People never get too old to remember their youth."

"Yes, they do. Hit's a long time; seems as fur away as if hit never was; and I'm a old woman—twenty-three year' old I am!"

"Twenty-three!" exclaimed Susanna, in utter amazement, for she had supposed Cory at least thirty-five. "Why, twenty-three is not old a bit—it's young. It's just my age."

It was Cory's turn to be astonished. "No woman couldn't look as young as you and be twenty-three," she said. "You hain't seed sixteen yet."

"I am twenty-three," insisted Susanna, "but I consider it young, not old. You must have been just a child when you married."

"Nigh fifteen I was."

"And at twenty-three the mother of six—Good Heavens!" exclaimed Susanna. "No wonder you are worn out! But you'll have a chance for a long rest in bed now, to get back your strength. I'm here to see that you do!"

Susanna cast an angry glance at the big, husky young man in the bed by the door. Of course it was his fault that poor Cory at twenty-three had forgotten her youth!

It was three days later, a week after her arrival, that one morning for the first time in the sick-room Dr. Benoni called Susanna by her surname. Uncle Tutt always addressed her and the other quare women by their Christian names. At the words "Miss Reeves," Cory sat up in bed and stared wildly about, only to fall back in a state of collapse when she saw Bill's eye fixed angrily upon her. Susanna and the doctor supposed it was only a manifestation of delirium, and thought no more about it. But when, in the afternoon, the patients were sleeping, and Susanna sat by Cory's bedside beginning a letter to Robert, she was surprised when Cory opened her eyes and whispered, "What name did he call you by?"

"Reeves," replied Susanna, in a low tone.

"Where do you live at?"

"In Lexington, in the Blue Grass."

"Is there many of the name of Reeves there?"

"Not now—our branch seems to have run largely to daughters, and I am the only one of the name left. My parents are dead, and I live with my married sister, who is much older than I. When I marry, the name will have died out—which is too bad, after a hundred years; for we were among the pioneers."

"Hit's a pretty name, Reeves—I love hit!" said Cory.

At that instant Bill, who had been apparently sleeping,

raised himself on his elbow and gave Cory a look that silenced her.

Susanna continued her letter:—

DEAR ROBERT,

How foolish of you to send that telegram! Of course it had to come across the mountains by mail, and it reached me at the same time as your letter. How foolish, too, to make both so mandatory! No, I will *not* "start home at once"—not if it were to my own wedding! I can't desert my post. You wouldn't have me if you knew the need. Poor Cory is in grave danger; Dr. Benoni says there is not a chance in fifty for her. And, oh, Robert, I have just found out that instead of being middle-aged, as I had supposed from her looks, the poor thing is only twenty-three, just my age—and the mother of six! With a horrid husband who lets her take the bottom row in hoeing corn and work herself to death in other ways. Also I believe she is the victim of some dreadful fear that hangs over her like a nightmare.

Glory for you, Doctor Helm! It's fine about old Boone Beverly and the thousand-dollar fee! I fervently hope that every rich old turf man and stockbreeder in the Blue Grass will have appendicitis this fall, and ask you to "cyarve" on him, so you can pay off those dreadful debts and marry

YOUR DEVOTED SUSANNA

Two nights after this the crisis of Cory's illness was reached. Dr. Benoni had spent both nights at the cabin, to relieve Susanna, so that one of them might be always at the bedside with the required heart-stimulant. At times the poor woman seemed almost too weak to breathe. The second night Dr. Benoni had called Susanna at three o'clock, himself lying down beside the little girls for a desperately needed nap. Bill snored loudly, and the three children were fast asleep. Susanna sat by Cory, holding one of her wasted hands. Suddenly she felt a feeble pressure, and heard a whisper: "Closter!"

She put her head down.

"I'm nigh gone, hain't I?"

"Oh, I hope not—we don't intend to let you go!"

"The young uns—what'll become of them?"

"Don't worry about them; they'll be cared for. They have their father."

"But if the Bentons gets him? Ssh—don't speak; whisper—they're atter him, and Black Shade he won't never stop till he finds him. And then the pore leetle orphants, without ary paw or maw! Listen," she whispered, desperately, "you must take 'em to my paw and maw when I'm gone; they'll forgive me then for running off with Anse—Bill, I mean. He was sech a pretty boy, I had to have him."

"Where does your father live, and what is his name?"

"In Harlan, on Reeves's Fork of Marrowbone. His name's same as yourn. There's a whole tribe of Reeveses there."

"Reeves!" gasped Susanna. "What's his first name?"

"Ssh—George."

"George Reeves!" exclaimed Susanna. "What other names are in your family—your grandfather? your great-grandfather?"

"Old Winfield was my grandsir', and behind him was another George. Them two is the main chiefest names all through."

Susanna took the sick woman's hands in both hers. "Cory," she said, "Winfield Reeves was the name of my father, and also of my pioneer forefather who came out from Virginia to Kentucky more than a hundred years ago. Near Cumberland Gap his young brother, George, left the wagon train to hunt a deer, and was never afterward heard of. My people went on to the Blue Grass, fought the Indians, subdued the wilderness, and became prosperous and prominent. They always supposed George had been killed by Indians. Instead, he must have found the hunting good, and have wandered from year to year in these mountains, at last settling down and founding the family to which you belong. The names tell the story. You and I are the same blood, and blood means a great deal to a Reeves! So now you can trust me to take care of your children if anything happens to you. I will do for them as if they were my own, and will adopt little George and change his name to Reeves. But you must n't die—you must live; for now you have found a sister who will always love you and take care of you!"

The entire conversation, tense as it was, had been carried on in whispers. Through it all Bill's snores had risen regularly; not a child had stirred; Dr. Benoni had slept profoundly.

Cory clutched Susanna's hand. "You and me the same blood? I hain't surprised, for I loved you when I seed you. Listen! A Reeves allus stands by a Reeves—you won't never tell what I tell you?"

"No, indeed."

"Well, Anse and the Bentons they had a furse, and he killed two of 'em. Then he give it out he had went West, and hid out in the high rocks awhile, and then we traveled here by nights. And, being a Reeves, you won't never tell on him, and will keep watch with me for Black Shade, and hide Anse if he comes?"

"Certainly, if it's possible. I'll protect him in every way, for your sake. You can depend on me. And now try to rest and sleep, and leave the worry and the watching to me. Remember you have found a sister."

Kneeling beside the bed, she folded the thin form to her breast; and lying thus, poor Cory relaxed, smiled, and soon fell asleep.

The unloading of that "perilous stuff that weighs upon the heart" was the beginning of better things. When Dr. Benoni left at six, Cory was still sleeping; her pulse was better, her temperature down two degrees. When at last she awoke, it was only by a glance of the eyes, a pressure of the hands, that she and Susanna indicated their remembrance of what had passed in the night. Bill, sullen and watchful as ever, had evidently heard nothing. Cory's eyes, instead of being fixed in that dreadful stare on the doorway, now followed Susanna constantly, hung upon her, feasted upon her.

That evening Susanna wrote again:

Dear Robert,

I have something amazing to tell you. You have heard us speak of the young brother of our pioneer Reeves ancestor, who went hunting one day as they came long the Wilderness Trail and was never heard of again. Well, he is found,—at least, his descendants are,—and one of them is poor Cory, the sick woman I am nursing! She belongs in Harlan County. Family names—everything—show there can be no mistake. And she and I are the same age. How easily I might have been in her place, and suffered what she has suffered! How selfish we prosperous Blue Grass people are, and how little we realize what is going on in this forgotten section of our state, where many of the people, doubtless, are of the same blood as our boasted aristocracy!

Almost three more weeks passed. Cory had gained steadily. The three children sat up for a while every morning, usually on Susanna's cot on the porch, and Bill, his splendid frame little impaired by illness, also sat in a chair there, pistol on his knees. This particular afternoon, all had come in for their rest and naps. Cory, the hunted look almost gone from her face, was sleeping, and Susanna sat by her bed reading a month-old magazine. Uncle Tutt had gone up in the timber to measure and mark the poplar trees he was giving to the quare women for their big settlement-house, taking little George with him.

Suddenly a shadow darkened the doorway. The curtain of mosquito netting was swept aside. A dark man, on noiseless feet, stepped in. Susanna rose, startled. At the same instant Cory's eyes flew open and she screamed in terror. With a single movement Bill, waking, drew his hand from beneath his pillow and fired, meeting the cross-fire of the intruder. Both men continued firing, swiftly as they could pull trigger, till at the same instant both lurched forward—Bill on his bed, the stranger full-length on the floor, neither so much as twitching a muscle thereafter.

The whole thing had happened in a flash. Cory's shrieks rent the air. Susanna flew to Bill, raised his heavy body, felt for his heart. Not a beat. But a slow trickle of blood welled out upon her fingers. Laying him back, she dashed a cup of water in his face. No response. Turning then to the intruder, beneath whose body a red pool was spreading on the floor, she looked for a sign of life. None there, either. Rushing then to the porch, she took down the gourd horn Uncle Tutt had left with her in case of need, and blew it loudly—once—twice—thrice.

The sound must have carried some of the poignancy of

her suffering, for in an incredibly short time Uncle Tutt came plunging down the slope.

They wasted no time on the dead men, but put in all their energies on the fainting, apparently dying Cory, forcing liquor between her lips, rubbing her cold hands and feet, at last seeing the tide of life flow slowly back again.

"Hit might be better to leave the pore creetur die," said Uncle Tutt. "She's seed enough trouble without this here."

"No," said Susanna, with determination, "that's the very reason she must live— to see something besides trouble; to get back the youth she has forgotten. I have found, Uncle Tutt, that she is a Reeves, that we are the same blood. I shall make it my business to take care of her and her children—to make life easier and happier for her. Of course she'll grieve for Bill; but grief never kills. A dead sorrow is better than a living one; in time it will wear away. She is young enough to forget."

Uncle Tutt received the news calmly. "I'm proud for her," he said. "I allow she has fell into good hands." Then, surveying the scene before him with philosophical eyes, he remarked, "I knowed hell was to pay somehow. Well, I better get them corps drug out of sight afore she comes to."

This gruesome task performed, the pistols taken from the clutch of the dead hands, the bodies laid on the porch out of Cory's line of vision, coins pressed down over the staring eyes, the old man stood in the doorway, looking down meditatively at his work.

"Hit hain't often," he said, "lightning strikes in the right spot. Hit's more gen'ally apter to strike wrong. I hain't seed hit fall right sence Heck was a pup. But this time hit went spang, clean, straight to the mark. I allow both needed killing and needed hit bad. I know Bill did! Well, hit's a sight of satisfaction to see jestice fall—kindly cheers a body up and holps up their confidence in the running of things. I'll say this much for Him—God Almighty is a pyore puzzle and myxtery and vexation of sperrit a big part of the time; but now and again, oncet or twicet maybe in a long lifetime, He does take Him a notion to do a plumb thorough, downright, complete, ondivided, effectual good job!"

SERENA AND WILD STRAWBERRIES*

By OLIVE TILFORD DARGAN

SHE WAS not an unalloyed joy that first year of our friendship. Her imperturbability did not always seem a restful evergreen wall, in whose shadow I could sit until perplexities lost their heat. At times it was a "no thoroughfare" with the meadows of desire gleaming beyond.

I called one day and found her churning by the spring, a pleasing picture, too, under the trees. Her rounded, youngish figure gave no hint of her sevenfold maternity, and however ragged the rest of her family might be, she always magically managed to be neat. She was singing leisurely and churning in rhythm—a most undomestic performance; but my eye was not Mrs. Poyser's, and if it had been, it could not have embarrassed Serena.

"I'm takin' my time," she said, "fer this is my last churnin' fer a good spell, I reckon."

"Your last? Why, is the cow sick?—dead? And you have just bought her?" I asked, my concern sharpened perhaps by the thought of a very inconvenient loan that had gone abysmally into her purchase.

"She got so many sweet apples last night she's foundered herself—clear light ruined, granpap says."

"Surely you didn't turn her into the orchard?"

"Why, a few apples wouldn't hurt her. But there was a whole passel on the ground that I couldn't see fer the weeds an' briers. An' she got 'em."

"But I lent Ben my scythe to cut those briers."

"His poppie needed him in the field, an' he couldn't git the time right off. When he did, we couldn't find that

* Reprinted from *Highland Annals* by Olive Tilford Dargan through arrangement with the holders of the copyright, Charles Scribner's Sons.

scythe nowheres. I hate it about the cow," she assured me cheerfully; "but it had to happen, I reckon."

I looked about me. At that moment I could see nothing artistic in Ned's half of a shirt looped about one shoulder; there was only pathos in little Lissie's naked, buttonless back; and I could not placidly think of Len, as I had passed him a few moments before, showing ankles as sockless as ever was Simpson. But perhaps it was the thought of that loan, with its indefinite time extension, that made me wish to set a shade of anxiety on Serena's unclouded brow. At any rate, I began to sermonize on the merits of discontent and the virtue of ambition.

Her face brimmed with astonishment that finally broke into speech: "But I've four beds, and bread on my table! What more do I want?"

What more could I say? So man, in some grateful season, may look up to the seated gods: "I've four religions and a bumper crop; what more do I want?" And what can the seated gods do but smile patiently?

I retreated, seeking my usual solace after all defeats—the unreproachful woods. Near a small clearing, in the quiet shield of some bushes, I overheard the latter end of an argument. One voice was Len's, the other a neighbor's.

"A tater's a tater, anyhow," the neighbor was affirming.

"You might as well say a woman's a woman," came the retort from Len.

"Well, ain't she?" said the neighbor.

"Lord, no!" said Len, with contempt freely flowing.

"Oh, course there ain't nobody like Reenie. Pity the Lord didn't think o' makin' her fer Adam. We'd all be in Eden yit, loaferin' by the river of life, 'stead o' diggin' taters out o' rocks."

"When you're spilin' to talk about a woman, Dan Goforth, you needn't travel furder'n your own doorstep," answered Len, his voice, like drawling fire, creeping on without pause. "Reenie mayn't be stout enough to wear out a hoe-handle, but she's never jowerin' when I come in , 'n' there's always a clean place in the house big enough fer me to set my cheer down in, I ain't layin' up much more'n debts, but they's easy carried when nobody's naggin' yer strenth out, a woman's smile ain't no oak-tree in harvest-time, but it's jest as good to set by, my coat's raggeder'n yourn, but I'd ruther Reenie 'ud lose her needle onct on a while than her temper all the time, neighbors can go by my house day or night an' never hear no fire aspittin', which kain't be said o' yourn, an' you scootle from here, Dan Goforth; don't you tech nary nuther tater in this patch!"

The neighbor scootled, backward it seemed, to the road. I took the trouble myself to go down to a trail and come up casually from another direction, in full view of Len. He was working mightily, digging up a hill with two strokes of his hoe.

"Dan gone?" I asked indifferently.

"Ay, he lit out. Old Nance wanted him, I reckon. He dassen't stay a minute after she fixes the clock fer him."

"That's a kind of trouble you and Reenie don't have."

"You've said it now. Reenie don't keep no time on me. If I want to drap over the mountain to see if I can git old man Diller's mule fer extry ploughin', 'cause the crab-grass is elbowin' along the ground 'most rootin' up my corn, an' tells Reenie I'll be back by twelve, an' I find the old man spilin' a ox-yoke, an' I shapes it up fer him an' stays to dinner, an' comes back by the meetin'-house where they's puttin' in the new windows an' not gittin' 'em plumb, an' I stays till sundown settin' 'em in so they won't make everybody 'at passes think he's gone cross-eyed, an' I remembers we've got no coffee, so I slips round by the store an' stays till dark talkin' with Tim Frizbie about the best way to grow fat corn an' lean cobs, 'cause I know you want me to git all the new idies I can, an' when I strikes Granny Groom's place she's at the gate wantin' me to talk to her Lizy's girl who's fixin' to leave an' strollop over the country, an' I says to that girl when you're at home you're eatin' welcome bread, and when you're out in the world you don't know what you're eatin', an' a lot more that was aplenty, an's I pass Mis' Woodlow's, who's got a powerful bad risin', I thinks I'll stop and see if her jaw's broke yit, an' I finds ol' Jim so out o' heart about her, I stays to help him put over a couple o' hours, an' when I walks in home about midnight, Reenie she's gone to bed sensible, an' says there's bread an' beans in the cupboard. Now that's what I call some comfort to a man, to know he can take what happens 'long the road, an' know his wife ain't frettin' till her stomach's gone an' she's as lean as a splinter like ol' Nance Goforth."

"You nearly got what you wanted when you married, didn't you, Len?"

"Well, I reckon, but I didn't know it from the start-off. Reenie was powerful to be agoin', an' I couldn't git used to draggin' off every Saturday night to stay till Monday mornin'. But I felt different about it after I'd nearly killed her an' the baby."

"Gracious, was it that bad?"

"I didn't do it a purpose. It was back in Madison, where I married Reenie, an' jest two days 'fore Christmas. She'd put in to go to her pap's, an' I thought I'd git up a nice lot o' wood, make me a big fire, an' have my Christmas at home. I'd told her I thought she'd feel different about stayin' in her own house after she'd got a little 'un in it, but she 'lowed her sight an' hearin' was as good as 'fore she had a baby, an' she could enjoy usin' 'em just the same. So I got out by good daylight an' went up the hill above the house to cut a big, dead chestnut that I was tired o' lookin' at; then I means to slip over to By Kenny's an' git him an' his wife to come over fer Christmas 'fore Reenie got away. There'd come a skift o' snow a few days back, bare enough to make the ground gray, then a little warm rain, an' on top o' that a freeze that stung yer eyeballs, an' you never saw anything as slick as that hill was 'fore the sun riz that mornin'. When my chestnut fell she crackled off every limb agin the hard ground clean as a sled-runner. Boys, if she didn't shoot off, makin' smoke out o' that frost! I saw she was pinted fer our little shack an' I tries to yell to Reenie to git out, but I never made more'n a peep like a chicken. When the log struck, it shaved by the corner o' the house an' took the chimbly. Boys, it made bug-bites o' that chimbly! I knowed Reenie was settin' by the fire with the baby, an' I'd killed 'em both. I felt 'most froze to the ground, an' I thought if Reenie was only livin' I'd let her do her own 'druthers the rest of her days. An' when I got down to the house an' sees her an' the baby not hurt, with the rocks all piled around 'em, I says to myself I ain't ever goin' back on what I promised her unbeknownst. An' I ain't."

"What was she doing?"

"She was jest settin' there."

"What did she say?"

"She 'lowed we'd got to go to pap's fer Christmas. An' we did."

* * *

I STOOD on the door-step one morning, balancing destiny.

Should I take the downward road to the post-office, and thereby connect with the distant maelstrom called progress, or should I choose the upward trail to the still crests of content?

Serena, happening designedly by, saved me the wrench of decision.

"If you want any strawberries this year," she said, "you'd better go before the Mossy Creek folks have rumpaged over Old Cloud field. They slip up from the west side an' don't leave a berry for manners. I'm goin' now. I always go once."

I provided buckets and cups, as expected, and we started. The high ridge field where the berries rambled had its name from an Indian, Old Cloud, who, it was said, had lived there behind the cloud that always rested on the ridge before so many of the peaks had been stripped of their pine and poplar and balsam that had held the clouds entangled and the sky so close. After it had passed to the settlers it has taken forty years of ignorant and monotonous tillage to reduce the rich soil to a half-wild pasture enjoying the freedom of exhaustion.

I had been under roof for three days, and the spring air produced the usual inebriation. Several times I left Serena far behind, but she always caught up, and we reached the top of the ridge together. Here, panting, I dropped to a bed of cinquefoil, while Serena stood unheated and smiling.

"Did you ever run, Serena?" I asked.

"I always take the gait I can keep," she said, her glance already roving the ground for berries. "The other side o' that gully's red with 'em. We've got ahead o' Mossy Creek this time."

I was looking at the world which the lifted horizon had given me. North by east the Great Smokies drew their lilac-blue veil over impenetrable wildernesses of laurel. I could see the round dome of Clingman, and turned quickly from the onslaught of a remembered day when my body was wrapped in the odor of its fir-trees and its heathery mosses cooled my feet. South lay the Nantahalas, source of clear waters. West—but what were names before that array of peaks like characters in creation's alphabet, whose key was kept in another star? They rose in every form, curved, swaying, rounded, a loaf, a spear, shadowed and unshadowed, their splotches of green, gold, and hemlock-black flowing into blue, where distance balked the eyes and imagination stepped the crests alone. It seemed easier to follow than to stay behind with feet clinging to earth. Affinity lay with the sky.

Serena was steadily picking berries.

"But, Serena," I called, "just see!"

"I come here once a year," she said, standing up, "an' I never take my look till I've filled my bucket." And she was on her knees again.

Rebuke number two, I thought, and set to work. Avoiding Serena's discovered province, I crossed to the next dip of the slope, and there the field was covered with morning-glories, still radiantly open. All hues were there, from the purple of night to snow without tint and the clusters of berries under them seemed in sanctuary. I plucked them away, feeling like a ravager of shrines. A breeze flowed over the field, and every color quivered dazzlingly. It was plainly a protest. I gave up my robberies and passed to another part of the field, where rapine seemed legitimate. Here the rank grass of yesteryears was deeply rooted and matted, and I sank adventurously in the tripping tangles. The slope was steeper, too, and I slipped, slid, and stumbled from patch to patch before theft was well begun, losing half my captures in the struggle. It was tinglingly arduous, however, and I continued a happy game of profit and loss until I scrambled from a gully into whose depths I had followed my rolling bucket, and confronted Serena. She looked as if she had coolly swum the lake of color behind us; but her fresh apron was unstained, while mine was a splash of coral. I advised her to return. The picking was better above.

"I know it is," she answered, "but them mornin'-glories keep me fluttery, lookin' at me all the time. I got to fill my bucket *first*. I promised Len all he could eat in a pie, an' it takes a big one fer ten of us. Granpap's stayin' at our house now. But we'd better move furder over, out o' this soddy grass. They's rattlers here."

With her word we saw him. He was partly coiled not more than three feet from Serena's undulating gingham. The black diamonds shining on his amber skin assured me of his variety—the kind that, as natives tell me, Indians will not kill because "he gives a man a chance." Certainly he was giving us a chance. His eyes seemed half-shut, but not sleepy, as if he did not need his full power of vision to comprehend our insignificant world. His poised head was motionless. Only his tail quivered, not yet erected for his gentlemanly warning. He glistened with newness, and was evidently a youngish snake, with dreams of knighthood still unbattered. His parents had bequeathed him none of the hatred that belongs to a defeated race. Serena seemed as motionless as he. I took her hand, drawing her a few paces back, and we stood watching. Sir Rattle slowly uncoiled, quivered throughout his variegated length, and moved indifferently from us, disappearing in the clumps of grass.

"Well," said a pale Serena, "I feel like I did after I was baptized. The preacher, he was old man Diller, put his hand on my shoulder an' said, 'Love the Lord, my sister'; but I was so full o' lovin' everything and everybody I couldn't think about the Lord. Do you reckon snakes have brothers and sisters that they know about? Think o' that feller throwin' away sech a chance to git even!" She could not stop talking any more than I could begin. "Let's get to the top o' the field where it's cooler. It's got so hot I'm afeard a shower's comin'."

By the time we reached the top we knew that the shower was to be a heavy one. There was a cave over the ridge on the Mossy Creek side, where we could take shelter. But we would wait a little for what the heavens could show us. The doors of the sky were to be thrown open. There would be no reservation of magic. Earth knew it by the quick wind that pressed every grass-blade to the ground and made the strawberry-blossoms look like little white, whipped flags; and by the grove of tall, young poplars that bent like maidens, their interlaced branches resting, a silver roof, on their curved shoulders. The lightning rippled, and earth was a golden rose spreading her mountain petals. It was the signal for the assembling of the dragons. They came swelling from the west, pulling one great paw after another from behind the walls of distance and puffing black breath half across the sky. The lightning again, and this time earth was a golden butterfly under the paws of the dragons. Then the conflict began, the beasts mingled, and the sound of their bones massively breaking struck and shook the ground under our feet. A gray sea rose vertically on the horizon and marched upon us. We fled, blinded, to the cave, tearing off our aprons to protect our buckets.

Even here Serena did not pant or gasp.

"How dry it is!" she said, examining the berries. "They're not hurt. My, you didn't cap yourn!"

"But I'd never fill my bucket if I stopped to cap them."

"You don't stop. You leave the cap on the vine. It's as quick done as not. Now it'll take you longer to cap than it did to pick. O' course you didn't know. Some folks knows one thing and some another," she added kindly. "Ain't it a thick rain? But we got a good place. Some say this cave's ha'nted, an' won't come anigh it. Uncle Sim Goforth died here, but he was a good man an' wouldn't harm nobody if he did come back."

"How did he happen to die here?"

"They killed him. It was in time o' the war way back. Folks are better now. They say they're doin' awful over the sea, but they'd never be so mean as they were to Uncle Sim. He hid here, an' brought his wife an' childern. But they found him."

"Was he a Unionist or Confederate?"

"I never could make out 'tween 'em. The Unionists, they wanted to free the black people, but the Unionists here in the mountains didn't favor 'em. So I never could git it clear. Anyway, Uncle Sim was a good man. I've heard granpap tell about him many a night. The men, when they found him, cut down a tree an' hewed out some puncheons fer a coffin, an' made Uncle Sim sit on it an' play his fiddle. He could play the best that ever was, an' they say he played up fine that night. They kept him playin' till near daylight; then they shot him, an' his wife an' childern lookin' right on. I used to cry, hearin' granpap tell it, out in Madison, but it don't make me feel bad now, 'cause I know folks are better than what they were them days."

Such naïveté was possible in the period of our national innocence, before "the boys" began to drift back home with certain truths on their tongue.

"Looky! the rain's stopped quicker'n it come. We can go right back, fer the ridge dreens off soon as the water strikes it. Ain't it cool, an' the air like gold!"

She tried to catch a handful of it to show me its quality. We went back, and in a minute, as she said, our buckets were full, though we lost a few seconds while I learned of Serena how to cap and pick at the same time. Then we started along the ridge to the gap where we had entered the field. Walking back, I lingered to pluck a giant white trillium that shone from the fringe of wood. No loss to the forest; there were thousands more lighting up the cove farther down. As I came out of the wood, the air over the field seemed visibly to precipitate some of its gold. A swarm—no, the word is too heavy for anything so delicately bodied—a band of butterflies, moving in a slow wave over the ridge, had at that moment broken into myriads of distinct flakes—a shattered blaze. Nearer, their gold became tinily specked, and showed flashes and fringes of pearl; the silver-bordered fritillaries, perhaps, or some kin of theirs. I started to call Serena, but paused softly, for she was gazing over the mountains, having her "look." I was left to the butterflies. Were they as unconscious of their grubby origin as they seemed, holding no memory of a life bounded by a sassafras twig, or of the cove behind us where a violet leaf may have been both food and heaven?

The butterfly ought to be the symbol on every Christian's flag. It is the perfect pietist. Its confidence in the Infinite is as patent as its wings. Serena, amid that airy fluttering, seemed, in her own shining way, the sovereign of the band. Deep as piety was her trust in the morrow. Food would come to her, raiment would be found.

The butterflies floated past, becoming a dim, coppery tremble in the shade of the valley. Serena was still gazing in the distance. At last I said that we must be going; Len was expecting his pie.

"These berries ain't goin' into a pie," she answered. "They're worth more than a pie'll come to. They're goin' into jam."

Was Serena taking forethought? No; I could trust her lighted face and wet eyes. She was still piously improvident.

* * *

ONCE MORE it was May, and early morning. I was out before breakfast, gathering sticks for my hearth-fire. There had been showers in the night, and an inch of new grass trembled over the ground. I tugged at a pile of brush made by my oldest apple-tree, which had fallen in a winter storm. The limbs, and even the million twigs, were all gray and green and slate blue in their wrappings of moss, and in among them, like a burning heart, sat a cardinal.

"You ought to be singing from a tree-top," said I.

"But I'm getting my breakfast. This is the *cafeteria* of Wingland. Are you going to demolish it?"

"Indeed, no!" I answered, picking up some peripheral sticks and leaving his stronghold unshaken.

To thank me, he hopped to the top of the pile, and, right in my face, sang his most shamelessly seductive song. Serena put her head out of the kitchen window to listen. He paused, and deserted me for a tree-top. But sweet was air and earth. Delight summoned an antithesis. I thought of forgotten pains, some monitions of the night before. Suppose I were to die, and never again stand in that dip of the mountain when it was a brimming bowl of springtime? Perhaps there was no other planet where I might gather in my arms such beautiful gray and green and slate-blue fagots. I turned to go in, and met rebuke in the eyes of my Chicago guest.

"I wonder if you are going to tell me that your woman does not know how to pick up brush."

My woman! If Serena had heard that!

"And after last night! Did you take your medicine?"

Verily I had. She was unconvinced.

"The bottle seems full."

"Oh, I took it from the cardinal's throat," said I, surrendering.

She laughed, for there was sweetness in her, and we went in to breakfast. I had prepared it before going out, leaving Serena on guard. She was with me, not so much for the help she gave, as to save the feelings of my guest.

"Do you have much of this soggy weather?" said Chicago, airily tolerant, as we took our seats.

"Why, I've never noticed."

"We shore do," said Serena, with gloom that was ludicrously alien to her face. "It's li'ble to rain now fer two weeks steady."

"But I had decided not to go home to-day," cried the guest, almost resentfully declining the hot biscuit Serena urged upon her. "Two weeks! Do you mean two weeks?"

"I've known it to hang wet fer a month."

"Why, Serena!"

"Showery like. You know it's so, Mis' Dolly."

"Well, we're going to have perfect weather now. Tender, bright, with maybe a bit of dew in the air. Stay, and I promise you a miracle among springs." I held up a glass of strawberry jam. "The kind of a spring that produced this." And I offered her the food of heaven.

"Thanks, but I've cut out sweets."

I caught my breath, and looked at Serena, in whose eyes sparkled a triumph that said plainly: "Now you see!"

My guest did not notice that I sat dumb, bewildered, bereft. She was talking.

"No, I think, my dear, that if you wish to memorialize a passing folk, you will find material more worthy of your pen in the twilight of the bourgeoisie. They have lived in the main line of evolution, and will leave their touch on the race. Faint it may be, but indelible. In art, in literature, perhaps in certain predilections of character and temperament, it will be possible to trace them. These mountain people will not have even a fossilized survival. They live in a *cul-de-sac*, a pocket of society, so to speak. Your mind has an epic cast, and will never fit into its limits."

There was more; then Serena's voice glided into the monologue.

"Mis' Dolly, I don't like to tell you, seein' you were ailin' last night, but Johnny Diller went by here this mornin', and he said Mis' Ludd's little Marthy wasn't expected to keep breath in her till sundown."

"I must go," said I, getting up.

"I don't approve of it," said my friend.

"I must. You don't understand—"

"Please don't tell me that again, my dear."

"But you don't!"

"Your hat's on the porch," said Serena.

"You can't leave to-day, Marie, because I haven't time to tell you good-by now," I said, and hurried away.

Home again at ten in the evening, I found Serena sitting by a bright kitchen fire humming "Old Time Religion."

"Is Miss Brooks asleep?" I asked.

"I reckon she is. She said she was goin' to take a sleeper."

"She's gone?"

Serena's affirming nod did not interrupt her tune.

"Please stop that humming, Serena, and tell me what you did the minute my back was turned."

"Nothin' at all. That was the matter, maybe."

"You didn't do *anything* for her?"

"I fixed her a snack to eat on the train."

"Oh, thank you! It was a nice one, wasn't it?"

"I give her some pickled beets, an' turnip-kraut, an' 'tater salad made with that blackberry vinegar."

I dizzily recalled a remark of Len's. "That blackberry vinegar 'ud pickle a horseshoe."

"Serena," I began faintly.

She had crossed to a shelf and was looking fondly at a jar of strawberry jam.

My voice died away; I could not reproach her.

Sweets, my friend had called it. And, my God, it was May morning on a mountain-top!

ON THE MOUNTAIN-SIDE*

By ELIZABETH MADOX ROBERTS

THERE was a play-party at the school-house at the bottom of the cove. Newt Reddix waited outside the house, listening to the noises as Lester Hunter, the teacher, had listened to them—a new way for Newt. Sound at the bottom of a cove was different from sound at the top, he noticed, for at the top voices spread into a wide thinness. Before Lester came Newt had let his ears have their own way of listening. Sounds had then been for but one purpose—to tell him what was happening or what was being said. Now the what of happenings and sayings was wrapped about with some unrelated feeling or prettiness, or it stood back beyond some heightened qualities.

"Listen!" Lester had said to him one evening, standing outside a house where a party was going on. "Listen!" And there were footsteps and outcries of men and women, happy cries, shrill notes of surprise and pretended anger, footsteps on rough wood, unequal intervals, a flare of fiddle playing and a tramp of dancing feet. Down in the cove the sounds from a party were different from those that came from a house on the side of a hill, the cries of men bent and disturbed, distorted by the place, by the sink and rise of land. While he listened the knowledge that Lester Hunter would soon go out of the country, the school term being over, brought a loneliness to his thought.

He went inside the school-house and flung his hat on the floor beside the door; he would take his part now in the playing. His hat was pinned up in front with a thorn and was as pert a hat as any of those beside the door,

* Reprinted from *The American Mercury* through the courtesy of the publishers and of Elizabeth Madox Roberts.

and no one would give it dishonor. The school teacher was stepping about in the dance, turning Corie Yancey, and the fiddle was scraping the top of a tune. For him the entire party was filled with the teacher's impending departure.

"Ladies change and gents the same," the fiddler called, his voice unblended with the tune he played. Newt fell into place when an older man withdrew in his favor and gave him Ollie Mack for his partner. The teacher danced easily, bent to the curve of the music, neglectful and willing, giving the music the flowing lightness of his limp body.

Newt wanted to dance as the teacher did, but he denied himself and kept the old harsh gesture, pounding the floor more roughly now and then with a deeply accented step. He wanted to tread the music lightly, meeting it halfway, but he would not openly imitate anybody. While he danced he was always, moment by moment, aware of the teacher, aware of him standing to wait his turn, pulling his collar straight, pushing his hands into the pockets of his coat, looking at Ollie Mack when she laughed, looking full into her face with pleasure, unafraid. The teacher had given an air to the dance, and had made it, for him, more bold in form, more like itself or more true to its kind. The dance drawing to an end, he realized again that in two days more the teacher would go, for he had set his head upon some place far away, down in the settlements, among the lower counties from which he had come six months earlier.

There was pie for a treat, baked by Marthy Anne Sands and brought to the school-house in a great hickory basket. Standing about eating the pie, all were quiet, regretting the teacher's going. Newt wove a vagrant path in and out among them, hearing the talk of the older men and women.

"My little tad, the least one, Becky, is plumb bereft over 'im," one said, a woman speaking.

"Last year at the school there wasn't hardly anybody would go, and look at this. I had to whop Joel to make him stay on the place one day to feed and water the property whilst I had to go. Hit appears like Joel loves book-sense since Les Hunter come up the mountain."

"What makes you in such a swivet to go nohow?" one asked.

"Did you come up the gorge to borrow fire you're in such a swivet to get on?"

"There's a big meeten over to Kitty's branch next light moon. Why don't you stay? No harm in you to be broguen about a small spell."

"You could loafer around a spell and wait for the meeten."

"Big meeten. And nohow the meeten needs youens to help sing."

"What's he in such a swivet to go off for?"

"I got to go. I got to see the other end of the world yet."

"What's he a-sayen?"

"I got to go to the other end of the world."

"That's too far a piece."

"That surely undoubtedly is a right smart piece to go."

"He could stay a spell at my place and welcome. I'd be real proud to have him stay with my folks a spell. And Nate, he'd keep youens a week, that I right well know. Youens could loafer around awhile as well as not."

"He always earns his way and more, ever since he kem up the mountain, always earns his keep, nohow."

"I've got to go. I'm bound for the other end of this

old globe. I'm obliged all the same, but I got a heap to see yet. I'm bound to go."

* * *

NEWT PLOUGHED the corn in the rocky field above the house where he lived, one horse to the plow, or he hoed where the field lay steepest. The teacher was gone now. On Sunday Newt would put on his clean shirt his mammy had washed on Friday, and climb up the gorge to the head of the rise and meet there Tige English and Jonathan Evans. Then they would go to see Lum Baker's girls. He would contrive to kiss each girl before the night fell and Lum would cry out, "Come on, you gals now, and milk the cow brutes." Or sometimes they would go down the way to see Corie Yancey and Ollie Mack. To Newt all the place seemed still since the teacher had left, idle, as if it had lost its uses and its future. Going to the well for water he would stare at the winch, at the soft rot of the bucket, at the stones inside the well curb, or he would listen intently to the sounds as the vessel struck the water or beat against the stones.

The noises gave him more than the mere report of a bucket falling into a well to get water; they gave him some comprehension of all things that were yet unknown. The sounds, rich with tonality, as the bucket struck the water, rang with some strange sonority and throbbed with a beat that was like something he could not define, some other, unlike fiddle playing but related to it in its unlikeness. A report had come to him from an outside world and a suspicion of more than he could know in his present state haunted him. He cried out inwardly for the answer, or he looked about him and listened, remembering all that he could of what Lester Hunter had taught—capitals of countries, seaports, buying and selling, nouns, verbs, numbers multiplied together to make other numbers. Now he looked intently and listened. He detected a throb in sound, but again there was a beat in the hot sun over a moist field. One day he thought that he had divined a throb in numbers as he counted, a beat in the recurrences of kinds, but this evaded him. He listened and looked at the well happenings, at the house wall, at the rail fence, at the barn, at the hills going upward toward the top of the gorge.

On every side were evasions. These sights and sounds could not give him enough; they lay flat against the air; they were imbedded within his own flesh and were sunk into his own sense of them. He would stare at the green and brown moss on the broken frame of the well box and stare again at the floating images in the dark of the well water. The rope would twine over the axle as he turned the wooden handle, and the rounds of the rope would fall into orderly place, side by side, as he knew too casually and too well. Since the teacher had gone the place had flattened to an intolerable staleness that gave out meager tokens of withheld qualities and beings—his mother leaning from the door to call him to dinner, his sister dragging his chair to the table and setting his cup beside his place, the old dog running out to bark at some varment above in the brush. He could hardly separate the fall of his own bare foot from the rock door-step over which he had walked since he could first walk at all. His thirst and his water to drink were one now. His loneliness, as he sat to rest at noon beside the fence, merged and was identified with the still country from brush-grown slope to brush-grown slope.

His father began to clear a new patch below the house; they grubbed at the roots all day when the corn was laid by. One morning in September, when the sun, moving North, was just getting free of Rattlesnake Hill, it came to him that he would go down to the settlements, that he would go to Merryman. All Summer he had known that there was a school at Merryman, but he had not thought to go there, for he had no money. It came to him as a settled fact that he would go there and look about at the place. Three high ridges with numberless breaks and gorges intervened; he had heard this said by men who knew or had heard of what lay beyond. The determination to set forth and the wish to go came to him at one instant. "My aim, hit's to go there," he said. "I lay off to do that-there, like I say."

He remembered the teacher more clearly at this moment, saw him in a more sharply detailed picture, his own breath jerked deeply inward as he was himself related, through his intended departure, to the picture. Hunter was remembered cutting wood for the schoolhouse fire, sweethearting the girls and turning them lightly in the dance, or sitting by the fire at night, reading his book, holding the page low to the blaze. He was remembered hallooing back up the mountain the day he left, his voice calling back as he went down the ridge and he himself answering until there was not even a faint hollow whoopee to come up the slope. By the fire Newt had often taken Hunter's book into his hands, but he could never read the strange words nor in any way know what they meant when they were read, for they had stood four-square and hostile against his understanding. His father's voice would fall dully over the slow clearing: "You could work on this-here enduren the while that I cut the corn patch."

He knew that he would go. His determination rejected the clearing, knowing that he would be gone before the corn was ready to cut. It rejected the monotonous passing of the days, the clatter of feet on the stones by the door, the dull, inconspicuous corn patch above. He would walk, taking the short cut over the mountains. Two ridges to go and then there would be a road for his feet, some one had said. He announced his plan to his father one day while they leaned over their grub hoes. There was no willingness offered, but his mind was set, and three days later he had established his plan. His mammy had washed his shirts clean and had rolled them into a bundle with his spare socks, and she had baked him bread and a joint of ham. She and his sister stood by the doorway weeping after he had driven back the dog and had shouted his goodbye.

* * *

IT WAS mid-afternoon and the sun beat down into the cove where he traveled. He worked his way through the thick-set laurel, struggling to keep his bundle tied to his shoulders where the brush stood most dense.

The dry clatter of the higher boughs came to his ears, but it was so mingled with the pricking snarls of the twigs on his face that the one sense was not divided from the other. "This durned ivy," he said when the laurel held him back. He matched his strength against boughs or he flashed his wits against snarls and rebounds, hot and weary, tingling with sweat and with the pricking twigs. Pushed back at one place where he tried to find an opening, he assailed another and then another, throwing all his strength angrily against the brush and tearing himself through the mesh with *god-damns* of relief. A large shaded stone that bulged angrily out of the mountain-side gave him a space of rest. He stretched himself on the slanting rock, his face away from the sun, and lay for an hour, thinking nothing, feeling the weariness as it beat heavily upon his limbs.

"I'm bodaciously tired," he said, after a long period of

torpor. "Could I come by a spring branch I'd drink me a whole durned quart of it."

Another tree-grown mountain arose across the cove, misty now in the afternoon and in the first haze of Autumn, and beyond lay other blue mountains, sinking farther and farther into the air. Back of him it was the same; he had been on the way two weeks now. Before him he knew each one would be dense with laurel until he came to the wagon road. He took to the pathless way after his hour of rest, going forward. When the sun was setting behind Bee Gum Mountain he saw a house down in the cove, not far as the crow would fly but the distance of two hours' going for him. When he saw the cabin he began to sing, chanting:

Right hands across and howdy-do,
Left and back and how are you.

Oh, call up yo' dog, oh, call up yo' dog,
Ring twang a-whoddle lanky day.

The sight of the house quickened his desire for Merryman and the cities in the settlements, and this desire had become more definite in his act of going. His wish was for sure, quick gestures and easy sayings that would come from the mouth as easily as breath. There were for him other things, as yet unrelated to any one place—men playing ball with a great crowd to watch, all the crowd breaking into a laugh at one time; men racing fine horses on a hard, smooth track; music playing; men having things done by machinery; lovely girls not yet imagined; and things to know beyond anything he could recall, and not one of them too fine or too good for him. He sang as he went down the slope, his song leaping out of him. He had heard it said that the lights of Merryman could be seen from Coster Ridge on a clear night, and Coster was now visible standing up in the pale air, for a man had pointed him the way that morning. Singing, he set himself toward the house at the bottom of the cove.

Night was falling when he called "Hello" at the foot of Bee Gum Mountain. The man of the house asked his name and told his own, making him welcome. Supper was over, but the host, whose name was Tom Bland, ordered Nance, his woman, to give the stranger a snack of biscuit bread and bacon, and this Newt ate sitting beside the fire. Another stranger was sitting in the cabin, an old man who kept very still while Nance worked with the utensils, his dim eyes looking into the fire or eyeing Newt who stared back and searched the looks of the stranger. Then Tom told Nance how they would sleep that night, telling her to give the old man her place in the bed beside himself.

"You could get in bed along with the young ones," he said to her. "The boy here, he could sleep on a shakedown along-side the fireplace."

From gazing into the fire the old stranger would fall asleep, but after a moment he would awake, opening dim, ashamed eyes that glanced feebly at Newt, faintly defying him. Then Nance put some children to bed, her own perhaps, and sat quietly in the corner of the hearth, her hands in her lap. Newt had looked at the host, acquainting himself with him. He was a strong man, far past youth, large-boned and broad-muscled. His heavy feet scraped on the floor when he moved from his chair to the water bucket on the window sill. Newt saw that he on his side had been silently searching out the old stranger. After a while the host and the old man began to talk, Tom speaking first.

"There's a sight of travel now."

"Hit's a moven age."

Between each speech there was a slow pause as each saying was carefully probed before the reply was offered.

Tom said, "Two in one night, and last week there was one come by." And then after a while he asked, "Where might youens be bound for, stranger?"

"I'm on my way back," the man said.

There was a long season of quiet. The ideas were richly interspersed with action, for Nance softly jolted back and forth in her chair, her bare feet tapping lightly on the boards of the floor.

"You been far?" Tom asked.

"I been a right far piece. I been to the settle-ments in Froman county, and then I been to the mines around Tateville and Beemen."

Newt bit nervously at his knuckles and looked at the man, taking from him these signs of the world. The fire burned low, and breaking the long silence Tom said once or twice, "There's a sight of travel now." Newt looked at the old man's feet in their patched shoes, feet that had walked the streets in towns. Indefinite wonders touched the man's feet, his crumpled knees, and his crooked hands that were spread on his lap.

Then Tom said, "Froman county, I reckon that's a prime good place to be now."

"Hit may be so, but I wouldn't be-nasty my feet with the dust of hit no longer. Nor any other place down there. I'm on my way back."

The old man's voice quavered over his words toward the close of this speech, and after a little while he added, his voice lifted, "Hit's a far piece back, but a man has a rather about where he'd like to be." Finally he spoke in great anger, his arm raised and his hand threatening, "I've swat my last drop of sweat in that-there country and eat my last meal's victuals. A man has a rather as to the place he likes to be."

This thought lay heavily over the fire-place, shared by all but uncomprehended by Nance, whose skin was rich with blood and life. She sat complacently rocking back and forth in her small chair.

After the long quiet which surrounded this thought the old man began to speak softly, having spent his passion, "I'm on my way back. I been in a study a long time about goen back but seems like I couldn't make hit to go. Work was terrible pressen. But now I'm on my way back where I was borned and my mammy and pappy before me. I was a plumb traitor to my God when I left the mountains and come to the settle-ments. Many is the day I'd study about that-there and many is the night I lay awake to study about the way back over Coster Ridge, on past Bear Mountain, past Hog Run, past Little Pine Tree, up and on past Louse Run, up, then on over Long Ridge and up into Laurel, into Grady Creek and on up the branch, past the Flat Rock, past the saw-mill, past the grove of he-balsams, and then the smoke a-comen outen the chimney and the door open and old Nomie's pup a-comen down the road to meet me. I'd climb the whole way whilst I was a-layen there, in my own mind I would, and I'd see the ivy as plain as you'd see your hand afore your face, and the coves and the he-balsams. In my own mind I'd go back, a step at a time, Coster, Bear Mountain and the Bee Gum, Little Pine Tree, Louse Run, Grady, and I'd see the rocks in the way to go, and a log stretched out in my way maybe. I wouldn't make hit too easy to go. Past Bear Mountain, past Hog Run and the cove, scratchen my way through ivy brush. Then I'd come to myself and there I'd be, a month's travel from as much as a sight of the Flat Rock, and I'd groan and shake and turn over again. I was a traitor to my God."

* * *

NANCE LAID a little stick on the fire, with a glance at Tom, he allowing it without protest. Then she sat back in her stiff chair with a quick movement, her bare feet light on the boards. The old man was talking again.

"Where my mammy was borned before me and her mammy and daddy before again. And no water in all Froman or Tateville but dead pump waters, no free-stone like you'd want. How could a man expect to live? Many's the night I've said, could I be on the shady side of the Flat Rock, up past the saw-mill, up past the grove of he-balsams, where the spring branch runs out over the horse-shoe rock, and could I get me one drink of that there cold crystal water I'd ask ne'er thing more of God Almighty in life."

"I know that there very spring branch," Newt now said. He was eager to enter the drama of the world, and his time now had come. "I know that there very place. You come to a rock set on end and a hemlock bush set off to the right, she-balsams all off to the left like."

"Mankind, that's just how hit's set. I believe you been right there!"

"A mountain goes straight up afore you as you stand, say this here is the spring, and the water comes out and runs off over a horse-shoe rock."

"Mankind, that's just how hit's set. I do believe you know that there very place. You say hit's there just the same?"

"I got me a drink at that there very spring branch Tuesday 'twas a week ago."

"You drank them waters!" And then he said after

a period of wonder, "To think you been to that very spring branch! You been there!"

"We can burn another stick," Tom said, as if in honor of the strange event, and Nance mended the fire again. Outside Newt heard dogs howling far up the slope and some small beast cried.

"To think you been there! You are a-setten right now in hearen of my voice and yet a Tuesday 'twas a week ago you was in the spot I call home. Hit's hard to study over. You come down the mountain fast. That country is powerful hard goen."

"Yes, I come right fast."

"I couldn't make hit back in twice the time and more. Hard goen it was. What made you travel so hard, young man?"

"I'm a-maken hit toward the settle-ments."

"And what you think to find in the settle-ments, God knows! What you think to see, young man?"

"Learnen. I look to find learnen in the settle-ments."

In the pause that followed the old man gazed at the hearth as if he were looking into time, into all qualities, and he fell momentarily asleep under the impact of his gaze. But presently he looked at Newt and said, "And to think you tasted them waters Tuesday 'twas a week ago."

"You come to a rock set on end, and here's the hemlock off to the right like, and here to the left goes the gorge."

The old man was asleep, his eyes falling away before the fire. But he waked suddenly and said with kindling eyes, his hand uplifted, "You come from there at a master pace, young man, come from the place I hope to see if God Almighty sees fitten to bless me afore I lay me down and die. You walked, I reckon, right over the spot I pined to see a many is the year, God knows, and it was nothing to you, but take care. The places you knowed when you was a little shirt-tail boy won't go outen your head or outen your recollections."

Then he said, another outbreak after a long pause, his hand again uplifted, "I reckon you relish learnen, young man, and take a delight in hit, and set a heap of store by the settle-ments. But the places you knowed when you was a little tad, they won't go outen your remembrance. Your insides is made that way, and made outen what you did when you was a shirt-tail boy, and you'll find it's so. Your dreams of a night and all you pine to see will go back. You won't get shed so easy of hit. You won't get shed."

Newt looked into the fire and a terror grew into his thought. He saw minutely the moss on the well curb and the shapes in which it grew, and saw the three stones that lay beside the well, that lifted his feet out of the mud. The sound made by the bucket in the well as it rocked from wall to wall, as it finally struck the water, rolled acutely backward into his inner hearing. He saw the rope twine over the beam as he turned the wooden handle, drawing the full bucket to the top. Three long steps then to the door of the house, the feel of the filled bucket drawing at his arm. Up the loft ladder to his room, his hands drawing up his body, the simple act of climbing, of emerging from some lower place to a higher, and he was buried in the act, submerged in a deep sense of it.

"You may go far and see a heap in life," the old stranger said, slowly, defiantly prophetic, "you may go far, but mark me as I say it, the places you knowed when you was a little tad will be the strongest in your remembrance. Your whole insides is made outen what you done first."

Newt saw in terror what he saw as he gazed into the sinking embers. His mother calling him from the house door, calling him to come to his dinner, her hand uplifted to the door frame. His sister, a little girl, dragging his chair in place and pushing his cup up against his plate. His tears for them dimmed the fire to a vague, red, quivering glow. The floating images in the dark of the well water, the bright light of the sky in the middle as a picture in a frame and his own head looking into the heart of the picture—these were between him and the fire, moving more inwardly and dragging himself with them as they went. He was bereft, divided, emptied of his every wish, and he gazed at the fire, scarcely seeing it.

There was moving in the room, figures making a dim passage of shadows behind him. Presently he knew that the old man had gone to his sleeping place and that Nance was spreading quilts on the floor to the side of the fireplace. Her strong body was pleasant to sense as she flung out the covers and pulled them into line, and a delight in the strange room, the strange bed, welled over him. His breath was then set to a fluted rhythm as he drew suddenly inward a rich flood of air, a rhythm flowing deeply until it touched the core of his desire for the settle-ments, laid an amorous pulse on its most quick and inner part. Learning was the word he cherished and kept identified with his quickened breath. He remembered that the lights of Merryman and the settlements would be brightly dusted over the low valley when he reached Coster.

By the end of the week he would, his eager breath told him, be looking down on to the farther valley.

UNC' EDINBURG'S DROWNDIN'*

A Plantation Echo

By THOMAS NELSON PAGE

"WELL, suh, dat's a fac—dat's what Marse George al'ays said. 'Tis hard to spile Christmas anyways."

The speaker was "Unc' Edinburg," the driver from Werrowcoke, where I was going to spend Christmas; the time was Christmas Eve, and the place the muddiest road in eastern Virginia—a measure which, I feel sure, will, to those who have any experience, establish its claim to distinction.

A half-hour before he had met me at the station, the queerest-looking, raggedest old darky conceivable, brandishing a cedar-staffed whip of enormous proportions in one hand, and clutching in the other a calico letter-bag with a twisted string; and with the exception of a brief interval of temporary suspicion on his part, due to the unfortunate fact that my luggage consisted of only a hand-satchel instead of a trunk, we had been steadily progressing in mutual esteem.

"Dee's a boy standin' by my mules; I got de ker'idge heah for you," had been his first remark on my making myself known to him. "Mistis say as how you might bring a trunk."

I at once saw my danger, and muttered something about "a short visit," but this only made matters worse.

"Dee don' nobody nuver pay short visits dyah," he said decisively, and I fell to other tactics.

"You couldn' spile Christmas den noways," he repeated, reflectingly, while his little mules trudged knee-

* Reprinted from *In Ole Virginia* by Thomas Nelson Page through arrangement with the holders of the copyright, Charles Scribner's Sons.

deep through the mud. "'Twuz Christmas den, sho' 'nough," he added, the fires of memory smouldering, and then, as they blazed into sudden flame, he asserted positively: "Dese heah free-issue niggers don' know what Christmas is. Hawg meat an' pop crackers don' meck Christmas. Hit tecks ole times to meck a sho'-'nough, tyahin'-down Christmas. Gord! I's seen 'em! But de wuss Christmas I ever seen tunned out de best in de een," he added, with sudden warmth, "an' dat wuz de Christmas me an' Marse George an' Reveller all got drownded down at Braxton's Creek. You's hearn 'bout dat?"

As he was sitting beside me in solid flesh and blood, and looked as little ethereal in his old hat and patched clothes as an old oak stump would have done, and as Colonel Staunton had made a world-wide reputation when he led his regiment through the Chickahominy thickets against McClellan's intrenchments, I was forced to confess that I had never been so favored, but would like to hear about it now; and with a hitch of the lap blanket under his outside knee, and a supererogatory jerk of the reins, he began:

"Well, you know, Marse George was jes' eighteen when he went to college. I went wid him, 'cause me an' him wuz de same age; I was born like on a Sat'day in de Christmas, an' he wuz born in de new year on a Chuesday, an' my mammy nussed us bofe at one breast. Dat's de reason maybe huccome we took so to one nurr. He sutney set a heap o' sto' by me; an' I 'ain' nuver see nobody yit wuz good to me as Marse George."

The old fellow, after a short reverie, went on:

"Well, we growed up togerr, jes as to say two stalks in one hill. We cotch ole hyahs togerr, an' we hunted 'possums togerr, an' 'coons. Lord! he wuz a climber! I 'member a fight he had one night up in de ve'y top of a big poplar tree wid a 'coon, whar he done gone up after, an' he flung he hat over he head; an' do' de varmint leetle mo' tyah him all to pieces, he fotch him down dat tree 'live; an' me an' him had him at Christmas. 'Coon meat mighty good when dee fat, you know?"

As this was a direct request for my judgment, I did not have the moral courage to raise an issue, although my views on the subject of 'coon meat are well known to my family; so I grunted something which I doubt not he took for assent, and he proceeded:

"Dee warn' nuttin he didn' lead the row in; he wuz the bes' swimmer I ever see, an' he handled a skiff same as a fish handle heself. An' I wuz wid him constant; wharever you see Marse George, dyah Edinburg sho', jes' like he shadow. So twuz, when he went to de university; 'twarn' nuttin would do but I got to go too. Master he didn' teck much to de notion, but Marse George wouldn' have it no urr way, an' co'se mistis she teck he side. So I went 'long as he body-servant to teck keer on him an' help meck him a gent'man. An' he wuz, too. From time he got dyah tell he cum 'way he wuz de head man.

"Dee warn' but one man dyah didn' compliment him, an' dat wuz Mr. Darker. But he warn' nuttin! not dat he didn' come o' right good fambly—'cep' dee politics; but he wuz sutney pitted, jes' like sometimes you see a weevly runty pig in a right good litter. Well, Mr. Darker he al'ays 'ginst Marse George; he hate me an' him bofe, an' he sutney act mischeevous todes us; 'cause he know he warn' as we all. De Stauntons dee wuz de popularitiest folks in Virginia; an' dee wuz high-larnt besides. So when Marse George run for de medal, an' wuz to meck he gret speech, Mr. Darker he speak 'ginst him.

Dat's what Marse George whip him 'bout. 'Ain' nobody nuver told you 'bout dat?"

I again avowed my misfortune; and although it manifestly aroused new doubts, he worked it off on the mules, and once more took up his story:

"Well, you know, dee had been speakin' 'ginst one nurr ev'y Sat'dy night; an' ev'ybody knowed Marse George wuz de bes' speaker, but dee give him one mo' sho', an' dee was bofe gwine spread deeselves, an' dee wuz two urr gent'mens also gwine speak. An' dat night when Mr. Darker got up he meck sich a fine speech ev'ybody wuz s'prised; an' some on 'em say Mr. Darker done beat Marse George. But shuh! I know better'n dat; an' Marse George face look so curious; but, suh, when he riz I knowed der wuz somen gwine happen—I wuz leanin' in de winder. He jes' step out in front an' throwed up he head like a horse wid a rank kyurb on him, and den he begin; an' twuz jes like de river when hit gits out de bank. He swep' ev'ything. When he fust open he mouf I knowed twuz comin'; he face wuz pale, an' he wuds tremble like a fiddle-string, but he eyes wuz blazin', an' in a minute he wuz jes reshin'. He voice soun' like a bell; an' he jes wallered dat turr man, an' wared him out; an' when he set down dee all yelled an' hollered so you couldn' heah you' ears. Gent'mans, twuz royal!

"Den dee tuck de vote, an' Marse George got it munanimous, an' dee all hollered agin, all 'cep' a few o' Mr. Darker's friends. An' Mr. Darker he wuz de second. An' den dee broke up. An' jes den Marse George walked thoo de crowd straight up to him, an' lookin' him right in de eyes, says to him, 'You stole dat speech you made to-night.' Well, suh, you ought to 'a hearn 'em; hit soun' like a mill-dam. You couldn' heah nuttin 'cep' roarin', an' you couldn' see nuttin 'cep' shovin'; but, big as he wuz, Marse George beat him; an' when dee pulls him off, do' he face wuz mighty pale, he stan' out befo' 'em all, dem whar wuz 'ginst him, an' all, jes as straight as an arrow, an' say: 'Dat speech wuz written an' printed years ago by somebody or nurr in Congress, an' this man stole it; had he beat me only, I should not have said one word; but as he has beaten others, I shall show him up!' Gord, suh, he voice wuz clear as a game rooster. I sutney wuz proud on him.

"He did show him up, too, but Mr. Darker ain' wait to see it; he lef' dat night. An' Marse George he wuz de popularitiest gent'man at dat university. He could handle dem students dyah same as a man handle a hoe.

"Well, twuz de next Christmas we meet Miss Charlotte an' Nancy. Mr. Braxton invite we all to go down to spen' Christmas wid him at he home. An' sich a time as we had!

"We got dyah Christmas Eve night—dis very night—jes befo' supper, an' jes natchelly froze to death," he pursued, dealing in his wonted hyperbole, "an' we jes had time to git a apple toddy or two when supper was ready, an' wud come dat dee wuz waitin' in de hall. I had done fix Marse George up gorgeousome, I tell you; and when he walk down dem stairs in dat swaller-tail coat, an' dem paten'-leather pumps on, dee warn nay one dyah could tetch him; he looked like he own 'em all. I jes rest my mind. I seen him when he shake hands wid 'em all roun', an' I say, 'Um-m-m! he got 'em.'

"But he ain' teck noticement o' none much tell Miss Charlotte come. She didn' live dyah, had jes come over de river dat evenin' from her home, 'bout ten miles off, to spen' Christmas like we all, an' she come down de stairs jes as Marse George finish shakin' hands. I seen he eye light on her as she come down de steps smilin', wid her dim blue dress trainin' behind her, an' her little blue foots peepin' out so pretty, an' holdin' a little hankcher, lookin' like a spider-web, in one hand, an' a gret blue fan in turr, spread out like a peacock tail, an' jes her roun' arms an' th'oat white, an' her gret dark eyes lightin' up her face. I say, 'Dyah 'tis!' and when de old Cun'l stan' aside an' interduce 'em, an' Marse George step for'ard an' meck he gran' bow, an' she sort o' swing back an' gin her curtchy, wid her dress sort o 'dammed up 'ginst her, an' her arms so white, an' her face sort o' sunsetty, I say, 'Yes, Lord! Edinburg, dyah you mistis.' Marse George look like he think she done come right down from de top o' de blue sky an' bring piece on it wid her. He ain' nuver took he eyes from her dat night. Dee glued to her, mun! an' she—well, do' she mighty rosy, an' look mighty unconsarned, she sutney ain' hender him. Hit look like kyarn nobody else tote dat fan an' pick up dat hankcher skusin o' him; an' after supper, when dee all playin' blindman's-buff in de hall—I don' know how twuz—but do' she jes as nimble as a filly, an' her ankle jes as clean, an' she kin git up her dress an' dodge out de way o' ev'ybody else, somehow or nurr she kyarn help him ketchin' her to save her life; he al'ays got her corndered; an' when dee'd git fur apart, dat ain' nuttin, dee jes as sure to come togerr agin as water is whar you done run you hand thoo. An' do' he kiss ev'ybody else under de mistletow, 'cause dee be sort o' cousins, he ain' nuver kiss her, nor nobody else ain't nurr, 'cep' de old Cun'l. I wuz standin' down at de een de hall wid de black folks, an' I notice it 'tic'lar, 'cause I done meck de 'quaintance o' Nancy; she wuz Miss Charlotte's maid; a mighty likely young gal she wuz den, an' jes as impident as a fly. She see it too, do' she ain' 'low it.

"Fust thing I know I seen a mighty likely light-skinned gal standin' dyah by me, wid her hyah mos' straight as white folks, an' a mighty good frock on, an' a clean apron, an' her hand mos' like a lady, only it brown, an' she keep on 'vidin her eyes twix me an' Miss Charlotte; when I watchin' Miss Charlotte she watchin' me, an' when I steal my eye 'roun' on her she noticin' Miss Charlotte; an' presney I sort o' sidle 'longside her, an' I say, 'Lady, you mighty sprightly to-night.' An' she say she 'bleeged to be sprightly, her mistis look so good; an' I ax her which one twuz, an' she tell me, 'Dat queen one over dyah,' an' I tell her dee's a king dyah too, she got her eye set for; an' when I say her mistis tryin' to set her cap for Marse George, she fly up, an' say she an' her mistis don' have to set dee cap for nobody; *dee* got to set dee cap an' all de clo'es for dem, an' den dee ain' gwine cotch 'em, 'cause dee ain' studyin' 'bout no up-country folks whar dee ain' nobody know nuttin 'bout.

"Well, dat oudaciousness so aggrivate me, I lite into dat nigger right dyah. I tell her she ain' been nowhar 'tall ef she don' know we all; dat we wuz de bes' of quality, de ve'y top de pot; an' den I tell her 'bout how gret we wuz; how de ker'idges wuz al'ays hitched up night an' day, an' niggers jes thick as weeds; an' how Unc' Torm he wared he swaller-tail ev'y day when he wait on de table; and Marse George he won' wyah a coat mo'n once or twice anyways, to save you life. Oh! I sutney 'stonish dat nigger, 'cause I wuz teckin up for de fambly, an' I meck out like dee use gold up home like urr folks use wood, an' sow silver like urr folks sow wheat; an' when I got thoo dee wuz all on 'em listenin', an' she 'lowed dat Marse George he were ve'y good, sho 'nough, ef twarn for he nigger; but I ain' tarrifyin' myself none 'bout dat, 'cause I know she jes projickin, an' she couldn' help bein' impident ef you wuz to whup de frock off her back.

"Jes den dee struck up de dance. Dee had wheel de pianer out in de hall, and somebody say Jack Forester had come cross de river, an' all on 'em say dee must' git Jack; an' presney he come in wid he fiddle, grinnin' and scrapin', 'cause he wuz a notable fiddler, do' I don' think he wuz equal to we all's Tubal, an' I know he couldn' tech Marse George, 'cause Marse George wuz a natchel fiddler, jes like 'coons is natchel pacers, an' mules an womens is natchel kickers. Howsomever, he sutney jucked a jig sweet, an' when he shake dat bow you couldn' help you foot switchin' a leetle—not ef you wuz a member of de chutch. He was a mighty sinful man, Jack wuz, an' dat fiddle had done drawed many souls to torment.

"Well, in a minute dee wuz all flyin', an' Jack he wuz rockin' like boat rockin' on de water, an' he face right shiny, an' he teef look like ear o' corn he got in he mouf, an' he big foot set 'way out keepin' time, an' Marse George he was in de lead row dyah too; ev'y chance he git he tunned Miss Charlotte—'petchel motion, right hand across, an' cauliflower, an' croquette—dee croquette plenty o' urrs, but I notice dee ain' nuver fail to tun one nurr, an' ev'y tun he gin she wrappin' de chain roun' him; once when dee wuz 'prominadin-all' down we all's een o' de hall, as he tunned her somebody step on her dress an' to' it. I heah de screech o' de silk, an' Nancy say, 'O Lord!' den she say, 'Nem mine! now I'll git it!' an' dee stop for a minute for Marse George to pin 't up, while turrers went on, an' Marse George wuz down on he knee, an' she look down on him mighty sweet out her eyes, an' say, 'Hit don' meck no difference,' an' he glance up an' cotch her eye, an', jes 'dout a wud, he tyah a gret piece right out de silk an' slipt it in he bosom, an' when he got up, he say, right low, lookin' in her eyes real deep, 'I gwine wyah dis at my weddin',' an' she jes look sweet as candy; an' ef Nancy ever wyah dat frock I ain' see it.

"Den presney dee wuz talkin' 'bout stoppin'. De ole Cun'l say hit time to have prars, an' dee wuz beggin' him to wait a leetle while; an' Jack Forester lay he fiddle down nigh Marse George, an' he picked 't up an' drawed de bow 'cross it jes to try it, an' den jes projickin' he struck dat chune 'bout 'You'll ermember me.' He hadn' mo'n tech de string when you coulda' heah a pin drap. Marse George he warn noticin', an' he jes lay he face on de fiddle, wid he eyes sort o' half shet, an' drawed her out like he'd do some nights at home in de moonlight on de gret porch, tell on a sudden he looked up an' cotch Miss Charlotte eye leanin' for'ards so earnest, an' all on 'em list'nin', an' he stopt, an' dee all clapt dee hands, an' he sudney drapt into a jig. Jack Forester ain' had to play no mo' dat night. Even de ole Cun'l ketched de fever, an' he stept out in de flo' in he long-tail coat an' high collar, an' knocked 'em off de 'Snow-bud on de Ash-bank,' an' 'Chicken in de Bread-tray,' right natchel.

"Oh, he could jes plank 'em down!

"Oh, dat wuz a Christmas like you been read 'bout! An' twuz hard to tell which gittin cotch most, Marse George or me; 'cause dat nigger she jes as confusin' as Miss Charlotte. An' she sutney wuz sp'ilt dem days; ev'y nigger on dat place got he eye on her, an' she jes az oudacious an' aggrivatin as jes womens kin be.

"Dees monsus 'ceivin' critters, womens is, jes as onreliable as de hind-leg of a mule; a man got to watch 'em all de time; you kyarn break 'em like you kin horses.

"Now dat off mule dyah" (indicating, by a lazy but not light lash of his whip the one selected for his illustration), "dee ain' no countin' on her at all; she go 'long all day, or maybe a week, jes dat easy an' sociable, an' fust thing you know you ain' know nuttin. She done knock you brains out; dee ain' no 'pendence to be placed in 'em 'tall, suh; she jes as sweet as a kiss one minute, an' next time she come out de house she got her head up in de air, an' her ears backed, an' goin' 'long switchin' herself like I ain' good 'nough for her to walk on.

" 'Fox-huntin's?' oh, yes, suh, ev'y day mos'; an' when Marse George didn' git de tail, twuz 'cause twuz a bob-tail fox—you heah me! He play de fiddle for he pas-time, but he fotched up in de saddle—dat he cradle!

"De fust day dee went out I heah Nancy quoilin 'bout de tail layin' on Miss Charlotte dressin'-table gittin' hyahs over ev'ything.

"One day de ladies went out too, Miss Charlotte 'mongst 'em, on Miss Lucy gray myah Switchity, an' Marse George he rid Mr. Braxton's chestnut Willful.

"Well, suh, he stick so close to dat gray myah, he leetle mo' los' dat fox; but, Lord! he know what he 'bout—he monsus 'ceivin' 'bout dat—he know de way de fox gwine jes as well he know heself; an' all de time he leadin' Miss Charlotte whar she kin heah de music, but he watchin' him too, jes as narrow as a ole hound. So, when de fox tun de head o' de creek, Marse George had Miss Char-lotte on de aidge o' de flat, an' he de fust man see de fox tun down on turr side wid de hounds right rank after him. Dat sort o' set him back, 'cause by rights de fox ought to 'a double an' come back dis side: he kyarn git out dat way; an' two or three gent'mens dee had see it too, an' wuz jes layin de horses to de groun' to git roun' fust, 'cause de creek wuz heap too wide to jump, an' wuz 'way over you head, an hit cold as Christmas, sho 'nough; well, suh, when dee tunned, Mr. Clarke he wuz in de lead (he wuz ridin' for Miss Charlotte too), an' hit fyah set Marse George on fire; he ain' said but one wud, 'Wait,' an' jes set de chestnut's head straight for de creek, whar de fox comin' wid he hyah up on he back, an' de dogs ravlin mos' on him.

"De ladies screamed, an' some de gent'mens hollered for him to come back, but he ain' mind; he went 'cross dat flat like a wild-duck; an' when he retch de water he horse try to flinch, but dat hand on de bridle, an' dem rowels in he side, an' he 'bleeged to teck it.

"Lord! suh, sich a screech as dee set up! But he wuz swimmin' for life, an' he wuz up de bank an' in de middle o' de dogs time dee tetched old Gray Jacket; an' when Mr. Clarke got dyah Marse George wuz stan'in' holdin' up de tail for Miss Charlotte to see, turr side de creek, an' de hounds wuz wallerin' all over de body, an' I don' think Mr. Clarke done got up wid 'em yit.

"He cotch de fox, an' he cotch some'n else besides, in my 'pinion, 'cause when de ladies went upstairs dat night Miss Charlotte had to wait on de steps for a glass o' water, an' couldn' nobody git it but Marse George; an' den when she tell him goodnight over de banisters, he couldn' say it good enough; he got to kiss her hand; an' she ain' do nuttin but jes peep upstairs ef anybody dyah lookin'; an' when I come thoo de do' she juck her hand 'way an' run upstairs jes as farst as she could. Marse George look at me sort o' laughin', an' say: 'Confound you! Nancy couldn' been very good to you.' An' I say, 'She le' me squench my thirst a leetle kissin' her hand'; an' he sort o' laugh an' tell me to keep my mouf shet.

"But dat ain' de on'y time I come on 'em. Dee al'ays gittin' corndered; an' de evenin' befo' we come 'way I wuz gwine in thoo de conservity, an' dyah dee wuz sort o' hide 'way. Miss Charlotte she wuz settin' down, an' Marse George he wuz leanin' over her, got her hand to he face, talkin' right low an' lookin' right sweet, an' she ain' say nuttin; an' presney he drapt on one knee by her, an' slip he arm roun' her, an' try to look in her eyes, an' she so 'shamed to look at him she got to hide her face on he shoulder, an' I slipt out.

"We come 'way next mornin'. When marster heah 'bout it he didn't teck to de notion at all, 'cause her pa—dat is, he warn' her own pa, 'cause he had married her ma when she wuz a widder after Miss Charlotte pa died—an' he politics warn' same as ourn. 'Why, you kin never stand him, suh,' he said to Marse George. 'We won't mix any mo'n fire and water; you ought to have found that out at college; dat fellow Darker is his son.'

"Marse George he say he know dat; but he on'y de step-brurr of de young lady, an' ain' got a drap o' her blood in he veins, an' he didn' know it when he meet her, an' anyhow hit wouldn' meck any diffence; an' when de mistis see how sot Marse George is on it she teck he side, an' dat fix it; 'cause when ole mistis warn marster to do a thing, hit jes good as done. I don' keer how much he rar roun' an' say he ain' gwine do it, you jes well go 'long an' put on you hat; you gwine see him presney doin' it jes peaceable as a lamb. She tun him jes like she got bline-bridle on him, an' he ain' nuver know it.

"So she got him jes straight as a string. An' when de time come for Marse George to go, marster he mo' consarned 'bout it 'n Marse George; he ain' say nuttin 'bout it befo'; but now he walkin' roun' an' roun' axin mistis mo' questions 'bout he cloes an' he horse an' all; an' dat mornin' he gi him he two Sunday razors, an' gi' me a pyah o' boots an' a beaver hat, 'cause I wuz gwine wid him to kyar he portmanteau, an' git he shavin' water, sense marster say ef he wuz gwine marry a Locofoco, he at least must go like a gent'man; an' me an' Marse

George had done settle it 'twixt us, cause we al'ays set bofe we traps on de same hyah parf.

"Well, we got 'em, an' when I ax dat gal out on de wood-pile dat night, she say bein' as her mistis gwine own me, an' we bofe got to be in de same estate, she reckon she ain' nuver gwine to be able to git shet o' me; an' den I clamp her. Oh, she wuz a beauty!"

A gesture and guffaw completed the recital of his conquest.

"Yes, suh, we got 'em sho!" he said presently. "Dee couldn' persist us; we crowd 'em into de fence an' run 'em off dee foots.

"Den come de 'gagement; an' ev'ything wuz smooth as silk. Marse George an' me wuz ridin' over dyah constant, on'y we nuver did git over bein' skeered when we wuz ridin' up dat turpentine road facin' all dem winders. Hit 'pear like ev'ybody in de wull 'mos' wuz lookin' at us.

"One evenin' Marse George say, 'Edinburg, d' you ever see as many winders p'intin' one way in you life? When I git a house,' he say, 'I gwine have all de winders lookin' turr way.'

"But dat evenin', when I see Miss Charlotte come walkin' out de gret parlor wid her hyah sort o' rumpled over her face, an' some yaller roses on her bres, an' her gret eyes so soft an' sweet, an' Marse George walkin' 'long hinst her, so peaceable, like she got chain roun' him, I say, 'Winders ain' nuttin.'

"Oh, twuz jes like holiday all de time! An' den Miss Charlotte come over to see mistis, an' of co'se she bring her maid wid her, 'cause she 'bleeged to have her maid, you know, an' dat wuz de bes' of all.

"Dat evenin', 'bout sunset, dee come drivin' up in de big ker'idge, wid de gret hyah trunk stropped on de seat behind, an' Nancy she settin' by Billy, an' Marse George settin' inside by he rose-bud, 'cause he had done gone down to bring her up; an' marster he done been drest in he blue coat an' yaller westket ever sence dinner, an' walkin' roun', watchin' up de road all de time, an' tellin' de mistis he reckon dee ain' comin', an' old mistis she try to pacify him, an' she come out presney drest, an' rustlin' in her stiff black silk an' all; an when de ker'idge come in sight, ev'ybody wuz runnin'; an' when dee draw up to de do', Marse George he help her out an' in'duce her to marster an' ole mistis; an' marster he start to meck her a gret bow, an' she jes put up her mouf like a little gal to be kissed, an' dat got him. An' mistis teck her right in her arms an' kiss her twice, an' de servants dee wuzz all peepin' an' grinnin'.

"Ev'ywhar you tun you see a nigger teef, 'cause dee all warn see de young mistis whar good 'nough for Marse George.

"Dee ain' gwine be married tell de next fall, 'count o' Miss Charlotte bein' so young; but she jes good as b'longst to we all now; an' ole marster and mistis dee jes as much in love wid her as Marse George. Hi! dee warn pull de house down an' buil' it over for her! An' ev'y han' on de place he peepin' to try to git a look at he young mistis whar he gwine b'longst to. One evenin' dee all on 'em come roun' de porch an' send for Marse George, an' when he come out, Charley Brown (he al'ays de speaker, 'cause he got so much mouf, kin' talk pretty as white folks), he say dee warn interduce to de young mistis, an' pay dee bespects to her; an' presney Marse George lead her out on de porch laughin' at her, wid her face jes rosy as a wine-sop apple, an' she meck 'em a beautiful bow, an' speak to 'em ev'y one, Marse George namin' de names; an' Charley Brown he meck her a pretty speech, an' tell her we mighty proud to own her; an' one o' dem impident gals ax her to gin her dat white frock when she git married; an' when she say, 'Well, what am I goin' wear?' Sally say, 'Lord, honey, Marse George gwine dress you in pure gol'!' an' she look up at him wid sparks flashin' out her eyes, while he look like dat ain' good 'nough for her. An' so twuz, when she went 'way, Sally Marshall got dat frock, an' proud on it I tell you.

"Oh, yes; he sutney mindin' her tender. Hi! when she go to ride in evenin' wid him, de ain' no horse-block good 'nough for her! Marse George got to have her step in he hand; an' when dee out walkin' he got de umbrellar holdin' 't over her all de time, he so feared de sun 'll kiss her; an' dee walk so slow down dem walks in de shade you got to sight 'em by a tree to tell ef dee movin' 'tall. She use' to look like she used to it too, I tell you, 'cause she wuz quality, one de white-skinned ones; an' she'd set in dem big cheers, wid her little foots on de cricket whar Marse George al'ays set for her, he so feared dee'd tetch de groun', jes like she on her throne; an' ole marster he'd watch her mos' edmirin as Marse George; an' when she went 'way, hit sutney was lonesome. Hit look like daylight gone wid her. I don' know which I miss mos', Miss Charlotte or Nancy.

"Den Marse George was 'lected to de Legislature, an' old Jedge Darker run for de Senator, an' Marse George vote gin him and beat him. An' dat commence de fuss; an' den dat man gi' me de whuppin, an' dat breck 'tup an' breck he heart.

"You see, after Marse George wuz 'lected ('lections wuz 'lections dem days; dee warn' no baitgode 'lections, wid ev'y sort o' wurrms squirmin' up 'ginst one nurr, wid piece o' paper d' ain' know what on, drappin' in a chink; didn' nuttin but gent'mens vote den, an' dee took dee dram, an' vote out loud, like gent'mens)—well, arter Marse George wuz 'lected, de parties wuz jes as even balanced as stilyuds, an' wen dee ax Marse George who wuz to be de Senator, he vote for de Whig, 'ginst de old jedge, an' dat beat him, of co'se. An' dee ain' got sense to know he 'bleeged to vote wid he politics. Dat he sprinciple; he kyarn vote for Locofoco, I don' keer ef he is Miss Charlotte pa, much less her step-pa. Of co'se de old jedge ain' speak to him arter dat, nur is Marse George ax him to. But who dat gwine s'pose women-folks got to put dee mouf in too? Miss Charlotte she write Marse George a letter dat pester him mightily; he set up all night answerin' dat letter, an' he mighty solemn, I tell you. An' I wuz gittin' right grewjousome myself, 'cause I studyin' 'bout dat gal down dyah whar I done gi' my wud to, an' when dee ain' no letters come torectly hit hard to tell which one de anxiouser, me or Marse George. Den presney I so 'straughted 'long o' it I ax Aunt Haly 'bouten it: (She know all sich things, 'cause she 'mos' a hunderd years ole, an' seed evil sperits, an' got skoripins up her chimley, an' knowed conjure); an' she ax me what wuz de signication, an' I tell her I ain' able nuther to eat nor to sleep, an' dat gal come foolin' 'long me when I sleep jes as natchel as ef I see her sho 'nough. An' she say I done conjured; dat de gal done tricked me.

"Oh, Gord! dat skeered me!

"You white folks, marster, don' believe nuttin like dat; y' all got too much sense, 'cause y' all kin read; but niggers dee ain' know no better, an' I sutney wuz skeered, 'cause Aunt Haly say my coffin done seasoned, de planks up de chimley.

"Well, I got so bad Marse George ax me 'bout it, an' he sort o' laugh an' sort o' cuss, an' he tell Aunt Haly ef she don' stop dat foolishness skeerin' me he'll sell her an' tyah her ole skoripin house down. Well, co'se he jes talkin', an' he ax me next day how'd I like to go an' see my sweetheart. Gord, suh, I got well torectly. So I set off next evenin', feelin' jes big as ole marster, wid my pass in my pocket, which I warn' to show nobody 'douten I 'bleeged to, 'cause Marse George didn' warn nobody to know he le' me go. An' den dat rascallion teck de shut off my back. But ef Marse George didn' pay him de wuth o' it!

"I done git 'long so good, too.

"When Nancy see me she sutney wuz 'stonished. She come roun' de cornder in de back yard whar I settin' in Nat's do' (he wuz de gardener), wid her hyah all done ontwist, an' breshed out mighty fine, an' a clean ap'on wid fringe on it, meckin' out she so s'prised to see me (whar wuz all a lie, 'cause some on 'em done notify her I dyah), an' she say, 'Hi! what dis black nigger doin' heah?'

"An' I say, 'Who you callin' nigger, you impident, kercumber-faced thing, you?' Den we shake hands, an' I tell her Marse George done set me free—dat I done buy myself; dat's de lie I done lay off to tell her.

"An when I tole her dat, she bust out laughin', an' say, well, I better go 'long 'way, den, dat she don' warn no free nigger to be comp'ny for her. Dat sort o' set me back, an' I tell her she kickin' 'fo' she spurred, dat I ain' got her in my mine; I got a nurr gal at home whar grievin' 'bout me dat ve'y minute. An' after I tell her all sich lies as dat presney she ax me ain' I hongry; an' ef dat nigger didn' git her mammy to gi' me de bes' supter! Umm-m! I kin mos' tas'e it now. Wheat bread off de table, an' zerves, an' fat bacon, tell I couldn' put a nurr moufful nowhar sep'n I'd teck my hat. Dat night I tote Nancy water for her, an' I tell her all about ev'ything, an' she jes sweet as honey. Next mornin', do', she done sort o' tunned some, an' ain' so sweet. You know how milk gits sort o' bonny-clabberish? An' when she see me she 'gin to 'buse me—say I jes' tryin' to fool her, an' all de time got nurr wife at home, or gittin' ready to git one, for all she know, an' she ain' know wherr Marse George ain' jes 'ceivin' as I is; an' nem mine, she got plenty warn marry her; an' as to Miss Charlotte, she got de whole wull; Mr. Darker he ain' got nobody in he way now, dat he deah all de time, an' ain' gwine West no mo'. Well, dat aggrivate me so I tell her ef she say dat 'bout Marse George I gwine knock her; an' wid dat she got so oudacious I meck out I gwine 'way, an' lef' her, an' went up todes de barn; an' up dyah, fust thing I know, I come across dat ar man Mr. Darker. Soon as he see me he begin to cuss me, an' he ax me what I doin' on dat land, an' I tell him 'Nuttin'.' An' he say, well, he gwine gi' me some'n; he gwine teach me to come prowlin' round gent'men's houses. An' he meck me go in de barn an' teck off my shut, an' he beat me wid he whup tell de blood run out my back. He sutney did beat me scandalous, 'cause he done hate me an' Marse George ever since we wuz at college togurr. An' den he say: 'Now you git right off dis land. Ef either you or you marster ever put you foot on it, you'll git de same thing agin.' An' I tell you, Edinburg he come way, 'cause he sutney had worry me. I ain' stop to see Nancy or nobody; I jes come 'long, shakin' de dust, I tell you. An' as I come 'long de road I pass Miss Charlotte walkin' on de lawn by herself, an' she call me: 'Why, hi! ain' dat Edinburg?'

"She look so sweet, an' her voice soun' so cool, I say, 'Yes'm; how you do, missis?' An' she say, she ve'y well, an' how I been, an' whar I gwine? I tell her I ain' feelin' so well, dat I gwine home. 'Hi!' she say, 'is anybody treat you bad?' An' I tell her, 'Yes'm.' An' she say, 'Oh! Nancy don' mean nuttin by dat; dat you mus'n mine what womens say, an' do, 'cause dee feel sorry for it next minute; an' sometimes dee kyarn help it, or maybe hit you fault; an' anyhow, you ought to be willin' to overlook it; an' I better go back an' wait till to-morrow—ef—ef I ain' bleeged to git home to-day.'

"She got mighty mixed up in de een part o' dat, an' she looked mighty anxious 'bout me an' Nancy; an' I tell her, 'No'm, I 'bleeged to git home.'

"Well, when I got home Marse George he warn know all dat gwine on; but I mighty sick—dat man done beat me so; an he ax me what de marter, an' I upped an' tell him.

"Gord! I nuver see a man in sich a rage. He call me in de office an' meck me teck off my shut, an' he fyah bust out cryin'. He walked up an' down dat office like a caged lion. Ef he had got he hand on Mr. Darker den, he'd 'a kilt him, sho!

"He wuz most 'stracted. I don't know what he'd been ef I'd tell him what Nancy tell me. He call for Peter to get he horse torectly, an' he tell me to go an' git some'n from mammy to put on my back, an' to go to bed torectly, an' not to say nuttin to nobody, but to tell he pa he'd be away for two days, maybe; an' den he got on Reveller an' galloped 'way hard as he could, wid he jaw set farst, an' he heaviest whup clamped in he hand. Gord! I wuz most hopin' he wouldn' meet dat man, 'cause I feared ef he did he'd kill him; an' he would, sho, ef he had meet him right den; dee say he leetle mo' did when he fine him next day, an' he had done been ridin' den all night; he cotch him at a sto' on de road, an' dee say he leetle mo' cut him all to pieces; he drawed a weepin on Marse George, but Marse George wrench it out he hand an' flung it over de fence; an' when dee got him 'way he had weared he whup out on him; an' he got dem whelps on him now, ef he ain' dead. Yes, suh, he ain' let nobody else do dat he ain' do heself, sho!

"Dat done de business!

"He sont Marse George a challenge, but Marse George sont him wud he'll cowhide him agin ef he ever heah any mo' from him, an' he ain't. Dat perrify him, so he shet he mouf. Den come he ring an' all he pictures an, things back—a gret box on 'em, and not a wud wid 'em. Marse George, I think he know'd dee wuz comin', but dat ain' keep it from huttin' him, 'cause he done been 'gaged to Miss Charlotte, an' got he mine riveted to her; an' do' befo' dat dee had stop writin', an' a riff done git 'twixt 'em, he ain' satisfied in he mine dat she ain't gwine 'pologizee—I know by Nancy; but now he got de confirmation dat he done for good, an' dat de gret gulf fixed 'twixt him an' Aberham bosom. An', Gord, suh, twuz torment, sho 'nough! He ain' say nuttin 'bout it, but I see de light done pass from him, an' de darkness done wrap him up in it. In a leetle while you wouldn' a knowed him.

"Den ole mistis died.

"B'lieve me, ole marster he 'most much hut by Miss Charlotte as Marse George. He meck a 'tempt to buy Nancy for me, so I find out arterward, an' write Jedge Darker he'll pay him anything he'll ax for her, but he letter wuz sont back 'dout any answer. He sutney was mad 'bout it—he say he'd horsewhip him as Marse George did dat urr young puppy, but ole mistis wouldn' le' him do nuttin, and den he grieve heself to death. You see he mighty ole, anyways. He nuver got over ole mistis' death. She had been failin' a long time, an' he ain' tarry long 'hinst her; hit sort o' like breckin up a holler—de ole 'coon goes 'way soon arter dat; an' marster nuver could pin he own collar or buckle he own stock—mistis she al'ays do dat; an' do' Marse George do de bes' he kin, an' mighty willin', he kyarn handle pin like a woman; he hand tremble like a p'inter dog; an' anyways he ain' ole mistis. So ole marster foller her dat next fall, when dee wuz gittin in de corn, an' Marse George he ain' got nobody in de wull left; he all alone in dat gret house, an' I wonder sometimes he ain' die too, 'cause he sutney wuz fond o' old marster.

"When ole mistis wuz dyin', she tell him to be good to ole marster, an' patient wid him, 'cause he ain' got nobody but him now (ole marster he had jes step out de room to cry); an' Marse George he lean over an' kiss her an' promise her faithful he would. An' he sutney wuz tender wid him as a woman; an' when ole marster die, he set by him an' hol' he hand an' kiss him sorf, like he wuz ole mistis.

"But, Gord! twuz lonesome arter dat, an' Marse George eyes look wistful, like he al'ays lookin' far 'way.

"Aunt Haly say he see harnts whar walk 'bout in de gret house. She say dee walk dyah constant of nights sence ole marster done alterate de rooms from what dee wuz when he gran'pa buil' 'em, an' dat dee huntin' for dee ole chambers an' kyarn git no rest 'cause dee kyarn fine 'em. I don't know how dat wuz. I know Marse George *he* used to walk about heself mightily of nights. All night long, all night long, I'd heah him tell de chickens crowin' dee second crow, an' some mornin's I'd go dyah an' he ain' even rumple de bed. I thought sho he wuz gwine die, but I suppose he done 'arn he days to be long in de land, an' dat save him. But hit sutney wuz lonesome, an' he nuver went off de plantation, an' he got older an' older, tell we all thought he wuz gwine die.

"An' one day come jes befo' Christmas, 'bout nigh two year after marster die, Mr. Braxton ride up to de do'. He had done come to teck Marse George home to spen'

Christmas wid him. Marse George warn git out it, but Mr. Braxton won' teck no disapp'intment; he say he gwine baptize he boy, an' he done name him after Marse George (he had marry Marse George cousin, Miss Peggy Carter, an' he vite Marse George to de weddin', but he wouldn' go, do' I sutney did want him to go, 'cause I heah Miss Charlotte was nominated to marry Mr. Darker, an' I warn know what done 'come o' dat bright-skinned nigger gal, whar I used to know down dyah); an' he say Marse George got to come an' stan' for him, an' gi' him a silver cup an' a gol' rattle. So Marse George he finally promise to come an' spend Christmas Day, an' Mr. Braxton went 'way next mornin', an' den hit tun in an' rain so I feared we couldn' go, but hit cler off de day befo' Christmas Eve an' tun cold. Well, suh, we ain' been nowhar for so long I wuz skittish as a young filly; an den you know twuz de same ole place.

"We didn' git dyah till supper-time, an 'twuz a good one too, 'cause seventy miles dat cold a weather hit whet a man's honger jes like a whetstone.

"Dey sutney wuz glad to see we all. We rid roun' by de back yard to gi' Billy de horses, an' we see dee wuz havin' gret fixin's; an' den we went to de house, jest as some o' de folks run in an' tell 'em we wuz come. When Marse George stept in de hall, dee all clustered roun' him like dee gwine hug him, dee faces fyah dimplin' wid pleasure, an' Miss Peggy she jes reched up and teck him in her arms an' hug him.

"Dee tell me in de kitchen dat dee wuz been 'spectin' of Miss Charlotte over to spend Christmas too, but de river wuz so high dee s'pose dee couldn' git cross. Chile, dat sutney disapp'int me!

"Well, after supper de niggers had a dance. Hit wuz down in de wash-house, an' de table wuz set in de carpenter shop jes' by. Oh, hit sutney wuz beautiful! Miss Lucy an' Miss Ailsy dee had superintend ev'ything wid dee own hands. So dee wuz down dyah wid dee ap'ons up to dee chins, an' dee had de big silver strandeliers out de house, two on each table, an' some o' ole mistis's best damas' tablecloths, an' ole marster's gret bowl full o' egg-nog; hit look big as a mill-pond settin' dyah in de cornder; an' dee had flowers out de greenhouse on de table, an' some o' de chany out de gret house, an' de dinin'-room cheers set roun' de room. Oh! oh! nuttin warn too good for niggers dem times; an' de little niggers wuz runnin' roun' right 'stracted, squealin' an' peepin' an' gittin in de way onder you foots; an' de mens dee wuz totin' in de wood—gret hickory logs, look like stock whar you gwine saw—an' de fire so big hit look like you gwine kill hawgs, 'cause hit sutney wuz cold dat night. Dis nigger ain' nuver gwine forgit it! Jack Forester he had come 'cross de river to lead de fiddlers, an' he say he had to put he fiddle onder he coat an' poke he bow in he breeches leg to keep de strings from poppin', an' dat de river would freeze over sho ef twarn so high; but twuz jes snortin', an' he had hard wuk to git over in he skiff, an' Unc' Jeems say he ain' gwine come out he boat-house no mo' dat night —he done tempt Providence often 'nough for one day.

"Den ev'ything wuz ready, an' de fiddlers got dee dram an' chuned up, an' twuz lively, I tell you! Twuz jes as thick in dyah as blackberries on de blackberry bush, 'cause ev'y gal on de plantation wuz dyah shakin' her foot for some young buck, an' back-steppin' for to go 'long. Dem ole sleepers wuz jes a-rockin', an' Jack Forester he wuz callin' de figgers for to wake 'em up. I warn' dancin', 'cause I done got 'ligion an 'longst to de chutch sence de trouble done tech us up so rank; but I tell you my foots wuz pintedly eechchin for a leetle sop on it, an'

I had to come out to keep from crossin' 'em onst, anyways. Den, too, I had a tetch o' misery in my back, an' I lay off to git a tas'e o' dat egg-nog out dat big bowl, wid snow-drift on it, from Miss Lucy—she al'ays mighty fond o' Marse George; so I slip into de carpenter shop, an' ax her kyarn I do nuttin for her, an' she laugh an' say, yes, I kin drink her health, an' gi' me a gret gobletful, an' jes den de white folks come in to 'spec' de tables, Marse George in de lead, an' dee all fill up dee glasses an' pledge dee health, an' all de servants', an' a merry Christmas; an' den dee went in de wash-house to see de dancin', an' maybe to teck a hand deeself, 'cause white folks' 'ligion ain' like niggers', you know; dee got so much larnin dee kin dance, an' fool de devil too. An' I stay roun' a little while, an' den went in de kitchen to see how supper gittin' on, 'cause I wuz so hongry when I got dyah I ain' able to eat 'nough at one time to 'commodate it, an' de smell o' de tuckeys an' de gret saddlers o' mutton in de tin-kitchens wuz mos' 'nough by deeself to feed a right hongry man; an' dyah wuz a whole parcel o' niggers cookin' an' tunnin 'bout for life, an' dee faces jes as shiny as ef dee done bas'e 'em wid gravy; an' dyah, settin' back in a cheer out de way, wid her clean frock up off de flo', wuz dat gal! I sutney did feel curiosome.

"I say, 'Hi! name o' Gord! whar'd you come from?' She say 'Oh, Marster! ef heah ain' dat free nigger agin!' An' ev'ybody laughed.

"Well, presney we come out, cause Nancy warn see de dancin', an' we stop a leetle while 'hind de cornder out de wind while she tell me 'bout ev'thing. An' she say dat's all a lie she tell me dat day 'bout Mr. Darker and Miss Charlotte; an' he done gone 'way now for good 'cause he so low down an' wuthless dee kyarn nobody stand him; an' all he warn marry Miss Charlotte for is to git her niggers. But Nancy say Miss Charlotte nuver could abide him; he so 'sateful, 'spressly sence she fine out what a lie he told 'bout Marse George. You know, Mr. Darker he done meck 'em think Marse George sont me dyah to fine out ef he done come home, and den dat he fall on him wid he weepin when he ain' noticin' him, an' sort o' out de way too, an' git two urr mens to hold him while he beat him, all 'cause he in love wid Miss Charlotte. D'you ever, ever heah sich a lie? An' Nancy say, do' Miss Charlotte ain' b'lieve it all togerr, hit look so reasonable she done le' de ole jedge an' her ma, who wuz 'pending on what she heah, 'duce her to send back he things; an' dee ain' know no better not tell after de ole jedge die; den dee fine out 'bout de whuppin me, an' all; an' den Miss Charlotte know huccome I ain' gwine stay dat day; an' she say dee was sutney outdone 'bout it, but it too late den; an' Miss Charlotte kyarn do nuttin but cry 'bout it, an' dat she did, pintedly, 'cause she done lost Marse George, an' done 'stroy he life; an' she nuver keer 'bout nobody else sep Marse George, Nancy say. Mr. Clarke he hangin' on, but Miss Charlotte she done tell him pintedly she ain' nuver gwine marry nobody. An' dee jes done come, she say, 'cause dee had to go 'way roun' by de rope ferry 'long o' de river bein' so high, an' dee ain' know tell dee done git out de ker'idge an' in de house dat we all wuz heah; an' Nancy say she glad dee ain', 'cause she 'feared ef dee had, Miss Charlotte wouldn' 'a come.

"Den I tell her all 'bout Marse George, 'cause I know she 'bleeged to tell Miss Charlotte. Twuz powerful cold dyah, but I ain' mine dat, chile. Nancy she done had to wrop her arms up in her ap'on an' she kyarn meck no zistance, 'tall, an' dis nigger ain' keerin' nuttin 'bout cold den.

"An' jes den two ladies come out de carpenter shop 'an went 'long to de wash-house, an' Nancy say, 'Dyah Miss Charlotte now'; an' twuz Miss Lucy an' Miss Charlotte; an' we heah Miss Lucy coaxin' Miss Charlotte to go, tellin' her she kin come right out; an' jes den dee wuz a gret shout, an' we went in hinst 'em. Twuz Marse George had done teck de fiddle, an' ef he warn' natchelly layin' hit down! he wuz up at de urr een o' de room, 'way from we all, 'cause we wuz at de do', nigh Miss Charlotte whar she wuz standin' 'hind some on 'em, wid her eyes on him mighty timid, like she hidin' from him, an' ev'y nigger in de room wuz on dat flo'. Gord! suh, dee wuz grinnin' so dee warn' a toof in dat room you couldn' git you tweezers on; an' you couldn' heah a wud, dee so proud o' Marse George playin' for 'em.

"Well, dee danced tell you couldn' tell which wuz de clappers an' which de back-steppers; de whole house look like it wuz rockin'; an' presney somebody say supper, an' dat stop 'em, an' dee wuz a spell for a minute, an' Marse George standin' dyah wid de fiddle in he hand. He face wuz tunned away, an' he wuz studyin'—studyin' 'bout dat urr Christmas so long ago—an' sudney he face drapt down on de fiddle, an' he drawed de bow 'cross de strings, an' dat chune 'bout 'You'll ermember me' begin to whisper right sorf. Hit begin so low ev'ybody had to stop talkin' an' hold dee mouf to heah it; an Marse George he ain' know nuttin 'bout it, he done gone back, an' standin' dyah in de gret hall playin' it for Miss Charlotte, whar done come down de steps wid her little blue foots an' gret fan, an' standin' dyah in her dim blue dress an' her fyah arms, an' her gret eyes lookin' in he face so earnest, whar he ain' gwine nuver speak to no mo.' I see it by de way he look—an' de fiddle wuz jes pleadin.' He drawed it out jes as fine as a stran' o' Miss Charlotte's hyah.

"Hit so sweet, Miss Charlotte, mun, she couldn' stan' it; she made to de do'; an' jes while she watchin' Marse George to keep him from seein' her he look dat way, an' he eyes fall right into hern.

"Well, suh, de fiddle drapt down on de flo'—perlang! —an' he face wuz white as a sycamore limb.

"Dee say twuz a swimmin' in de head he had; an' Jack say de whole fiddle warn wuff de five dollars.

"Me an Nancy followed 'em tell dee went in de house, an' den we come back to de shop whar de supper wuz gwine on, an' got we all supper an' a leetle sop o' dat yaller gravy out dat big bowl, an' den we all rejourned to de wash-house agin, an' got onder de big bush o' misseltow whar hangin' from de jice, an' ef you ever see scufflin', dat's de time.

"Well, me an' she had jes done lay off de whole Christmas, when wud come dat Marse George want he horses.

"I went, but it sutney breck me up; an' I wonder whar de name o' Gord Marse George gwine sen' me dat cold night, an' jes as I got to de do' Marse George an' Mr. Braxton come out, an' I know torectly Marse George wuz gwine 'way. I seen he face by de light o' de lantern, an' twuz set jes rigid as a rock.

"Mr. Braxton he wuz baiggin him to stay; he tell him he ruinin' he life, dat he sho dee's some mistake, an' twill be all right. An' all de answer Marse George meck wuz to swing heself up in de saddle, an' Reveller he look like he gwine fyah 'stracted. He al'ays mighty fool anyways, when he git cold, dat horse wuz.

"Well, we come 'long 'way, an' Mr. Braxton an' two mens come down to de river wid lanterns to see us cross, 'cause twuz dark as pitch, sho 'nough.

"An' jes 'fo' I started I got one o' de mens to hol' my

horses, an' I went in de kitchen to git warm, an' dyah Nancy wuz. An' she say Miss Charlotte upsteairs cryin' right now, 'cause she think Marse George gwine cross de river 'count o' her, an' she whimper a little herself when I tell her good-by. But twuz too late den.

"Well, de river wuz jes natchelly b'ilin', an' hit soun' like a mill-dam roarin' by; an' when we got dyah Marse George tunned to me an' tell me he reckon I better go back. I ax him whar he gwine, an' he say, 'Home.' 'Den I gwine wid you,' I says. I wuz mighty skeered, but me an' Marse George wuz boys togerr; an' he plunged right in, an' I after him.

"Gord! twuz cold as ice; an' we hadn' got in befo' bofe horses wuz swimmin' for life. He holler to me to byah de myah head up de stream; an' I did try, but what's a nigger to dat water! Hit jes pick me up an' dash me down like I ain' no mo'n a chip, an' de fust thing I know I gwine down de stream like a piece of bark, an' water washin' all over me. I knowed den I gone, an' I hollered for Marse George for help. I heah him answer me not to git skeered, but to hold on; but de myah wuz lungin' an' de water wuz all over me like ice, an' den I washed off de myah back, and got drownded.

"I 'member comin' up, an' hollerin' agin for help, but I know den 'tain' no use, dee ain' no help den, an' I got to pray to Gord, an' den some'n hit me an' I went down agin' an'—de next thing I know I wuz in de bed, an' I heah 'em talkin' 'bout wherr I dead or not, an' I ain' know myself tell I taste de whiskey dee po'rin' down my jugular.

"An den dee tell me 'bout how when I hollered Marse George tun back an' struck out for me for life, an' how jes as I went down de last time he cotch me an' helt on to me tell we wash down to whar de bank curve, an dyah de current wuz so rapid hit yuck him off Reveller back, but he helt on to de reins tell de horse lunge so he hit him wid he fo' foot an' breck he collar-bone, an' den he had to let him go, an' jes helt on to me; an' den we wash up agin de bank an' cotch in a tree, an' de mens got dyah quick as dee could, an' when dee retched us Marse George wuz holdin' on to me, an' had he arm wropped round' a limb, an' we wuz lodged in de crotch, an' bofe jes as dead as a nail; an' de myah she got out, but Reveller he wuz drowned, wid his foot cotch in de rein an' de saddle tunned onder he side; an' dee ain' know wherr Marse George ain' dead too, 'cause he not only drownded, but he lef' arm broke up nigh de shoulder.

"An' dee say Miss Charlotte she 'mos' 'stracted; dat de fust thing anybody know 'bout it wuz when de servants bust in de hall an' holler, an' say Marse George an' me bofe done washed 'way an' drownded, an' dat she drapt down dead on de flo', an' when dee bring her to she 'low to Miss Lucy dat she de 'casion on he death; an' dee say dat when de mens wuz totin' him in de house, an' wuz shufflin de feets not to make no noige, an' a little piece o' wet blue silk drapt out he breast whar somebody picked up an' gin Miss Lucy, Miss Charlotte breck right down agin; an' some on 'em say she sutney did keer for him; an' now when he layin' upstairs dyah dead, hit too late for him ever to know it.

"Well, suh, I couldn't teck it in dat Marse George and Reveller wuz dead, an' jes den somebody say Marse George done comin' to an' dee gi' me so much whiskey I went to sleep.

"An' next mornin' I got up an' went to Marse George room, an' see him layin' dyah in de bed, wid he face so white an' he eyes so tired-lookin', an' he ain' know me no mo' 'n ef he nuver see me, an' I couldn' stan' it; I jes drap down on de flo' an' bust out cryin'. Gord! suh, I couldn' help it, 'cause Reveller wuz drownded, an' Marse George he wuz mos' gone.

"An' he came nigher goin' yit, 'cause he had sich a strain, an' been so long in de water, he heart done got numbed, an' he got 'lirium, an' all de time he thought he tryin' to git 'cross de river to see Miss Charlotte, an' hit so high he kyarn git dyah.

"Hit sutney wuz pitiful to see him layin' dyah tossin' an' pitchin', not knowin' whar he wuz, tell it teck all Mr. Braxton an' me could do to keep him in de bed, an' de doctors say he kyarn hol' out much longer.

"An' all dis time Miss Charlotte she wuz gwine 'bout de house wid her face right white, an' Nancy say she don' do nuttin all day long in her room but cry an' say her pra'rs, prayin' for Marse George, whar dyin' upsteairs by 'count o' not knowin' she love him, an' I tell Nancy how he honin' all de time to see her, an' how he constant cravin' her name.

"Well, so twuz, tell he mos' done wyah heself out; an' jes lay dyah wid his face white as de pillow, an' he gret pitiful eyes rollin' 'bout so restless, like he still lookin' for her whar he all de time callin' her name, an' kyarn git 'cross dat river to see.

"An' one evenin' 'bout sunset he 'peared to be gwine; he weaker'n he been at all, he ain' able to scuffle no mo', an' jes layin' dyah so quiet, an' presney he say, lookin' mighty wistful:

"'Edinburg, I'm goin' to-night; ef I don' git 'cross dis time, I'll gin't up.'

"Mr. Braxton wuz standin' nigh de head o' de bed, an' he say, 'Well, by Gord! he *shell* see her!'—jes so. An' he went out de room, an' to Miss Charlotte do', an' call her, an' tell her she got to come, ef she don't, he'll die dat night; an' fust thing I know, Miss Lucy bring Miss Charlotte in, wid her face right white, but jes as tender as a angel's, an' she come an' stan' by de side de bed, an' lean down over him an' call he name, 'George!'—jes so.

"An' Marse George he ain' answer; he jes look at her study for a minute, an' den he forehead got smooth, an' he tun he eyes to me, an' say, 'Edinburg, I'm 'cross.' "

WHY THE CONFEDERACY FAILED*

By JOEL CHANDLER HARRIS

WHEN the surrender of Lee's army brought the Southern Confederacy to a sudden end, in 1865, not one Southerner in a hundred had prepared his mind for the event. It came as a stroke of lightning out of a clear sky. But there were a few who thought they knew why the surrender came; who had anticipated it, in a vague way, a year or more before the event; and of these few there were two men who regarded the outcome as the result of the direct interposition of Providence, although this belief did not cause them to bear with resignation the cruel wounds which the result inflicted on their hopes and their fortunes. They gave good reasons for their foreknowledge of the collapse—reasons which the attentive reader will doubtless be able to discover for himself when the facts are laid before him.

When the deadly game of war began in earnest, the Southern leaders found it necessary to depend almost entirely on blockade-running as the means of communicating with their agents abroad. But this method was a "skittish" one at best. Comparatively few men could be induced to engage in it, and those who were willing were just the men whose services could be better employed in other directions. More than that the blockade was becoming more real and, consequently, more serious every day. No plan to elude the increasing vigilance of the blockaders could be looked upon as certain or definite. It was a game of hazard, thrilling enough to attract the reckless and the adventurous, but dangerous enough to repel

* From *The Kidnapping of Lincoln* by Joel Chandler Harris, copyright 1900 by Esther LaRose Harris and reprinted by permission of Doubleday, Doran & Company, Inc., Publishers.

all others. One day with another, the advantages all lay with the grim war-vessels that rocked lazily up and down just outside the Southern harbors.

Therefore it was necessary to hit upon some plan more definite and systematic to enable the Confederate Government to communicate with its agents in the North, in Canada, and in Europe. Communication with Washington was easy, as John Omahundro (well known after the war as "Texas Jack") and his companion scouts were demonstrating every day; but it had also been demonstrated that it was a risky business for any scout or spy to walk out of Washington, day or night, with an incriminating map or drawing or document concealed on his person. Many an innocent countryman, going away from Washington after selling his produce, was suddenly seized and stripped naked, being compelled to remain in this plight while the lining was ripped from his coat, if he had one, and from his boots. He might protest tearfully, or threaten loudly; it was all one to those who were submitting him to this rough investigation.

Events of this kind necessarily went far to make the traffic in contraband information across the Potomac as dangerous as running the blockade. Omahundro kept it up from pure love of excitement and adventure, and played his cards with such apparent boldness and indifference that the cold eye of suspicion never once glanced in his direction. But he and the few others who followed his initiative were not equal to the necessities of the Confederate Government, and so it was decided that the New York Hotel, so popular with Southerners before the war, should be the centre to which information should be sent and from which it should be distributed.

I saw an announcement the other day to the effect that the old hotel had been closed to the public, and by this time no doubt its place has been taken by one of those unsightly and ridiculous structures which stand for pretty much all that is concrete and real in our commercial environment. In that event the old building has been demolished and carted away as so much rubbish; but if that rubbish should find a voice, how many strange stories it could tell! The flat roof covered and the dull, unattractive walls concealed, a thousand mysteries.

Now, as Mr. Lincoln used to put it, no Government could sleep soundly while such a man as Secretary Stanton was stamping about in the corridors, kicking chairs over, and breaking bell-cords. The Government, consequently, was not asleep. The great Secretary had early knowledge that something suspicious was going on in and around the New York Hotel, as the agents of the secret service, as well as the most expert detectives the world could produce, gave it their undivided attention for many weary months. They followed many a promising clew to its unpretentious entrance, only to see it disappear, or entered its plain and silent corridors only to come away baffled and amazed. For while the Government was wide-awake, the hotel seemed to be asleep. Porters, waiters, bell-boys, even the guests moved about with a noiseless politeness. To enter the dining room of the hotel was to take refuge from the chaotic rumble and rattle of Broadway; was to go, in fact, many steps toward the subdued literary atmosphere of Washington Square.

The hotel itself, in its own proper person, was supposed to have no knowledge of the interest which the Government was taking in the movements of its guests. At any rate, it betrayed no irritation, and was neither surprised nor alarmed. It went to bed early, arose at dawn, and lay sprawling in sun or rain day after day, to all appearances blissfully ignorant of the secret inquest which the Government was holding over its corpus. As a matter of fact, however, there was not an hour of the twenty-four when the old hotel was not wide-awake, and fairly quivering with eagerness to take advantage of every instant's carelessness on the part of the cordon of gentlemanly spies and detectives: fairly quivering and quaking with eagerness, and yet as silent, as motionless, and as patient as the animals whose instincts and necessities compel them to catch and kill their prey. No writer has ever hit off this natural characteristic in a phrase. To describe it you need a term that is a hundred times more expressive than wariness or cunning, and that gives a new illumination and a deeper meaning to patience.

On the day before Christmas, in the year 1863, about four o'clock in the afternoon, Captain Fontaine Flournoy (he was made a Colonel later) alighted from a cab and entered the office of the clerk's desk and looked about him, as if in doubt or perplexity, or as if seeking for a familiar face. Though dressed in the garb of a civilian, his figure was still military.

"I was expecting to meet my son," he explained to the smiling clerk.

"I think he arrived this morning," said that functionary. "Is that his handwriting?" He pointed to a signature on the register, "Emory W. Hunt, Montpelier, Vermont."

Captain Flournoy gave a grunt of satisfaction, and signed beneath it, "Frederic J. Hunt, U. S. A." A gentlemanly-looking person, promenading about the office, approached the desk and inspected the signature.

"Show the gentleman to 322," said the clerk to a porter, and the two went upstairs. The porter, inspecting the tag of the key, saw that it was for room 328. He did not pause to correct the error but showed the guest to

322, went in, closed the door carefully, and proceeded to usher the Captain through connecting rooms until 328 was reached. In that apartment a half-dozen men were grouped around a table. They appeared to be playing dominoes, and were so intent on the game that only one of them looked up. Meanwhile Captain Flournoy unfastened his valise, took out a bundle of papers, and laid it upon the table. Then he rearranged the contents of the satchel and was escorted back to 322, one of the group playfully throwing a kiss after him.

In all this he was simply following to the letter the careful instructions that had been given him in Washington with respect to his movements. This was his first experience in work of this kind, and the precautions he saw taken in his behalf, at every turn and crossing, brought home to him in the most vivid way the dangerous character of his mission. If this danger had taken tangible shape, or had assumed actual proportions such as may be seen when a battery of guns spits out shot and shell from its red and smoking mouths, he would have known how to face it; but to be walking in the dark, to be groping blindly, as it were, with the possibility of a long imprisonment, or even the gallows, at the end of the tangle—this was enough to put even his stout nerves to the test.

More than this, on his own responsibility he had taken it upon himself to deliver in person to the authorities in Richmond the most important document he had received at the Federal capital. This document he had detached from the rest, and now had it stored away in the lining of an undergarment. It would have been no relief to Captain Flournoy if he had known that the document had been missed by the War Department not twenty minutes subsequent to its delivery into his hands; that the worthy official who had it in charge had been promptly clapped into the Old Capital prison; and that he himself had been accompanied from Washington by a special detective in whom Secretary Stanton had the utmost confidence.

This official had long desired an opportunity to uncover the conspiracy that had its site in the New York Hotel, and he rejoiced now to find that he had run his game to earth in that quarter. His name, which was Alonzo Barnum, will have a familiar sound to those who saw it on the title-page of one of the most interesting volumes published directly after the war. It was entitled, "From Harlem to the Antarctic."

Mr. Barnum shook himself as he entered the hotel, and smiled when he contemplated the registry-book.

"When did Hunt arrive?" he asked, as he signed what he called his "travelling name."

"Which one?" the clerk asked blandly.

"Why, Frederic, of course."

"About ten minutes ago. Want a room? Well, I'm sorry, but we are full to the roof. It often happens close to the holiday season. We may have one vacant before night; shall I save it for you?"

"Certainly," said Mr. Barnum. "Will you send my card up to Hunt?"

The bland and rosy clerk turned to a tall, dignified-looking man who was standing near the counter. He was in evening dress, and the garb showed that he was either a gentleman preparing to attend some social function or a dining-room servant. His countenance and his air were those of the man of the world. As a matter of fact, he was the head waiter of the hotel and something more.

"McCarthy," said the clerk, "will you shove this into room 322 on your way to the dining room? The porter will bring an answer."

"With pleasure, sir," replied the head waiter. He took the card and marched up the stairway. At room 322 he stopped and knocked, and entered without an invitation.

"I beg your pardon, sir," he said; "I am the head waiter. A gentleman has sent up his card."

"Well, I must shake hands with you, McCarthy. Omahundro has been telling me about you."

"What a boy that is!" exclaimed the head waiter. "And so this is Captain Flournoy? Upon my word, sir, we are well met. Do you know this man Barnes? Amos Barnes, it is. The cabman was telling me that he came on your train from Washington. He ordered his cab to follow yours, and he has no baggage."

Captain Flournoy frowned slightly and then smiled. "I'm green in this business," he said; "but my impulse is to take the bull by the horns. I shall invite this man up, and then deal with him as circumstances suggest."

"I'll shake your hand once more," exclaimed McCarthy, jubilantly. "Barring Omahundro, you're the only one of the whole crew that didn't want to crawl under the bed on the first trip."

He went to the door, called to the porter, who was waiting outside, and said, "Johnny, go down and tell Mr. Barnes that Major Hunt will be glad to see him in 322."

When Mr. Barnes entered the room, McCarthy, the head waiter, was standing by the fireplace talking. He was saying, "That boy of yours, Major, has grown since last summer. I saw a good deal of him when I went to Montpelier, and the questions he asked about the city, sir! 'Twould amaze you. He's uptown at a matinée. Excuse me, sir"—this to the redoubtable Mr. Barnes, or Barnum.

Captain Flournoy was politeness itself. He placed a chair for his visitor and seated himself on the side of the bed in an unceremonious way. The head waiter bowed himself out. There was a moment's hesitation on the part of the detective. He also was to take the bull by the horns.

"My friend," he said, squaring himself in his chair, "let us deal plainly with each other. Your name is not Hunt, and my name is not Barnes."

"In regard to personal matters you will speak only for yourself," said Captain Flournoy with a smile.

"Very well. I will speak now of a matter impersonal. During the last few days a document of immense importance has been abstracted from the War Department."

"I am well aware of that," remarked Captain Flournoy. "Otherwise I should be elsewhere at this moment."

"It contains the outlines of plans that cannot be changed at a moment's notice."

"Precisely."

"Now that document," said the detective, "is worth to the Government at least five thousand dollars in gold, —much more, perhaps,—certainly not less."

Captain Flournoy placed one pillow on another and leaned back in a restful attitude. "If I thought the Government would pay no more than five thousand dollars for the recovery of that document, I wouldn't move a hand in the matter," he declared.

The detective arose from his chair, and Captain Flournoy sat bolt upright on the bed.

"Now what is the use of beating about the bush?" asked the detective.

"Don't be impertinent, my friend," said the Captain.

"You are a Southerner."

"Why, so is General Thomas."

"I'll bet you ten dollars that the document is in your valise there," declared the detective.

"Done!" said the Captain, reaching out and placing a gold piece on the table. Mr. Barnum did likewise, whereupon Flournoy kicked the valise toward him and pocketed the money. But the detective refused to search the valise. Perhaps he feared some trick. The frankness of his opponent was calculated to baffle him.

"I was mistaken," he said and then hesitated.

At that moment the door opened and McCarthy stuck his head in. His face was convulsed with laughter. "Excuse me, sir," he said, "but I thought maybe you'd like to see a funny sight. Two Government detectives have cornered a chap in 328, and they're making him unload papers enough to line the hotel pantry. If you want to see 'em, sir, step right this way."

He came into the room, unlocked the connecting door, and pointed with his hand. Two rooms away angry voices could be heard in altercation. The three went as rapidly as they could, McCarthy bringing up the rear.

In 328 the gas was turned low. In one corner was a man apparently at bay. He had a pistol in his hand. Over against him were two men who had him covered with Colt's revolvers. "I'll not surrender the paper to you," he was saying. "I'll see you dead and die myself first. You have treated me like a dog."

"What is it all about?" asked Mr. Barnum, advancing into the room. The door behind him closed, and the three men lowered their weapons.

The man who had been at bay in the corner lounged up to the detective with a grin, saying, "Well, I'll be switched, Colonel, if you ain't a daisy from the county next adjoinin'."

"Come, sir!" cried the head waiter. His voice was harsh and stern, and his attitude was that of a commanding officer. "Come, sir! this is no time for buffoonery!"

"All right, Cap; I only allowed for to kiss him for his ma."

The head waiter laid his hand on the shoulder of Mr. Alonzo Barnum. "You have no need to be told what has happened. You were doing your duty as you see it; we are doing ours. It rests with you whether you leave this house with your life."

McCarthy paused, passed his hand over his face, and the gesture transformed him into a head waiter again. He turned to Captain Flournoy with a deferential smile. "Will you have dinner now, sir? It is ready."

It is not necessary to relate here the experience of Mr. Alonzo Barnum. It is sufficient to say that he awoke one morning and found himself on a vessel that a puffy little tug was towing through the bay. In a little while the tug loosed its grip, and the vessel, a Swedish bark, swung slowly around in the current as the wind filled her sails. Slowly city and harbour faded from view, and Mr. Barnum was at the beginning of the long voyage which he has so graphically described in his book. What a pity he did not take it upon himself to begin it by presenting the details of his experiences immediately previous to his voyage. Such an introduction would have given it a human as well as historical interest.

Captain Flournoy followed the head waiter down the stairway to the second story, and so into the dining room. He observed quite a flutter among the waiters when their chief entered. It was as if a military company had been suddenly given the command, "Attention!"

Captain Flournoy was conducted to the first table to the left of the door as he entered. At this table he had no company, but before he had finished the first course a guest had seated himself in the chair opposite. This newcomer had hardly given his order for soup and fish before the head waiter approached Captain Flournoy with the most deprecatory air, remarking:—

"I'm *very* sorry sir; but the sauterne is out. Is there nothing else on the card to your taste?" He held the card out, and across its face Captain Flournoy saw written, "Watch out!"

"No; I'll have a pony of brandy after dinner, but that I can get at the bar," said the Captain.

"I'm sorry enough, sir. You could do better than that in Montpelier; at your house, I mean, sir—not at the hotel. Oh, no—not at the hotel," the head waiter went on, keeping an eye on the men under him.

"And yet," said the Captain with a smile, transferring his thoughts to his own home in the far Southern town, "I used to think that the old hotel was a very fine affair."

"Give me your wine card," the guest opposite suddenly demanded.

"Certainly, sir," replied the head waiter, producing it instantly. The guest who took it, turned it over, and remarked, "Why, I saw you writing on it a while ago."

"What I wrote, sir, is in a very blunt hand. I simply marked out the pints of sauterne." He pointed to the erasure with the pencil which he had in readiness for the guest's order.

Captain Flournoy leaned back in his chair and wondered in what school of experience this hotel servant had learned his adroitness, his tact, and the composure which marked his acts and his utterances. It was all so admirable and yet so simple; and there was a certain incongruity about it, too, that caused the Captain to laugh inwardly though outwardly he was gravity itself. If the whole scene had been especially devised to compel the guest opposite to show his hand, it could not have succeeded better.

Before the guest could return the card the head waiter had gone to the door to usher in a number of newcomers. When these had been comfortably seated, he returned, took the card and examined it.

"No order, sir?"

"A half pint of claret," said the guest, curtly. Evidently his temper was somewhat ruffled. In fact, he was hot, though the weather outside was cold enough to make a pig squeal. He was restless and expectant, too, for he moved nervously in his chair, and drummed on the table, and kept his eyes on the entrance. And his anxiety betrayed itself even when his dinner had been served.

Several times the head waiter was called to the door and had conferences with persons in the corridor. After one of the interviews, he returned with a slip of paper in his hand, and went about from guest to guest, showing it and apparently making inquiries. Finally he came to Captain Flournoy, still holding the slip of paper.

"Do you happen to know, sir, a gentleman by the name of Barnes—Amos Barnes? His voice was modulated to the pitch of respectful anxiety.

"Why, I know him casually," Captain Flournoy responded carelessly. "He called at my room an hour ago."

"Do you see him in the dining room, sir? There is great inquiry for him; he seems to be wanted at the nearest telegraph office."

The Captain turned in his chair, putting on his glasses as he did so, and glanced at the occupants of the various tables. "No," he said presently; "I see no one that resembles him."

"May I ask you an impertinent question?" remarked the Captain's vis-à-vis, as the head waiter resumed his place near the entrance.

"If it is a necessary one—certainly."

"Why did Barnes go to your room?"

"May I give you a frank reply?"

"I should appreciate it."

"Well," said Captain Flournoy, "he called on me because I was a stranger."

"Did he explain his visit?"

"He did; he suspected that I was a Confederate spy. He explained that a very important document had been abstracted from one of the departments at Washington. To take the edge off his duty he wagered that the document was in my valise. He laid the wager and lost."

"If you will pardon me, sir, I'll say that you don't look like a person who would permit his valise to be searched in this way."

"Well, when Mr. Lincoln permits Stanton to send him word that he's a —— fool, why should the small fry resent the liberties taken with them by those who are doing their duty?"

Captain Flournoy leaned back in his chair and regarded his opponent with a smile. As he did so, the head waiter came forward with a deferential bow.

"Two gentlemen at the farther table, sir, request that you join them before you go out," he said. "They have a bottle between them, sir, and it would be as well for some one to share it with them." A peal of gleeful laughter and the clinking of glasses justified the suggestion.

"I'll be with them in a moment," Flournoy remarked. "Your venison is famous to-day, McCarthy."

"So it is, sir; so it is," assented the head waiter, as he moved away. In a moment he had returned, ushering a new guest to the table at which Captain Flournoy sat. This new guest by preference took the chair next to the gentleman who had engaged Flournoy in conversation.

"He can't be found," said the newcomer to his neighbor.

"Well, he knows what he is about," remarked the other, and then the two put their heads together and engaged in a confidential talk.

Flournoy took advantage of this to accept the invitation extended him by the lively occupants of another table at the farther end of the room. He had never seen either of them before, but under the circumstances this made no difference. They made a very noisy demonstration over his arrival, slapped him on the back, and displayed a familiarity which at any other time Captain Flournoy would have resented. They told jokes at his expense.

"Did you ever hear what Hunt said to his Brigadier when the latter reprimanded him for not falling back before the rebels at Stony Creek?" asked one in a loud voice.

"No! no!" cried the others; "let's have it."

"Why," said the first one, drawing himself up, and screwing a good-humoured countenance into an appearance of severity, "he asked this question, 'When was a soldier ever censured for standing his ground?' "

There were cries of "Good!" the sound of enthusiastic thumping on the table, and other symptoms of unusual hilarity that carry their own explanation with them.

But in the midst of it all, one of Flournoy's unknown friends gave him to understand that the officers and detectives of the Secret Service were stationed in the corridors, and that in all probability he would be placed under arrest the moment he left the dining room.

"Well, what is to be will be" remarked the Captain.

"McCarthy is coming this way," said the other, "and as he's smiling we'll watch his manoeuvres."

In fact, the somewhat stern features of the head waiter

were beaming. He snapped his fingers, and a waiter stationed himself behind the Captain's chair. The head waiter snapped his fingers again, and from the kitchen entry came swarming a dozen waiters. They moved about from table to table, crossing, and recrossing one another, and creating quite a stir, though the tables were now well emptied of guests. From the front of the dining room this movement must have seemed to be very much like confusion, but to an experienced eye it was the result of much drilling and practice. What it lacked was formality.

"There is a towel by your chair, sir," said the head waiter to Flournoy. "When you stoop to pick it up, throw it over your left shoulder, turn your back to the front, allow your head and shoulders to droop, and then go out into the kitchen."

There was no difficulty in following these instructions. The scheme was simplicity itself, so transparent, indeed, that even suspicion would pass it by. Before it was carried out the head waiter had returned to the front, where he stood almost immovable until the activity of the waiters had subsided. In a few minutes the hilarious guests who had called Flournoy to their table came out.

"Didn't Hunt say he'd wait for us?" asked one, as they came out.

"No, confound him!" replied another loudly. "He had to go to the telegraph office. He's nothing but business."

"Pity, too," exclaimed a third; "he'sh fine feller." His voice was somewhat thick.

On each side of the door two men were stationed. They made no display of their presence, but stood in the attitude of men who had met by chance and who had something interesting to say to one another. But they narrowly eyed each guest as he came out. Presently the last one, a stout, middle-aged gentleman, a well-known habitué of the hotel sauntered forth and took from the long rack the last hat left, and walked down the corridor to the stairway in the most amiable frame of mind. He had made a big deal at the gold exchange. He had bought the metal for a rise, and greenbacks had dropped several cents on the dollar.

As he disappeared, the head waiter came to the entrance and closed one side of the double door. The four men in the corridor regarded one another with looks of mingled surprise and dismay. One of them—the man who had sat opposite to Captain Flournoy at the table—beckoned to the head waiter.

"Are you closing the dining room?" he asked.

"Not entirely, sir. We close the doors at four. It is now three-fifty."

The questioner went to the door and looked in. The dining room was entirely empty of guests, and some of the waiters had begun to snip at one another with their towels.

"What has become of the gentleman who sat at table with me?" he asked with some emphasis. "There were two, sir," replied the head waiter, deferentially.

"I mean the one who sat opposite."

"Major Hunt? Why, he joined a party at another table, but the bottle was moving too fast to suit his taste, sir. He had been there not more than ten minutes when he excused himself. I think he went out before you did, sir."

"That is impossible," exclaimed the man, vigorously.

"I am simply giving you my impression, sir," rejoined the head waiter, politely.

"Why, I'll swear—" the man began excitedly. Then, as if remembering himself, he paused and stared helplessly.

"It seems unnatural, sir, that you shouldn't see him come out if you were standing here." The extreme suavity and simplicity of the head waiter were in perfect keeping with his position. "He left me a message for his son who is here. Says he, 'Mack'—he always calls me Mack, sir—'Mack', says he, 'when the lad comes in tell him not to be uneasy if I fail to come in to-night. Tell him,' says he, 'that I'm engaged on some important Government business, and tell him to meet me at the custom-house at ten to-morrow morning.' It's a pity you didn't make an engagement with him, sir, if you're obliged to see him. He's a fine man, a fine man."

With that he turned and went into the dining room. In a few minutes the door was closed and locked, but the four men in the corridor still stared at one another. Three of them were amazed, the fourth seemed to be amused.

"Well, what did I tell you?" he asked.

"I've made up my mind to arrest the head waiter," said the one who had questioned McCarthy.

"This isn't Washington," said the amused one. "Arrest him and in ten minutes you'll have an Irish riot on your hands in which nobody would be hurt but ourselves. Our orders are plain on that score. We can't afford to stir up the population. I suggest a cocktail all around. It will give us strength to admit that we are mere bunglers by the side of Barnum."

"I believe you," acquiesced another. "He has been here, got what he came for, and is by this time on his way to Washington."

It was this belief that shed a faint gleam of light over a prospect otherwise gloomy.

Meanwhile, when Captain Flournoy went through the swinging doors of the dining room and found himself in the entryway leading to the kitchen, he was in a quandary as to his further movements. But every step he took seemed to have been foreseen and provided for. He knew that he had talked too freely to the guest who sat at his table, but how could this emergency have been forestalled? He had left his hat on the rack or shelf in the front of the dining room; a waiter presented it to him the moment he slipped into the entryway. He was in doubt what course to pursue; an elderly gentleman beckoned him with a smile. Following this venerable guide, Flournoy went down a short flight of stairs and into an apartment which he recognized as the drying room of the laundry. Thence he went into a narrow corridor, ascended three flights of stairs, and was ushered into the apartment which had served as a trap for Mr. Barnum, or, as he chose to call himself, Mr. Amos Barnes.

Some changes had been made. Two hours ago the room was bare but for a few chairs and a table, but now there was a bed in the corner, a lounge, and a comfortable-looking rocker. The table held pens, ink, and writing-paper, and a brisk fire was burning in the grate. Everything had a comfortable and cosey appearance.

After the strain under which he had been, it was not difficult for Captain Flournoy to adapt himself to such circumstances. He drew the rocker before the fire and gave himself up to reflections which, whether pleasing or not, were of a character to engross his mind so completely that he failed to hear the door swing open. Presently a hand was laid on his shoulder and he came back to earth with a start. The head waiter stood over him smiling.

"Have a chair, my friend," said Flournoy. "You have placed me under great obligations."

"We have had a very close shave, and that's a fact," remarked McCarthy, "but you are under no obligations to me. It's all in the way of duty." The air, the attitude of an upper servant had vanished completely, and Flournoy was experienced enough to know that he was talking to a man of the world capable of commanding men. "I am a head waiter for precisely the same reason that you are a—"

"Spy?" suggested Flournoy, as the other hesitated.

"No; there's a flavour to that word that doesn't suit my taste. Let's call it scout, or inspector, or better still military attaché."

"I am simply a messenger," said Flournoy, modestly.

"It is your first experience, I imagine," suggested McCarthy. "You are a soldier, and you don't relish the undertaking."

"That is the truth," Flournoy assented.

"Well, I was a Captain in the Navy," explained McCarthy, "and now I am—what you see me."

"You are still a Captain of the Navy," said Flournoy; "the house is your ship, and the dining room is your quarter-deck."

McCarthy laughed gleefully. "I have had the same conceit—oh, hundreds of times!"

They talked a long time, touching on a great variety of topics, and found themselves in hearty agreement more often than not. Finally they drifted back to the matter in hand, and Flournoy confided to McCarthy that one of the papers with which he had been intrusted was of so much importance that he had decided to deliver it in person.

"Should this document reach Richmond by the first of February," he said, "the Federal Army will be captured, Washington will fall, and the war will be over by the first of May."

"Are you sure?" McCarthy inquired.

"Quite sure," the other assented.

At this McCarthy ceased to ask questions or to make comments, but sat for a long time gazing in the fire. Flournoy forbore to interrupt his reflections, and the most absolute silence reigned in the room.

Presently McCarthy straightened himself in his chair. "The documents you left with the committee this afternoon will reach Richmond in five days," he remarked somewhat dryly. "They start at midnight."

This seemed to be so much in the nature of a suggestion that Flournoy was moved to ask his advice.

"Shall I include this document with the other papers?" he inquired earnestly.

McCarthy shook his head slowly and indecisively. "It's a serious question," he said. "Ten minutes ago, on an impulse, I should have said send it with the rest by all means—by all means; but now—Do you know," he went on, with great earnestness, "I am getting to be superstitious about this war. Look at it for yourself." He waved his hand as if calling attention to a panorama spread out on the walls of the room. "First, there is Mr. Lincoln. He went to Washington a country boor. What is he now? Why, he manages the politicians, the officials,—the whole lot,—precisely as a chess-player manages his pieces, and he never makes a mistake. Doesn't that seem queer?"

Captain Flournoy, gazing in the glowing grate, nodded his head. Some such idea had already crossed his mind.

"Then there's the first Manassas—Bull Run," McCarthy went on. "Does it seem natural that a victorious army which had utterly routed its enemy would fail to pursue the advantage? Is it according to human nature?"

Again Flournoy nodded.

"Finally, take into consideration the case of the *Merrimac*," continued McCarthy. "She had barely begun to perform the work she was cut out to do when around the corner came the *Monitor*, a match and more than a match for her. Does that look like an accident, or even a coincidence?"

At this Captain Flournoy turned in his chair and regarded his companion with a very grave countenance.

"Do you know," remarked McCarthy, "that I had everything arranged to take charge of the *Merrimac?* It was a very great disappointment to me when it was found that she couldn't be manoeuvred to advantage."

"You think, then, that Providence—" Flournoy hesitated to speak the words in his mind.

"Judge for yourself. You have the facts. I could mention other circumstances, but these three stand out. As an old friend of mine used to say, they toot out like pot-legs."

"But if you think Providence has a hand in the matter, why call yourself superstitious?" Flournoy inquired.

"'Twas a convenient way of introducing what I had to say," replied McCarthy.

Silence fell on the two for a time. Finally McCarthy resumed the subject. "You say this document will enable the Confederates to win the day and put an end to the war?"

"I do," Flournoy insisted; "I believe so sincerely. It embodies plans that cannot possibly be altered because the success of the Federals depends upon them, and it will enable General Lee and the Confederate authorities to checkmate every move made by our enemies on land from now on. Do you know that in the early spring Grant is to be given command of all the Federal forces? That is the least important information the document contains."

"A truly comprehensive paper," remarked McCarthy gravely. "It falls directly in the category of Lincoln,

Manassas, and the *Merrimac*, and we shall see what we shall see."

"You are certain the rest of the papers will reach Richmond safely?" Flournoy asked.

"Those you turned over to the committee? As certain as that I am sitting here."

"Then let us place this other document with them," suggested Flournoy.

"If you think it best, certainly," said McCarthy with alacrity.

Flournoy reflected a moment. "No; I'll carry out my first impulse," he declared. He rose and paced across the room once or twice. Then he turned suddenly to McCarthy. "Shall we toss a penny?" he asked.

"No! no!" cried the other, with a protesting gesture. "It is folly to match chance against Providence."

"Then the matter is settled," said Flournoy, decisively.

"It was settled long ago," McCarthy remarked solemnly.

The Southern soldier looked hard at his companion, trying to find in his countenance an interpretation of his remark. But McCarthy's face was almost grim in its impassiveness.

He arose as Flournoy resumed his seat. "You will have your supper here, and your breakfast also. To-morrow morning you may be able to start on your journey. Do you go west or north? Ah, west; but it is a long way round. Did you ever try the Cumberland route? Omahundro would know which is the easiest."

"He advised the western route because I am familiar with it," explained Flournoy.

McCarthy bowed, and in doing so became the head waiter again. The deferential smile flickered about his stern mouth, and then flared up, as it were, changing all the lines of the face; and the straight and stalwart shoulders stooped forward a little so that humility might seat itself in the saddle.

"I must be going about my duties, sir," he said. "I may call to bid you good night. If I should not, may your dreams be pleasant." He bowed himself out, and Flournoy sat wondering at the fortunes of war and the curious demands of duty which had made a spy of him and a head waiter of Lawrence McCarthy. He mused over the matter until he fell asleep in his chair, where he nodded comfortably until a waiter touched him on the arm and informed him his supper was served.

"Did you think I had company?" Flournoy asked. "You've brought enough for Company B of the Third Georgia."

"'Tis a sayin', sir, that travel sharpens the appetite," said the waiter, smiling brightly. Then, "The Third Georgia is Colonel Nisbet's ridgment; 'tis in Ranse Wright's brigade. To be sure, I know 'em well, sir. Should ye be goin' to Augusty, an' chance to see James Nagle, kindly tell 'im ye've seen Terence an' he's doin' well. He's me father, sir, an' he thinks I'm in Elmiry prison."

"How did you get out? Did you take the oath?"

"Bless ye, sir, 'twas too strong for me stomach. I'll never tell ye, sir, whether I escaped by accident or design. 'Twas this way, sir. I was in the hospital, sir, an' whin I got stronger, Father Rafferty, seein' my need of trousers, brought me a pair of blue ones. The next day he comes in a barouche along with an officer. He says to me, 'Terence, here's a coat to go with the trousers,' says he. 'Ye see the man drivin' the barouche?' says he. 'Well,' says he, 'whin I go inside, he'll fall down an' have a fit,' says he, 'an' do ye be ready,' he says, 'to hold the horses whiles I sind out the doctor,' he says. Well, sir, 'twas like a theatre advertisement. Down comes the man with a fit, an' if he had one spasm, he had forty. The horses were for edging away, sir, but I caught 'em an' helt 'em. 'Take 'im inside,' says the officer, 'an' 'tend to 'im,' he says, 'an' do ye, me man,' he says to me, 'get up there an' drive me back to quarters,' he says. 'How about Father Rafferty?' I says. 'Oh, as fer that,' he says, 'he'll be took with a fever if son Terence turns out to be a drivelin' idjut,' he says. I looked at 'im hard, sir, an' he looked at me. Says he, 'D—— ye, will ye drive on?' It was Captain McCarthy, sir."

Flournoy laughed, though he would have found it difficult to explain why. The reason doubtless was that such boldness and simplicity seemed so foreign to our complex civilization that they struck the note on incongruity. "He is a queer man," he remarked.

"Queer, sir?" said the waiter. "Oh, no, sir; not queer. He's simple as a little child. He's a grand man, sir—nothin' less than that." There was no doubt of Terence Nagle's enthusiastic loyalty to his employer.

Supper was duly despatched, the waiter enlivening the meal with many anecdotes of his own experience in the Confederate Army and in prison. Flournoy found that they had many acquaintances in common, and more than once when Terence was for returning to the dining room, the guest found various excuses for detaining him.

But he went at last, after replenishing the fire, and Captain Flournoy sat long before it, wondering over the chain of circumstances by which he had been dragged, rather than led, into his present position. He took no thought of time, and was surprised when he heard a clock in a distant room strike eleven. By the time the sound had died away a gentle tap at the door attracted his attention, and, following his invitation, Terence Nagle came in, bearing a waiter on which was a bowl, a silver ladle, and three glasses. In another moment the head waiter came in. He had doffed his evening dress, the badge of his position, and with it dropped the air and manner he assumed in the dining room. He was now himself, the educated Irishman, a fine specimen of a class that can be matched in few of the nations of the earth.

"Do you know the day?" he asked when, obeying Flournoy's gesture, he seated himself.

"Yes, replied the Southerner, "it is Christmas Eve."

"And hard upon Christmas," said McCarthy. "I hope that our Lord who is risen will have mercy upon us all, and help us to carry out all our plans that are not contrary to His own."

"Amen!" responded Flournoy. It was like grace before meat, only simpler and less formal.

"Remembering the day, and the custom we have at the South," McCarthy explained, "I have taken the liberty of brewing you a bowl of nog. 'Twill be a reminder of old times, if nothing else."

Flournoy's face brightened. "My friend, you seem to think of everything," he declared. "The very flavour of it will carry me straight home."

"'Twas no thought of mine. I have a little lass who comes to fetch me my toggery in the afternoons. I was telling her of the Southern gentleman so far from home, and her eyes filled with tears, and says she, 'Dada, darling, why not make the gentleman a bowl of nog for his Christmas gift? It is wonderful how thoughtful the womenfolk are, and how tender-hearted. I'll fill your glass, sir."

"And yours," insisted Flournoy.

"To be sure," cried McCarthy, "and one for my

lieutenant, Terence Nagle. See the lad blush! You'd thing he was a girl by the way he reddens. Yet with half a dozen men like him I could meet a company of regulars."

"He's overdoin' it, sir!" Terence protested; "he's overdoin' it." The lad was so overcome he dropped a glass on the floor, but the carpet saved it.

"Were you ever drunk?" McCarthy asked, after they had made away with the nog. The inquiry was bluntly put, and Flournoy looked hard at his companion.

"Yes; once when I was a youngster of fourteen. It was at a corn-shucking," he replied.

"Well, recall your feelings and actions if you can. To-morrow morning you must not only be drunk—you must be very drunk."

"I don't understand," said Flournoy.

"To-morrow morning a cabman will be waiting for a fare on the other side of the street, opposite this window. The blinds must be opened early, but some one will attend to that. If the sun is shining, the cabman will take out his watch. The hour will be anywhere from nine to ten. The sun will shine on the face of the watch, and the reflection will be thrown on the wall of your room. If the sun is obscured, you will hear a policeman's rattle. Then your spree must begin. And make it a jolly one. Here is a small pistol loaded with blank cartridges. Use it at your discretion. At the head of the stairs you will fall into the arms of a big policeman, who will be joined by another. Take no offense if they hustle you. A bruise or two won't hurt you. It is all for the good of the cause."

"But—"

"It is our only chance. I can see that you have a temper; don't lose it with our friends, the policemen. They will have a very critical crowd to play to, and must play as if they meant business. I must bid you good night."

"One moment," said Flournoy. He drew from his pocket a five-dollar gold piece and laid it on the table.

McCarthy drew back, his face flushing. "What is that for?" he asked sternly.

"It is a Christmas gift for your daughter."

"For Nora!" cried the other; "why, she'll be the happiest lass in the town!" His eyes sparkled and his whole manner changed. "This must be my real good night," he went on. "I have work to do and you will need rest." He went out, followed by Terence.

Captain Flournoy was up betimes, his plantation habits following him wherever he went. But he was not a man on whose hands time hung heavily. Just now one of his windows commanded a view of about twenty feet of Broadway, and he watched, with more interest than usual, the fluctuating stream of humanity that flowed through it. When he grew tired of that panorama, he had his own thoughts for company, and the thoughts that are bred by a cheerful disposition are the best of companions. And then he had in his pocket a copy of Virgil. Under such circumstances only a man with a bad conscience could be either lonely or gloomy.

Presently his breakfast came, and by the time Terence had cleared away the fragments nine o'clock had struck, and the sky, which had been overcast in the early morning hours, was clear. At nine, too, a closed cab came leisurely from the direction of Washington Square and took up its position in the side street opposite the ladies' entrance of the hotel. From behind the curtains Flournoy watched the driver closely, and never once did the man give so much as a side glance at the upper windows of the hotel. His curiosity seemed to be dead. For a while he read a newspaper, nor did he cease from reading when a man, passing quickly by, pitched a small valise into the cab. But presently the paper palled on him, and he folded it neatly and tucked it away under the cushion. Then he looked at the sun, and, as if to verify the time of day, pulled out his watch and sprung the case open. The reflection from the crystal, or from the burnished case, flashed through Flournoy's window, and danced upon the wall, once, twice, thrice.

Now was the time to act, and act promptly, but Flournoy paused and drew a long breath. The whole business seemed to be child's play. He seized his overcoat by one sleeve, slung it over his shoulder, threw open the door, gave a fox-hunter's view—halloo,—the same that is called the "rebel yell,"—fired two blank cartridges, and went staggering blindly along the corridor, crying, "There 'e goes! there 'e goes! I'll shoot 'im. Out o' the way an' lemme shoot 'im!"

At the head of the stairs a policeman loomed up as big as a giant. "Come out o' this, ye maunderin' divil!" he cried. "They tell me ye've been kapin' the house awake the livelong night. Be aisy, or I'll twist yure dommed neck, ye dribblin' idjit!"

"Fling 'im down to me, Tim, while I whale the jimmies out av 'im. 'Tis the second time the howlin' divil has broke loose the fortnight." This from the policeman at the foot of the stairs.

Now, while these policemen were talking, they were also acting. They cuffed Flournoy about between them, and knocked and dragged and bundled him along with a zeal that was almost unbearable. By the time they reached the sidewalk he was limp and exhausted, but he did not fail to notice that Terence Nagle was prominent in the considerable crowd collected there.

"Take 'im to the hospital, Tim; 'tis the only way to clear the jimmies from his head."

"The hospital!" cried Terence Nagle; "an' if he was a poor man, he'd be hauled to the station an' be left there."

"Ain't it the truth!" exclaimed a keen-faced, shabby-looking man.

"Cheese it!" cried the policeman who had been left behind; "cheese it an' move on, ivery livin' sowl av ye!"

By this time the cab was rattling away up Fifth Avenue. "You fellows have heavy hands," said Flournoy to his companion when he had pulled himself together.

"Faith, we had to limber ye up, Cap. Why, ye don't know the A B C av a jag. Whin ye landed me one in the jaw, I says to meself, 'Bedad, av he goes down hittin' straight an' hard like this, he'll be nabbed be thim keenies at the dure,' says I, an' I tipped the wink to Moike an' we doubled ye up same es jinin' the Improved Order av Red Min, sorr. All we needed to give the job reg'larity, sorr, was the pile-driver."

At Fortieth Street the cab halted, the policeman shook hands with Flournoy and got out, and in a very short time thereafter the latter found himself at the passenger station of the New York Central. He descended from the cab, and was about to pay the fare when the cabman lifted his hat with "Good luck to you, sir," touched up his horse and went whirling away.

Two weeks afterward, Captain Flournoy, with a companion, a scout who knew the country well, was feeling his way southward through West Virginia. They had good horses, but travelled mainly at night. As they drew near the Virginia line, Flournoy's uneasiness became perceptible. The important document he carried became a burden almost intolerable to him, whereas the scout, one James Kirkpatrick, grew gayer and gayer with each passing hour. While Flournoy was riding gloomily along, Kirkpatrick was whistling or singing softly all the lilting tunes he knew. One night, in a heavily wooded valley, the wayfarers scented danger. They heard a horse whinnying, the clinking of spurs, and the rattling of sabres or carbines.

"It's the Yanks," said Kirkpatrick.

"You know this country, you say?" queried Flournoy.

"Like a book," replied the other.

"Well, here is a paper as important to the Confederacy as Lee's army. Stow it in an inner pocket, and if anything should happen to me, do you ride right on to Richmond. You have the fate of your country in your hands."

"Phew!" whistled Kirkpatrick softly. Instantly a voice cried "Halt!"

"Do you save yourself," said Flournoy, and spurred forward, while Kirkpatrick turned to the left, struck a footpath, and went clattering away in the gloom. Captain Flournoy spurred forward and found himself in the arms of the Confederate videttes. In a moment he heard shots as of skirmishers firing and falling back. In the distance they heard the drums beating to arms.

"Your friend has stampeded a whole Yankee brigade," remarked one of the videttes.

But this was a mistake. Kirkpatrick was lying dead not a mile away, killed by a stray bullet. It was his horse running wild that disturbed the Federal camp.

Next morning the Federals advanced, feeling their way cautiously. One of their skirmishers, a German, found Kirkpatrick stark and stiff. He appropriated the dead man's overcoat, searched his pockets for valuables, and found the document that was to decide the fate of the Confederacy. He looked at it critically, crumpled it in his hand, and made as if to throw it away. A second thought caused him to cram it in one of his pockets, where it remained until he needed something with which to light his pipe.

On the fourth of the following March Grant was made General-in-Chief of the land forces of the United States, and the programme set forth in the paper—Grant's move on Virginia and Sherman's march to the sea—was promptly begun and carried out.

WORDS AND MUSIC*

By IRVIN S. COBB

WHEN Breck Tandy killed a man he made a number of mistakes. In the first place, he killed the most popular man in Forked Deer County—the county clerk, a man named Abner J. Rankin. In the second place, he killed him with no witnesses present, so that it stood his word—and he a newcomer and a stranger—against the mute, eloquent accusation of a riddled dead man. And in the third place, he sent north of the Ohio River for a lawyer to defend him.

* * *

ON THE FIRST Monday in June—Court Monday—the town filled up early. Before the field larks were out of the grass the farmers were tying their teams to the gnawed hitch-racks along the square. By nine o'clock the swapping ring below the wagonyard was swimming in red dust and clamorous with the chaffer of the horse-traders. In front of a vacant store the Ladies' Aid Society of Zion Baptist Church had a canvas sign out, announcing that an elegant dinner would be served for twenty-five cents from twelve to one, also ice cream and cake all day for fifteen cents.

The narrow wooden sidewalks began to creak and churn under the tread of many feet. A long-haired medicine doctor emerged from his frock-coat like a locust coming out of its shell, pushed his high hat off his forehead and ranged a guitar, sundry bottles of a potent mixture, his tooth-pulling forceps, and a trick-handkerchief upon the narrow shelf of his stand alongside the Drummers' Home Hotel. In front of the little dingy tent of the

* *Back Home*, George H. Doran Company.

Half Man and Half Horse a yellow negro sat on a split-bottom chair limbering up for a hard day. This yellow negro was an artist. He played a common twenty-cent mouth organ, using his left hand to slide it back and forth across his spread lips. The other hand held a pair of polished beef bones, such as end men wield, and about the wrist was buckled a broad leather strap with three big sleigh-bells riveted loosely to the leather, so that he could clap the bones and shake the bells with the same motion. He was a whole orchestra in himself. He could play on the mouth organ almost any tune you wanted, and with his bones and his bells to help out he could creditably imitate a church organ, a fife-and-drum corps, or, indeed, a full brass band. He had his chair tilted back until his woolly head dented a draggled banner depicting in five faded primary colors the physical attractions of the Half Man and Half Horse—Marvel of the Century—and he tested his mouth organ with short, mellow, tentative blasts as he waited until the Marvel and the Marvel's manager finished a belated breakfast within and the first ballyhoo could start. He was practicing the newest of the ragtime airs to get that far South. The name of it was The Georgia Camp-Meeting.

The town marshal in his shirt sleeves, with a big silver shield pinned to the breast of his unbuttoned blue waistcoat and a hickory stick with a crook handle for added emblem of authority, stalked the town drunkard, fair game at all seasons and especially on Court Monday. The town gallant whirled back and forth the short hilly length of Main Street in his new side-bar buggy. A clustering group of negroes made a thick, black blob, like hiving bees, in front of a negro fishhouse, from which came the smell and sounds of perch and channel cat frying on spitting-hot skillets. High upon the squat cupola of the court-house, a red-headed woodpecker clung, barred in crimson, white, and blue-black, like a bit of living bunting, engaged in the hopeless task of trying to drill through the tin sheathing. The rolling rattle of his beak's tattoo came down sharply to the crowds below. Mourning doves called to one another in the trees round the red-brick courthouse, and at ten o'clock, when the sun was high and hot, the sheriff came out and, standing between two hollow white pillars, rapped upon one of them with a stick and called upon all witnesses and talesmen to come into court for the trial of John Breckinridge Tandy, charged with murder in the first degree, against the peace and dignity of the commonwealth of Tennessee and the statutes made and provided.

But this ceremonial by the sheriff was for form rather than effect, since the witnesses and the talesmen all sat in the circuit-court chamber along with as many of the population of Forked Deer County as could squeeze in there. Already the air of the crowded chamber was choky with heat and rancid with smell. Men were perched precariously in the ledges of the windows. More men were ranged in rows along the plastered walls, clunking their heels against the cracked wooden baseboards. The two front rows of benches were full of women. For this was to be the big case of the June term—a better show by long odds than the Half Man and Half Horse.

Inside the low railing that divided the room and on the side nearer the jury box were the forces of the defense. Under his skin the prisoner showed a sallow paleness born of his three months in the county jail. He was tall and dark and steady eyed, a young man, well under thirty. He gave no heed to those who sat in packed rows behind him, wishing him evil. He kept his head turned front, only bending it sometimes to whisper with one of his lawyers or one of his witnesses. Frequently, though, his hand went out in a protecting, reassuring way to touch his wife's brown hair or to rest a moment on her small shoulder. She was a plain, scared, shrinking little thing. The fingers of her thin hands were plaited desperately together in her lap. Already she was trembling. Once in a while she would raise her face, showing shallow brown eyes dilated with fright, and then sink her head again like a quail trying to hide. She looked pitiable and lonely.

The chief attorney for the defense was half turned from the small counsel table where he might study the faces of the crowd. He was from Middle Indiana, serving his second term in Congress. If his party held control of the state he would go to the Senate after the next election. He was an orator of parts and a pleader of almost a national reputation. He had manly grace and he was a fine, upstanding figure of a man, and before now he had wrung victories out of many difficult cases. But he chilled to his finger-nails with apprehensions of disaster as he glanced searchingly about the close-packed room.

Wherever he looked he saw no friendliness at all. He could feel the hostility of that crowd as though it had substance and body. It was a tangible thing; it was almost a physical thing. Why, you could almost put your hand out and touch it. It was everywhere there.

And it focused and was summed up in the person of Aunt Tilly Haslett, rearing on the very front bench with her husband, Uncle Fayette, half hidden behind her vast and overflowing bulk. Aunt Tilly made public opinion in Hyattsville. Indeed she was public opinion in that town. In her it had its upcomings and its out-flowings. She held herself bolt upright, filling out the front of her black bombazine basque until the buttons down its front strained at their buttonholes. With wide, deliberate strokes she fanned herself with a palm-leaf fan. The fan had an edging of black tape sewed round it—black tape signifying in that community age or mourning, or both. Her jaw was set like a steel latch, and her little gray eyes behind her steel-bowed specs were leveled with a baleful, condemning glare that included the strange lawyer, his client, his client's wife, and all that was his client's.

Congressman Durham looked and knew that his presence was an affront to Aunt Tilly and all those who sat with her; that his somewhat vivid tie, his silken shirt, his low tan shoes, his new suit of gray flannels—a masterpiece of the best tailor in Indianapolis—were as insults, added up and piled on, to this suspendered, gingham-shirted constituency. Better than ever he realized now the stark hopelessness of the task to which his hands were set. And he dreaded what was coming almost as much for himself as for the man he was hired to defend. But he was a trained veteran of courtroom campaigns, and there was a jauntily assumed confidence in his bearing as he swung himself about and made a brisk show of conferring with the local attorney who was to aid him in the choosing of the jurors and the questioning of the witnesses.

But it was real confidence and real jauntiness that radiated from the other wing of the inclosure, where the prosecutor sat with the assembled bar of Forked Deer County on his flanks, volunteers upon the favored side, lending to it the moral support of weight and numbers. Rankin, the dead man, having been a bachelor, State's Attorney Gilliam could bring no lorn widow and children to mourn before the jurors' eyes and win added sympathy for his cause. Lacking these most valued assets of a murder trial he supplied their places with the sisters of the dead man—two sparse-built elderly women in heavy black, with sweltering thick veils down over their faces. When the proper time came he would have them raise these veils and show their woeful faces, but now they sat shrouded all in crepe, fit figures of desolation and sorrow. He fussed about busily, fiddling the quill toothpick that hung perilously in the corner of his mouth and evening up the edges of a pile of law books with freckled calfskin covers. He was a lank, bony garfish of a man, with a white goatee aggressively protruding from his lower lip. He was a poor speaker but mighty as a cross-examiner, and he was serving his first term and was a candidate for another. He wore the official garbing of special and extraordinary occasions—long black coat and limp white waistcoat and gray striped trousers, a trifle short in the legs. He felt the importance of his place here almost visibly—his figure swelled and expanded out his clothes.

"Look yonder at Tom Gilliam," said Mr. Lukins, the grocer, in tones of whispered admiration to his next-elbow neighbor, "jest prunin' and honin' hisse'f to git at that there Tandy and his dude Yankee lawyer. If he don't chaw both of 'em up together I'll be dad-burned."

"You bet," whispered back his neighbor—it was Aunt Tilly's oldest son, Fayette, Junior—"it's like Maw says—time's come to teach them murderin' Kintuckians they can't be a-comin' down here a-killin' up people and not pay for it. I reckon, Mr. Lukins," added Fayette, Junior, with a wriggle of pleased anticipation, "we shore are goin' to see some carryin's-on in this cotehouse today."

Mr. Lukins' reply was lost to history because just then the judge entered—an elderly, kindly-looking man—from his chambers in the rear, with the circuit-court clerk right behind him bearing large leather-clad books and sheaves of foolscap paper. Their coming made a bustle. Aunt Tilly squared herself forward, scrooging Uncle Fayette yet farther into the eclipse of her shapeless figure. The prisoner raised his head and eyed his judge. His wife looked only at the interlaced, weaving fingers in her lap.

The formalities of the opening of a term of court were mighty soon over; there was everywhere manifest a haste to get at the big thing. The clerk called the case of the Commonwealth versus Tandy. Both sides were ready. Through the local lawyer, delegated for these smaller purposes, the accused man pleaded not guilty. The clerk spun the jury wheel, which was a painted wooden drum on a creaking wooden axle, and drew forth a slip of paper with the name of a talesman written upon it and read aloud:

"Isom W. Tolliver."

In an hour the jury was complete: two townsmen, a clerk and a telegraph operator, and ten men from the country—farmers mainly and one blacksmith and one horse-trader. Three of the panel who owned up frankly to a fixed bias had been let go by consent of both sides. Three more were sure they could give the defendant a fair trial, but those three the local lawyer had challenged peremptorily. The others were accepted as they came. The foreman was a brownskinned, sparrowhawk-looking old man, with a smoldering eye. He had spare, knotted hands, like talons, and the right one was marred and twisted, with a sprayed bluish scar in the midst of the crippled knuckles like the mark of an old gunshot wound. Juror No. 4 was a stodgy old man, a small planter from the back part of the county, who fanned himself steadily with a brown-varnished straw hat. No. 7 was even older, a white-whiskered patriarch on crutches. The twelfth juryman was the oldest of the twelve—he looked to be almost seventy, but he went into the box after he had sworn that his sight and hearing and general health were good and that he still could do his ten hours a day at his blacksmith shop. The juryman chewed tobacco without pause. Twice after he took his seat at the back end of the double line he tried for a wooden cuspidor ten feet away. Both were creditable attempts, but he missed each time. Seeing the look of gathering distress in the eyes the sheriff brought the cuspidor nearer, and thereafter No. 12 was content, chewing steadily like some bearded contemplative ruminant and listening attentively to the evidence, meanwhile scratching a very wiry head of whity-red hair with a thumbnail that through some injury had taken on the appearance of a very thick, very black Brazil nut. This scratching made a raspy, filing sound that after a while got on Congressman Durham's nerves.

It was late in the afternoon when the prosecution rested its case and court adjourned until the following morning. The state's attorney had not had so very much evidence to offer, really—the testimony of one who heard the single shot and ran in at Rankin's door to find Rankin upon the floor, about dead, with a pistol, unfired, in his hand and Tandy standing against the wall with a pistol, fired, in his; the constable to whom Tandy surrendered; the physician who examined the body; the persons who knew of the quarrel between Tandy and Rankin growing out of a land deal into which they had gone partners—not much, but enough for Gilliam's purposes. Once in the midst of examining a witness the state's attorney, seemingly by accident, let his look fall upon the two black-robed, silent figures at his side, and as though overcome by the sudden realization of a great grief, he faltered and stopped dead and sank down. It was an old trick, but well done, and a little humming murmur like a breeze coming through treetops swept the audience.

Durham was sick in his soul as he came away. In his mind there stood the picture of a little, scared woman's drawn, drenched face. She had started crying before the last juror was chosen and thereafter all day, at half-minute intervals, the big, hard sobs racked her. As Durham came down the steps he had almost to shove his way through a knot of natives outside the doors. They grudged him the path they made for him, and as he showed them his back he heard a snicker and some one said a thing that cut him where he was already bruised—in his egotism. But he gave no heed to the words. What was the use?

At the Drummers' Home Hotel a darky waiter sustained a profound shock when the imported lawyer declined the fried beeksteak with fried potatoes and also the fried ham and eggs. Mastering his surprise the waiter offered to try to get the Northern gentleman a fried pork chop and some fried June apples, but Durham only wanted a glass of milk for his supper. He drank it and smoked a cigar, and about dusk he went upstairs to his room. There he found assembled the forlorn rank and file of the defense, the local lawyer and three character witnesses—prominent citizens from Tandy's home town who were to testify to his good repute in the place where he was born and reared. These would be the only witnesses, except Tandy himself, that Durham meant to call. One of them was a bustling little man named Felsburg, a clothing merchant, and one was Colonel Quigley, a banker and an ex-mayor, and a third was Judge Priest, who sat on a circuit-court bench back in Kentucky. In contrast to his size, which was considerable, this Judge Priest had a voice that was high and whiny. He also had the trick, common to many men in politics in his part of the South, of being purposely ungrammatical at times.

This mannerism led a lot of people into thinking that the judge must be an uneducated man—until they heard him charging a jury or reading one of his rulings. The judge had other peculiarities. In conversation he nearly always called men younger than himself, son. He drank a little bit too much sometimes; and nobody had ever beaten him for any office he coveted. Durham didn't know what to make of this old judge—sometimes he seemed simple-minded to the point of childishness almost.

The others were gathered about a table by a lighted kerosene lamp, but the old judge sat at an open window with his low-quarter shoes off and his white-socked feet propped against the ledge. He was industriously stoking at a home-made corncob pipe. He pursed up his mouth, pulling at the long cane stem of his pipe with little audible sucks. From the rocky little street below the clatter of departing farm teams came up to him. The Indian medicine doctor was taking down his big white umbrella and packing up his regalia. The late canvas habitat of the Half Man and Half Horse had been struck and was gone, leaving only the pole-holes in the turf and a trodden space to show where it had stood. Court would go on all week, but Court Monday was over and for another month the town would doze along peacefully.

Durham slumped himself into a chair that screeched protestingly in all its infirm joints. The heart was gone clean out of him.

"I don't understand these people at all," he confessed. "We're beating against a stone wall with our bare hands."

"If it should be money now that you're needing, Mister Durham," spoke up Felsburg, "that boy Tandy's father was my very good friend when I first walked into that town with a peddling pack on my back, and if it should be money—?"

"It isn't money, Mr. Felsburg," said Durham. "If I didn't get a cent for my services I'd still fight this case out to the end for the sake of that game boy and that poor little mite of a wife of his. It isn't money or the lack of it—it's the damned hate they've built up here against the man. Why, you could cut it off in chunks—the prejudice that there was in that courthouse today."

"Son," put in Judge Priest in his high, weedy voice, "I reckon maybe you're right. I've been projectin' around courthouses a good many years, and I've taken notice that when a jury look at a prisoner all the time and never look at his women folks it's a monstrous bad sign. And that's the way it was all day today."

"The judge will be fair—he always is," said Hightower, the local lawyer, "and of course Gilliam is only doing his duty. Those jurors are as good solid men as you can find in this country anywhere. But they can't help being prejudiced. Human nature's not strong enough to stand out against the feeling that's grown up round here against Tandy since he shot Ab Rankin."

"Son," said Judge Priest, still with his eyes on the darkening square below, "about how many of them jurors would you say are old soldiers?"

"Four or five that I know of," said Hightower—"and maybe more. It's hard to find a man over fifty years old in this section that didn't see active service in the Big War."

"Ah, hah," assented Judge Priest with a squeaky little grunt. "That foreman now—he looked like he might of seen some fightin'?"

"Four years of it," said Hightower. "He came out a captain in the cavalry."

"Ah, hah." Judge Priest sucked at his pipe.

"Herman," he wheezed back over his shoulder to Felsburg, "did you notice a tall sort of a saddle-colored darky playing a juice harp in front of that there side-show as we came along up? I reckon that nigger could play almost any tune you'd a mind to hear him play?"

At a time like this Durham was distinctly not interested in the versatilities of strange negroes in this corner of the world. He kept silent, shrugging his shoulders petulantly.

"I wonder now is that nigger left town yet?" mused the old judge half to himself.

"I saw him just a while ago going down toward the depot," volunteered Hightower. "There's a train out of here for Memphis at 8:50. It's about twenty minutes of that now."

"Ah, hah, jest about," assented the judge. When the judge said "Ah, hah!" like that it sounded like the striking of a fiddle-bow across a fiddle's tautened E-string.

"Well, boys," he went on, "we've all got to do the best we can for Breck Tandy, ain't we? Say, son"—this was aimed at Durham—"I'd like mightily for you to put me on the stand the last one tomorrow. You wait until you're through with Herman and Colonel Quigley here, before you call me. And if I should seem to ramble somewhat in giving my testimony—why, son, you just let me ramble, will you? I know these people down here better maybe than you do—and if I should seem inclined to ramble, just let me go ahead and don't stop me, please?"

"Judge Priest," said Durham tartly, "if you think it could possibly do any good, ramble all you like."

"Much obliged," said the old judge, and he struggled into his low-quarter shoes and stood up, dusting the tobacco fluff off himself.

"Herman have you got any loose change about you?"

Felsburg nodded and reached into his pocket. The judge made a discriminating selection of silver and bills from the handful that the merchant extended to him across the table.

"I'll take about ten dollars," he said. "I didn't come down here with more than enough to jest about buy my railroad ticket and pay my bill at this here tavern, and I might want a sweetenin' dram or somethin'."

He pouched his loan and crossed the room.

"Boys," he said, "I think I'll be knockin' round a little before I turn in. Herman, I may stop by your room a minute as I come back in. You boys better turn in early and git yourselves a good night's sleep. We are all liable to be purty tolerable busy tomorrow."

After he was outside he put his head back in the door and said to Durham:

"Remember, son, I may ramble."

Durham nodded shortly, being somewhat put out by the vagaries of a mind that could concern itself with trivial things on the imminent eve of a crisis.

As the judge creaked ponderously along the hall and down the stairs those he had left behind heard him whistling a tune to himself, making false starts at the air and halting often to correct his meter. It was an unknown tune to them all, but to Felsburg, the oldest of the four, it brought a vague, unplaced memory.

The old judge was whistling when he reached the street. He stood there a minute until he had mastered the tune to his own satisfaction, and then, still whistling, he shuffled along the uneven board pavement, which, after rippling up and down like a broken-backed snake, dipped downward to a little railroad station at the foot of the street.

IN THE MORNING nearly half the town—the white half—came to the trial, and enough of the black half to put a dark hem, like a mourning border, across the back width of the courtroom. Except that Main Street now drowsed in the heat where yesterday it had buzzed, this day might have been the day before. Again the resolute woodpecker drove his bloodied head with unimpaired energy against the tin sheathing up above. It was his third summer for that same cupola and the tin was pocked with little dents for three feet up and down. The mourning doves still pitched their lamenting note back and forth across the courthouse yard; and in the dewberry patch at the bottom of Aunt Tilly Haslett's garden down by the creek the meadow larks strutted in buff and yellow, with crescent-shaped gorgets of black at their throats, like Old Continentals, sending their clear-piped warning of "Laziness 'gwine kill you!" in at the open windows of the steamy, smelly courtroom.

The defense lost no time getting under headway. As his main witness Durham called the prisoner to testify in his own behalf. Tandy gave his version of the killing with a frankness and directness that would have carried conviction to auditors more even-minded in their sympathies. He had gone to Rankin's office in the hope of bringing on a peaceful settlement of their quarrel. Rankin had flared up; had cursed him and advanced on him, making threats. Both of them reached for their guns then. Rankin's was the first out, but he fired first—that was all there was to it. Gilliam shone at cross-examination, taking hold like a snapping turtle and hanging on like one.

He made Tandy admit over and over again that he carried a pistol habitually. In a community where a third of the male adult population went armed this admission was nevertheless taken as plain evidence of a nature bloody-minded and desperate. It would have been just as bad for Tandy if he said he armed himself especially for his visit to Rankin—to these listeners that could have meant nothing else but a deliberate, murderous intention. Either way Gilliam had him, and he sweated in his eagerness to bring out the significance of the point. A sinister little murmuring sound, vibrant with menace, went purring from bench to bench when Tandy told about his pistol-carrying habit.

The cross-examination dragged along for hours. The recess for dinner interrupted it; then it went on again, Gilliam worrying at Tandy, goading at him, catching him up and twisting his words. Tandy would not be shaken, but twice under the manhandling he lost his temper and lashed back at Gilliam, which was precisely what Gilliam most desired. A flary fiery man, prone to violent outbursts—that was the inference he could draw from these blaze-ups.

It was getting on toward five o'clock before Gilliam finally let his bedeviled enemy quit the witness-stand and go back to his place between his wife and his lawyer. As for Durham, he had little more to offer. He called on Mr. Felsburg, and Mr. Felsburg gave Tandy a good name as man and boy in his home town. He called on Banker Quigley, who did the same thing in different words. For these character witnesses State's Attorney Gilliam had few questions. The case was as good as won now, he figured; he could taste already his victory over the famous lawyer from up North, and he was greedy to hurry it forward.

The hot round hub of a sun had wheeled low enough to dart its thin red spokes in through the westerly windows when Durham called his last witness. As Judge Priest settled himself solidly in the witness chair with the deliberation of age and the heft of flesh, the leveled rays caught him full and lit up his round pink face, with the short white-bleached beard below it and the bald white-bleached forehead above. Durham eyed him half doubtfully. He looked the image of a scatter-witted old man, who would potter and philander round a long time before he ever came to the point of anything. So he appeared to the others there, too. But what Durham did not sense was that the homely simplicity of the old man was of a piece with the picture of the courtroom, that he would seem to these watching, hostile people one of their own kind, and that they would give to him in all likelihood a sympathy and understanding that had been denied the clothing merchant and the broadclothed banker.

He wore a black alpaca coat that slanted upon him in deep, longitudinal folds, and the front skirts of it were twisted and pulled downward until they dangled in long, wrinkly black teats. His shapeless gray trousers were short for him and fitted his pudgy legs closely. Below them dangled a pair of stout ankles encased in white cotton socks and ending in low-quarter black shoes. His shirt was clean but wrinkled countlessly over his front. The gnawed and blackened end of a cane pipestem stood out of his breast pocket, rising like a frosted weed stalk.

He settled himself back in the capacious oak chair, balanced upon his knees a white straw hat with a string band round the crown and waited for the question:

"What is your name?" asked Durham.

"William Pitman Priest."

Even the voice somehow seemed to fit the setting. Its high nasal note had a sort of whimsical appeal to it.

"When and where were you born?"

"In Calloway County, Kintucky, July 27, 1839."

"What is your profession or business?"

"I am an attorney-at-law."

"What position if any do you hold in your native state?"

"I am presidin' judge of the first judicial district of the state of Kintucky."

"And have you been so long?"

"For the past sixteen years."

"When were you admitted to the bar?"

"In 1860."

"And you have ever since been engaged, I take it, either in the practice of the law before the bar or in its administration from the bench?"

"Exceptin' for the four years from April, 1861, to June, 1865."

Up until now Durham had been sparring, trying to fathom the probable trend of the old judge's expected meanderings. But in the answer to the last question he thought he caught the cue and, though none save those two knew it, thereafter it was the witness who led and the questioner who followed his lead blindly.

"And where were you during those four years?"

"I was engaged, suh, in takin' part in the war."

"The War of the Rebellion?"

"No, suh," the old man corrected him gently but with firmness, "the War for the Southern Confederacy."

There was a least bit of a stir at this. Aunt Tilly's tape-edged palmleaf blade hovered a brief second in the wide regular arc of its sweep and the foreman of the jury involuntarily ducked his head, as if in affiance of an indubitable fact.

"Ahem!" said Durham, still feeling his way, although now he saw the path more clearly. "And on which side were you engaged?"

"I was a private soldier in the Southern army," the

old judge answered him, and as he spoke he straightened up.

"Yes, suh," he repeated, "for four years I was a private soldier in the late Southern Confederacy. Part of the time I was down here in this very county," he went on as though he had just recalled that part of it. "Why, in the summer of '64 I was right here in this town. And until yistiddy I hadn't been back since."

He turned to the trial judge and spoke to him with a tone and manner half apologetic, half confidential.

"Your Honor," he said, "I am a judge myself, occupyin' in my home state a position very similar to the one which you fill here, and whilst I realize, none better, that this ain't all accordin' to the rules of evidence as laid down in the books, yet when I git to thinkin' about them old soldierin' times I find I am inclined to sort of reminiscence round a little. And I trust your Honor will pardon me if I should seem to ramble slightly?"

His tone was more than apologetic and more than confidential. It was winning. The judge upon the bench was a veteran himself. He looked toward the prosecutor.

"Has the state's attorney any objection to this line of testimony?" he asked, smiling a little.

Certainly Gilliam had no fear that this honest-appearing old man's wanderings could damage a case already as good as won. He smiled back indulgently and waved his arm with a gesture that was compounded of equal parts of toleration and patience, with a top-dressing of contempt. "I fail," said Gilliam, "to see wherein the military history and achievements of this worthy gentleman can possibly affect the issue of the homicide of Abner J. Rankin. But," he added magnanimously, "if the defense chooses to encumber the record with matters so trifling and irrelevant I surely will make no objection now or hereafter."

"The witness may proceed," said the judge.

"Well, really, Your Honor, I didn't have so very much to say," confessed Judge Priest, "and I didn't expect there'd be any to-do made over it. What I was trying to git at was that comin' down here to testify in this case sort of brought back them old days to my mind. As I git along more in years—" he was looking toward the jurors now—"I find that I live more and more in the past."

As though he had put a question to them several of the jurors gravely inclined their heads. The busy cud of Juror No. 12 moved just a trifle slower in its travels from the right side of the jaw to the left and back again.

"Yes, suh," he said musingly, "I got up early this mornin' at the tavern where I'm stoppin' and took a walk through your thrivin' little city." This was rambling with a vengeance, thought the puzzled Durham. "I walked down here to a bridge over a little creek and back again. It reminded me mightily of that other time when I passed through this town—in '64—just about this season of the year—and it was hot early today just as it was that other time—and the dew was thick on the grass, the same as 'twas then."

He halted a moment.

"Of course your town didn't look the same this mornin' as it did that other mornin'. It seemed to me there are twicet as many houses here now as there used to be—it's got to be quite a little city."

Mr. Lukins, the grocer, nodded silent approval of this utterance, Mr. Lukins having but newly completed and moved into a two-story brick store building with a tin cornice and an outside staircase.

"Yes, suh, your town has grown mightily, but"—and the whiny, humourous voice grew apologetic again—"but your roads are purty much the same as they were in '64—hilly in places—and kind of rocky."

Durham found himself sitting still, listening hard. Everybody else was listening too. Suddenly it struck Durham, almost like a blow, that this simple old man had somehow laid a sort of spell upon them all. The flattering sunrays made a kind of pink glow about the old judge's face, touching gently his bald head and his white whiskers. He droned on:

"I remember about those roads particularly well, because that time when I marched through here in '64 my feet was about out of my shoes and them flints cut 'em up some. Some of the boys, I recollect, left bloody prints in the dust behind 'em. But shucks—it wouldn't a-made no real difference if we'd wore the bottoms plum off our feet! We'd a-kept on goin'. We'd a-gone anywhere—or tried to—behind old Bedford Forrest."

Aunt Tilly's palmleaf halted in air and the twelfth juror's faithful quid froze in his cheek and stuck there like a small wen. Except for a general hunching forward of shoulders and heads there was no movement anywhere and no sound except the voice of the witness:

"Old Bedford Forrest hisself was leadin' us, and so naturally we just went along with him, shoes or no shoes. There was a regiment of Northern troops—Yankees—marchin' on this town that mornin', and it seemed the word had traveled ahead of 'em that they was aimin' to burn it down.

"Probably it wasn't true. When we got to know them Yankees better afterward we found out that there really wasn't no difference, to speak of, between the run of us and the run of them. Probably it wasn't so at all. But in them days the people was prone to believe 'most anything—about Yankees—and the word was that they was a comin' across country, a-burnin' and cuttin' and slashin', and the people here thought they was going to be burned out of house and home. So old Bedford Forrest he marched all night with a battalion of us—four companies—Kintuckians and Tennesseeans mostly, with a sprinklin' of boys from Mississippi and Arkansas—some of us ridin' and some walkin' afoot, like me—we didn't always have horses enough to go round that last year. And somehow we got here before they did. It was a close race though between us—them a-comin' down from the North and us a-comin' up from the other way. We met 'em down there by that little branch just below where your present railroad depot is. There wasn't no depot there then, but the branch looks just the same now as it did then—and the bridge too. I walked acros't it this mornin' to see. Yes, suh, right there was where we met 'em. And there was a right smart fight.

"Yes, suh, there was a right smart fight for about twenty minutes—or maybe twenty-five—and then we had breakfast."

He had been smiling gently as he went along. Now he broke into a throaty little chuckle.

"Yes, suh, it all come back to me this mornin'—every little bit of it—the breakfast and all. I didn't have much breakfast, though, as I recall—none of us did—probably just corn pone and branch water to wash it down with." And he wiped his mouth with the back of his hand as though the taste of the gritty cornmeal cakes was still there.

There was another little pause here; the witness seemed to be through. Durham's crisp question cut the silence like a gash with a knife.

"Judge Priest, do you know the defendant at the bar, and if so, how well do you know him?"

"I was just comin' to that," he answered with simplicity, "and I'm obliged to you for puttin' me back on the track. Oh, I know the defendant at the bar mighty well—as well as anybody on earth ever did know him, I reckin, unless 'twas his own maw and paw. I've known him, in fact, from the time he was born—and a gentler, better-disposed boy never grew up in our town. His nature seemed almost too sweet for a boy—more like a girl's—but as a grown man he was always manly, and honest, and fair—and not quarrelsome. Oh, yes, I know him. I knew his father and his mother before him. It's a funny thing too—comin' up this way—but I remember that his paw was marchin' right alongside of me the day we came through here in '64. He was wounded, his paw was, right at the edge of that little creek down yonder. He was wounded in the shoulder—and he never did entirely git over it."

Again he stopped dead short, and he lifted his hand and tugged at the lobe of his right ear absently. Simultaneously Mr. Felsburg, who was sitting close to a window beyond the jury box, was also seized with nervousness, for he jerked out a handkerchief and with it mopped his brow so vigorously that, to one standing outside, it might have seemed that the handkerchief was actually being waved about as a signal.

Instantly then there broke upon the pause that still endured a sudden burst of music, a rollicking, jingling air. It was only a twenty-five-cent mouth organ, three sleigh bells, and a pair of the rib bones of a beef-cow being played all at once by a saddle-colored negro man but it sounded for all the world like a fife-and-drum corps:

If you want to have a good time,
If you want to have a good time,
If you want to have a good time,
If you want to ketch the devil—
Jine the cavalree!

To some who heard it now the tune was strange; these were the younger ones. But to those older men and those older women the first jubilant bars rolled back the years like a scroll.

If you want to have a good time,
If you want to have a good time,
If you want to have a good time,
If you want to ride with Bedford—
Jine the cavalree!

The sound swelled and rippled and rose through the windows—the marching song of the Southern trooper—Forrest's men, and Morgan's, and Jeb Stuart's and Joe Wheeler's. It had in it the jingle of saber chains, the creak of sweaty saddle-girths, the nimble clunk of hurrying hoofs. It had in it the clanging memories of a cause and a time that would live with these people as long as they lived and their children lived and their children's children. It had in it the one sure call to the emotions and the sentiments of these people.

And it rose and rose and then as the unseen minstrel went slouching down Main Street, toward the depot and the creek it sank lower and became a thin thread of sound and then a broken thread of sound and then it died out altogether and once more there was silence in the courthouse of Forked Deer County.

Strangely enough not one listener had come to the windows to look out. The interruption from without had seemed part and parcel of what went on within. None faced to the rear, every one faced to the front.

There was Mr. Lukins now. As Mr. Lukins got upon his feet he said to himself in a tone of feeling that he be dad-fetched. But immediately changing his mind he stated that he would preferably be dad-blamed, and as he moved toward the bar rail one overhearing him might have gathered from remarks let fall that Mr. Lukins was going somewhere with the intention of being extensively dad-burned. But for all these threats Mr. Lukins didn't go anywhere, except as near the railing as he could press.

Nearly everybody else was standing up too. The state's attorney was on his feet with the rest, seemingly for the purpose of making some protest.

Had any one looked they might have seen that the ember in the smoldering eyes of the old foreman had blazed up to a brown fire; that Juror No. 4, with utter disregard for expense, was biting segments out of the brim of his new brown-varnished straw hat; that Juror No. 7 had dropped his crutches on the floor, and that no one, not even their owner, had heard them fall; that all the jurors were half out of their chairs. But no one saw these things, for at this moment there rose up Aunt Tilly Haslett, a dominant figure, her huge wide back blocking the view of three or four immediately behind her.

Uncle Fayette laid a timid detaining hand upon her and seemed to be saying something protestingly.

"Turn loose of me, Fate Haslett!" she commanded. "Ain't you ashamed of yourse'f, to be tryin' to hold me back when you know how my only dear brother died a-follerin' after Gineral Nathan Bedford Forrest. Turn loose of me!"

She flirted her great arm and Uncle Fayette spun flutteringly into the mass behind. The sheriff barred her way at the gate of the bar.

"Mizz Haslett," he implored, "please, Mizz Haslett—you must keep order in the cote."

Aunt Tilly halted in her onward move, head up high and elbows out, and through her specs, blazing like burning-glasses, she fixed on him a look that instantly charred that unhappy official into a burning red ruin of his own self-importance.

"Keep it yourse'f, High Sheriff Washington Nash, Esquire," she bade him; "that's whut you git paid good money for doin'. And git out of my way! I'm a-goin' in there to that pore little lonesome thing settin' there all by herself, and there ain't nobody goin' to hinder me neither!"

The sheriff shrunk aside; perhaps it would be better to say he evaporated aside. And public opinion, reorganized and made over but still incarnate in Aunt Tilly Haslett, swept past the rail and settled like a billowing black cloud into a chair that the local attorney for the defense vacated just in time to save himself the inconvenience of having it snatched bodily from under him.

"There, honey," said Aunt Tilly crooningly as she gathered the forlorn little figure of the prisoner's wife in her arms like a child and mothered her up to her ample bombazined bosom, "there now, honey, you jest cry on me."

Then Aunt Tilly looked up and her specs were all blurry and wet. But she waved her palmleaf fan as though it had been the baton of a marshal.

"Now, jedge," she said, addressing the bench, "and you other gentlemen—you kin go ahead now."

The state's attorney had meant evidently to make some sort of an objection, for he was upon his feet through all this scene. But he looked back before he spoke and what he saw kept him from speaking. I believe I stated earlier that he was a candidate for reëlection. So he settled back down in his chair and stretched out his legs and buried his chin in the top of his limp white waistcoat in an attitude that he had once seen in a picture entitled, "Napoleon Bonaparte at St. Helena."

"You may resume, Judge Priest," said the trial judge in a voice that was not entirely free from huskiness, although its owner had been clearing it steadily for some moments.

"Thank you kindly, suh, but I was about through anyhow," answered the witness with a bow, and for all his homeliness there was dignity and stateliness in it. "I merely wanted to say for the sake of completin' the record, so to speak, that on the occasion referred to them Yankees did not cross that bridge."

With the air of tendering and receiving congratulations Mr. Lukins turned to his nearest neighbor and shook hands with him warmly.

The witness got up somewhat stiffly, once more becoming a commonplace old man in a wrinkled black alpaca coat, and made his way back to his vacant place, now in the shadow of Aunt Tilly Haslett's form. As he passed along the front of the jury-box the foreman's crippled right hand came up in a sort of a clumsy salute, and the juror at the other end of the rear row—No. 12, the oldest juror—leaned forward as if to speak to him, but remembered in time where his present duty lay. The old judge kept on until he came to Durham's side, and he whispered to him:

"Son, they've quit lookin' at him and they're all a-lookin' at her. Son, rest your case."

Durham came out of a maze.

"Your Honor," he said as he rose, "the defense rests."

* * *

THE JURY were out only six minutes. Mr. Lukins insisted

that it was only five minutes and a half, and that he'd be dad-rotted if it was a second longer than that.

As the lately accused Tandy came out of the courthouse with his imported lawyer—Aunt Tilly bringing up the rear with his trembling, weeping, happy little wife—friendly hands were outstretched to clasp his and a whiskered old gentleman with a thumbnail like a Brazil nut grabbed at his arm.

"Whichaway did Billy Priest go!" he demanded—"little old Fightin' Billy—whar did he go to? Soon as he started in talkin' I placed him. Whar is he?"

Walking side by side, Tandy and Durham came down the steps into the soft June night, and Tandy took a long, deep breath into his lungs.

"Mr. Durham," he said, "I owe a great deal to you."

"How's that?" said Durham.

Just ahead of them, centered in a shaft of light from the window of the barroom of the Drummers' Home Hotel, stood Judge Priest. The old judge had been drinking. The pink of his face was a trifle more pronounced, the high whine in his voice a trifle weedier, as he counted one by one certain pieces of silver into the wide-open palm of a saddle-colored negro.

"How's that?" said Durham.

"I say I owe everything in the world to you," repeated Tandy.

"No," said Durham, "what you owe me is the fee you agreed to pay me for defending you. There's the man you're looking for."

And he pointed to the old judge.

MT. PISGAH'S CHRISTMAS 'POSSUM*

By PAUL DUNBAR

NO MORE happy expedient for raising the revenues of the church could have been found than that which was evolved by the fecund brain of the Reverend Isaiah Johnson. Mr. Johnson was wise in his day and generation. He knew his people, their thoughts and their appetites, their loves and their prejudices. Also he knew the way to their hearts and their pocket-books.

As far ahead as the Sunday two weeks before Christmas, he had made the announcement that had put the congregation of Mt. Pisgah church into a flurry of anticipatory excitement.

"Brothahs an' sistahs," he had said, "you all reckernizes, ez well ez I does, dat de revenues of dis hyeah chu'ch ain't whut dey ought to be. De chu'ch, I is so'y to say, is in debt. We has a mo'gage on ouah buildin', an' besides de int'rus' on dat, we has fuel to buy an' lightin' to do. Fu'thahmo', we ain't paid de sexton but twenty-five cents on his salary in de las' six months. In conserquence of de same, de dus' is so thick on de benches dat ef you 'd jes' lay a clof ovah dem, dey'd be same ez upholstahed fu'niture. Now, in o'dah to mitigate dis condition of affairs, yo' pastoh has fo'med a plan which he wishes to p'nounce dis mo'nin' in yo' hyeahin' an' to ax yo' 'proval. You all knows dat Chris'mus is 'proachin', an' I reckon dat you is all plannin' out yo' Chris'mus dinnahs. But I been a-plannin' fu' you when you was asleep, an' my idee is dis,—all of you give up yo' Chris'mus dinnahs, tek fifteen cents er a qua'tah apiece an' come hyeah to chu'ch an' have a 'possum dinnah."

"Amen!" shouted one delighted old man over in the corner, and the whole congregation was all smiles and acquiescent nods.

"I puceive on de pa't of de cong'egation a disposition to approve of de pastoh's plan."

"Yes, yes, indeed," was echoed on all sides.

"Well, den I will jes' tek occasion to say fu'thah dat I already has de 'possums, fo' of de fattes' animals I reckon you evah seen in all yo' bo'n days, an' I's gwine to tu'n 'em ovah to Brothah Jabez Holly to tek keer of dem an' fatten 'em wuss ag'in de happy day."

The eyes of Jabez Holly shone with pride at the importance of the commission assigned to him. He showed his teeth in a broad smile as he whispered to his neighbor, 'Lishy Davis, "I 'low when I gits thoo wif dem 'possums dey won't be able to waddle"; and 'Lishy slapped his knee and bent double with appreciation. It was a happy and excited congregation that filed out of Mt. Pisgah church that Sunday morning, and how they chattered! Little knots and clusters of them, with their heads together in deep converse, were gathered all about, and all the talk was of the coming dinner. This, as has already been said, was the Sunday two weeks before Christmas. On the Sunday following, the shrewd, not to say wily, Mr. Johnson delivered a stirring sermon from the text, "He prepareth a table before me in the presence of mine enemies," and not one of his hearers but pictured the Psalmist and his brethren sitting at a 'possum feast with the congregation of a rival church looking enviously on. After the service that day, even the minister sank into insignificance beside his steward, Jabez Holly, the custodian of the 'possums. He was the most sought man on the ground.

"How dem 'possums comin' on?" asked one.

"Comin' on!" replied Jabez. " 'Comin' on' ain't no name fu' it. Why, I tell you, dem animals is jes' a-waddlin' a'ready."

"O-o-mm!" groaned a hearer, "Chris'mus do seem slow a'comin' dis yeah."

"Why, man," Jabez went on, "it 'u'd mek you downright hongry to see one o' dem critters. Evah time I looks at 'em I kin jes' see de grease a-drippin' in de pan, an' dat skin all brown an' crispy, an' de smell a-risin' up—"

"Heish up, man!" exclaimed the other; "ef you don't, I'll drap daid befo' de time comes."

"Huh-uh! no, you won't; you know dat day's wuf livin' fu'. Brothah Jackson, how'd yo' crap o' sweet pertaters tu'n out dis yeah?"

"Fine, fine! I's got dem mos' plenteous in my cellah."

"Well, don't eat 'em too fas' in de nex' week, 'ca'se we 'spects to call on you fu' some o' yo' bes'. You know dem big sweet pertaters cut right in two and laid all erroun' de pan teks up lots of de riches' grease when ol' Mistah 'Possum git too wa'm in de oven an' git to sweatin' it out."

"Have mercy!" exclaimed the impressionable one. "I know ef I don't git erway f'om dis chu'ch do' right now, I'll be foun' hyeah on Chris'mus day wif my mouf wide open."

But he did not stay there until Christmas morning, though he arrived on that momentous day bright and early like most of the rest. Half of the women of the church had volunteered to help cook the feast, and the other half were there to see it done right; so by the time for operations to commence, nearly all of Mt. Pisgah's congregation was assembled within its chapel walls. And what laughing and joking there was!

"O-omph!" exclaimed Sister Green, "I see Brothah Bill Jones' mouf is jes' sot fu' 'possum now."

"Yes, indeed, Sis' Green; hit jes' de same 's a trap an' gwine to spring ez soon ez dey any 'possum in sight."

"Hyah, hyah, you ain't de on'iest one in dat fix, Brothah Jones; I see some mo' people roun' hyeah lookin' mighty 'spectious."

"Yes, an' I's one of 'em," said some one else. "I do wish Jabez Holly 'ud come on, my mouf's jest p'intly worterin'."

"Let's sen' a c'mittee aftah him, dat'll be a joke." The idea was taken up, and with much merriment the committee was despatched to find and bring in the delinquent Jabez.

Every one who has ever cooked a 'possum—and who has not?—knows that the animal must be killed the day before and hung out of doors over night to freeze "de wil' tas'e outen him." This duty had been intrusted to Jabez, and shouts of joy went up from the assembled people when he appeared, followed by the committee and bearing a bag on his shoulder. He set the bag on the floor, and as the crowd closed round him, he put his arm far down into it, and drew forth by the tail a beautiful white fat cleaned 'possum.

"O-m, jes' look at dat! Ain't dat a 'possum fu' you? Go on, Brothah Jabez, let's se anothah." Jabez hesitated.

"Dat's one 'possum dah, ain't it?" he said.

"Yes, yes, go on, let's see de res'." Those on the inside of the circle were looking hard at Jabez.

"Now, dat's one 'possum," he repeated.

"Yes, yes, co'se it is." There was breathless expectancy.

"Well, dat's all dey is."

The statement fell like a thunder-clap. No one found voice till the Reverend Isaiah Johnson broke in with, "Wha', what dat you say, Jabez Holly?"

"I say dat's all de 'possum dey is, dat's what I say."

"Whah's dem othah 'possums, huh! whah's de res'?"

"I put 'em out to freeze las' night, an' de dogs got 'em."

A groan went up from the disappointed souls of Mt. Pisgah. But the minister went on: "Whah 'd you hang dem?"

"Up ag'in de side o' de house."

"How 'd de dogs git 'em dah?"

"Mebbe it mout 'a' been cats."

"Why, why—'ca'se—'ca'se—Oh, don't questun me, man. I want you to know dat I's a honer'ble man."

"Jabez Holly," said the minister, impressively, "don't lie hyeah in de sanctua'y. I see 'possum grease on yo' mouf."

Jabez unconsciously gave his lips a wipe with his sleeve. "On my mouf, on my mouf!" he exclaimed. "Don't you say you see no 'possum grease on my mouf! I mek you prove it. I's a honer'ble man, I is. Don't you 'cuse me of nuffin'!"

Murmurs had begun to arise from the crowd, and they had begun to press in upon the accused.

"Don't crowd me!" he cried, his eyes bulging, for he saw in the faces about him the energy of attack which should have been directed against the 'possum all turned upon him. "I did n't eat yo' ol' 'possum, I do' lak 'possum nohow."

"Hang him," said some one, and the murmur rose louder as the culprit began to be hustled. But the preacher's voice rose above the storm.

"Ca'm yo'se'ves, my brethren," he said; "let us thank de Lawd dat one 'possum remains unto us. Brothah Holly has been put undah a gret temptation, an' we believe dat he has fell; but it is a jedgment. I ought to knowed bettah dan to 'a' trusted any colo'ed man wif fo' 'possums. Let us not be ha'd upon de sinnah. We mus' not be violent, but I tu'ns dis assembly into a chu'ch meetin' of de brothahs to set on Brothah Holly's case. In de mean time de sistahs will prepah de remainin' 'possum."

The church-meeting promptly found Brother Holly guilty of having betrayed his trust, and expelled him in disgrace from fellowship with Mt. Pisgah church.

The excellence of the one 'possum which the women prepared only fed their angry feelings, as it suggested what the whole four would have been; but the hungry men, women, and children who had foregone their Christmas dinners at home ate as cheerfully as possible, and when Mt. Pisgah's congregation went home that day, salt pork was in great demand to fill out the void left by the meagre fare of Christmas 'possum.

SIS' BECKY'S PICKANINNY*

By CHARLES W. CHESNUTT

WE HAD not lived in North Carolina very long before I was able to note a marked improvement in my wife's health. The ozone-laden air of the surrounding piney woods, the mild and equable climate, the peaceful leisure of country life, had brought about in hopeful measure the cure we had anticipated. Toward the end of our second year, however, her ailment took an unexpected turn for the worse. She becam the victim of a settled melancholy, attended with vague forebodings of impending misfortune.

"You must keep up her spirits," said our physician, the best in the neighboring town. "This melancholy lowers her tone too much, tends to lessen her strength, and, if it continues too long, may be fraught with grave consequences."

I tried various expedients to cheer her up. I read novels to her. I had the hands on the place come up in the evening and serenade her with plantation songs. Friends came in sometimes and talked, and frequent letters from the North kept her in touch with her former home. But nothing seemed to rouse her from the depression into which she had fallen.

One pleasant afternoon in spring, I placed an armchair in a shaded portion of the front piazza, and filling it with pillows led my wife out of the house and seated her where she would have the pleasantest view of a somewhat monotonous scenery. She was scarcely placed when old Julius came through the yard, and, taking off his tattered straw hat, inquired, somewhat anxiously:—

* Reprinted from *The Conjure Woman* by Charles W. Chesnutt with the permission of and by arrangement with Houghton Mifflin Company.

"How is you feelin' dis atternoon, m'am?"

"She is not very cheerful, Julius," I said. My wife was apparently without energy enough to speak for herself.

The old man did not seem inclined to go away, so I asked him to sit down. I had noticed, as he came up, that he held some small object in his hand. When he had taken his seat on the top step, he kept fingering this object, —what it was I could not quite make out.

"What is that you have there, Julius?" I asked, with mild curiosity.

"Dis is my rabbit foot, suh."

This was at a time before this curious superstition had attained its present jocular popularity among white people, and while I had heard of it before, it had not yet outgrown the charm of novelty.

"What do you do with it?"

"I kyars it wid me fer luck, suh."

"Julius," I observed, half to him and half to my wife, "your people will never rise in the world until they throw off these childish superstitions and learn to live by the light of reason and common sense. How absurd to imagine that the fore-foot of a poor dead rabbit, with which he timorously felt his way along through a life surrounded by snares and pitfalls, beset by enemies on every hand, can promote happiness or success, or ward off failure or misfortune!"

"It is ridiculous," assented my wife, with faint interest.

"Dat's w'at I tells dese niggers roun' heah," said Julius. "De fo'foot ain' got no power. It has ter be de hin'-foot, suh,—de lef' hin'-foot er a grabe-ya'd rabbit, kilt by a cross-eyed nigger on a da'k night in de full er de moon."

"They must be very rare and valuable," I said.

"Dey is kinder ska'ce, suh, en dey ain' no 'mount er money could buy mine, suh. I mought len' it ter anybody I sot sto' by, but I would n' sell it, no indeed, suh, I would n'."

"How do you know it brings good luck?" I asked.

"'Ca'se I ain' had no bad luck sence I had it, suh, en I's had dis rabbit foot fer fo'ty yeahs. I had a good marster befo' de wah, en I wa'n't sol' erway, en I wuz sot free; en dat 'uz all good luck."

"But that does n't prove anything," I rejoined. "Many other people have gone through a similar experience, and probably more than one of them had no rabbit's foot."

"Law, suh! you doan hafter prove 'bout de rabbit foot! Eve'ybody knows dat; leas'ways eve'ybody roun' heah knows it. But ef it has ter be prove' ter folks w'at wa'n't bawn en raise' in dis naberhood, dey is a' easy way ter prove it. Is I eber tol' you de tale er Sis' Becky en her pickaninny?"

"No," I said, "let us hear it." I thought perhaps the story might interest my wife as much or more than the novel I had meant to read from.

"Dis yer Becky," Julius began, "uster b'long ter ole Kunnel Pen'leton, who owned a plantation down on de Wim'l'ton Road, 'bout ten miles fum heah, des befo' you gits ter Black Swamp. Dis yer Becky wuz a fiel'-han', en a monst'us good 'un. She had a husban' oncet, a nigger w'at b'longed on de nex' plantation, but de man w'at owned her husban' died, en his lan' en his niggers had ter be sol' fer ter pay his debts. Kunnel Pen'leton 'lowed he 'd 'a' bought dis nigger, but he had be'n bettin' on hoss races, en did n' hab no money, en so Becky's husban' wuz sol' erway ter Fuhginny.

"Co'se Becky went on some 'bout losin' her man, but

she could n' he'p herse'f; en 'sides dat, she had her pickaninny fer ter comfo't her. Dis yer little Mose wuz de cutes', blackes', shiny-eyedes' little nigger you eber laid eyes on, en he wuz ez fon' er his mammy ez his mammy wuz er him. Co'se Becky had ter wuk en did n' hab much time ter was'e wid her baby. Ole Aun' Nancy, de plantation nuss down at de qua'ters, useter take keer er little Mose in de daytime, en atter de niggers come in fum de cotton-fiel' Becky 'ud git her chile en kiss 'im en nuss 'im, en keep 'im 'tel mawnin'; en on Sundays she'd hab 'im in her cabin wid her all day long.

"Sis' Becky had got sorter useter gittin' 'long widout her husban', w'en one day Kunnel Pen'leton went ter de races. Co'se w'en he went ter de races, he tuk his hosses, en co'se he bet on 'is own hosses, en co'se he los' his money; fer Kunnel Pen'leton did n' nebber hab no luck wid his hosses, ef he did keep hisse'f po' projeckin' wid 'em. But dis time dey wuz a hoss name' Lightnin' Bug, w'at b'longed ter ernudder man, en dis hoss won de sweepstakes; en Kunnel Pen'leton tuk a lackin' ter dat hoss, en ax' his owner w'at he wuz willin' ter take fer 'im.

" 'I'll take a thousan' dollahs fer dat hoss,' says dis yer man, who had a big plantation down to'ds Wim'l'ton, whar he raise' hosses fer ter race en ter sell.

"Well, Kunnel Pen'leton scratch' 'is head, en wonder whar he wuz gwine ter raise a thousan' dollahs; en he did n' see des how he could do it, fer he owed ez much ez he could borry a'ready on de skyo'ity he could gib. But he wuz des boun' ter hab dat hoss, so sezee:—

" 'I'll gib you my note fer 'leven hund'ed dollahs fer dat hoss.'

"De yuther man shuck 'is head, en sezee:—

" 'Yo' note, suh, is better 'n gol', I doan doubt; but I is made it a rule in my bizness not ter take no notes fum nobody. Howsomeber, suh, ef you is kinder sho't er fun's, mos' lackly we kin make some kin' er bahg'in. En w'iles we is talkin', I mought 's well sey dat I needs ernudder good nigger down on my place. Ef you is got a good one ter spar', I mought trade wid you.'

"Now Kunnel Pen'leton did n' r'ally hab no niggers fer ter spar', but he 'lowed ter hisse'f he wuz des bleedzd ter hab dat hoss, en so he sez, sezee:—

" 'Well, I doan lack ter, but I reckon I'll haf ter. You come out ter my plantation ter-morrow en look ober my niggers, en pick out de one you wants.'

"So sho' 'nuff nex' day dis yer man come out ter Kunnel Pen'leton's place en rid roun' de plantation en glanshed at de niggers, en who sh'd he pick out fum 'em all but Sis Becky.

" 'I needs a noo nigger 'oman down ter my place,' sezee, 'fer ter cook en wash, en so on; en dat young 'oman 'll des fill de bill. You gimme her, en you kin hab Lightnin' Bug.'

"Now, Kunnel Pen'leton did n' lack ter trade Sis' Becky, 'ca'se she wuz nigh 'bout de bes' fiel-han' he had; en' sides, Mars Kunnel did n' keer ter take de mammies 'way fum dey chillun w'iles de chillun wuz little. But dis man say he want Becky, er e'se Kunnel Pen'leton could n' hab de race hoss.

" 'Well,' sez de kunnel, 'you kin hab de 'oman. But I doan lack ter sen' her 'way fum her baby. W'at'll you gimme fer dat nigger baby?'

" 'I doan want de baby,' sez de yuther man. 'I ain' got no use fer de baby.'

" 'I tell yer w'at I'll do,' 'lows Kunnel Pen'leton, 'I'll th'ow dat pickaninny in fer good measure.'

"But de yuther man shuck his head. 'No,' sezee, 'I's much erbleedzd, but I doan raise niggers; I raise hosses, en

I doan wanter be both'rin' wid no nigger babies. Nemmine de baby. I'll keep dat 'oman so busy she'll fergit de baby; fer niggers is made ter wuk, en dey ain' got no time fer no sick foolis'ness ez babies.'

"Kunnel Pen'leton didn' wanter hu't Becky's feelin's, —fer Kunnel Pen'leton wuz a kin'-hea'ted man, en nebber lack' ter make no trouble fer nobody,—en so he tol' Becky he wuz gwine sen' her down ter Robeson County fer a day er so, ter he'p out his son-in-law in his wuk; en bein' ez dis yuther man wuz gwine dat way, he had ax' 'im ter take her 'long in his buggy.

" 'Kin I kyar little Mose wid me, marster?' ax' Sis' Becky.

" 'N-o,' sez de kunnel, ez ef he wuz studyin' whuther ter let her take 'im er no; 'I reckon you better let Aun' Nancy look atter yo' baby fer de day er two you'll be gone, en she 'll see dat he gits ernuff ter eat 'tel you gits back.'

"So Sis' Becky hug en kiss' little Mose, en tol' 'im ter be a good little pickaninny, en take keer er hisse'f, en not fergit his mammy w'iles she wuz gone. En little Mose put his arms roun' his mammy en lafft en crowed des lack it wuz monst'us fine fun fer his mammy ter go 'way en leabe 'im.

"Well, dis yer hoss trader sta'ted out wid Becky, en bimeby, atter dey 'd gone down de Lumbe'ton Road fer a few miles er so, dis man tu'nt roun' in a diffe'nt d'rection, en kep' goin' dat erway, 'tel bimeby Sis' Becky up 'n ax' 'im if he wuz gwine to Robeson County by a noo road.

" 'No, nigger,' sezee, "I ain' gwine ter Robeson County at all. I's gwine ter Bladen County, whar my plantation is, en whar I raises all my hosses.'

" 'But how is I gwine ter git ter Mis' Laura's plantation down in Robeson County?' sez Becky, wid her hea't in her mouf, fer she 'mence' to git skeered all er a sudden.

"'You ain' gwine ter git dere at all,' sez de man. 'You b'longs ter me now, fer I done traded my bes' race hoss fer you, wid yo' ole marster. Ef you is a good gal, I'll treat you right, en ef you doan behabe yo'se'f—w'y, w'at e'se happens 'll be yo' own fault.'

"Co'se Sis Becky cried en went on 'bout her pickaninny, but co'se it did n' do no good, en bimeby dey got down ter dis yer man's place, en he put Sis' Becky ter wuk, en fergot all 'bout her habin' a pickaninny.

"Meanw'iles, w'en ebenin' come, de day Sis' Becky wuz tuk 'way, little Mose, 'mence' ter git res'less, en bimeby, w'en his mammy did n' come, he sta'ted ter cry fer 'er. Aun' Nancy fed 'im en rocked 'im en rocked 'im, en fin'lly he des cried en cried 'tel he cried hisse'f ter sleep.

"De nex' day he did n' 'pear ter be as peart ez yushal, en w'en night come he fretted en went on wuss'n he did de night befo'. De nex' day his little eyes 'mence' ter lose dey shine, en he would n' eat nuffin, en he 'mence' ter look so peaked dat Aun' Nancy tuk 'n kyared 'im up ter de big house, en showed 'im ter her ole missis, en her ole missis gun her some med'cine fer 'im, en 'lowed ef he did n' git no better she sh'd fetch 'im up ter de big house ag'in, en dey'd hab a doctor, en nuss little Mose up dere. Fer Aun' Nancy's ole missis 'lowed he wuz a lackly little nigger en wu'th raisin'.

"But Aun' Nancy had l'arn' ter lack little Mose, en she did n' wanter hab 'im tuk up ter de big house. En so w'en he didn' git no better, she gethered a mess er green peas, and tuk de peas en de baby, en went ter see ole Aun' Peggy, de cunjuh 'oman down by the Wim'l'ton Road. She gun Aun' Peggy de mess er peas, en tol' her all 'bout Sis' Becky en little Mose.

" 'Dat is a monst'us small mess er peas you is fotch' me,' sez Aun' Peggy, sez she.

" 'Yas, I knows,' 'lowed Aun' Nancy, 'but dis yere is a monst'us small pickaninny.'

" 'You'll hafter fetch me sump'n mo',' sez Aun' Peggy, 'fer you can't 'spec' me ter was'e my time diggin' roots en wukkin' cunj'ation fer nuffin.'

" 'All right,' sez Aun' Nancy, 'I'll fetch you sump'n mo' nex' time.'

" 'You bettah,' sez Aun' Peggy, 'er e'se dey'll be trouble. W'at dis yer little pickaninny needs is ter see his mammy. You leabe 'im heah 'tel ebenin' en I'll show 'im his mammy.'

"So w'en Aun' Nancy had gone 'way, Aun' Peggy tuk 'n' wukked her roots, en tu'nt little Mose ter a hummin'-bird, en sont 'im off fer ter fin' his mammy.

"So little Mose flewed, en flewed, en flewed away, 'tel bimeby he got ter de place whar Sis' Becky b'longed. He seed his mammy wukkin' roun' de ya'd, en he could tell fum lookin' at her dat she wuz trouble' in her min' 'bout sump'n, en feelin' kin' er po'ly. Sis' Becky heard sump'n hummin' roun' en roun' her, sweet en low. Fus' she 'lowed it wuz a hummin'-bird; den she thought it sounded lack her little Mose croonin' on her breas' way back yander on de ole plantation. En she des 'magine' it wuz her little Mose, en it made her feel bettah, en she went on 'bout her wuk pearter 'n she'd done sence she'd be'n down dere. Little Mose stayed roun' 'tel late in de ebenin', en den flewed back ez hard ez he could ter Aun' Peggy. Ez fer Sis' Becky, she dremp all dat night dat she wuz holdin' her pickaninny in her arms, en kissin' him, en nussin' him, des lack she useter do back on de ole plantation whar he wuz bawn. En fer th'ee er fo' days Sis' Becky went 'bout her wuk wid mo' sperrit dan she 'd showed sence she 'd be'n down dere ter dis man's plantation.

"De nex' day atter he come back, little Mose wuz mo' pearter en better 'n he had be'n fer a long time. But to'ds de een' er de wek he 'mence' ter git res'less ag'in, en stop' eatin', so Aun' Nancy kyared 'im down ter Aun' Peggy once mo', en she tun't 'im ter a mawkin'-bird dis time, en sont 'im off ter see his mammy ag'in.

"It did n' take him long fer ter git dere, en w'en he did, he seed his mammy standin' in de kitchen, lookin' back in de d'rection little Mose wuz comin' fum. En dey wuz tears in her eyes, en she look' mo' po'ly en peaked 'n she had w'en he wuz down dere befo'. So little Mose sot on a tree in de ya'd en sung, en sung, en sung, des fittin' ter split his th'oat. Fus' Sis' Becky did n' notice 'im much, but dis mawkin'-bird kep' stayin' roun' de house all day, en bimeby Sis' Becky des 'magine' dat mawkin'-bird wuz her little Mose crowin' en crowin', des lack he useter do w'en his mammy would come home at night fum de cotton-fiel'. De mawkin'-bird stayed roun' dere' mos' all day, en w'en Sis' Becky went out in de ya'd one time, dis yer mawkin'-bird lit on her shoulder en peck' at de piece er bread she wuz eatin', en fluttered his wings so dey rub-up agin de side er her head. En w'en he flewed away 'long late in de ebenin', 'fo' sundown, Sis' Becky felt mo' better 'n she had sence she had heared dat hummin'-bird a week er so pas'. En dat night she dremp 'bout ole times ag'in, des lack she did befo'.

"But dis yer totin' little Mose down ter ole Aun' Peggy, en dis yer gittin' things fer ter pay de cunjuh 'oman, use' up a lot er Aun' Nancy's time, en she begun ter git kinder ti'ed. 'Sides dat, w'en Sis' Becky had be'n on de plantation, she had useter he'p Aun' Nancy wid de young uns ebenin's en Sundays; en Aun' Nancy 'mence' ter miss er monst'us, 'speshly sence she got a tech er de rheumatiz herse'f, en so she 'lows ter ole Aun' Peggy one day:—

" 'Aun' Peggy, ain' dey no way you kin fetch Sis' Becky back home?'

" 'Huh!' sez Aun' Peggy, 'I dunno 'bout dat. I'll hafter wuk my roots en fin' out whuther I kin er no. But it 'll take a monst'us heap er wuk, en I can't was'e my time fer nuffin. Ef you'll fetch me sump'n ter pay me fer my trouble, I reckon we kin fix it.'

"So nex' day Aun' Nancy went down ter see Aun' Peggy ag'in.

" 'Aun' Peggy,' sez she, 'I is fotch' you my bes' Sunday head-hankercher. Will dat do?'

"Aun' Peggy look' at de head-hankercher, en run her han' ober it, en sez she:—

" 'Yas, dat'll do fus'-rate. I's be'n wukkin' my roots sence you be'n gone, en I 'lows mos' lackly I kin git Sis' Becky back, but it's gwine take fig'rin' en studyin' ez well es cunj'in'. De fus' thing ter do'll be ter stop fetchin' dat pickaninny down heah, en not sen' 'im ter see his mammy no mo'. Ef he gits too po'ly, you lemme know, en I'll gib you some kin' er mixtry fer ter make 'im fergit Sis' Becky fer a week er so. So 'less'n you comes fer dat, you neenter come back ter see me no mo' 'tel I sen's fer you.'

"So Aun' Peggy sont Aun' Nancy erway, en de fus' thing she done wuz ter call a hawnet fum a nes' unner her eaves.

" 'You go up ter Kunnel Pen'leton's stable, hawnet,' sez she, 'en sting de knees er de race hoss name' Lightnin' Bug. Be sho 'en git de right one.'

"So de hawnet flewed up ter Kunnel Pen'leton's stable en stung Lightnin' Bug roun' de laigs, en de nex' mawnin' Lightnin' Bug's knees wuz all swoll' up, twice't ez big ez dey oughter be. W'en Kunnel Pen'leton went out ter de stable en se de hoss's laigs, hit would 'a' des made you trimble lack a leaf fer ter heah him cuss dat hoss trader. Howsomeber, he cool' off bimeby en tol' de stable boy fer ter rub Lightnin' Bug's laigs wid some linimum. De boy done ez his marster tol' 'im, en by de nex' day de swellin' had gone down consid'able. Aun' Peggy had sont a sparrer, w'at had a nes' in one er de trees close ter her cabin, fer ter watch w'at wuz gwine on 'roun' de big house, en w'en dis yer sparrer tol' 'er de hoss wuz gittin' ober de swellin', she sont de hawnet back fer ter sting 'is knees some mo', en de nex' mawnin' Lightnin' Bug's laigs wuz swoll' up wuss'n befo'.

"Well, dis time Kunnel Pen'leton wuz mad th'oo en th'oo, en all de way 'roun', en he cusst dat hoss trader up en down, fum *A* ter *Izzard*. He cusst so ha'd dat de stable boy got mos' skeered ter def, en went off en hid hisse'f in de hay.

"Ez fer Kunnel Pen'leton, he went right up ter de house en got out his pen en ink, en tuk off his coat en roll' up his sleeves, en write a letter ter dis yer hoss trader, en sezee:—

" 'You is sol' me a hoss w'at is got a ringbone er a spavin er sump'n, en w'at I paid you fer wuz a soun' hoss. I wants you ter sen' my nigger 'oman back en take yo' ole hoss, er e'se I'll sue you, sho's you bawn.'

"But dis yer man wa'n't skeered a bit, en he writ back ter Kunnel Pen'leton dat a bahg'in wuz a bahg'in; dat Lightnin' Bug wuz soun' w'en he sol' 'im, en ef Kunnel Pen'leton did n' knowed ernuff, 'bout hosses ter take keer er a fine racer, dat wuz his own fune'al. En he say Kunnel Pen'leton kin sue en be cusst fer all he keer, but he ain' gwine ter gib up de nigger he bought en paid fer.

"W'en Kunnel Pen'leton got dis letter he wuz madder'n he wuz befo', 'speshly 'ca'se dis man 'lowed he did n' know how ter take keer er fine hosses. But he could n' do nuffin but fetch a lawsuit, en he knowed, by his own 'spe'ience, dat lawsuits wuz slow ez de seben-yeah eetch and cos' mo' d'n dey come ter, en he 'lowed he better go slow en wait awhile.

"Aun' Peggy knowed w'at wuz gwine on all dis time, en she fix' up a little bag wid some roots en one thing en ernudder in it, en gun it ter dis sparrer er her'n, en tol' 'im ter take it 'way down yander whar Sis' Becky wuz, en drap it right befo' de do' er her cabin, so she'd be sho' en fin' it de fus' time she come out'n de do'.

"One night Sis' Becky dremp' her pickaninny wuz dead, en de nex' day she wuz mo'nin' en groanin' all day. She dremp' de same dream th'ee nights runnin', en den, de nex' mawnin' atter de las' night, she foun' dis yer little bag de sparrer had drap' in front her do'; en she 'lowed she'd be'n cunju'd, en wuz gwine ter die, en ez long ez her pickaninny wuz dead dey wa'n't no use tryin' ter do nuffin nohow. En so she tuk 'n went ter bed, en tol' her marster she 'd be'n cunju'd en wuz gwine ter die.

"Her marster lafft at her, en argyed wid her, en tried ter 'suade her out'n dis yer fool notion, ez he called it,—fer he wuz one er dese yer w'ite folks w'at purten' dey doan b'lieve in cunj'in',—but hit wa'n't no use. Sis' Becky kep' gittin' wusser en wusser, 'tel fin'lly dis yer man 'lowed Sis' Becky wuz gwine die, sho'nuff. En ez he knowed dey had n' be'n nuffin de matter wid Lightnin' Bug w'en he traded 'im, he 'lowed mebbe he could kyo' 'im en fetch 'im roun' all right, leas'ways good 'nuff ter sell ag'in. En anyhow, a lame hoss wuz better 'n a dead nigger. So he sot down en writ Kunnel Pen'leton a letter.

" 'My conscience,' sezee, 'has be'n troublin' me 'bout dat ringbone' hoss I sol' you. Some folks 'lows a hoss trader ain' got no conscience, but dey doan know me, fer dat is my weak spot, en de reason I ain' made no mo' money hoss tradin'. Fac' is,' sezee, 'I is got so I can't sleep nights fum studyin' 'bout dat spavin' hoss; en I is made up my min' dat, w'iles a bahg'in is a bahg'in, en you seed Lightnin' Bug befo' you traded fer 'im, principle is wuth mo' d'n money er hosses er niggers. So ef you 'll sen' Lightnin' Bug down heah, I'll sen' you' nigger 'oman back, en we' ll call de trade off, en be ez good frien's ez we eber wuz, en no ha'd feelin's.'

"So sho' nuff, Kunnel Pen'leton sont de hoss back. En w'en de man w'at come ter bring Lightnin' Bug tol' Sis Becky her pickaninny wa'n't dead, Sis' Becky wuz so glad dat she 'lowed she wuz gwine ter try ter lib 'tel she got back whar she could see little Mose once mo'. En w'en she retch' de ole plantation en seed her baby kickin' en crowin' en holdin' out his little arms to'ds her, she wush' she wuz n' conju'd en did n' hafter die. En w'en Aun' Nancy tol' 'er all' bout Aun' Peggy, Sis Becky went down ter see de cunjah 'oman, en Aun' Peggy tol' her she had conju'd her. En den Aun' Peggy tuk de goopher off'n her, en she got well, en stayed on de plantation, en raise' her pickaninny. En w'en little Mose growed up, he could sing en whistle des lack a mawkin'-bird, so dar de w'ite folks useter hab 'im come up ter de big house at night, en whistle en sing fer 'im, en dey useter gib 'im money en vittles en one thing er ernudder, w'ich he alluz tuk home ter his mammy; fer he knowed all, 'bout w'at she had gone th'oo. He tu'nt out ter be a sma't man, en l'arnt de blacksmif trade; en Kunnel Pen'leton let 'im hire his time. En bimeby he bought his mammy en sot her free, en den he bought hisse'f, en tuk keer er Sis' Becky ez long ez dey bofe libbed."

My wife had listened to this story with greater interest

than she had manifested in any subject for several days. I had watched her furtively from time to time during the recital, and had observed the play of her countenance. It had expressed in turn sympathy, indignation, pity, and at the end lively satisfaction.

"That is a very ingenious fairy tale, Julius," I said, "and we are much obliged to you."

"Why, John!" said my wife severely, "the story bears the stamp of truth, if ever a story did."

"Yes," I replied, "especially the humming-bird episode, and the mocking-bird digression, to say nothing of the doings of the hornet and the sparrow."

"Oh, well, I don't care," she rejoined, with delightful animation; "those are mere ornamental details and not at all essential. The story is true to nature, and might have happened half a hundred times, and no doubt did happen, in those horrid days before the war."

"By the way, Julius," I remarked, "your story does n't establish what you started out to prove,—that a rabbit's foot brings good luck."

"Hit's plain 'nuff ter me, suh," replied Julius. "I bet young missis dere kin 'splain it herse'f."

"I rather suspect," replied my wife promptly, "that Sis' Becky had no rabbit's foot."

"You is hit de bull's-eye de fus' fire, ma'm," assented Julius. "Ef Sis' Becky had had a rabbit foot, she nebber would 'a' went th'oo all dis trouble."

I went into the house for some purpose, and left Julius talking to my wife. When I came back a moment later he was gone.

My wife's condition took a turn for the better from this very day, and she was soon on the way to ultimate recovery. Several weeks later, after she had resumed her afternoon drives, which had been interrupted by her illness, Julius brought the rockaway round to the front door one day, and I assisted my wife into the carriage.

"John," she said, before I had taken my seat, "I wish you would look in my room, and bring me my handkerchief. You will find it in the pocket of my blue dress."

I went to execute the commission. When I pulled the handkerchief out of her pocket, something else came with it and fell on the floor. I picked up the object and looked at it. It was Julius's rabbit's foot.

A RIEVER OF THE BLACK BORDER*

By AMBROSE E. GONZALES

MONDAY PARKER and his brothers and sisters—a large family—were all intelligent and capable, inheriting these qualities from their mother, Maum Pender—an unusual name, and a Negro of unusual ability, tall and slender, with small and well-shaped hands and feet, high aquiline nose, thin lips, and distinguished carriage. Maum Pender transmitted the shapeliness of her hands and feet, with their tapering fingers and arched insteps, to all her offspring, and the gift of slender fingers made them famous cotton-pickers. But, in respect to husbands, Pender having been as comprehensive as a Smart-Set New Yorker of the present day, her prepotency did not impress her aquiline nose upon more than half her quiver-full, and as Monday had been sired by one of his mother's flatnosed affiliations, no nasal promontory jutted forth to break the broad expanse of his flat, good-natured face.

Monday walked rapidly, with long springy steps, and swung his arms in exaggerated fashion, perhaps through pride in his ancestry, for he claimed descent from an African king—a "Foulah" he said; but as the Foulahs, an intelligent people, are tawny in color, while the members of Monday's clan were all of a rich, shiny, brownish black, it is probable that the Foulah tradition, stuck in the memory of some breech-clouted captive from the West Coast, was no better authenticated than some of the Mayflower pedigrees that have stretched so many masculine hatbands and swelled so many feminine corsages throughout the North and West!

* Reprinted from *The Captain* by Ambrose E. Gonzales with the courteous permission of the publishers, The State Company.

But whether of Foulah, Gullah, or Mandingo blood, it is certain that Monday's ancestral arms must have borne a boar—a boar not rampant, but quiescent, a boar singed or scalded and hung by the heels, for Monday's instinct for the cloven-footed quadruped forbidden to the children of Israel was as that of the rill for the river, the river for the sea! As he padded noiselessly through the woods forbidden to poachers or prowlers his ears were always pricked for squeal or squeak or grunt—the sweetest music that could come to them—and Monday knew how to interpret their faintest inflection—fear, hope, hunger, satiety, were all expressed as the half-wild shoats foraged through the woods, nosing about under the oaks for the fallen acorns, or rooting in the swampy places for grubs or snails, and if their voices seemed sympathetic, indicating mental serenity, Monday would utter a soft, crooning swine-herd's call, "*peeg, peeg, peeg.*"

Repeating this at intervals as they neared him with furtive steps and questioning grunts, he would throw wide a handful of corn from his knapsack, then other handfuls nearer and yet nearer, until he had tolled them to his very feet. By now, Monday would have dropped his axe to the ground and his appraising eye would have fixed upon the fattest shoat in the bunch, which by the abundance of his largesse he patiently coaxed into his confidence. When the intended victim had been skilfully maneuvered into position for vicarious sacrifice, with his tail toward the slaughterer, Monday would stoop as swiftly as a hawk from the blue, seize the animal by a hind leg and throw him, when a blow between the eyes from the ready axe, and the knife slipped into his throat, silenced all but the poor pig's first squeal of protest at the betrayal of his confidence.

As the squeal never reached the ears of "de Buckruh" —for two-legged marauders seldom adventured within a mile of the farmstead—Monday was safe, and slipping his prize into a sack cached it in some convenient thicket near his cabin until nightfall should make its butchery reasonably safe. If the shoat were but a small one, he kept its theft to himself, for its scalding and dressing could be contrived within the privacy of his own cabin, and, needing no help, he took none into his confidence; but for the more ambitious captures, his cronies were called in. If any among these had pigs of his own, and if the weather were cool enough to avert suspicion, the matter was simple, for the pig owner boldly boiled the water on his own premises, and those who passed by believed him to be preparing the product of his own pen; but if none among the Free Companions could thus offer justification for the possession of pork, or if the weather were too warm to make lawful butchery reasonable, the confederates would slip a large iron pot into a sack, build a fire near some woodland branch or spring, scald and dress the porcine carcass, and divide the meat.

In this brotherhood of the frying-pan his cronies sometimes shared with Monday such spoils as they were able to lift from the pens, the kraals, or the wide pastures of the palefaces, but their contributions to the common good were negligible compared with those of one whose attainments had exalted him among his fellows as Rob Roy was exalted among the cattle-rievers of the Scottish border, or King Arthur among the Knights of the Table Round!

Nor among these lowly jungle folk was a Prophet without honor, nor was a lifter's prowess denied cordial, even generous recognition.

"Paa'kuh, him sho' hab uh giftid han' fuh ketch hog."

"Yaas, man, you talk trute. Him ketch'um en' 'e hol'um alltwo. W'en Gawd mek Buh Monday, Him sho' g'em uh fait'ful han' fuh hol' hog! Ef Buh Monday ebbuh graff hog by 'e hine foot! da' hog done mek up 'e min' fuh dead! 'E nebbuh fuh loose'um 'tel t'unduh roll!"

While Monday, fond of the sound of his own voice, was gregariously inclined during his working hours, and dearly loved the gatherings at the Cross-roads store on pay days or Saturday nights, he was seldom willing to live on a plantation street, preferring the privacy of an isolated cabin some distance away from the "quarters" or "Negro-house-yard." By thus "keeping his distance," Monday not only kept his chickens and his children from mixing too indiscriminately with those of his brothers in black, but these brothers in black, together with the sisters thereunto appertaining—all of them inclined to be inquisitive, if not inquisitorial—were prevented from knowing too much about Monday's business; and as long as Monday's business was light, whenever the stolen shoats were small enough to be scalded without help, Monday adhered to a Lodge-like policy of isolation, greasing his own jowls though all those about him were dry, and only when confronted with an animal too heavy to be handled alone, did he impose upon himself entangling alliances, carrying as they did the obligation to divide the spoils.

In a certain autumn, the plantation pig crop had been unusually good, and, as the mast crop, too, was very abundant, there was promise of a full smokehouse by the end of the winter, for in the wild pastures of the Low-Country shoats are turned out in the fall to forage for acorns, pig-nuts, and haws, and when these are plentiful the porkers need little other food. So, before the first light frost of October, the ground under live-oak, water-oak and Spanish-oak was covered with fallen acorns, while the heavy boughs of white-oak and chestnut-oak were loaded with the big "overcups" that would fall with the coming of the cold nights. Everywhere in the woods there was both promise and fulfillment, and the porkers throve amazingly.

The Captain rode the woods almost daily, and, while looking for deer-tracks, was not unmindful of other cloven hoof-prints that mingled with those of wildcat, fox, and raccoon in the soft mud of the swampy places. The Captain was observant, and one day he noticed among the pig-tracks leading into the "seven-acre" field the impression of a plantation brogan—a number six, an extraordinarily small shoe for a Negro—and the Captain knew the shoe for Monday's and knew at once what had become of three or four fine shoats that had, one by one, failed to respond to the far-flung "*whoop-ee*" at the plantation round-up in the forest, whither they were called by the master's voice every two or three days to be counted and inspected, as they squealed and scuffled for the ears of nubbin corn thrown among them.

The Captain rode without pencil or paper, but the Captain was resourceful and, dismounting, he picked up a handful of the richly colored brown needles of the great long-leaf pines. They were of different lengths, but he sorted them over until he found a cluster that exactly measured the length of the footprint. Breaking another off to cover the width of the shoe at its greatest breadth, the Captain carefully put his evidence in his pocket, mounted his horse, and rode away.

The next morning, finding occasion to put Monday at some ditching near the pond, the Captain watched until the ditcher had made plain tracks in the mud, and then, sending him to the lot for a shovel, pulled out the pine needles and proved by length and breadth that the pig thief of seven-acre had worn Monday's shoes!

With such convincing evidence against him, Monday, if tried by a jury of white men, would have spent two years in the State penitentiary at Columbia; but Monday was a good hand and, if committed to the law, the plantation would lose his labor and, at the same time, be charged with the responsibility for the maintenance of his young and dependent family. On the other hand, Monday's absence from the stock-range would undoubtedly result in a large increase in the four-legged population—so, as to economics, 'twas a stand-off whether Monday stayed or went; but the Captain, a kindly man, had withal a sneaking fondness for the former slave, whose frailties he knew so well, and for which he had so often made allowances. Instead of having him arrested, therefore, he resolved upon a punishment so unusual, so subtle in its psychology, so exquisite in its mental torture, that its conception was worthy of Machiavelli himself! The Captain determined to commit the lamb to the watchful care of the wolf, the grunting herd to the custody of the most expert smotherer of grunts in St. Paul's Parish; in short, to make Monday the plantation pig-minder!

"Great Gawd, Mas' Rafe!" Monday groaned, "Wuh de—! yuh de debble now! Mas' Rafe, you duh fun, enty? Put *me* fuh min' *hog!*"

"Yes, Monday, you know every hog-track in the woods and every hog-thief in the Parish. Of course you never stole one, Monday, but if you ever had you would know how it was done, and you would be the thief set to catch a thief; but, as you never stole hogs in your life, I know I can trust you to keep others from stealing those under your charge."

"Great Gawd!" and Monday threw his black wool hat on the ground and looked at it long and silently.

"Mas' Rafe, w'en you wan' me fuh tek chaa'ge?"

"Right away, today."

"Great Gawd! Mas' Rafe, enty Chris-mus come een t'ree week?"

"Yes, but what has that to do with it?"

Monday chuckled shamefacedly and looked down with shaking shoulders, while he scratched the thick nap of his woolly head slowly and reflectively. When at last he looked up quickly and cheerfully, his "berrywellden, suh," told the Captain that Monday had bethought him of how to come by his Christmas pork unlawfully without violating the trust but now so rudely imposed upon him!

The news of Monday's elevation, which he had resisted with less success but far more sincerity than Caesar put away the crown upon the Lupercal, bore heavily upon the dusky band whose war-cry was a squeal and whose password was a grunt. Believing that Monday's guardianship would be taken in a Pickwickian sense, they hoped the way would still be open to the herd, and they proceeded to sound the keeper of the portcullis.

"Paa'kuh, Mas' Rafe sho' mek you fuh rich. Him pit de hog een you han'! You jaw gwine greesy fuh true."

"Rich de debble! Hukkuh Mas' Rafe fuh mek me rich? Him pit de hog een me han' fuh true, but wuh use fuh pit hog een you han' w'en alltwo you han' tie? W'en Mas' Rafe mek' me 'sponsubble fuh dem hog him tie me han' en' me foot alltwo sukkuh hog tie! Him count ebb'ry Gawd hog on de place en' pit'um onduh my 't'oruthy. Him know berrywell suh me, 'self ent able fuh t'ief'um, en' him know same time suh none you t'odduh Nigguh ent fuh t'ief'um. Yuh de debble now! Me haffuh look 'puntop dem hog ebb'ry day, en' shum git mo' fattuh 'tel dem tail quite tight 'puntop dem back sukkuh snake quile. Man! W'en Uh look 'puntop dem barruh en' yeddy'um grunt, me h'aa't hebby en' watuh run out me mout'! Mas' Rafe! Mas' Rafe schemy *tummuch!*"

The Free Companions, convinced that their former chief would be forced, for a time at least, to live up to his responsibilities, exchanged knowing glances and dispersed, intending to meet again and lay plans for the spoliation of some "po'-buckruh' " pasture across the railway toward Caw-Caw Swamp. Realizing that the Captain had hamstrung Monday to the disadvantage of the hunting pack, his compatriots did not take him into their confidence, but decided to leave him to bear, without their spiritual support, his Tantalus task.

For two weeks Monday walked the woods and watched with heavy heart the fattening drove whose every grunt brought anguish to his soul. And as he walked, his busy thoughts pictured every band or litter whose range he knew lay beyond the borders of the plantation, for from among these, whether owned by poor-white or thrifty black, his Christmas pork must come, if it came at all.

At last "one fine day," when the holiday to which the Negroes look forward so ardently was almost upon him, Monday recalled having seen early in the fall a bunch of half-grown shoats foraging for new-fallen acorns under the heavy water-oaks that fringed the far side of the Cypress swamp, almost at the boundary of the plantation. Monday remembered them for their rich auburn color and knew them as the property of a well-to-do Negro who rented and maintained a comfortable little farmstead at Moss Hill. So to the belt of oaks Monday made his way, and, as he entered the timber the rustling of the dead leaves and the low grunts of the feeding pigs told him that he had found that for which he was looking. Before they came in sight, however, he uttered softly his coaxing call, hoping to establish an *entente*, but the frightened "*goof, goof,*" and the scurrying feet of the shoats as they hurried away, told him as plainly as sound can tell that the wary creatures had recognized the voice of their hereditary enemy, and, realizing that, as the imminence of Christmas would not allow him time to establish friendly relations and capture his quarry by direct attack, he would have to resort to strategy, he swiftly laid his plans.

Monday resolved to build a trap! As a preliminary, he scattered under the oaks a few handfuls of corn from his well-filled knapsack, and laid a thin trail of grain to a point in the thicker woods nearby, where he intended making his capture. The pig-lifters among the Negroes of the Low-Country often catch their game in log-traps, simple pens eight or ten feet square and five feet high, made of pine saplings and fitted with a suspended door sliding in grooves and released by a cord when the animals, feeding upon the bait spread within the trap, touch the trigger to which it is attached. Similar devices are often used for taking wild turkeys, and sometimes an entire flock is captured in a single bag.

Had Monday been hunting in company and needed a large haul, he would have built a pen, but as the Knights of the Round Table would assemble at another board at which swineherds would, by the nature of their calling, be unwelcome guests, Monday knew that if he would feast at all he must feast alone; so, to supply his small needs, he determined upon a deadfall as an effective device requiring a minimum of labor. His first concern was to get his intended captives used to the instrument with which he intended to rob them at once of life, liberty, and the pursuit of happiness.

Selecting a comparatively open spot, Monday with ready axe cut two forked hardwood saplings about eight feet long, and sharpened the lower ends which, after first loosening the soil with the blade of his axe, he rammed into the ground as far as he could and packed the earth about their bases. These uprights were set about five feet apart and, resting in their forked tops seven feet above the ground, a pole was laid. Having rigged up his rustic horizontal bar that looked like a miniature football goal post, Monday cut near at hand a heavy log twelve feet long, which taxed all his strength and skill to maneuver into position at right angles to the goal post. With the aid of a stout forked pole he raised the heavy end of his log to the top of the bar, upon which it rested securely. The deadfall was now almost complete, lacking only a trigger, and Monday, well pleased with his day's work, scattered corn freely about the little glade and went his ways.

On the following morning and again on the second day, the hunter returned to the Cypress to find that all the scattered corn had been eaten and that the unsuspecting shoats had rooted freely under and around the trap. On successive days, he threw wide his seductive bait under the oaks and laid his train from the oaks to the little glade where the grain was strewn with a heavy hand.

Christmas eve broke clear and cold. The roads were frozen iron hard, the water left by the recent rains in the wheel ruts and in the tracks of horses and cattle had turned to ice, and frost crystals burst from the sides of the damp ditches along the way. Monday, engaged in the preparation of the plantation bacon until a late hour on the preceding night, was not astir until toward noon, and the sun was well in the west before he set out for his private hunting-ground. Here he at once began his preparations to put teeth into the hitherto harmless trap, to which his intended quarry had now become accustomed. First bringing his log to earth with the aid of his forked pole, he beveled with his sharp axe one side of the heavy end, and when this had been smoothed to his satisfaction he rubbed the polished surface with a piece of bacon rind and hoisted it again into position upon the bar, with the beveled side downward, carefully propping it up with his forked pole for additional support until he could adjust his "trigger," a narrow piece of plank, beveled at one end, which he had prepared in advance and brought with him. Scraping out a shallow hole in the ground directly under the heavier end of the log, he filled it with corn, and in the grain he set the lower end of the trigger, while the smooth upper end was fitted snugly against the greased surface of the heavy timber with such nicety that the slightest jar against the lower end would spring the trap and release the lethal log upon the pigs that fed below. Then, once more he laid his trail of corn from the trap to the oaks and, scattering the grain that remained, he returned to his cabin.

An hour after dark, when Venus blazed in the west and the young moon, a golden proa with upturned ends, rode on an even keel nearby, Monday slipped away by woodland paths to his trap, and was rewarded by finding under his deadfall a tawny sixty pound shoat which the heavy log, falling on his spine, must have killed instantly. Removing the log, Monday put his pig into a sack and, upon reaching home, came to his cabin from the rear. In response to a stealthy tap, his window was opened from within, and through the narrow aperture he first thrust his sack and then pulled himself. His children were abed, but his trusty wife, Hannah, having implicit faith in the prowess of her lord, had kept the home fires burning under a large caldron of water. The auburn shoat was soon scalded, scraped, and dressed, and the pork was carefully concealed in the cabin loft. Then Monday crept out and threw the handful of red hair far over the fence among the gallberry bushes.

On Christmas day, Monday's jaws, like those of all who called his roof their own, glistened with fatness, and throughout the three-day holiday the comforting sizzling of the frying-pan told those who passed his cabin that Monday's family "fared sumptuously every day."

At last his sometime hunting companions, becoming suspicious, questioned the swineherd, who proudly displayed a pork shoulder that had been given him by the master of the plantation on Christmas eve. From this shoulder only a few slices had been cut, but Monday shrewdly used these as justification for the almost incessant frying within his habitation.

"Paa'kuh, you mout' sho' greesy dis Chris'mus!"

"Yaas, man, me jaw greesy fuh true. Enty you see da' hebby gham wuh Mas' Rafe gimme fuh Chris'mus? Him gimme dat 'cause Uh min' him hog so good 'en keep oonuh Nigguh' mout' off'um."

"Yaas, Uh yeddy 'bout da' gham, en' Uh yeddy de Lawd' wu'd wuh de sukkus preachuh resplain 'bout how Jedus, Him tek da' string uh fish en' dem t'ree loaf uh bread en' feed 'leb'm t'ous'n man 'tel dem hongry done gone, but 'e tek Jedus fuh do da' t'ing. *Nigguh* ent fuh do'um!"

A few days later, one of the Free Companions, passing through the gallberry thicket near Monday's cabin, saw a wad of auburn hair and a great light, for he remembered the ruddy band from Moss Hill, and knew that Monday, holding inviolate the plantation drove committed to his care, had deserted his quondam associates and hunted successfully far afield!

"Paa'kuh! Paa'kuh smaa't *tummuch!* W'enebbuh Paa'kuh' jaw greesy, w'edduh de hog red, uh w'edduh 'e black, w'edduh 'e stan' close uh fudduh, *somebody' hog done dead!*"

GREEN THURSDAY*

By JULIA PETERKIN

THE DAY was bright and hot. Cotton and cornfields glittered green. Dancing, quivering heat waves blurred the distant woods and cabins.

Killdee could not see a single soul anywhere. He was the only man working to-day. Green Thursday.

Slowly, steadily, patiently, he walked behind his plow. Up and down the long rows. Back and forth. Thinking. Reasoning with himself. Was he right or wrong to work to-day? The day Jesus went back to heaven.

He watched indifferently the spurts of red dust that rose with each step his mule took. The ground was dry. Baked. Parched. The stiff clay broke into clods as the plow's edge cut through its rigid crust. The lumps of earth that fell awkwardly away from each other were fettered with tough, jointed grass. Tense grass roots had burrowed deep. They had wound a strong net to choke and strangle the crop. They were sucking all the moisture out of the ground. They were eating all the fertilizer. They'd leave nothing but starvation for the cotton and corn.

The grass had to be killed. Every root must be torn up and cut. Every green blade must be turned under and buried.

The sun stood blinding white straight overhead. The sun was a friend in the fight against the grass. Its heat to-day would kill every root that was cut.

The long shadow that had started out traveling beside him early this morning had shortened and darkened until now it crept small and black right under his feet.

* Reprinted from *Green Thursday* by Julia Peterkin by and with permission of and special arrangement with Alfred A. Knopf, Inc., authorized publishers.

It seemed to be trying to hide from the sun. It must be near noon. Time for Mike and himself to stop and eat and drink and rest.

With a low-spoken "Whoa, Mike," he reined in the tall, bony beast that he had plowed and cast a swift glance up at the sun. Yes, it was noon. He could tell, although the sun's brilliance clouded his vision.

"Le's go home, Mike," he said, and he stuck the plow's point deep into the earth to stand alone until noon was over.

The loosened joints of the old plow stock creaked with the strain and reminded him to be careful how he wrenched them. They were giving out in the hard fight with the grass. If they came apart, broken, no good, he had no money to buy new ones. He must remember to be easy with them.

He unhooked the trace chains from the singletree and tossed them over Mike's back. As he slipped the frayed rope lines through the rings in the bit, Mike's rib-marked hide swelled with a grateful sigh. Mike's long, shaggy neck stretched and his cloudy eyes closed as he gave a long whicker of approval.

Killdee laughed. His strong white teeth gleamed through the soft sparse beard that covered his mouth and chin as he murmured:

"You hongry, enty, Mike? I is too. Come on. Le's go home. You got sense like people, son."

He smoothed the rough hair on the hollowed back and stroked the haggard neck while Mike nibbled at grass in the furrow ahead.

When Killdee started across the uneven ground toward the line of woods where a tiny, drab-colored cabin showed dim in the smoky distance, Mike stopped eating and followed him.

Killdee scanned the quiet fields. Not a soul was in sight. He and Mike seemed to be the only living things in the world to-day.

Small cabins scattered at intervals over the landscape showed no sign of life at all. Narrow red roads that ran by them were empty. Idle. The day itself was still. Stiller than Sunday. Green Thursday. Ascension day. The day Jesus went back to God.

Maybe it was a holier day than Sunday.

All Killdee's life he had heard that to stir the earth on Green Thursday was a deadly sin. Fields plowed, or even hoed to-day would be struck by lightning and killed so they couldn't bear life again. God would send fire down from heaven to punish men who didn't respect this day. Yet here he and Mike were plowing. Risking the wrath of the great I-am.

Everybody else on the whole plantation had gone fishing in the river swamp. Dry weather made the fish bite fast. Rose would have been trying her luck too if she had been able to walk so far. But it was near time now for her to "go down." She wouldn't risk walking so far from home.

Rose asked him to hitch Mike to the wagon and take her and baby Rose to fish for a while. Meat was mighty scarce and when a woman is pregnant, fish bite better for her than for anybody else. Rose wanted to go and try them. She wanted to go even if the crop was eaten up with grass. She was worried and hurt right now because he and Mike were out in the field plowing.

Last night he lay awake and thought it all over. He made up his mind. He would fight the grass this year to the end. He would make a crop. God ought to know Rose hadn't been able to hoe a lick since the crop was planted. And how old and slow Mike was! Mike couldn't step fast like the grass. He never had plowed on Green Thursday before. Never. But this year he was too far behind to miss a day. God ought to know how it was.

Clear drops of sweat trickled down Mike's thin flanks and down Kildee's lean black face. Kildee's faded patched shirt was blotched with wetness. It clung to his shoulders and outlined his strong, straight back. Its unbuttoned, opened neck let the hot breeze reach his big throat and breast.

Ragged overalls turned high at the bottom slouched along with each step he took and laid open their torn places for the sun to shine through on the firm black flesh of his narrow hips and sinewy legs.

He stopped where a path divided. Instead of going straight home, he took the path that dropped down the steep hill behind it.

The trees made a cool, dark shade. Leaves fluttered and let bits of white light fall on the ground. The path became even and wet and comforting to his hot, bare feet.

He trampled on ferns and white violets as he hurried forward and dropped on his knees to drink from the spring that bubbled out from under great brown rock. Water ran smooth for the length of an old rotting trough, then fell with a bright splash on its bed of white sand and clean pebbles.

When a spring puppy clung to the side of the trough not far from his mouth, Killdee laughed.

"You better be glad dis is me 'stead o' Mike, son. I kin see you. I ain' gwine swallow you. Mike ain' got good eyes like me. You'd be ruint ef you got een dat big, ol' mout' o' his'n. It 'ud sen' you down dat big ol' t'roat an' Mike wouldn't know nuttin' 'bout it."

When his own thirst was quenched, Killdee sat and watched Mike's shaggy throat forcing the water up until

Mike raised his head and looked at him with gentle, somber eyes. He was ready to go home and eat dinner.

Man and mule suddenly paused stock-still while a snake writhed through the green shadows. Tufts of grass and slender vines with satiny leaves almost hid its silent, stealthy slipping.

Killdee watched with serious eyes, then spoke to the reptile.

"I know I ought to kill you an' hang you up on a limb to mek it rain. De groun' is awful dry. De plow can' ha'dly cut 'em. But I ain' got de heart fo' kill nuttin' today. I gwine le' you go home to you' fambly."

As Killdee got to his feet a strong-smelling he-goat rustled through the bushes and stopped to look.

"Hey!" Killdee called to him.

"How-come you dis close to water, ol' man? You better come wash. You smell powerful rank to me. I don' see how lil Nan kin stan' you. No, my Gawd! But 'oman is strange. Nan t'ink nobody ain' fine ez you. Nobody. An' you know dat, too."

Killdee picked up a pebble and threw it and the goat scampered away. Killdee laughed. Preachers say sinners are like goats and Christians are like sheep. He'd a lot rather be a goat than a sheep. Goats have sense.

Old Bill yonder went home to sleep with the other goats at night. He was afraid of the dark. But in the daytime he ran around by himself and went where he liked and ate what he pleased and had a good time. He was too smart to huddle with others of his kind. Bill was a sinner maybe, but he was better off than the foolish, scary sheep that stayed in a flock all the time.

Mike's head was close to his shoulder. Killdee looked at the quiet, smoky eyes. One of them was covered over with a milky film and the other was dim and cloudy.

Soon Mike would be blind. Good, faithful, old Mike. God ought not to make Mike blind. Not a good fellow like Mike.

Mike's ribs stuck out bold too, and the corn pile was low, and the new crop didn't promise much. If it didn't rain soon, everything would dry up. The corn's hands were shut tight to-day. The corn's feet were scorched till they were yellow. The cotton leaves were hanging limber.

Maybe that was the way they all prayed for rain. And yet—if it rained, the grass would eat them up.

Killdee looked at the path leading up the hill to his cabin. He was tired. Rose would be cross, vexed with him, because he had plowed Green Thursday. He'd lie down and rest here a little while in the shade. He took Mike's bridle off and dropped it on the ground, saying sadly:

"Pick roun', Mike, an' git a lil fresh grass fo' taste you mout'. You teeth is too bad fo' chaw cawn anyhow."

Killdee stretched himself out on the damp ground. It was good to lie here in the cool, green shade. There was scarcely a sound but the water flowing over the pebbles.

It sounded so fresh. So cheerful. Not tired a bit. All day, all night, it ran like this. Creeping out of the earth like a living thing. Weak. Small. Yet too strong for anybody to hold it back. It was like life itself.

Two years ago this very month his little baby Rose was born. As soon as the moon changed, another baby would come. His baby too, the same as baby Rose was his.

Maybe this next child would be a boy-child. He hoped it would. Every man needs boy-children. Wants them.

Not that he didn't love baby Rose. He loved her better than life. God, yes! He would do for her what he'd do for nobody else in the world. He'd slave and sweat and struggle for her. He'd do anything to provide for her.

Yes, he'd plow on Green Thursday for her. He'd go to hell for her if he had to do it!

Funny how he felt about her at first. When Maum Hannah first told him a girl-child was born his heart fell. He wanted a son. But when the teeny little fingers closed tight over one of his big ones as he slipped it inside them that morning, his heart mighty near broke with joy. He shook all over, and laughed. He cried a little bit too.

That baby knew then he was hers. That they two were the same flesh. She was so like him. He could see it. Her little hands, her little feet, even her face, were all shaped like his from the very first.

The wonder of it made him feel humble and helpless and weak, yet it fired his pride and courage. He made up his mind to fend for her. Work for her. Suffer for her if it came to that. And he would. He was no poor fool of a sheep. No. He was a man. He'd plow today and not be afraid. If God was, He was fair. Kind. God would like a man better if He saw him doing his best.

He must soon go get Maum Hannah to come stay with Rose. He must take a bushel of corn over to Daddy Cudjoe and swap it for a quart of whiskey. Rose would soon need it. Maum Hannah said it helps a woman to "birth" a child better if she had a little whiskey to deaden the pain.

Rose wanted a bottle of castor oil from the cross-roads store, too. There was no money to buy it with. He'd have to take corn for it too. The corn pile was low. He and Rose and Baby Rose had to eat. Mike too. Grass got the crop last year. Mike crept too slow to keep up with the grass. But this year, he'd kill that grass or die trying! Plowing every day was the only way. Let lightning strike where it pleased!

Fire burned a house in Maum Hannah's yard yesterday. Nobody knew how it caught. Maum Hannah said Jesus burned it. How could fire know Jesus wanted it burned? And yet, the little baby that was coming would know when the moon changed. It would come then. Baby Rose came on the change of the moon.

How do things buried deep know when the moon changes? Seed in the ground know. The water in the river knows. The weather knows. The wind knows. All know more than men. Maum Hannah said Jesus tells His children a lot of things.

Killdee lay on his back and a spot of sunshine fell right in his eyes. The noon hour was passing and neither he nor Mike had eaten dinner. What a fool he was to lie here thinking!

He got slowly to his feet and looked around. Mike had wandered away to find grass that was tender and sweet. Killdee called him.

"Come on, Mike. You got to go home and eat some cawn. Grass won' gi' you de strengt' to pull de plow t'rough da tough grass. Come on. You too greedy. You gwine miss an' eat a pizen weed ef you don' mine. Den you'll hab belly-ache."

While Mike came, Killdee knelt beside the spring and with cupped hands dipped up water and cleansed his dusty face, then he trudged up the hill with Mike following behind him.

Once he stumbled on a root in the narrow crooked path. Thinking had made him unsteady. He had plowed on Green Thursday.

Already the sky was darkening. Thunder rumbled far over the river. It had a threatening loury sound.

Raising his eyes, he looked at his home. The low roof was half-hidden with smoke that rose out of the red-clay chimney at its side. Rose had a fire trying to keep his dinner hot for him there on the hearth inside. He was late to-day. As he hurried forward, a flick of lightning was followed by muted thunder. What if lightning should strike that cabin—burn it—burn all he had within it! God, what a thought!

Shucks! Thinking had made him a coward. When had he ever feared lightning? He was no woman. No he was a man. Hadn't he promised himself he'd be like a goat? Not a sheep. Not a frightened, huddling, scary fool. No.

The crop needed rain and it was coming. He'd feed Mike first, then eat himself. He had let the snake go, but it would rain anyway. The cloud was rolling nearer every minute.

As he got further up the hill, he could see that the back door had been whitened with some of the clay from the gully down near the spring. The wooden blinds, half open on each side of the chimney, were whitened inside and out. How nice it made the house look!

Rose had done it all since morning. She liked to have things clean. She was getting everything ready for her venture. Childbirth. Poor Rose! Soon pain would wrench her!

Some of these days he would build Rose a better house. If the crop made anything this year, he would "wash-white" the house all over and maybe build another shed room there at the back.

When he opened the door of Mike's stable, a shed room added to the log barn, streaks of light shone through the roof. Mike must have a better stable before next winter. Mike was old, but he was faithful.

If the crop was good, it might seem hard-hearted, but he must try to arrange somehow to get a better mule. The thought made Killdee feel guilty.

He shucked a few ears of corn and put them into the trough and watched Mike's feeble efforts to bite the grains off.

"You teet' ain' no count, not no mo', Mike. It make me sad fo' see you strive fo' chaw."

He'd have to take a sack of corn to mill and get it ground up for Mike. Mike's old teeth were worn out. They couldn't crack corn any more.

Killdee sighed as he closed the barn door and walked toward the cabin. The sun shone out with a sudden, dazzling flash of brilliance. The chinaberry tree beside the doorstep made a round, thick spot of shade. The wild-cherry tree cast light, leafy shadows that played up and down over the red-clay chimney.

Rose called out of the window:

"How-come you so late to-day? You been to see Maum Hannah? I know you didn' plow so long an' it Green Thursday."

Killdee shook his head wearily and walked inside.

"Yes," he admitted, "I been plowin' sence sunrise tell twelve o'clock. I lay down by de spring fo' res' a lil while."

Rose shook her head dolefully, then leaned to dip his dinner out of the pot. Her brows were knotted with a frown. She dropped a few peas on the clean hearth as she helped a pan for him. She was cross. She thought he had done wrong.

"Somet'ing bad'll happen to you sho as Gawd's een heaben. People ain' fo' plow to-day."

"Somet'ing bad'll happen ef I don't plow. Grass is got de crop now." Killdee answered meekly, but Rose's anger was not easy to quench.

"I know you mean I didn' he'p you none wid de crop, but I ain' able fo' do nuttin'—" She began crying.

"Now, now," Killdee went forward and petted her shoulder, "I didn' say nuttin' 'bout you. You mus'n fret, honey. No. You fo' be happy. Look wha' a nice lil gal we got. Mebbe dis time nex-week we would hab a nice lil boy. 'Member how de people say when we was ma'ied: 'I wish you joy, a gal an' a boy'? We gwine hab all two."

Rose drew away from him. She was not to be appeased so easily.

Killdee went and stood by the bed where Baby Rose, covered over with a patchwork quilt, lay asleep. Flies crawled over the child's delicate features. They rose and buzzed and crawled again.

"Whyn't you git on off!" Killdee growled angrily at them. He waved his hands violently to frighten them off.

"Do don' wake em, Killdee. Le'em sleep. Da chile ain' been still all day. 'E keep me busy watchin' 'em. I done tired. Le'em sleep. You come on an' eat you' dinner."

Killdee took the pan of food from Rose's hand and sat down in the doorway to eat. He looked at the cow-peas and bacon and cornbread and stirred among them absent-mindedly with his spoon.

Rose didn't look right. She was vexed because he had plowed to-day, but she didn't look well. Maybe he was wrong to worry her.

He glanced toward her heavy, bulging body, at her swollen ankles, and pity for her stirred him.

How could she breathe like that? Of course she

couldn't hoe. No. Yet she had struggled up and down the hill bringing water to scour the floor. How clean its bare boards were!

She had whitened the windows and doors. Getting the house ready. Poor Rose. She needed help here at home. Baby Rose was a frisky baby. The hill was long and steep. Bringing up water was hard work. After this he must bring it for her before he went to work in the field.

"Come set heah by me an' le's talk," he suggested kindly.

"I ain' able fo' set low ez dem steps, not now," Rose said with a wistful sigh.

"I haffer set high een chair now."

As she drew a chair to the door a flash of lightning lit the cabin and a peal of thunder crashed close behind it. Rose shivered and put up a hand.

"You see, enty!" she whispered. "Lightnin's gwine strike you field!"

Lightning flashed again and Rose's eyes shone white in the glare as she quavered.

"Git up out de do, Killdee. De wedder is too cross. 'E might miss an' strike you. I so faid em, Killdee. . . . "

Killdee wiped his mouth on his sleeve and got up. He put an arm around her and led her to the bed where Baby Rose slept peacefully.

"Lay down by de baby an' res', Honey. Don' be faid. Nuttin' ain' gwine hu't you. No. Rain'll do de crop good. De cawn an' cotton'll grow. Next fall I gwine buy you a fine dress and shoe an' hat. I'll git a wagon an' harness an' hitch up ol' Mike an' tek you to Mount Pleasant Church. De people'll say: 'Who is dat dress' up so fine comin' yonder?' "

Rose's fingers rested on the strongs thews of Killdee's

forearm. With him close beside her like this, she felt comforted. Dress—shoes—hat—she smiled to think of them all.

But the heavy cloud darkened the cabin. Lightning blazed in through the open windows and door. Thunder clapped savagely.

"Do shet de do, Killdee—an' de window—"

As Killdee got up to do it, there were muffled bangs from Mike's stable. He listened, then ran stumbling down the steps. Had Mike gotten fastened in a crack of the stable?

Hot stench filled his nostrils when he opened the stable door. Flies sung over the moist dung where Mike lay kicking, groaning, rolling with pain. Mike's belly was puffed with colic.

Bad corn. Bad teeth. Or—was it because Mike stirred the earth on Green Thursday? Something must be done. A mule can't last long swollen up like this.

Killdee shouted through the wind:

"Rose! Rose! See ef a kerosene is lef' een de bottle! Fetch em quick!"

Rose came hurrying across the yard, panting, trembling, ashy, with a quart bottle in her hand.

The wind twisted her skirts and blew the stable door shut with a bang. Killdee opened it and took the bottle from her shaking fingers.

"Jedus," she sobbed, "Ef Mike dead, wha' we gwine do!"

Killdee knelt and pulled the mule's great black lips open. He forced the worn, yellow teeth apart and poured the kerosene down the unwilling throat.

"Git up on you feet, Mike!" he called sternly.

"You can' leddown wid colic. You mus' walk 'em off. Das de only way."

Mike lay prone. Moaning, rolling. Killdee got the bridle and put it on him. He shook the bit and coaxed:

"Git up, Mike. Don' mek me git a whip. You mus' git up and walk, son."

Lightning blazed, and wind, mean and wet, sung through the cracks of the log barn. Rose whimpered and clung to Killdee's arm.

"You mus' go back to de house, Rose. De lightnin' know good you is faid em. Dat mek em do wusser. Go on een de house. I can' lef Mike fo' go wid you. Go leddown on de bed side de baby. Kiver up you haid. Try fo' go sleep tell I come."

Rose went and Killdee led Mike out into the yard to keep him walking. Spikes of water drove against his cheeks. Things dazzled a little before his eyes. He felt confused. Distracted. He must pull himself together. Mike and Rose depended on him. He must be strong. Not afraid. Rain fell in a solid flood and Mike stopped and tried to lie down. Killdee was firm and urged him on. Round and round the barn they went. Walking, walking.

Sheets of water hid the cabin. Beat and slashed on his shoulders. Chilled the very flesh on his bones. Made him shudder foolishly.

Something braced him. Maybe shame. Was he a man or not? What were wind and rain and thunder and lightning that he'd fear them?

Women and children mind such things. Not strong men.

Mike must not lie down and die. He must walk this colic off. Plowing Green Thursday had nothing to do with his sickness. Bad teeth. Rotten, weevily corn. They were worse than lightning. Or plowing Green Thursday.

Rose was scary. Chicken-hearted. All good women are so. It was right for them to be afraid of things. Right.

The rain battered down and Mike and Killdee walked on and on unheeding.

A voice piped shrill above the storm's roaring. Killdee smiled. Rose wanted him. She thought he could keep harm away from her. He'd go to her soon and put on dry clothes. A fire was still in the chimney. He would build it up and its light would make the cabin bright and cheerful. Mike was getting better. His belly was less near bursting. Soon he could go back to his stable. Thank God!

Rose was running toward him! Screaming! Was she sick? No, she had Baby Rose in her arms. She held Baby Rose out to him.

Killdee felt numb. Dazed. What had happened? He couldn't think. He was stunned—or drunk—

As he went into the cabin a fog of smoke filled his eyes. The air was rank with the smell of burned cloth—burned meat—

He stumbled to a chair and sat down in it. He was holding Baby Rose's fire-blackened, scorched little body in his arms. What must he do? What?

"Go git Maum Hannah," Rose said between teeth that chattered.

Killdee put the baby on the bed and went staggering blindly across the fields through the storm. Lightning mocked him. Thunderbolts flouted him. Made him go the wrong way. Made him stumble. Made him afraid. Told him it was Green Thursday, and this morning he stirred the earth!

At last he reached Maum Hannah's cabin. It sat safe behind the pile of ashes where a man's house had been.

Fire burned that house, yesterday. Maum Hannah said Jesus burned it.

* * *

ALL NIGHT Killdee and Rose sat beside the bed. Rose moaned incessantly. Her own burned hands were held out in front of her. She didn't seem to know he was there.

Maum Hannah kept putting white hog lard and white cotton over the little crisp ears and fingers. Mary West held the pan. The pan itself kept shaking. Killdee took it and tried to hold it steady, but it shook in his hand just the same.

Baby Rose never cried at all. Her breath came easy. Soft. Like whispering. It made Killdee weak and sick to hear the long gaps that came between.

All night he listened for it. Then just before day, it stopped. He kept trying to hear it. Just one more time. His own breast cramped with an effort to catch air! Baby Rose wasn't breathing! No! She was gone! Gone!

Rose got down on her knees and prayed and begged and called to her to come back. Not to go. Not to leave her. But she was gone. Gone.

Rose got up and shrieked and cried and waved her arms. She said God was hard. Unfair. Killdee had done wrong. He had stirred the earth on a holy day. He should suffer. Not her. Not her child. But Baby Rose lay still. Dead.

Maum Hannah talked to Rose and tried to quiet her. She told Rose that it was to be. The child's time had come. God called Baby Rose because her work here was over. Her time was out. To question what God had done was a sin. Rose must bear her sorrow with patience.

Killdee sat in the doorway and looked out at the thick, black night. His muscular hands shook helplessly and clutched at the rough board step. His strength had left him. He felt weak. Shaken. Afraid. The darkness came up close. It filled his eyes and ears and nostrils. It slipped past him into the fire-lit room. The fire still burned. There was no other light to be had. But darkness filled the corners. Silent darkness. Black, dumb darkness. It told nobody what it was, or what it was doing. It was like death. It came. It went. Nobody could keep it away. Nobody.

The wind had died. Faint flashes of lightning low in the sky were followed by thunder that muttered and mumbled. Killdee's heart was black. Bitter.

If God wanted to call Baby Rose, why did He burn her to death? She had never harmed God. Or anybody. She had never done anything wrong. She was too little to sin. If God was mad with him for plowing Green Thursday, why didn't he strike him with lightning and kill him? That would have been easy enough. But to burn a baby —it wasn't square.

How could God have the heart to burn a baby? Who made the baby so she loved to play in the fire, if God didn't? Yes. God did it!

Rose gave her other things to play with. Rose made her a pretty little cloth doll. He had gotten an empty cigar box from the cross-roads store and made her a nice little doll wagon. But she loved the fire more than anything else.

She didn't know it would burn her. He told her it would. Rose told her too. But she was a baby. She didn't understand.

Maybe she wasn't playing with fire! Who could tell? Rose was on the bed with her head covered up to keep from seeing the lightning. A gust of wind might have sucked a flame out to catch her little dress. The lightning might have sent a tongue of fire in through the window to kill her.

Rose didn't know. Rose was on the bed. With her eyes shut. Scared. A coward. She let her baby burn to death. She was to blame. Rose and God.

Something inside him made him shake and shiver as he sat there trying to make things out. Something kept telling him he had plowed the ground on Green Thursday. He had stirred the earth on a holy day.

Keen, blasting grief wrung him to the core. Resentment heated his blood like a fever. Burnt the marrow in his skull. Emboldened him. With set lips and rigid muscles, he glared at the overhead darkness. He was helpless. Yes. He had to take whatever came. There was nothing else to do. Nothing! He could fight men. Settle with them. But God—Ha!—that was a different matter. God kept out of reach. Yes. He did his worst. He cut men at the very roots. Blighted them. He burned tender girl-children. And nobody could ever get even with Him. Up there in the sky, He had the whole world in His cold-blooded reach.

* * *

A STAR BLINKED out between flying clouds and was gone. Where was Baby Rose? Was she up there? No. She was inside on the bed. Dead. Dead.

Maum Hannah laid a light hand on his shoulder.

"Son," she said, "better come eenside now. De night air'll gi' you a chill. Day'll soon be clean. Andrew mus' come mek a lil box to fit de baby. You haffer lay em way, you know."

Her hand waited. It must have felt his misery, for it shook just a little. Killdee knew she pitied him as she murmured:

"Try to fret out loud, son. You could bear de pain

mo better ef you would cry. Eenside frettin' kin bus' you' heart open."

* * *

THEY WAITED until the sun had set in the little grave, then Killdee and Andrew placed the small pine box that held Baby Rose, carefully down in the earth. Together they filled in the damp, red clay, and smoothed it over the top, into a mound. When it was done, Killdee fell to his knees on the ground and wept bitterly. But Andrew said solemnly to him:

"Don' cry, Killdee. De Lawd hab gi' em. De Lawd hab tek em away. Blessed be de name ob de Lawd."

Andrew walked home with him to Rose, who strove with Maum Hannah's help and encouragement to bring another child into the world.

Maum Hannah looked up at Killdee when he walked in, and said:

"Some duh comin' an' some duh gwinen. Him up-yonder duh tek an' sen. Be tanksful, son. Be tanksful."

But Killdee's eyes were fixed on a small cloth doll that had fallen out of its cigar-box wagon and that lay face down on the floor.

THE HALF PINT FLASK*

By DUBOSE HEYWARD

I PICKED up the book and regarded it with interest. Even its format suggested the author: the practical linen covered boards, the compact and exact paragraphing. I opened the volume at random. There he was again: "There can be no doubt," "An undeniable fact," "I am prepared to assert." A statement in the preface leaped from the context and arrested my gaze:

"The primitive American Negro is of a deeply religious nature, demonstrating in his constant attendance at church, his fervent prayers, his hymns, and his frequent mention of the Deity that he has cast aside the last vestiges of his pagan background, and has unreservedly espoused the doctrine of Christianity."

I spun the pages through my fingers until a paragraph in the last chapter brought me up standing:

"I was hampered in my investigation by a sickness contracted on the island that was accompanied by a distressing insomnia, and, in its final stages, extreme delirium. But I already had sufficient evidence in hand to enable me to prove—"

Yes, there it was, fact upon fact. I was overwhelmed by the permanence, the unanswerable last word of the printed page. In the face of it my own impressions became fantastic, discredited even in my own mind. In an effort at self-justification I commenced to rehearse my *impressions* of that preposterous month as opposed to Barksdale's *facts;* my feeling for effects and highly developed fiction writer's imagination on the one hand; and

* Reprinted with the courteous permission of the author and the publishers, Farrar and Rinehart.

on the other, his cold record of a tight, three dimensional world as reported by his five good senses.

Sitting like a crystal gazer, with the book in my hand, I sent my memory back to a late afternoon in August, when, watching from the shore near the landing on Ediwander Island, I saw the "General Stonewall Jackson" slide past a frieze of palmetto trees, shut off her steam, and nose up to the tenuous little wharf against the ebb.

Two barefooted Negroes removed a section of the rail and prepared to run out the gang plank. Behind them gathered the passengers for Ediwander landing; ten or a dozen Negroes back from town with the proceeds of a month's labor transformed into flaming calico, amazing bonnets, and new flimsy, yellow luggage; and trailing along behind them, the single white passenger.

I would have recognized my guest under more difficult circumstances and I experienced that inner satisfaction that comes from having a new acquaintance fit neatly into a preconceived pattern. The obstinacy of which I had been warned was evident in the thin immobile line of the mouth over the prognathous jaw. The eyes behind his thick glasses were a bright hard blue and moved methodically from object to object, allowing each its allotted time for classification then passing unhurriedly on to the next. He was so like the tabloid portrait in the letter of the club member who had sent him down that I drew the paper from my pocket and refreshed my memory with a surreptitious glance.

"He's the museum, or collector type," Spencer had written; "spends his time collecting facts—some he sells—some he keeps to play with. Incidentally his hobby is American glass, and he has the finest private collection in the state."

We stood eyeing each other over the heads of the

noisy landing party without enthusiasm. Then when the last Negro had come ashore he picked up his bag with a meticulousness that vaguely exasperated me, and advanced up the gang plank.

Perfunctory introductions followed: "Mr. Courtney?" from him, with an unnecessarily rising inflection; and a conventional "Mr. Barksdale, I presume," from me in reply.

The buckboard had been jogging along for several minutes before he spoke.

"Very good of Mr. Spencer to give me this opportunity," he said in a close clipped speech. "I am doing a series of articles on Negroid Primates, and I fancy the chances for observation are excellent here."

"Negroid Primates!" The phrase annoyed me. Uttered in that dissecting voice, it seemed to strip the human from the hundred or more Negroes who were my only company except during the duck season when the club members dropped down for the shooting.

"There are lots of Negroes here," I told him a little stiffly. "Their ancestors were slaves when the island was the largest rice plantation in South Carolina, and isolation from modern life has kept them primitive enough, I guess."

"Good!" he exclaimed. "I will commence my studies at once. Simple souls, I fancy. I should have my data within a month."

We had been travelling slowly through deep sand ruts that tugged at the wheels like an undertow. On either side towered serried ranks of virgin long-leaf pine. Now we topped a gentle rise. Before us was the last outpost of the forest crowning a diminishing ridge. The straight columned trees were bars against a released splendor of sunset sky and sea.

Impulsively I called his attention to it:

"Rather splendid, don't you think?"

He raised his face, and I was immediately cognizant of the keen methodical scrutiny that passed from trees to sea, and from sea back to that last wooded ridge that fell away into the tumble of dunes.

Suddenly I felt his wire-tight grasp about my arm.

"What's that?" he asked, pointing with his free hand. Then with an air of authority, he snapped: "Stop the cart. I've got to have a look at it."

"That won't interest you. It's only a Negro burying ground. I'll take you to the quarters tomorrow, where you can study your 'live primates.'"

But he was over the wheel with surprising alacrity and striding up the slight ascent to the scattered mounds beneath the pines.

The sunset was going quickly, dragging its color from the sky and sea, rolling up leagues of delicately tinted gauze into tight little bales of primary color, then draping these with dark colors for the night. In sharp contrast against the light the burying ground presented its pitiful emblems of the departed. Under the pine needles, in common with all Negro graveyards of the region, the mounds were covered with a strange litter of half-emptied medicine bottles, tin spoons, and other futile weapons that had failed in the final engagement with the last dark enemy.

Barksdale was puttering excitedly about among the graves, peering at the strange assortment of crockery and glass. The sight reminded me of what Spencer had said of the man's hobby and a chill foreboding assailed me. I jumped from the buckboard.

"Here," I called, "I wouldn't disturb those things if I were you."

But my words went unheeded. When I reached

Barksdale's side, he was holding a small flat bottle, half filled with a sticky black fluid, and was rubbing the earth from it with his coat sleeve. The man was electric with excitement. He held the flask close to his glasses, then spun around upon me.

"Do you know what this is?" he demanded, then rushed on triumphantly with his answer: "It's a first issue, half pint flask of the old South Carolina state dispensary. It gives me the only complete set in existence. Not another one in America. I had hoped that I might get on the trail of one down here. But to fall upon it like this!"

The hand that held the flask was shaking so violently that the little palmetto tree and single X that marked it described small agitated circles. He drew out his handkerchief and wrapped it up tenderly, black contents and all.

"Come," he announced, "we'll go now."

"Not so fast," I cautioned him. "You can't carry that away. It simply isn't done down here. We may have our moral lapses, but there are certain things that—well—can't be thought of. The graveyard is one. We let it alone."

He placed the linen covered package tenderly in his inside pocket and buttoned his coat with an air of finality; then he faced me truculently.

"I have been searching for this flask for ten years," he asserted. "If you can find the proper person to whom payment should be made I will give a good price. In the meantime I intend to keep it. It certainly is of no use to anyone, and I shan't hesitate for a silly superstition."

I could not thrash him for it and I saw that nothing short of physical violence would remove it from his person. For a second I was tempted to argue with him; tell him why he should not take the thing. Then I was frustrated by my own lack of reason. I groped with my instinctive knowledge that it was not to be done, trying to embody the abstract into something sufficiently concrete to impress him. And all the while I felt his gaze upon me, hard, very blue, a little mocking, absolutely determined.

Behind the low crest of the ridge sounded a single burst of laughter, and the ring of a trace chain. A strange panic seized me. Taking him by the arm I rushed him across the short distance to the buckboard and into his seat; then leaped across him and took up the lines.

Night was upon us, crowding forward from the recesses of the forest, pushing out beyond us through the last scattered trees, flowing over the sea and lifting like level smoke into the void of sky. The horse started forward, wrenching the wheels from the clutching sand.

Before us, coming suddenly up in the dusk, a party of field Negroes filled the road. A second burst of laughter sounded, warm now, volatile and disarming. It made me ashamed of my panic. The party passed the vehicle, dividing and flowing by on both sides of the road. The last vestiges of day brought out high lights on their long earth-polished hoes. Teeth were a white accent here and there. Only eyes, and fallen sockets under the brows of the very old, seemed to defy the fading glimmer, bringing the night in them from the woods. Laughter and soft Gullah words were warm in the air about us.

"Howdy, Boss."

"Ebenin', Boss."

The women curtsied in their high tucked up skirts; the men touched hat brims. Several mules followed, grotesque and incredible in the thickening dark, their trace chains dangling and chiming faintly.

The party topped the rise, then dropped behind it.

Silence, immediate and profound, as though a curtain had been run down upon the heels of the last.

"A simple folk," clipped out my companion. "I rather envy them starting out at zero, as it were, with everything to learn from our amazing civilization."

"Zero, hell!" I flung out. "They had created a Congo art before our ancestors drugged and robbed their first Indian."

Barksdale consigned me to limbo with his mocking, intolerable smile.

The first few days at the club were spent by my guest in going through the preliminary routine of the systematic writer. Books were unpacked and arranged in the order of study, looseleaf folders were laid out, and notes made for the background of his thesis. He was working at a table in his bedroom which adjoined my own, and as I also used my sleeping apartment as a study for the fabrication of the fiction which, with my salary as manager of the club, discharged my financial obligations, I could not help seeing something of him.

On the morning of the second day I glanced in as I passed his door, and surprised him gloating over his find. It was placed on the table before him, and he was gazing fixedly at it. Unfortunately, he looked up; our glances met and, with a self-consciousness that smote us simultaneously, remained locked. Each felt that the subject had better remain closed—yet there the flask stood evident and unavoidable.

After a strained space of time I managed to step into the room, pick up a book and say casually:

"I am rather interested in Negroes myself. Do you mind if I see what you have here?"

While I examined the volume he passed behind me and put the flask away, then came and looked at the book with me. "'African Religions and Superstitions,'" he said, reading the title aloud; then supplemented:

"An interesting mythology for the American Negro, little more. The African Gullah Negro, from whom these are descended, believed in a God, you know, but he only created, then turned his people adrift to be preyed upon by malign spirits conjured up by their enemies. Really a religion, or rather a superstition, of senseless terror."

"I am not so sure of the complete obsoleteness of the old rites and superstitions," I told him, feeling as I proceeded that I was engaged in a useless mission. "I know these Negroes pretty well. For them, Plat-eye, for instance, is a very actual presence. If you will notice the cook you will see that she seems to get along without a prayer book, but when she goes home after dark she sticks a sulphur match in her hair. Sulphur is a charm against Plat-eye."

"Tell me," he asked with a bantering light in his hard eyes, "just what is Plat-eye?"

I felt that I was being laughed at and floundered ahead at the subject, anxious to be out of it as soon as possible.

"Plat-eye is a spirit which takes some form which will be particularly apt to lure its victims away. It is said to lead them into danger or lose them in the woods and, stealing their wits away, leave them to die alone."

He emitted a short acid laugh.

"What amusing rot. And I almost fancy you believe it."

"Of course I don't," I retorted but I experienced the feeling that my voice was overemphatic and failed to convince.

"Well, well," he said, "I am not doing folk lore but religion. So that is out of my province. But it is amusing and I'll make a note of it. Plat-eye, did you say?"

The next day was Thursday. I remember that distinctly because, although nearly a week's wages were due, the last servant failed to arrive for work in the morning. The club employed three of them; two women and a man. Even in the off season this was a justifiable expense, for a servant could be hired on Ediwander for four dollars a week. When I went to order breakfast the kitchen was closed, and the stove cold.

After a makeshift meal I went out to find the yard boy. There were only a few Negroes in the village and these were women hoeing in the small garden patches before the cabins. There were the usual swarms of lean mongrel hounds, and a big sow lay nourishing her young in the warm dust of the road. The women looked up as I passed. Their soft voices, as they raised their heads one after another to say "Mornin', Boss," seemed like emanations from the very soil, so much a part of the earth did they appear.

But the curs were truculent that morning: strange, canny, candid little mongrels. If you want to know how you stand with a Negro, don't ask him—pat his dog.

I found Thomas, the hired boy, sitting before his cabin watching a buzzard carve half circles in the blue.

"When are you coming to work?" I demanded. "The day's half done."

"I gots de toot'ache, Boss. I can't git ober 'fore termorrer." The boy knew that I did not believe him. He also knew that I would not take issue with him on the point. No Negro on the island will say "no" to a white man. Call it "good form" if you will, but what Thomas had said to me was merely the code for "I'm through." I did not expect him and I was not disappointed.

Noon of the following day I took the buckboard, crossed the ferry to the mainland, and returned at dark with a cheerful wholesome Negress, loaned to me by a plantation owner, who answered for her faithfulness and promised that she would cook for us during the emergency. She got us a capital supper, retired to the room adjoining the kitchen that I had prepared for her, as I did not wish her to meet the Negroes in the village, and in the morning had vanished utterly. She must have left immediately after supper, for the bed was undisturbed.

I walked straight from her empty room to Barksdale's sanctum, entered, crossed to the closet where he had put the flask, and threw the door wide. The space was empty. I spun around and met his amused gaze.

"Thought I had better put it away carefully. It is too valuable to leave about."

Our glances crossed like the slide of steel on steel. Then suddenly my own impotence to master the situation arose and overwhelmed me. I did not admit it even to myself, but that moment saw what amounted to my complete surrender.

We entered upon the haphazard existence inevitable with two preoccupied men unused to caring for their own comfort: impossible makeshift meals, got when we were hungry; beds made when we were ready to get into them; with me, hours put into work that had to be torn up and started over the next day; with Barksdale, regular tours of investigation about the island and two thousand words a day, no more, no less, written out in longhand and methodically filed. We naturally saw less and less of each other—a fact which was evidently mutually agreeable.

It was therefore a surprise to me one night in the second week to leap from sleep into a condition of lucid consciousness and find myself staring at Barksdale who had opened the door between our rooms. There he stood like a bird of ill omen, tall and slightly stooping, with his ridiculous nightshirt and thin slightly bowed shanks.

"I'll leave this open if you don't mind," he said with a new note of apology in his voice. "Haven't been sleeping very well for a week or so, and thought the draft through the house might cool the air."

Immediately I knew that there was something behind the apparently casual action of the man. He was the type who could lie through conviction; adopt some expedient point of view, convince himself that it was the truth, then assert it as a fact; but he was not an instinctive liar, and that new apologetic note gave him away. For a while after he went back to bed, I lay wondering what was behind his request.

Then for the first time I felt it; but hemmed in by the appalling limitations of human speech, how am I to make the experience plain to others!

Once I was standing behind the organ of a great cathedral when a bass chord was pressed upon the keys; suddenly the air about me was all sound and movement. The demonstration that night was like this a little, except that the place of the sound was by an almost audible silence, and the vibrations were so violent as to seem almost a friction against the nerve terminals. The wave of movement lasted for several minutes, then it abated slowly. But this was the strange thing about it: the agitation was not dissipated into the air; rather it seemed to settle slowly, heavily, about my body, and to move upon my skin like the multitudinous crawling of invisible and indescribably loathsome vermin.

I got up and struck a light. The familiar disorder of the room sprang into high relief, reassuring me, telling me coolly not to be a fool. I took the lamp into Barksdale's room. There he lay, his eyes wide and fixed, braced in his bed with every muscle tense. He gave me the impression of wrenching himself out of invisible bonds as he turned and sat up on the edge of his bed.

"Just about to get up and work," he said in a voice that he could not manage to make casual. "Been suffering from insomnia for a week, and it's beginning to get on my nerves."

The strange sensation had passed from my body but the thought of sleep was intolerable. We went to our desks leaving the door ajar, and wrote away the four hours that remained until daylight.

And now a question arises of which due cognizance must be taken even though it may weaken my testimony. Is a man quite sane who has been without sleep for ten days and nights? Is he a competent witness? I do not know. And yet the phenomena that followed my first startled awakening entered into me and became part of my life experience. I live them over shudderingly when my resistance is low and memory has its way with me. I know that they transpired with that instinctive certainty which lies back of human knowledge and is immune from the skepticism of the cynic.

After that first night the house was filled with the vibrations. I closed the door to Barksdale's room, hoping a superstitious hope that I would be immune. After an hour I opened it again, glad for even his companionship. Only while I was wide awake and driving my brain to its capacity did the agitation cease. At the first drowsiness it would commence faintly, then swell up and up, fighting sleep back from the tortured brain, working under leaden eyelids upon the tired eyes.

Ten days and nights of it! Terrible for me: devastating for Barksdale. It wasted him like a jungle fever.

Once when I went near him and his head had dropped

forward on his desk in the vain hope of relief, I made a discovery. He was the *center*. The moment I bent over him my nerve terminals seemed to become living antennae held out to a force that frayed and wasted them away. In my own room it was better. I went there and sat where I could still see him for what small solace there was in that.

I entreated him to go away, but with his insane obstinacy he would not hear of it. Then I thought of leaving him, confessing myself a coward—bolting for it. But again, something deeper than logic, some obscure tribal loyalty, held me bound. Two members of the same race; and out there the palmetto jungle, the village with its fires bronze against the midnight trees, the malign, beleaguering presence. No, it could not be done.

But I did slip over to the mainland and arrange to send a wire to Spencer telling him to come and get Barksdale, that the man was ill.

During that interminable ten days and nights the fundamental difference between Barksdale and myself became increasingly evident. He would go to great pains to explain the natural causes of our malady.

"Simple enough," he would say, while his bloodshot eyes, fixed on me, shouted the lie to his words. "One of those damn swamp fevers. Livingstone complained of them, you will remember, and so did Stanley. Here in this sub-tropical belt we are evidently subject to the plague. Doubtless there is a serum. I should have inquired before coming down."

To this I said nothing, but I confess now, at risk of being branded a coward, that I had become the victim of a superstitious terror. Frequently when Barksdale was out I searched for the flask without finding the least trace of it.

Finally I capitulated utterly and took to carrying a piece of sulphur next to my skin. Nothing availed.

The strange commotion in the atmosphere became more and more persistent. It crowded over from the nights into the days. It came at noon; any time the drowsiness fell upon our exhausted bodies it was there, waging a battle with it behind the closed lids. Only with the muscles tense and the eyes wide could one inhabit a static world. After the first ten days I lost count of time. There was a nightmare quality to its unbreakable continuity.

I remember only the night I saw *her* in Barksdale's doorway, and I think that it must have been in the third week. There was a full moon, I remember, and there had been unusual excitement in the village. I have always had a passion for moonlight and I stood long on the piazza watching the great disc change from its horizon copper to gold, then cool to silver as it swung up into the immeasurable tranquillity of the southern night. At first I thought that the Negroes must be having a dance, for I could hear the syncopation of sticks on a cabin floor, and the palmettos and moss-draped live oaks that grew about the buildings could be seen the full quarter of a mile away, a ruddy bronze against the sky from a brush fire. But the longer I waited listening the less sure I became about the nature of the celebration. The rhythm became strange, complicated; and the chanting that rose and fell with the drumming rang with a new, compelling quality, and lacked entirely the abandon of dancers.

Finally I went into my room, stretched myself fully dressed on the bed, and almost achieved oblivion. Then suddenly I was up again, my fists clenched, my body taut. The agitation exceeded anything that I had before experienced. Before me, across Barksdale's room, were wide open double doors letting on the piazza. They molded the moonlight into a square shaft that plunged through the darkness of the room, cold, white, and strangely substantial among the half-obliterated familiar objects. I had the feeling that it could be touched. That hands could be slid along its bright surface. It possessed itself of the place. It was the one reality in a swimming, nebulous cube. Then it commenced to tremble with the vibrations of the apartment.

And now the incredible thing happened. Incredible because belief arises in each of us out of the corroboration of our own life experience; and I have met no other white man who has beheld Plat-eye. I have no word, no symbol which can awaken recognition. But who has not seen heat shaking upward from hot asphalt, shaking upward until the things beyond it wavered and quaked? That is the nearest approach in the material world. Only the thing that I witnessed was colored a cold blue, and it was heavy with the perfume of crushed jasmine flowers.

I stood, muscle locked to muscle by terror.

The center of the shaft darkened; the air bore upon me as though some external force exerted a tremendous pressure in an effort to render an abstraction concrete: to mold moving unstable elements into something that could be seen—touched.

Suddenly it was done—accomplished. I looked—I saw *her*.

The shock released me, and I got a flare from several matches struck at once. Yellow light bloomed on familiar objects. I got the fire to a lamp wick, then looked again.

The shaft of moonlight was gone. The open doors showed only a deep blue vacant square. Beyond them something moved. The lamplight steadied, grew. It warmed the room like fire. It spread over the furniture, making it real again. It fell across Barksdale's bed, dragging my gaze with it. *The bed was empty.*

I got to the piazza just as he disappeared under a wide armed live oak. The Spanish moss fell behind him like a curtain. The place was a hundred yards away. When I reached it, all trace of him had vanished.

I went back to the house, built a rousing fire, lit all the lamps, and stretched myself in a deep chair to wait until morning.

Then! an automobile horn on Ediwander Island. Imagine that! I could not place it at first. It crashed through my sleep like the trump of judgment. It called me up from the abysses into which I had fallen. It infuriated me. It reduced me to tears. Finally it tore me from unutterable bliss, and held me blinking in the high noon, with my silly lamps still burning palely about me.

"You're a hell of a fellow," called Spencer. "Think I've got nothing to do but come to this jungle in summer to nurse you and Barksdale."

He got out of a big muddy machine and strode forward laughing. "Oh, well," he said, "I won't row you. It gave me a chance to try out the new bus. That's why I'm late. Thought I'd motor down. Had a hell of a time getting over the old ferry; but it was worth it to see the niggers when I started up on Ediwander. Some took to trees—one even jumped overboard."

He ended on a hearty burst of laughter. Then he looked at me and broke off short. I remember how his face looked then, close to mine, white and frightened.

"My God, man!" he exclaimed, "what's wrong? You aren't going to die on me, are you?"

"Not today," I told him. "We've got to find Barksdale first."

We could not get a Negro to help us. They greeted Spencer, who had always been popular with them, warmly. They laughed their deep laughter—were just as they had always been with him. Mingo, his old paddler, promised to meet us in half an hour with a gang. They never showed up; and later, when we went to the village to find them, there was not a human being on the premises. Only a pack of curs there that followed us as closely as they dared and hung just out of boot reach, snapping at our heels.

We had to go it alone: a stretch of jungle five miles square, a large part of it accessible only with bush hooks and machetes. We dared not take the time to go to the mainland and gather a party of whites. Barksdale had been gone over twelve hours when we started and he would not last long in his emaciated condition.

The chances were desperately against us. Spencer, though physically a giant, was soft from office life. I was hanging on to consciousness only by a tremendous and deliberate effort. We took food with us, which we ate on our feet during breathing spells, and we fell in our tracks for rest when we could go no farther.

At night, when we were eating under the high, white moon, he told me more of the man for whom we were searching.

"I ought to have written you more fully at the start. You'd have been sorry for him then, not angry with him. He does not suggest Lothario now, but he was desperately in love once.

"She was the most fantastically imaginative creature, quick as light, and she played in circles around him. He was never dull in those days. Rather handsome, in the lean Gibson manner; but he was always—well—matter of fact. She had all there was of him the first day, and it was hers to do as she pleased with him. Then one morning she saw quite plainly that he would bore her. She had to have someone who could *play*. Barksdale could have died for her, but he could not play. Like that," and Spencer gave a snap of his fingers, "she jugged him. It was at a house party. I was there and saw it. She was the sort of surgeon who believes in amputation and she gave it to Barksdale there without an anæsthetic and with the crowd looking on.

"He changed after that. Wouldn't have anything he couldn't feel, see, smell. He had been wounded by something elusive, intangible. He was still scarred; and he hid behind the defenses of his five good senses. When I met him five years later he had gone in for facts and glass."

He stopped speaking for a moment. The August dark crowded closer, pressing its low, insistent nocturne against our ears. Then he resumed in a musing voice: "Strange the obsession that an imaginative woman can exercise over an unimaginative man. It is the sort of thing that can follow a chap to the grave. Celia's living in Europe now, married—children—but I believe that if she called him today he'd go. She was very beautiful, you know."

"Yes," I replied, "I know. Very tall, blonde, with hair fluffed and shining about her head like a madonna's halo. Odd way of standing, too, with head turned to one side so that she might look at one over her shoulder. Jasmine perfume, heavy, almost druggy."

Spencer was startled: "You've seen her!"

"Yes, here. She came for Barksdale last night. I saw her as plainly as I see you."

"But she's abroad, I tell you."

I turned to Spencer with a sudden resolve: "You've heard the Negroes here talk of Plat-eye?"

He nodded.

"Well, I've got to tell you something whether you believe it or not. Barksdale got in wrong down here. Stole a flask from the graveyard. There's been hell turned loose ever since: fires and singing every night in the village and a lot more. I am sure now what it all meant—conjuring, and Plat-eye, of course, to lead Barksdale away and do him in, at the same time emptying the house so that it might be searched for the flask."

"But Celia; how could they know about her?"

"They didn't. But Barksdale knew. They had only to break him down and let his old obsession call her up. I probably saw her on the reflex from him, but I'll swear she was there."

Spencer was leaning toward me, the moon shining full upon his face. I could see that he believed.

"Thank God you see it," I breathed. "Now you know why we've got to find him soon."

In the hour just before dawn we emerged from the forest at the far side of the island. The moon was low and reached long fingers of pale light through the trees. The east was a swinging nebula of half light and vapor. A flight of immense blue heron broke suddenly into the air before us, hurling the mist back into our faces from their beating wings. Spencer, who was ahead of me, gave a cry and darted forward, disappearing behind a palmetto thicket.

I grasped my machete and followed.

Our quest had ended. Barksdale lay face downward in the marsh with his head toward the east. His hands flung out before him were already awash in the rising tide.

We dragged him to high ground. He was breathing

faintly in spasmodic gasps, and his pulse was a tiny thread of movement under our finger tips. Two saplings and our coats gave us a makeshift litter, and three hours of stumbling, agonizing labor brought us with our burden to the forest's edge.

I waited with him there, while Spencer went for his car and some wraps. When he returned his face was a study.

"Had a devil of a time finding blankets," he told me, as we bundled Barksdale up for the race to town. "House looks as though a tornado had passed through it; everything out on the piazza, and in the front yard."

With what strength I had left I turned toward home. Behind me lay the forest, dark even in the summer noon; before me, the farthest hill, the sparse pines, and the tumble of mounds in the graveyard.

I entered the clearing and looked at the mound from which Barksdale had taken the flask. There it was again. While it had been gone the cavity had filled with water; now this had flooded out when the bottle had been replaced and still glistened gray on the sand, black on the pine needles.

I regained the road and headed for the club.

Up from the fields came the hands, dinner bound; fifteen or twenty of them; the women taking the direct sun indifferently upon their bare heads. Bright field hoes gleamed on shoulders. The hot noon stirred to deep laughter soft, Gullah accents:

"Mornin', Boss—howdy, Boss."

They divided and flowed past me, women curtsying, men touching hat brims. On they went; topped the ridge; dropped from view.

Silence, immediate and profound.

THE GAY DANGERFIELDS*

By LYLE SAXON

THE Dangerfields lived on Acacia Plantation in Louisiana, not far from the town of Baton Rouge. The house was a charming but dilapidated structure at the end of a long avenue of cedar trees, each tree shrouded with trailing Spanish moss. Beyond the cedars on each side of the avenue, were crepe-myrtle and acacia trees, and in summer the myrtles were rose-colored bouquets and the acacias were feathery green and gold. It was a romantic and beautiful place—rose and gold and green massed against black cedars and gray moss—and at the end of the avenue, seen through an arch of dark branches, were the white columns of the plantation-house.

The house was very old. Once white, it was now a creamy gray and the window-blinds had faded to a bluish green. There were eight large white columns across the façade, and a wide veranda upstairs and down. In fancy I can see it yet—and always I see, there between the columns, a red-haired woman in a long black riding-habit, surrounded by black-and-white spotted dogs. This was Kate Dangerfield, the mother of the children that I came to see.

They were all artists, the Dangerfields were. All the children had talent for drawing. The mother had received some training as a girl, and she believed that she had missed a great career by marrying and settling down. "Settling down" is hardly the phrase, for she was far from settled. She was nearly six feet tall, and she was very handsome. In her girlhood she had been known as a dashing young lady, and, even as the mother of six chil-

* From *Old Louisiana* by Lyle Saxon, copyright 1929 by The Century Company.

dren, she still dashed. She wore always a black riding-habit with trailing skirts which she would gather up and pin at her waist. In consequence, her skirt would be knee-high on one side and would trail behind her as she walked. She was dramatic; her gestures were wide and free. Her hair, now streaked with gray, she dyed bright-red in front; the back she disregarded entirely. Her oldest daughter, who was just my age, would always draw me aside and ask, "What do you think of Mama's hair, this time?"

Kate Dangerfield would stride about the house, a riding crop in her hand, a cigarette between her lips—a magnificent figure.

In those days ladies did not smoke except behind closed doors, and there was always an air of mystery about her smoking. When I first arrived there would be a pretense of hiding the cigarette; but soon I would come upon her puffing behind doors or in corners; later in my visit caution was abandoned, and the cigarette was always in her hand as she talked and gesticulated.

She was an artist, as I have said, or rather she painted pictures. She gloried in her artistic temperament. She called herself a "bohemian." It was the first time that I had ever heard the phrase. One of her eccentricities was that she never finished anything. She would take my arm and draw me along the hall of the plantation-house, pointing out a picture with her riding crop. "Now that," she would say, "is Paul and Virginia fleeing from the storm, but it isn't finished. It needs much more work on it. I have so little time, you know."

Or perhaps she would pause before a picture of three horses' heads. "Pharaoh's Horses," she would say. "How I love to paint animals! But it is unfinished. You can see that for yourself."

It was characteristic of her that she should do everything in the grand manner. I never saw her at work upon a painting, but I am sure that she painted with the same large magnificence with which she spoke and acted. In fact, the pictures looked like that. They had a startled expression—horses and men, as though surprised when confronted by the masterful woman who had created them.

Once, I remember, she paused before the portrait of a recumbent cow. "Now that," she said, "is what I call painting. But of course, it is not finished. Just a little old sketch that I made one day." Then she sighed and we went on to the next picture.

The daughters were like their mother, good-looking and erratic. Ada was the eldest. She was dark-eyed and olive-skinned and she was pretty in a gypsy sort of way. Magda was next, a girl of twelve, tall for her age, pale-skinned and with dark eyes and red hair. The youngest daughter was Dorothy (named for Dorothy Vernon of Haddon Hall!), a charming, dreamy child who was only eight years old, but who was already erratic about coming to meals or learning lessons or getting dressed in the morning. It was no unusual sight to see Dorothy on her calico pony, wearing her nightgown, racing down the avenue just as the breakfast bell was ringing. There were other children, twin red-haired boys, nicknamed Judge and Jury. I never knew their real names. And there was a baby in the arms of a negro nurse.

The younger children were kept in the background, but the three girls would have long arguments with their mother about horsemanship, in which they would squabble exactly as though they were all of the same age. There was constant warfare between Ada and her mother as to which of them was the better horsewoman. The mother was noted for miles around as an excellent and fearless rider, but at home the daughters disputed this. They would urge her on to bolder and more extravagant feats; they would wager that she could not ride this or that unbroken horse. And they would shriek with glee when she was thrown off—which happened frequently. Instead of spanking them all, as one would imagine, she would cringe before their criticism, and would accept their wildest dares in order to retain her supremacy. I don't know when she found time to paint, but paint she did, as scores of pictures in the house testified.

The family owned two plantations on opposite sides of the Mississippi, and Mr. Dangerfield was nearly always "over at the other place." He seldom appeared, but when he did it was always in the same way. He would ride slowly up the cedar avenue on a huge white horse, dismount, throw the reins to a waiting negro, kiss his wife and children if they were within range—and then disappear. He always shook hands with me gravely, and inquired as to my grandfather's health and my own, but he did not listen to my answers. He had a remote "office" in a wing of the house where he remained aloof; even his meals were carried there on a tray. I remember him as a shadowy figure, tall, distinguished-looking, and absent-minded, a man with a black beard and a soft drawl. But to me he was a minor actor in the drama enacted by the female members of the family. I remember this unsolicited statement from him: "My wife is a magnificent horsewoman, by God!"

He had good reason to be proud of her, for she was noted throughout that section of the State. She used to come galloping through the streets of Baton Rouge on a black stallion, and the shopkeepers would run to their doors to see her go by. News would spread through the streets— "Mrs. Dangerfield is in town. Watch out for the fun!"

She was the heroine of a score of mishaps. Once a horse that she was driving with a light buggy became restive on Main Street; it reared and snorted and ended by kicking the dashboard to pieces, while Kate Dangerfield, with feet firmly braced and with the reins wrapped around her wrists, gave shriek after shriek of wild laughter, and called out to those brave young men, who attempted to rescue her, that she needed no help; and she begged them to keep away until she got the horse under control. She did it, too, but not until the carriage was practically demolished.

On another day a frightened horse managed to pull the harness loose from the shafts of her carriage. She held the reins and was dragged over the dashboard into the road. But she held on through sheer stubbornness and it was not until the horse had dashed her against a tree that she let go.

She lay there in the dust while the horse went running down the street. Men and women came out to pick her up. Every one thought that she was dead, but she sat up and laughed.

"Why that's nothing," she said. "Just a little old wild colt that I'm breaking in!"

As she was casual about risking her life, so was she casual about the affairs of the plantation household; and while she was the most hospitable woman in the world, her guests sometimes suffered severe trials.

At Acacia Plantation there were nine hunting dogs—pointers and setters—that slept in the hall. All day long there would be growls and yelps as their tails were stepped upon by some of the Dangerfields, for it was nearly impossible to go from room to room without stepping on some sleeping animal. But the dogs must have been strangely good-natured, for no one was ever bitten. There was an army of cats, too, which no one ever remembered to feed, and they were always ravenous. Going to the dinner table was like going to war. We were surrounded on all sides by cats and dogs—animals ready to snatch the food out of our mouths.

As half of the family never came to meals anyway, there were always empty chairs at the table. Mrs. Dangerfield would sit at one end and I would sit beside her; then there would be, perhaps, four empty chairs, and, down at the opposite end of the table, Dorothy would be lolling, lost in a day-dream. The others would trail in at ten-minute intervals, as the spirit moved them.

One day the cat situation became acute.

Mrs. Dangerfield, Dorothy, and I were at table, and a servant had just placed a large silver platter of roast beef in the center of the board, beyond the reach of any of us. Scarcely had the servant left the room when a black cat sprang up and began eating from the dish. Kate Dangerfield regarded it languidly and said: "This is too much. Dorothy, knock that cat off the table."

The little girl came out of her day-dream with an effort, looked narrowly at the cat, and said: "I won't touch it. That's Ada's cat. Make her come and drive it away."

And the cat continued to eat.

"Oh, well . . . " said Kate Dangerfield, and reaching behind her she took a buggy whip from a rack, and came crashing down among the plates and glasses. It is true that this drove the cat away, but it also scattered gravy in every direction, inundating us in grease. Two goblets and a plate were broken, and dinner proceeded as usual.

One soon fell into the spirit of the occasion, or at least I did.

Although the house was overrun with servants, everything was left undone. Meals were always late, and sometimes forgotten altogether. One night at ten o'clock, Kate Dangerfield, who had been walking up and down the hall reciting poetry aloud, stopped suddenly, clutched her red hair, and cried out: "Good Lord! I forgot to have supper!" And to our surprise, we found that it was perfectly true. We went to the kitchen and to the ice-box; we foraged for the remains of dinner. Jars of preserved fruits were opened, cold biscuits appeared. At half past ten, instead of going prosaically to bed, we were sitting around the dining-room table in the midst of a meal.

Mrs. Dangerfield was a great teller of stories and many of them dealt with the sensational and romantic episodes of her girlhood. Her daughters scoffed openly and stifled exaggerated yawns, but they would listen for hours on end, and to their interruptions she paid not the least attention. She talked for the pleasure of talking; she "entertained us" for the sheer joy of entertaining.

One evening after dinner she walked up and down the floor of the drawing-room and recited Kipling's poems until long past midnight. She was like a woman in a dream. The poems seemed thrilling as she recited them, and though I heard midnight strike, I was far from sleepy. The candles burned low in their sconces and went guttering out, one by one, as she strode back and forth in the long room under the family portraits, her head up, her red hair coming down, her black riding-habit trailing after her, a cigarette in her hand.

> "This is the sorrowful story
> Told when the twilight fails,

And the monkeys walk together,
Holding each others' tails!"

It was after one o'clock when she ended. Then she got out a decanter and gave each of us a glass of Benedictine for a nightcap.

Once there was a guest in the house, a pale, aristocratic-looking woman from New Orleans. She was a distant relative who had come to spend a week at the plantation. She was totally unprepared for such a family as the Dangerfields, and her visit was not quite a success.

She had been given a room upstairs at the front of the house, a large room with a four-post bed, a sofa, two or three arm-chairs, and the other usual bedroom furniture. She appeared at breakfast the next morning looking wan and worn, and in answer to the question as to how she had slept, she answered somewhat hesitantly that she had been bothered by fleas. She said, in fact, that she had been forced to leave her bed and spend the night upon the sofa; and, as the sofa was covered with black horsehair and was very slippery, she had not slept at all.

Instead of being horrified, as the guest expected, Kate Dangerfield laughed.

"My poor Virginia! You, of all people in the world, to be bitten by fleas in my house. You, a Randolph of Roanoke!" And she was gone again in a gale of laughter.

The guest mustered a wry smile. "It was pretty bad, just the same," she said.

Mrs. Dangerfield sobered. "My dear, I *am* sorry. You have no idea how sorry I am. Really. Why didn't you come to me? There are other rooms empty here. Although," and here she laughed again, "there may be fleas in every one, for all I know."

Then she went on to explain: "You see, I haven't been

in that room for months. I supposed that the servants looked after it, but instead they've left the door open and the dogs got in. It's highly probable that a dozen dogs have been sleeping on that bed all summer. It's odd about negroes and doors. Why, do you know, I've made a discovery about negroes: it is absolutely impossible to teach them to close doors after them, even in cold weather. They won't. It's some racial trait, I suppose." And she went blithely on.

"But what will you do to get rid of the fleas?" the guest asked at last.

All through breakfast we talked of possible flea remedies. Some one suggested that a young lamb be put upon the bed, the theory being that the fleas would leave the bed and take refuge in the lamb's wool. This idea delighted Mrs. Dangerfield, as it promised immediate action. She ordered one of the negro men-servants to catch a lamb and bring it to her. But the negro demurred.

"Now you know, Miz Kate, dat dey ain't a single l'il lamb in de pasture, dis time a-yeah!"

"Well, then, catch me a sheep," ordered our undaunted hostess. "If a lamb is good, a sheep will be better. It's bigger, you know. More room for fleas."

A few minutes later two negro men appeared at the dining-room door; they carried a large, dirty, and very angry ram between them. The old ram's dignity was upset and he struggled to get down.

"Carry him upstairs!" ordered Kate Dangerfield.

But this was not as easy as it sounded. We all tried to help. We tugged, we pushed, we shoved, and the ram cried "*Baa-aa-aa!*" and set his hind legs. All of us took part in assisting the ram upstairs. All, that is, except the guest. She stood in the parlor door watching us, and she seemed annoyed and amused and miserable, all at once.

Finally the ram was brought into the bedroom and deposited upon the bed, and he lay there, panting and exhausted. We retired and closed the door, but we had scarcely reached the drawing-room, directly below, when there came a crash which set the crystals tinkling in chandelier. Mrs. Dangerfield, who had collapsed on a sofa, and who was smoking a cigarette in order to regain her composure, cried out, "He's jumped off the bed!"

We all ran upstairs again, dogs, children, white folks, and negroes. This time the ram gave battle. He charged us, knocking one of the children down. Chairs were overturned, children screamed, dogs barked. But in the end we were triumphant. This time the servants tied the ram's legs together and put him back in bed again.

"Cover him up!" Mrs. Dangerfield ordered.

Accordingly the blankets were drawn up over the ram, and he lay there, furious, his horns on the pillow, and looking for all the world like Red Riding Hood's grandmother.

However, it was not more than ten minutes later that the second crash came and the ram was free again. The struggle lasted all day. The room was a wreck, chairs and sofa overturned, a mirror broken and the disorder unbelievable. It was not odd that the guest remembered an important engagement in New Orleans and left suddenly in the afternoon.

Oh, charming people, the Dangerfields were, galloping about the country on horseback, a gay cavalcade, hunting, shooting clay pigeons, or riding to hounds. Looking back upon them now, across twenty years, I can think of no more delightful times than those I spent with the gay and eccentric family at Acacia Plantation.

When I grew older, I lost sight of them. I went away to school, then work took me out of Louisiana. Years passed before I returned. When I inquired for them I found that the girls had married, the father had died, and like so many other country families, they had lost their plantations. Kate Dangerfield, they told me, had moved to another plantation in the northern part of the State. I wrote to her, but the letter was returned unclaimed.

But it was only last year that I saw her again. It came about like this: I sat in the lobby of a New Orleans hotel, waiting for a man who had invited me to luncheon. Nearby sat two sunburned men who wore broad-brimmed Panama hats. So near they were that I could hear what they were saying, and suddenly my attention was caught by a bit of talk:

" . . . a most remarkable woman, I tell you. Why, just the other night she heard a noise in her hen-house, and she went out to see what was after the chickens. It was a wildcat. You'd think that any woman would be afraid, but not that one! Why, man, would you believe it, she put her foot on that wildcat's head and held it there until her son came with a pistol and shot it, right under her foot!"

"What did you say her name was?" asked the other.

"Mrs. Kate Dangerfield," he answered.

I sprang up. "Where is she?" I demanded. "I must see her. I knew her years ago."

"If you hurry, you can catch her at the station," the planter said. "She's in town for a day's shopping. I left her a few minutes ago. She's headed for the Union Station to catch the one-fifteen train."

I ran from the hotel, caught a taxi and reached the station with only two minutes to spare. The gateman let me through to the platform and I ran along beside the train, looking in at the windows. But just as I was about to give up the search, I saw her walking along the platform. She was strangely unchanged; still red-haired, still straight, and she wore a long black dress, cut like a riding-habit. A negro girl followed her, her arms full of parcels. I caught Kate Dangerfield's hand as she put her foot on the step of the coach.

She greeted me as though we had parted the day before. "How in the world did you know that I was in town to-day?" she asked.

"I overheard a conversation in a hotel," I answered. "It was about a remarkable woman who put her foot on a wildcat's head and held it until her son came with a pistol."

She laughed and made the sweeping gesture that I remembered so well.

"Why, that was nothing," she said. "It's just talk. It was a little bit of an old wildcat. I thought it was an owl."

THE BIRD AND THE GIRL*

By LAFCADIO HEARN

SUDDENLY, from the heart of the magnolia, came a ripple of liquid notes, a delirium of melody, wilder than the passion of the nightingale, more intoxicating than the sweetness of the night,—the mockingbird calling to its mate.

"*Ah, comme c'est coquet! — comme c'est doux!*"—murmured the girl who stood by the gateway of the perfumed garden, holding up her mouth to be kissed with the simple confidence of a child.

"Not so sweet to me as your voice," he murmured, with lips close to her lips, and eyes looking into the liquid jet that shone through the silk of her black lashes.

The little Creole laughed a gentle little laugh of pleasure. "Have you birds like that in the West?" she asked.

"In cages," he said. "But very few. I have seen five hundred dollars paid for a fine singer. I wish you were a little mockingbird!"

"Why?"

"Because I could take you along with me to-morrow."

"And sell me for five hundred dol—?" (A kiss smothered the mischievous question.)

"For shame!"

"Won't you remember this night when you hear them sing in the cages?—poor little prisoners!"

"But we have none where I am now going. It is all wild out there; rough wooden houses and rough men!—no pets—not even a cat!"

* Reprinted from *Fantastics and Other Fancies* by Lafcadio Hearn with the courteous permission of and by arrangement with the publishers, Houghton Mifflin Company.

"Then what would you do with a little bird in such a place? They would all laugh at you—would n't they?"

"No; I don't think so. Rough men love little pets."

"Little pets!"

"Like you, yes—too well!"

"Too well?"

"I did not mean to say that."

"But you did say it."

"I do not know what I say when I am looking into your eyes."

"Flatterer!"

* * *

THE MUSIC and perfume of those hours came back to him in fragments of dreams all through the long voyage;—in slumber broken by the intervals of rapid travel on river and rail; the crash of loading under the flickering yellow of pine-fires; the steam song of boats chanting welcome or warning; voices of mate and roustabout; the roar of railroad depots; the rumble of baggage in air heavy with the oily breath of perspiring locomotives; the demands of conductors; the announcements of stations;—and at last the heavy jolting of the Western stage over rugged roads where the soil had a faint pink flush, and great coarse yellow flowers were growing.

* * *

SO THE DAYS and weeks and months passed on; and the far Western village with its single glaring street of white sand, blazed under the summer sun. At intervals came the United States mail-courier, booted and spurred and armed to the teeth, bearing with him always one small satiny note, stamped with the postmark of New Orleans, and faintly perfumed as by the ghost of a magnolia.

"Smells like a woman—that," the bronzed rider sometimes growled out as he delivered the delicate missive with an unusually pleasant flash in his great falcon eyes,—eyes made fiercely keen by watching the horizon cut by the fantastic outline of Indian graves, the spiral flight of savage smoke far off which signals danger, and the spiral flight of vultures which signals death.

One day he came without a letter for the engineer—"She's forgotten you this week, Cap," he said in answer to the interrogating look, and rode away through the belt of woods, redolent of resinous gums and down the winding ways to the plain, where the eyeless buffalo skulls glimmered under the sun. Thus he came and thus departed through the rosiness of many a Western sunset, and brought no smile to the expectant face: "She's forgotten you again, Cap."

* * *

AND ONE TEPID NIGHT (the 24th of August, 18—), from the spicy shadows of the woods there rang out a bird-voice with strange exotic tones: "Sweet, sweet, sweet!"—then cascades of dashing silver melody!—then long, liquid, passionate calls!— then a deep, rich ripple of caressing mellow notes, as of love languor oppressed that seeks to laugh. Men rose and went out under the moon to listen. There was something at once terribly and tenderly familiar to at least One in those sounds.

"What in Christ's name is that?" whispered a miner, as the melody quivered far up the white street.

"It is a mockingbird," answered another who had lived in lands of palmetto and palm.

And as the engineer listened, there seemed to float to him the flower-odors of a sunnier land;—the Western hills faded as clouds fade out of the sky; and before him lay once more the fair streets of a far city, glimmering with the Mexican silver of Southern moonlight;—again he saw the rigging of masts making cobweb lines across the faces of stars and white steamers sleeping in ranks along the river's crescent-curve, and cottages vine-garlanded or banana-shadowed, and woods in their dreamy drapery of Spanish moss.

* * *

"GOT SOMETHING for you this time," said the United States mail-carrier, riding in weeks later with his bronzed face made lurid by the sanguine glow of sunset. He did not say "Cap" this time; neither did he smile. The envelope was larger than usual. The handwriting was the handwriting of a man. It contained only these words:—

DEAR——, Hortense is dead. It happened very suddenly on the night of the 24th. Come home at once. S——.

A MUNICIPAL REPORT*

By O. HENRY

The cities are full of pride,
    Challenging each to each—
This from her mountainside,
    That from her burthened beach.
            R. KIPLING.

Fancy a novel about Chicago or Buffalo, let us say, or Nashville, Tennessee! There are just three big cities in the United States that are "story cities"—New York, of course, New Orleans, and, best of the lot, San Francisco.—FRANK NORRIS.

EAST is East, and West is San Francisco, according to Californians. Californians are a race of people; they are not merely inhabitants of a State. They are the Southerners of the West. Now, Chicagoans are no less loyal to their city; but when you ask them why, they stammer and speak of lake fish and the new Odd Fellows Building. But Californians go into detail.

Of course they have, in the climate, an argument that is good for half an hour while you're thinking of your coal bills and heavy underwear. But as soon as they come to mistake your silence for conviction, madness comes upon them, and they picture the city of the Golden Gate as the Bagdad of the New World. So far, as a matter of opinion, no refutation is necessary. But, dear cousins all (from Adam and Eve descended), it is a rash one who will lay his finger on the map and say: "In this town there can be no romance—what could happen here?" Yes, it is a bold and a rash deed to challenge in one sentence history, romance, and Rand and McNally.

* From *Strictly Business* by O. Henry, copyright 1909 by Doubleday, Doran & Company, Inc.

NASHVILLE.—A city, port of delivery, and capital of the State of Tennessee, is on the Cumberland River and on the N. C. & St. L. and the L. & N. railroads. This city is regarded as the most important educational centre in the South.

I stepped off the train at 8 P. M. Having searched the thesaurus in vain for adjectives, I must, as a substitution, hie me to comparison in the form of a recipe.

Take of London fog 30 parts; malaria 10 parts; gas leaks 20 parts; dewdrops gathered in a brick yard at sunrise, 25 parts; odor of honeysuckle 15 parts. Mix.

The mixture will give you an approximate conception of a Nashville drizzle. It is not so fragrant as a mothball nor as thick as pea-soup; but 'tis enough—'twill serve.

I went to a hotel in a tumbril. It required strong self-suppression for me to keep from climbing to the top of it and giving an imitation of Sidney Carton. The vehicle was drawn by beasts of a bygone era and driven by something dark and emancipated.

I was sleepy and tired, so when I got to the hotel I hurriedly paid the fifty cents it demanded (with approximate lagniappe, I assure you). I knew his habits; and I did not want to hear it prate about its old "marster" or anything that happened "befo' de wah."

The hotel was one of the kind described as "renovated." That means $20,000 worth of new marble pillars, tiling, electric lights and brass cuspidors in the lobby, and a new L. & N. time table and a lithograph of Lookout Mountain in each one of the great rooms above. The management was without reproach, the attention full of exquisite Southern courtesy, the service as slow as the progress of a snail and as good-humored as Rip Van Winkle. The food was worth traveling a thousand miles for. There is no other hotel in the world where you can get such chicken livers *en brochette*.

At dinner I asked a Negro waiter if there was anything doing in town. He pondered gravely for a minute, then replied: "Well, boss, I don't really reckon there's anything at all doin' after sundown."

Sundown had been accomplished; it had been drowned in the drizzle long before. So that spectacle was denied me. But I went forth upon the streets in the drizzle to see what might be there.

It is built on undulating grounds; and the streets are lighted by electricity at a cost of $32,470 per annum.

As I left the hotel there was a race riot. Down upon me charged a company of freedmen, or Arabs, or Zulus, armed with—! no, I saw with relief that they were not rifles, but whips. And I saw dimly a caravan of black, clumsy vehicles; and at the reassuring shouts, "Kyar you anywhere in the town, Boss, fuh fifty cents," I reasoned that I was merely a "fare" instead of a victim.

I walked through long streets, all leading uphill. I wondered how those streets ever came down again. Perhaps they didn't until they were "graded." On a few of the "main streets" I saw lights in stores here and there; saw street cars go by conveying worthy burghers hither and yon; saw people pass engaged in the art of conversation, and heard a burst of semi-lively laughter issuing from a soda-water and ice-cream parlor. The streets other than "main" seemed to have enticed upon their borders houses consecrated to peace and domesticity. In many of them lights shone behind discreetly drawn window shades; in a few pianos tinkled orderly and irreproachable music. There was, indeed, little "doing." I wished I had come before sundown. So I returned to my hotel.

In November, 1864, the Confederate General Hood advanced against Nashville, where he shut up a National force under

General Thomas. The latter then sallied forth and defeated the Confederates in a terrible conflict.

All my life I have heard of, admired, and witnessed the fine marksmanship of the South in its peaceful conflicts in the tobacco-chewing regions. But in my hotel a surprise awaited me. There were twelve bright, new, imposing, capacious brass cuspidors in the great lobby, tall enough to be called urns and so wide-mouthed that the cracked pitcher of a lady baseball team should have been able to throw a ball into one of them at five paces distant. But, although a terrible battle had raged and was still raging, the enemy had not suffered. Bright, new, imposing, capacious, untouched, they stood. But, shades of Jefferson Brick! the tile floor—the beautiful tile floor! I could not avoid thinking of the battle of Nashville, and trying to draw, as is my foolish habit, some deductions about hereditary marksmanship.

Here I first saw Major (my misplaced courtesy) Wentworth Caswell. I knew him for a type the moment my eyes suffered from the sight of him. A rat has no geographical habitat. My old friend, A. Tennyson, said, as he so well said almost everything:

> Prophet, curse me the blabbing lip,
> And curse me the British vermin, the rat.

Let us regard the word "British" as interchangeable *ad lib.* A rat is a rat.

This man was hunting about the hotel lobby like a starved dog that had forgotten where he had buried a bone. He had a face of great acreage, red, pulpy, and with a kind of sleepy massiveness like that of Buddha. He possessed one single virtue—he was very smoothly shaven. The mark of the beast is not indelible upon a man until he goes about with a stubble. I think that if he had not used his razor that day I would have repulsed his advances, and the criminal calendar of the world would have been spared the addition of one murder.

I happened to be standing within five feet of a cuspidor when Major Caswell opened fire on it. I had been observant enough to perceive that the attacking force was using Gatlings instead of squirrel rifles; so I side-stepped so promptly that the major seized the opportunity to apologize to a non-combatant. He had the blabbing lip. In four minutes he had become my friend and had dragged me to the bar.

I desire to interpolate here that I am a Southerner. But I am not one by profession or trade. I eschew the string tie, the slouch hat, the Prince Albert, the number of bales of cotton destroyed by Sherman, and plug chewing. When the orchestra plays Dixie I do not cheer. I slide a little lower on the leather-cornered seat and, well, order another Würzburger and wish that Longstreet had— But what's the use?

Major Caswell banged the bar with his fist, and the first gun at Fort Sumter reëchoed. When he fired the last one at Appomattox I began to hope. But then he began on family trees, and demonstrated that Adam was only a third cousin of a collateral branch of the Caswell family. Genealogy disposed of, he took up, to my distaste, his private family matters. He spoke of his wife, traced her descent back to Eve, and profanely denied any possible rumor that she may have had relations in the land of Nod.

By this time I began to suspect that he was trying to obscure by noise the fact that he had ordered the drinks, on the chance that I would be bewildered into paying for them. But when they were down he crashed a silver dollar loudly upon the bar. Then, of course, another serving was obligatory. And when I had paid for that I took leave of him brusquely; for I wanted no more of him. But before I had obtained my release he had prated loudly of an income that his wife received, and showed a handful of silver money.

When I got my key at the desk the clerk said to me courteously: "If that man Caswell has annoyed you, and if you would like to make a complaint, we will have him ejected. He is a nuisance, a loafer, and without any known means of support, although he seems to have some money most of the time. But we don't seem able to hit upon any means of throwing him out legally."

"Why, no," said I, after some reflection; "I don't see my way clear to making a complaint. But I would like to place myself on record as asserting that I do not care for his company. Your town," I continued, "seems to be a quiet one. What manner of entertainment, adventure, or excitement have you to offer to the stranger within your gates?"

"Well, sir," said the clerk, "there will be a show here next Thursday. It is—I'll look it up and have the announcement sent up to your room with the ice water. Good night."

After I went up to my room I looked out the window. It was only about ten o'clock, but I looked upon a silent town. The drizzle continued, spangled with dim lights, as far apart as currants in a cake sold at the Ladies' Exchange.

"A quiet place," I said to myself, as my first shoe struck the ceiling of the occupant of the room beneath mine. "Nothing of the life here that gives color and variety to the cities in the East and West. Just a good, ordinary, humdrum, business town."

Nashville occupies a foremost place among the manufacturing centers of the country. It is the fifth boot and shoe market in the United States, the largest candy and cracker manufacturing city in the South, and does an enormous wholesale dry goods, grocery, and drug business.

I must tell you how I came to be in Nashville, and I assure you the digression brings as much tedium to me as it does to you. I was traveling elsewhere on my own business, but I had a commission from a Northern literary magazine to stop over there and establish a personal connection betwen the publication and one of its contributors, Azalea Adair.

Adair (there was no clue to the personality except the hand-writing) had sent in some essays (lost art!) and poems that had made the editors swear approvingly over their one o'clock luncheon. So they had commissioned me to round up said Adair and corner by contract his or her output at two cents a word before some other publisher offered her ten or twenty.

At nine o'clock the next morning, after my chicken livers *en brochette* (try them if you can find that hotel), I strayed out into the drizzle, which was still on for an unlimited run. At the first corner I came upon Uncle Cæsar. He was a stalwart Negro, older than the pyramids, with gray wool and a face that reminded me of Brutus, and a second afterwards of the late King Cettiwayo. He wore the most remarkable coat that I have ever seen or expect to see. It reached to his ankles and had once been a Confederate gray in colors. But rain and sun and age had so variegated it that Joseph's coat, beside, would have faded to a pale monochrome. I must linger with that coat, for it has to do with the story—the story that is so long in coming, because you can hardly expect anything to happen in Nashville.

Once it must have been the military coat of an officer. The cape of it had vanished, but all adown its front it had been frogged and tasseled magnificently. But now the frogs and tassels were gone. In their stead had been patiently stitched (I surmised by some surviving "black mammy") new frogs made of cunningly twisted common hempen twine. This twine was frayed and disheveled. It must have been added to the coat as a substitute for vanished splendors, with tasteless but painstaking devotion, for it followed faithfully the curves of the long-missing frogs. And, to complete the comedy and pathos of the garment, all its buttons were gone save one. The second button from the top alone remained. The coat was fastened by other twine strings tied through the buttonholes and other holes rudely pierced in the opposite side. There was never such a weird garment so fantastically bedecked and of so many mottled hues. The lone button was the size of a half-dollar, made of yellow horn and sewed on with coarse twine.

This Negro stood by a carriage so old that Ham himself might have started a hack line with it after he left the ark with the two animals hitched to it. As I approached he threw open the door, drew out a feather duster, waved it without using it, and said in deep, rumbling tones:

"Step right in, suh; ain't a speck of dust in it—jus' got back from a funeral, suh."

I inferred that on such gala occasions carriages were given an extra cleaning. I looked up and down the street and perceived that there was little choice among the vehicles for hire that lined the curb. I looked in my memorandum book for the address of Azalea Adair.

"I want to go to 861 Jessamine Street," I said, and was about to step into the hack. But for an instant the thick, long, gorilla-like arm of the Negro barred me. On his massive and saturnine face a look of sudden suspicion and enmity flashed for a moment. Then, with quickly returning conviction, he asked blandishingly: "What are you gwine there for, boss?"

"What is that to you?" I asked, a little sharply.

"Nothin', suh, jus' nothin'. Only it's a lonesome kind of part of town and few folks ever has business out there. Step right in. The seats is clean—jes' got back from a funeral, suh."

A mile and a half it must have been to our journey's end. I could hear nothing but the fearful rattle of the ancient hack over the uneven brick paving; I could smell nothing but the drizzle, now further flavored with coal smoke and something like a mixture of tar and oleander blossoms. All I could see through the streaming windows, were two rows of dim houses.

The city has an area of 10 square miles; 181 miles of streets, of which 137 miles are paved; a system of water-works that cost $2,000,000, with 77 miles of mains.

Eight-sixty-one Jessamine Street was a decayed mansion. Thirty yards back from the street it stood, outmerged in a splendid grove of trees and untrimmed shrubbery. A row of box bushes overflowed and almost hid the paling fence from sight; the gate was kept closed by a rope noose that encircled the gate post and the first paling of the gate. But when you got inside you saw that 861 was a shell, a shadow, a ghost of former grandeur and excellence. But in the story, I have not yet got inside.

When the hack had ceased from rattling and the weary quadrupeds came to a rest I handed my jehu his fifty cents with an additional quarter, feeling a glow of conscious generosity, as I did so. He refused it.

"It's two dollars, suh," he said.

"How's that?" I asked. "I plainly heard you call out at the hotel: 'Fifty cents to any part of the town.' "

"It's two dollars, suh," he repeated obstinately. "It's a long ways from the hotel."

"It is within the city limits and well within them," I argued. "Don't think that you have picked up a greenhorn Yankee. Do you see those hills over there?" I went on, pointing toward the east (I could not see them, myself, for the drizzle); "well, I was born and raised on their other side. You old fool nigger, can't you tell people from other people when you see 'em?"

The grim face of King Cettiwayo softened. "Is you from the South, suh? I reckon it was them shoes of yourn fooled me. They is somethin' sharp in the toes for a Southern gen'l'man to wear."

"Then the charge is fifty cents, I suppose?" said I inexorably.

His former expression, a mingling of cupidity and hostility, returned, remained ten seconds, and vanished.

"Boss," he said, "fifty cents is right; but I *needs* two dollars, suh; I'm *obleeged* to have two dollars. I ain't *demandin'* it now, suh; after I knows whar you's from; I'm jus' sayin' that I *has* to have two dollars to-night, and business is mighty po'."

Peace and confidence settled upon his heavy features. He had been luckier than he had hoped. Instead of having picked up a greenhorn, ignorant of rates, he had come upon an inheritance.

"You confounded old rascal," I said, reaching down to my pocket, "you ought to be turned over to the police."

For the first time I saw him smile. He knew; *he knew;* HE KNEW.

I gave him two one-dollar bills. As I handed them over I noticed that one of them had seen parlous times.

Its upper right-hand corner was missing, and it had been torn through in the middle, but joined again. A strip of blue tissue paper, pasted over the split, preserved its negotiability.

Enough of the African bandit for the present: I left him happy, lifted the rope, and opened the creaky gate.

The house, as I said, was a shell. A paint brush had not touched it in twenty years. I could not see why a strong wind should not have bowled it over like a house of cards until I looked again at the trees that hugged it close—the trees that saw the battle of Nashville and still drew their protecting branches around it against storm and enemy and cold.

Azalea Adair, fifty years old, white-haired, a descendant of the cavaliers, as thin and frail as the house she lived in, robed in the cheapest and cleanest dress I ever saw, with an air as simple as a queen's, received me.

The reception room seemed a mile square, because there was nothing in it except some rows of books, on unpainted white-pine bookshelves, a cracked marble-top table, a rag rug,a hairless horse-hair sofa, and two or three chairs. Yes, there was a picture on the wall, a colored crayon drawing of a cluster of pansies. I looked around for the portrait of Andrew Jackson and the pine-cone hanging basket but they were not there.

Azalea Adair and I had conversation, a little of which will be repeated to you. She was a product of the old South, gently nurtured in the sheltered life. Her learning was not broad, but was deep and of splendid originality in its somewhat narrow scope. She had been educated at home, and her knowledge of the world was derived from inference and by inspiration. Of such is the precious, small group of essayists made. While she talked to me I kept brushing my fingers, trying, unconsciously, to rid them guiltily of the absent dust from the half-calf backs of Lamb, Chaucer, Hazlitt, Marcus Aurelius, Montaigne, and Hood. She was exquisite, she was a valuable discovery. Nearly everybody nowadays knows too much—oh, so much too much—of real life.

I could perceive clearly that Azalea Adair was very poor. A house and a dress she had, not much else, I fancied. So, divided between my duty to the magazine and my loyalty to the poets and essayists who fought Thomas in the valley of the Cumberland, I listened to her voice, which was like a harpsichord's, and found that I could not speak of contracts. In the presence of the nine Muses and the three Graces one hesitated to lower the topic to two cents. There would have to be another colloquy after I had regained my commercialism. But I spoke of my mission, and three o'clock of the next afternoon was set for the discussion of the business proposition.

"Your town," I said, as I began to make ready to depart (which is the time for smooth generalities), "seems to be a quiet, sedate place. A home town, I should say, where few things out of the ordinary ever happen."

It carries on an extensive trade in stoves and hollow ware with the West and South, and its flouring mills have a daily capacity of more than 2,000 barrels.

Azalea Adair seemed to reflect.

"I have never thought of it that way," she said, with a kind of sincere intensity that seemed to belong to her. "Isn't it in the still, quiet places that things do happen? I fancy that when God began to create the earth on the first Monday morning one could have leaned out one's window and heard the drops of mud splashing from His trowel as He built up the everlasting hills. What did the noisiest project in the world—I mean the building of the tower of Babel—result in finally? A page and a half of Esperanto in the *North American Review*."

"Of course," said I platitudinously, "human nature is the same everywhere; but there is more color—er—more drama and movement and—er—romance in some cities than in others."

"On the surface," said Azalea Adair. "I have traveled many times around the world in a golden airship wafted on two wings—print and dreams. I have seen (on one of my imaginary tours) the Sultan of Turkey bowstring with his own hands one of his wives who had uncovered her face in public. I have seen a man in Nashville tear up his theatre tickets because his wife was going out with her face covered—with rice powder. In San Francisco's Chinatown I saw the slave girl Sing Yee dipped slowly, inch by inch, in boiling almond oil to make her swear she would never see her American lover again. She gave in when the boiling oil had reached three inches above her knee. At a euchre party in East Nashville the other night I saw Kitty Morgan cut dead by seven of her schoolmates and lifelong friends because she had married a house painter. The boiling oil was sizzling as high as her heart; but I wish you could have seen the fine little smile that she carried from table to table. Oh, yes, it is a humdrum town. Just a few miles of red brick houses and mud and stores and lumber yards."

Some one knocked hollowly at the back of the house. Azalea Adair breathed a soft apology and went to investigate the sound. She came back in three minutes with brightened eyes, a faint flush on her cheeks, and ten years lifted from her shoulders.

"You must have a cup of tea before you go," she said, "and a sugar cake."

She reached and shook a little iron bell. In shuffled a

small Negro girl about twelve, barefoot, not very tidy, glowering at me with thumb in mouth and bulging eyes.

Azalea Adair opened a tiny, worn purse and drew out a dollar bill, a dollar bill with the upper right-hand corner missing, torn in two pieces and pasted together again with a strip of blue tissue paper. It was one of the bills I had given the piratical Negro—there was no doubt of it.

"Go up to Mr. Baker's store on the corner, Impy," she said, handing the girl the dollar bill, "and get a quarter of a pound of tea—the kind he always sends me—and ten cents worth of sugar cakes. Now, hurry. The supply of tea in the house happens to be exhausted," she explained to me.

Impy left by the back way. Before the scrape of her hard, bare feet had died away on the back porch, a wild shriek—I was sure it was hers—filled the hollow house. Then the deep, gruff tones of an angry man's voice mingled with the girl's further squeals and unintelligible words.

Azalea Adair rose without surprise or emotion and disappeared. For two minutes I heard the hoarse rumble of the man's voice; then something like an oath and a slight scuffle, and she returned calmly to her chair.

"This is a roomy house," she said, "and I have a tenant for part of it. I am sorry to have to rescind my invitation to tea. It was impossible to get the kind I always use at the store. Perhaps to-morrow Mr. Baker will be able to supply me."

I was sure that Impy had not had time to leave the house. I inquired concerning street-car lines and took my leave. After I was well on my way I remembered that I had not learned Azalea Adair's name. But to-morrow would do.

That same day I started in on the course of iniquity

that this eventful city forced upon me. I was in the town only two days, but in that time I managed to lie shamelessly by telegraph, and to be an accomplice—after the fact, if that is the correct legal term—to a murder.

As I rounded the corner nearest my hotel the Afrite coachman of the polychromatic, nonpareil coat seized me, swung open the dungeony door of his peripatetic sarcophagus, flirted the feather duster, and began his ritual: "Step right in, boss. Carriage is clean—jes' got back from a funeral. Fifty cents to any—"

And then he knew me and grinned broadly. "'Scuse me, boss; you is de genl'man what rid out with me dis mawnin'. Thank you kindly, suh."

"I am going out to 861 again to-morrow afternoon at three," said I, "and if you will be here, I'll let you drive me. So you know Miss Adair?" I concluded, thinking of my dollar bill.

"I belonged to her father, Judge Adair, suh," he replied.

"I judge that she is pretty poor," I said. "She hasn't much money to speak of, has she?"

For an instant I looked again at the fierce countenance of King Cettiwayo, and then he changed back to an extortionate old Negro hack driver.

"She ain't gwine to starve, suh," he said slowly. "She has reso'ces, suh; she has reso'ces."

"I shall pay you fifty cents for the trip," said I.

"Dat is puffeckly correct, suh," he answered humbly. "I jus' had to have dat two dollars dis mawnin', boss."

I went to the hotel and lied by electricity. I wired the magazine: "A. Adair holds out for eight cents a word."

The answer that came back was: "Give it to her quick, you duffer."

Just before dinner "Major" Wentworth Caswell bore

down upon me with the greetings of a long-lost friend. I have seen few men whom I have so instantaneously hated, and of whom it was so difficult to be rid. I was standing at the bar when he invaded me; therefore I could not wave the white ribbon in his face. I would have paid gladly for the drinks, hoping, thereby, to escape another; but he was one of those despicable, roaring, advertising, bibbers who must have brass bands and fireworks attend upon every cent that they waste in their follies.

With an air of producing millions he drew two one-dollar bills from a pocket and dashed one of them upon the bar. I looked once more at the dollar bill with the upper right-hand corner missing, torn through the middle, and patched with a strip of blue tissue paper. It was my dollar bill again. It could have been no other.

I went up to my room. The drizzle and the monotony of a dreary, eventless Southern town had made me tired and listless. I remember that just before I went to bed I mentally disposed of the mysterious dollar bill (which might have formed the clew to a tremendously fine detective story of San Francisco) by saying to myself sleepily: "Seems as if a lot of people here own stock in the Hack-Driver's Trust. Pays dividends promptly, too. Wonder if—" Then I fell asleep.

King Cettiwayo was at his post the next day, and rattled my bones over the stones out to 861. He was to wait and rattle me back again when I was ready.

Azalea Adair looked paler and cleaner and frailer than she had looked on the day before. After she had signed the contract at eight cents per word she grew still paler and began to slip out of her chair. Without much trouble I managed to get her up on the antediluvian horsehair sofa and then I ran out on the sidewalk and yelled to the coffee-colored Pirate to bring a doctor. With a wisdom that I had not suspected in him, he abandoned his team and struck off up the street, afoot, realizing the value of speed. In ten minutes he returned with a grave, gray-haired, and capable man of medicine. In a few words (worth much less than eight cents each) I explained to him my presence in the hollow house of mystery. He bowed with stately understanding, and turned to the old Negro.

"Uncle Cæsar," he said calmly, "run up to my house and ask Miss Lucy to give you a cream pitcher full of fresh milk and a half a tumbler of port wine. And hurry back. Don't drive—run. I want you to get back sometime this week."

It occurred to me that Dr. Merriman also felt a distrust as to the speeding powers of the land-pirate's steeds. After Uncle Cæsar was gone, lumberingly, but swiftly, up the street, the doctor looked me over with great politeness and as much careful calculation until he had decided that I might do.

"It is only a case of insufficient nutrition," he said. "In other words, the result of poverty, pride, and starvation. Mrs. Caswell has many devoted friends who would be glad to aid her, but she will accept nothing except from that old Negro, Uncle Cæsar, who was once owned by her family."

"Mrs. Caswell!" said I, in surprise. And then I looked at the contract and saw that she had signed it "Azalea Adair Caswell."

"I thought she was Miss Adair," I said.

"Married to a drunken, worthless loafer, sir," said the doctor. "It is said that he robs her even of the small sums that her old servant contributes toward her support."

When the milk and wine had been brought the doctor soon revived Azalea Adair. She sat up and talked of the beauty of the autumn leaves that were then in season, and their height of color. She referred lightly to her fainting seizure as the outcome of an old palpitation of the heart. Impy fanned her as she lay on the sofa. The doctor was due elsewhere, and I followed him to the door. I told him that it was within my power and intentions to make a reasonable advance of money to Azalea Adair on future contributions to the magazine, and he seemed pleased.

"By the way," he said, "perhaps you would like to know that you have had royalty for a coachman. Old Cæsar's grandfather was a king in Congo. Cæsar himself has royal ways, as you may have observed."

As the doctor was moving off I heard Uncle Cæsar's voice inside: "Did he git bofe of dem two dollars from you, Mis' Zalea?"

"Yes, Cæsar," I heard Azalea Adair answer weakly. And then I went in and concluded business negotiations with our contributor. I assumed the responsibility of advancing fifty dollars, putting it as a necessary formality in binding our bargain. And then Uncle Cæsar drove me back to the hotel.

Here ends all of the story as far as I can testify as a witness. The rest must be only bare statements of facts.

At about six o'clock I went out for a stroll. Uncle Cæsar was at his corner. He threw open the door of his carriage, flourished his duster, and began his depressing formula: "Step right in, suh. Fifty cents to anywhere in the city—hack's puffickly clean, suh—jus' got back from a funeral—"

And then he recognized me. I think his eyesight was getting bad. His coat had taken on a few more faded shades of color, the twine strings were more frayed and ragged, the last remaining button—the button of yellow horn—was gone. A motley descendant of kings was Uncle Cæsar!

About two hours later I saw an excited crowd besieging the front of a drug store. In a desert where nothing happens this was manna; so I wedged my way inside. On an extemporized couch of empty boxes and chairs was stretched the mortal corporeality of Major Wentworth Caswell. A doctor was testing him for the immortal ingredient. His decision was that it was conspicuous by its absence.

The erstwhile Major had been found dead on a dark street and brought by curious and ennuied citizens to the drug store. The late human being had been engaged in terrific battle—the details showed that. Loafer and reprobate though he had been, he had been also a warrior. But he had lost. His hands were yet clinched so tightly that his fingers would not be opened. The gentle citizens who had known him stood about and searched their vocabularies to find some good words, if it were possible, to speak of him. One kind-looking man said, after much thought: "When 'Cas' was about fo'teen he was one of the best spellers in the school."

While I stood there the fingers of the right hand of "the man that was," which hung down the side of a white pine box, relaxed, and dropped something at my feet. I covered it with one foot quietly, and a little later on I picked it up and pocketed it. I reasoned that in his last struggle his hand must have seized that object unwittingly and held it in a death grip.

At the hotel that night the main topic of conversation, with the possible exceptions of politics and prohibition, was the demise of Major Caswell. I heard one man say to a group of listeners:

"In my opinion, gentlemen, Caswell was murdered by

some of these no-account niggers for his money. He had fifty dollars this afternoon which he showed to several gentlemen in the hotel. When he was found the money was not on his person."

I left the city the next morning at nine, and as the train was crossing the bridge over the Cumberland River I took out of my pocket a yellow horn overcoat button the size of a fifty-cent piece, with frayed ends of coarse twine hanging from it, and cast it out of the window into the slow, muddy waters below.

I wonder what's doing in Buffalo!

HER HUSBAND*

By GEORGE MADDEN MARTIN

IT HAD come with its swift threatening consequences. And now that it was here, it seemed to Edith Thornberry she had known all her life that this moment would confront her.

An up-country black boy newly come in the locality had appeared in the kitchen doorway of an unprotected white woman, the wife of a section hand employed by the railroad, living on the outskirts of the mill settlement. The woman, fleeing by way of a front door as the boy stepped in at the back and screaming as she ran, spread the word.

This was in the forenoon. The black boy, emerging from the kitchen doorway to find the alarm given, fled. Since noon the hunt for him was on.

* * *

IT WAS FOUR in the afternoon now. Edith had not known the world about her could be so still. A region of sandy loam and long-leaf pine, the community was made up of mill hands—white and black—their families, the half dozen clerks in the office, her husband who was the owner of the mill, and herself; these with the mill, the railroad station, and the switches.

A sluggish stream, half creek, half bayou, and spanned by a bridge, drained the low country about, and cut the mill and its population off from the high lands. Beyond the plant and the clustering shacks and cottages of the employees stretched the canebrake, a peninsula of relatively solid land, which out-thrust itself into the farther marshlands.

* Reprinted from *Harpers Magazine* with the courteous permission of the publishers and the author.

Within fifteen minutes after the woman passed Edith's gate, crying her terror as she ran, the mill had shut down—the scream of the saws eating into the logs and the pant of the escaping steam stopping abruptly.

In less time than this, indeed, as Edith, once she had gathered the meaning of what had happened, hurried into the house to call the mill and warn her husband. She found the place empty, the negro cook and negro housegirl gone, pantry, kitchen, and kitchen-porch deserted.

A moment ago Viney the laundress, busy over her tubs under the pecan tree, had lifted her voice in mounting, quavering song.

This laundress, who claimed she came from Edith's native town in a neighboring state, was an old negress. The cook and the housegirl were young women. Outbursts of song over their work, songs of their race such as were outpoured by the older woman, never came from them. The three, however, old and young alike, were gone now.

As Edith, coming back into the body of the house, went to the telephone, David, her husband, appeared, running up the steps of the front porch and into the hall where she stood. He thrust her aside, telling her the boy had fled into the canebrake and that a posse was getting ready to follow, calling this back as he went up the stairs at a leap.

She followed him, standing with him in his room as he flung off his coat, her fear being that he find the servants gone and she here in the house alone.

She had told herself from the moment she heard the woman's story that it would be David—with possibly the clerks—against the certain wills and the inevitable purpose of the white mill hands.

Horror at what might have been but for the woman's

escape still submerged her; horror that stifled and choked her and sent shuddering tremors through her body. But beneath its recurring floods the ground on which she always believed she stood remained firm, and for this she thanked God.

If, as she feared, there was to be attempted violence here to-day, the more it fell to her now to hurry David back to his post. Cut off from the surrounding regions as the mill was, the issue was between him and these white mill hands, his employees.

That her heart thudded as she stood watching him while he drew in his belt and slipped his revolver in his pocket mattered not at all, her eyes gathering up into her consciousness his features, his carriage, his person. She was the personal equation, and as such was subordinate to the larger, the immediate claim. She was here to aid him, to speed him, to wish him on his way back to the mill and his men.

He was thirty-three, a man still young who had prospered beyond even his own belief in himself, and marked by a white heat of energy and driving will. His features were bold and aquiline, his skin was tanned to a fine clear brown, his expression now as always was intent and keen.

Granting that in the event of trouble the clerks failed him. Boys they seemed as she thought of them now. Then it was David alone. It was David and herself, their backs to the wall against the odds if it became necessary.

Tears burned behind her eyelids. Together with her affection for her husband, she was conscious always of a yearning, a brooding, a passion of longing over him which would not be quieted; conscious that along certain lines instinctive and habitual with her, her taken-for-granted premises and assumptions, she spoke a language he did not always understand—or understanding, did not, accept.

"You'll have your dinner before you go, David? It'll take only a minute to get something together?"

"I can't stop for it, Edie."

Hurrying down, she had two sandwiches waiting for him when he joined her a moment later, swiftly and deftly made, and ice-cold tea in a glass. She watched him while he ate, one of those women who, giving themselves, give wholly and with marvelous tenderness, the simplicity of devotion expressed through ministry.

"Sadie Henderson mustn't go back to the section-house, David. I told some of the women to bring her here."

"She's at her cousin's up near the mill. She'll be better off with her own sort."

He turned as he reached the doorway leading to the porch, and kissed her. She put a hand on each of his shoulders, a woman ordinarily of few gestures, and in her turn kissed him, the rare expression of spirit which, once its affection is given, does not waver. This swift David with his eagle-keen features was beautiful—oh, beautiful to the eye, and she, the woman, delighted in his beauty.

He paused again, this time on the gravel at the foot of the porch steps, and turned to speak to her on the steps above. His eyes had narrowed as if they were seeing not her but his course ahead, and his voice was curt. She was secondary in his thoughts, she saw—as indeed at this moment she should be.

"Promise me you won't let yourself get worked up, Edie. God knows I'm sorry you have to be here at a time like this. Forget it if you will. Cut it out. Find a book. Write letters. Get busy at your piano."

"Have you talked yet with Chinquapin, David? And with Mr. Delahunt?"

His eyes and consciousness alike had come round to her

now. Chinquapin was the county seat and nearest town, twenty miles away. Delahunt, who lived at Chinquapin, was the sheriff. Her question left David frowning.

"Listen to me. This is a man's, not a woman's job. Get that, Edie? Yes, since you want to know, Delahunt, or rather his wife, has been on the line. Now listen again and I'll promise *you*. There shan't be a thing out of hand. Five minutes after the first word reached the mill of what happened, every man had his orders. It's in our several hands, and we'll keep it there. There'll be no interference or trouble from the outside, because we're leaving no chance for any. First word as I've said, and we sent a posse of men, *white* men, twenty-odd, to patrol the bridge on the other side. Forget it now. I ask you to, I want you to."

She repeated his phrases, dwelling on them, finding in them reassurance and comfort.

"In your hands—everything seen to—every man has his orders. I'm so glad you've told me, David."

And still she stood there, stood after he had gone, the gate in the hedge at the end of the gravel walk swinging to behind him.

She was his junior by one year, a woman with the charm of simplicity and comeliness. There was a directness about her, and in general an opulence of frank enjoyment and well-being.

David was from the same neighboring state and locality as herself, having removed to this state of his adoption in his boyhood. Reticent as to his background and his kindred, Edith took him for himself, as he would have her do. What he wanted her to know he would tell her in his own time and way.

The first time she met him and heard his name, Thornberry, an unexplainable thing occurred. This was four years ago and in Washington, at the home of Big Albion Burns, as his world calls him, maker and un-maker of senators and congressmen in David's adopted, as well as his native, state. Edith at the time was secretary of the big man's wife. And the unexplainable thing was this:

As she heard the name Thornberry, a picture arose in her mind out of her childhood's past, of a straggling line of hill-billies, six men upon starved and bony nags, picking their way along the street of the old Southern town that was her home. And, perched behind the squeaking saddle of one of the six, a boy about her own age and size. They were come to court, offenders against the federal law; and her grandfather, with whom she lived an orphaned child, was the federal judge who tried them; her grandfather who removed to Washington the next year, and she with him, called to a seat upon the supreme bench.

She saw this grandfather in memory now, recalled him in his physical aspect. He was of big stature, his eyes far-set beneath craggy brows, his lips accurately closed—a just and comprehending man, beloved and adored in his own household, a great judge.

Yes, this sense with her always and overwhelmingly of the authority of the law, of its sovereignty, its godhead, this was hers by tradition and inheritance. There was decent stock in the line of men back of Edith. As for that, there was decent stock in the women back of her, too, mothers of these men.

A judge upon the supreme bench, unless he brings his competency with him to office, leaves no fortune when he dies. Edith, with a yearly few hundreds of her own only, was earning her living happily and contentedly when she met David.

It was Big Albion Burns, her old friend in whose house

she was living, who presented him and smilingly defined him:

"Thornberry and I are of the *new* South, Edith, my dear. As I've told you times before, *my* grandfather was a blacksmith, putting shoes on his neighbors' horses. My father was a molder, making castings in the foundry I own to-day. I carried a dinner-bucket at my start. *Your* South the *old* South, if it believes in democracy and its workings at all, must believe in the *new* South, which means Thornberry and me."

Edith did believe in the *new* South; she believed in it then and she believed in it now. She had her few hundreds a year and her work, and was capable and happy in it, but she was alone in the world, and felt her loneliness. Within a surprisingly short time she believed in David Thornberry because he urged it, and because she was glad to. Within a year she had married him.

In the three years of her married life she had been charmed and delighted that man and wife could be such playfellows and companions. She was an outdoor creature by instinct and early habit, brought up to like dogs and horses, and David was a skilled and natural woodsman. They rode, they hunted, they tramped, they motored, they went for days together in their houseboat through the creeks and bayous to the coast and open water. He was on the speedy way to wealth and competency, and declared that within the next few years he would turn the mill over to a manager, and he and she would go out into the world, *her* world, he called it, and live!

Her world? And was it true then, this consciousness which, haunting the serenity of her new life, would not down, this gathering realization that she and her world spoke a language, a speech born of a common tradition, a common acceptance, a common conduct, which David did not understand, and which Big Albion Burns and his motherly and kindly wife *did?*

Again tears burned behind her eyelids. David had flung his hat on a table when he arrived, and when he went had worn an old motor cap. Lifting the hat as she came into the house, she pressed it to her with a yearning, a brooding passion of longing.

* * *

IT WAS FOUR in the afternoon now. The assurance born of David's words had left Edith. She had called up the mill twice and been there in her car once, to no purpose. She had found the place deserted except for Cass Boswell, the boss of the yard crew, who was in charge. He was noncommittal and gave her no satisfaction beyond the statement that Mr. Thornberry wasn't there.

Returning, she stopped her car at the door of Sadie Henderson's cousin. There was no answer to her tap, the two women, as she believed, disappearing out the back door as she knocked at the front.

She stopped at the houses of certain other women. Gaunt figures for the most part these women were, in skimpy cotton skirts and faded cotton waists, spiritless creatures with spiritless eyes. Noncommittal, furtive, what did they and Cass Bosswell know that she did not? Not a negro—man, woman, or child—did she see.

Reaching home, the house with its big rooms and bigger porches front and back seemed more silent, more deserted, and even more removed and apart from all knowledge of what was happening, alone in a sense poignant and terrifying. She went again through the empty lower floor, and came as aimlessly back to the front porch.

The tramp of feet reached her. A score of men in groups of three and four came in sight, their heads and shoulders rising and falling above her hedge with their striding gait. Following these some hundred yards, came a second score.

She realized the gravity which had come into the situation with this new element. She was dismayed at its appearance here. These sand-hillers, tramping along the wooden sidewalk outside her hedge, must have crossed the bridge. And to cross the bridge they must have passed the twenty-odd men put there to guard it. Edith had little of her husband's confidence in these mill hands; she shared none of his faith in their reliability.

She in her neighboring state had known this class of poor whites now tramping by her gate, not as sand-hillers, but as hill-billies, a term signifying the same thing and interchangeable. Under whatever name, the thing it signified was a breed so poor of spirit, so mean of courage, that the world about it, white and black, despised it. Cass Boswell was of sand-hiller stock himself.

These men must have passed the patrol at the bridge. She went in and called the mill again. As before, Cass answered.

"Mr. Thornberry's still away, yes'm."

"Go and find him."

"Reckon I mought ez wal' let ye hev it, Mis' Thornberry. He's outen wi' th' posse beatin' the brake. He mought be back in er hour, yit mought be midnight, yit mought be mawnin'."

She rang off and called for Chinquapin. She knew the sheriff and she knew his wife. David was a bit of a politician in local and also in state affairs, and was proud of his acquaintance and his popularity in the county.

Mrs. Delahunt answered the call:

"Yes, oh, yes, we got the news all right, Mrs. Thornberry—got it right away after it happened, I guess. The sand-hillers are comin' in, you say? Well, that looks bad, surely. Mr. Delahunt was off in the county on a summons when the word came; I took the message myself, and he had to be found. Getting back here to Chinquapin, he had to swear in some extra deputies. These things take time, you see. They got away from here twenty minutes ago, yes, all of twenty minutes. The bunch o' 'em filled three flivvers."

Edith went back to the porch. The gate in the hedge banged. Jim Hester, the foreman of the drying shed at the mill, came in. Lean and shambling, he too was of sand-hiller stock, and to Edith's mind of a common stripe with Cass Boswell, whom she did not like.

She had long since noticed that Hester's wife had a timid glance and that his children were afraid of him. She had said so to David, and he had laughed at her, saying it took all kinds to run a mill here in the backwoods.

She knew that Jim Hester in his turn did not like her, knew that he belittled to the other men her attempts to better conditions for the families of the mill hands, and she believed he would do her an ill turn if the opportunity came his way. She had once seen him kick a female dog—his own dog, the creature soon to litter—and this for no visible reason but for his own gratification. And she saw him leer when she, Edith, cried out, pleased when he knew that it hurt her too.

"Wanter use yo' telephone, Mis' Thornberry. I'm jus' come in f'om th' bridge en' I got ter git back."

A third group of sand-hillers passed.

Edith questioned him:

"You say you're just from the bridge? What's happened? How did these men get by you? They're coming in right along."

He eyed her, as he had that time in the case of the dog, with a leering satisfaction. His tongue licked his lips.

He had her again, it would seem, where it pleased him to have her.

"Git by? How'd you mean 'git by,' Mis' Thornberry? They cyant come tew fas' ner tew many, d'yer reckon? Th' more we air th' quicker hell fer th' nigger, ain't it?"

He turned to the telephone and in his turn called for the mill. His hair that lay over long on his sallow neck was dank and heavy, and his person was slovenly.

"Ary news come in f'om th' brake, Cass?"

Apparently there was none.

"Ary thing furder heerd f'om Chinquapin? Delahunt made his git-erway f'om thar yit?"

Cass evidently gave Jim the same news that Mrs. Delahunt had given Edith.

"Wall, trust us'n, Cass. Delahunt'll never git by us'n holdin' th' bridge, till it's over. With a shotgun tew ev'y mammy's son uv us'n waitin' thar fur him, he mought ez well turn eroun' en go back tew home, him an' his crowd, en they know it."

Edith watched him out through the gate. Going back to the telephone, this time to spread the news far and wide, she found the wire cut. Jim had done it. He mistrusted her. It merely meant she must run her car to the mill again and get her message over the mill telephone to Chinquapin and the region at large.

The sun was dropping beyond the bridge and behind the hills when Edith returned.

As on her first visit, Cass met her as her car stopped. He let her descend. But when she said she'd come to use the office telephone, he stepped between her and the office doorway.

"The line's dead."

She believed that he lied. A middle-aged man, his stubby red beard did not cover the cunning line of the mouth. But when she pushed by him she found the door locked, and turning to demand the key, he had disappeared.

She went across the yard and the tracks to the box-like little railroad station. The place was empty and the door here too was locked.

Coming and returning, again she passed groups of women who, talking together, fell silent at her approach, or turning, slipped within doors.

Reaching her gate, here came more sand-hillers. Their gaze as their eyes met hers was hostile.

She went in and sank on a step of her porch, her head bowed, her heart chilled. She thought of her grandfather, she thought of Big Albion Burns, she thought of— and her heart cried out and her hands out-stretched to— David!

Evening was here, cool and pure and still. Edith, still sitting upon her step, stood up. She'd go in and have supper ready in case David should return.

Going through the house, she came on Cynthia, her cook, sitting on a step of the back porch, bowed in her turn, her head upon her knees.

"Cynthy, you're here! You're back. Oh, I'm *glad!*"

Cynthia, lifting her head, stood up. She was a young married woman with little children. Her set face was without expression.

"Reckon I'll go in an' start supper."

"Cynthia, what do those shots mean I've been hearing?"

Three at a time they'd been, and from time to time repeated, starting in the distance from the direction of the brake and coming nearer.

She took a step closer and, laying a hand on the brown wrist, compelled Cynthia to look up.

"We're both women. Tell me what you know. It means. . . ?"

Cynthia raised her eyes far enough to rest on and search Edith's face. The gaze fell and she spoke, looking straight ahead. Her words came in shifting cadences, now fiercely and bitterly full and clear, now without inflection in a dull monotony. Past and present were met in her now, she was at once the young and the old negro.

"It means they caught him."

"And then?"

"They're bringin' him in."

"In where?"

"Where the road out of the brake crosses the switches an' the track. They're waitin' for him there."

"Who's bringing him in? Who's waiting for him? Waiting for what?"

Edith's gaze was riveted to Cynthia's face. Her questions came sharp, like cries. She had a choking, stifling sense that Cynthia, in common with the mill women earlier in the afternoon, was sparing her, was withholding from her some knowledge which must rend and hurt her.

Sudden passion flared through Cynthia's words. It was the young negro in her speaking now. Her head was upflung and she looked at Edith squarely.

"Mr. Thornberry an' his posse are bringin' him in. He ain't nothin' but a boy. He ain't twenty years old. My mother knows his folks. Mrs. Henderson, she's been allowin' up to her cousin's she ain't no ways certain what he came to her kitchen door for."

"They're bringing him in—go on."

"Cass Boswell an' his sand-hiller kinfolks are waitin' for them on the road the other side of the switches. Jim

Hester an' his crowd are at the bridge holdin' the sheriff up till it's over. They know their parts, ev'y man of 'em. Mr. Thornberry tol' 'em off himse'f, ev'y man to his place."

And still Edith's eyes were riveted on Cynthia's face. Her own face took on a growing remoteness, a whitening pallor.

And still she gazed. Out of the meaning that punctuated Cynthia's words, streams of horror seemed to pour toward her and envelop her. David, her husband. David, the father of the child she had reason to believe in these last few days, she was to bear.

"You're wrong about Mr. Thornberry, Cynthia. You're wrong, wrong! I tell you you're *wrong!*"

She felt a shuddering and reeling of all her known world.

The dusk had thickened, and here and there a star was gleaming through. Edith climbed into the car still standing at her gate. She had pulled a sweater over her muslin dress. Her hand on the wheel, the car moved swiftly off.

She was thinking of David as she urged it on. Her face was bloodless and her eyes stared ahead. Her mind went back to that first meeting with him, back to the words of Big Albion Burns, his sponsor:

"Your South, the *old* South, if it believes in democracy and its workings at all, must believe in David and me."

She believed in David. She was on her way to him now. He only could shake her faith in him.

* * *

It was over when she got there. For all the mad speed of her coming, it was over even to some scattering shots to insure the completeness of the business.

The moon was coming up, emerging over the horizon.

Edith, on reaching the railroad crossing, had rushed her car at the steep roadbed and mounting the track had paused there abruptly; ahead of her the switches, the road emerging out of the canebrake, and the massed crowd about to disperse.

Had secrecy been her end, perversity would have proclaimed her. Indifferent as to who saw her, she backed down the roadbed, across the sandy road by which she had come, over the coarse weeds of the open ground, into the lee of the drying shed of the mill. The mill truck and the flivver of the office force already stood there.

Sitting with her hand on the wheel, concerned only with her need of finding and hearing from David, she let the returning crowd pour by.

They came silently and swiftly, pouring up over the track and down the descent of the road in front of her, moving as by a common haste, a common spur. For a moment a silent continuous stream, and then they would be gone.

Edith's teeth suddenly chattered and her body shook. These were white men, American born. No imported foreign labor as yet had reached this portion of the state. These were American-born white men who, having lent themselves to an act, were fleeing secretly and undeclared. These were American-born Southern white men who under the test were showing yellow. A night wind had sprung up, and again she shivered.

With the last of the dispersing crowd appearing over the roadbed came David. A moment for him to make the descent, and Edith gliding forward would intercept and meet him, would hear from his own lips his refutation of any part in this unlawful act.

She saw him come, clean cut in the light of the mounting moon intent, alert. One of his clerks was with him.

His hand came down on the boy's shoulder, and he spoke abruptly:

"By God, we had it to do, Jimmy, and we've done it! The world couldn't hold that black boy and any woman you and I care for."

* * *

THEY HAD PASSED now to the last one of them—mill hands, sand-hillers, Cass Boswell, David, the boy clerk—melted into the haze of the shining night. Their dispersal was a thing of moments, not minutes, a going as sinister as it was craven.

Edith shuddered violently anew. She was deadly pale. Then she sat erect, in her countenance that intent stillness which speaks absorption and concentration. The next moment her car slid forward, and this time mounted and crossed the track. It stopped at the foot of the descent on the other side, and she stepped out. Taking a cinder path which led across the open ground to an unpainted shack that, facing the switches, stood apart under a clump of pines, she tapped at the door, calling her name as she knocked.

"It's Mrs. Thornberry, Edith Thornberry."

The door opened on Viney, the old laundress who lived there alone. Edith spoke to her beseechingly, laying a hand on her arm and drawing her out beyond the doorsill. The skin of the old creature was gray, witness to her knowledge of the business just over with beyond the switches. But she listened as Edith talked, regarding her with clear, scrutinizing eyes.

"Viney, when I first came here you told me that you knew Mr. David when he was a boy, and you and he lived in the piney woods near my old home. I didn't ask you more then. I ask you now—who was he, Viney?"

The eyes of the two women met and held. The hand of Edith resting on the arm of Viney, tightened.

"One uv th' Laurel Cove hill-billy crowd. His pappy war shot daid in yo' gran'pa's co'te-room, on account uv him profferin' evi-*dence* against th' y'uther five men in th' case, calkilatin' tew save his own skin. Yo' gran'pa paid th' boy's way here to his daid mammy's folks, seein' he hadn't nary person lef' thar ter look to."

And still the eyes of the two women held. Then Edith was conscious that her head drooped, that it was against Viney, that it leaned, supported; that her lips moved, buried against Viney's shoulder; that she prayed—prayed as she thought of David, well on his way to fortune, but in soul and spirit *poor white* still, by him showing himself a coward, craven inbred.

Big Albion Burns was wrong when he bracketed himself with David. Bracketed with Big Albion were those thousands of Southern men and women who speak a universal language of decency. Bracketed with David was a pusillanimous multitude, skulkers ever behind the decent South, lynchers, night-riders, white-caps, Ku Klux.

A great weariness was upon her. If, as she had reason to believe, she was with child, then in her own eyes she was carrying the child of a malefactor.

Her head lifted. Her face was gray and bleak. In her eyes was a terrible despair.

* * *

When the first flivver rushed up, followed by two others, and Mr. Delahunt the sheriff sprang out of the first, he found the two women here, in their faces something immutable and fatelike, their heads high and their eyes stern. Seeing in him the authority of the law, they moved aside, and the hand of the white woman clasping the arm of the black woman, they turned to go.

THE BASEBALL*

By BENJAMIN BRAWLEY

ALL his life Lias had been used to a coarse bill of fare and a scanty wardrobe, but when it seemed that he must give up the narrow margin of pleasure that made life bearable he thought it was time to do something radical.

Why should he be unhappy? What had he to do with ambitions, he, an ordinary Negro boy in the uplands of South Carolina? As far back as he could remember his father had lived like other tenants on the land of Cooper, the white man who owned half the county. Why should he not be willing some day to settle down and do the same?

Something of all this he was thinking tonight. He had called a meeting of his baseball team at the home of Ed Ellington, not far from the little country schoolhouse. Somehow the boys liked to come to Ed's. Old man Ellington was different from the other men around Pineville. He owned his land and did not have to work on shares with Cooper; and although he himself was notoriously close-fisted, things somehow seemed just a little more free around his home than elsewhere.

Lias had asked the boys to come together in order that he might collect the dollar and a quarter necessary for the purchase of the ball that he was to use in the game with Jonesboro the next Saturday. As captain of the home team he would have to furnish the new ball to be used in the game.

One by one the husky fellows arrived. It was too warm to go indoors; so they sat on the benches and old

* Reprinted from *The Crisis* with the courteous permission of the publishers and the author.

chairs in front of the house. Here was Sid Samuels, the pitcher, a tall, young man who had already developed a round shoulder. Then there was Ben Waters, the first base, immense in physique, but with a forehead that too soon sloped backward from his eyes; and Ed Ellington, the second base, a pleasant-looking young fellow with a face of the utmost frankness. Ned Jackson, the short stop, was a squatty little creature with bow-legs. Bud Jennings, the third base, had great, thick lips, and still bore the marks of a recent fight down by the railroad one night when he was drunk. Jim Moses, the left fielder, was tall and agile, with a step as light as that of a cat. The other fielders, the Stevens brothers, arrived late. They were always late. They lived a good distance away. Some people said that the two fellows were just naturally slow and shiftless, but at any rate the boys had learned to make allowance for them.

Until Lias began to talk business the conversation was very merry. There was the big meeting at Silver Creek the last Sunday, and the game the next Saturday, to say nothing of the girls. A peculiar hush, however, fell on the crowd when Lias passed the hat and asked each man for fifteen cents. After all, he could hope at this rate to collect only one dollar and thirty-five cents. He did not yet know what he would do about his wornout catcher's mitt.

The hat brought back sixty-five cents. Each man declared half sullenly, half shamefacedly, that he did not have any money.

Lias had been in pretty good humor all the evening. His mood of depression had vanished in the presence of the other boys. Especially did he remind Samuels of the previous performances of their famous battery. When the hat came back to him, however, the silence that ensued for a moment was embarrassing.

Then the captain arose to speak.

"Men," said he, "what's de matter? Why can't you gi' me a dollar an' a quarter for a baseball? We all wo'ks hard. I got up dis mornin' at sunup an' wo'ked till sundown, an' ev'y one o' you done de same. Yet when I call you here an' asks you for money for a baseball, you all say you ain't got it, an' I know you ain't got it. Sumpin's wrong."

He walked home that night with Jennings. He did not have much to do with this man, because he was a good deal older than the other boys, but tonight Jennings was going his way, and the two fell in together.

For some time Lias walked on in silence. Then he suddenly blurted out something about the money for the baseball.

"Well, Lias, we is down, you know," said Jennings. "We is down, an' we can't hope to do much better."

The next day the boy worked in the field where the sun, not yet at its zenith, seemed to blaze like a ball of fire. The hot waves of air danced before him as he looked away in the distance at the yellowing corn.

What did it all mean anyway? Why should he be working on and on, getting nowhere? What good had come of it so far? Where would he be next year at this season but right here, doing the same work over again, never a bit better off, and without even the price of a baseball?

Who was Cooper, anyway, that he should be slaving for him in this fashion?

Why couldn't the boys, nine hard-working fellows, get at least enough money for one baseball? Why did they not have just a little more to spare?

It was bad enough not to have much of a house to live in, and to eat bacon and cornbread every day, but if one could not even buy a baseball, why, life was hardly worth living.

Then it was that Lias resolved to run away.

At dinner he was more than usually patient. Andy turned his cup of water over on the oilcloth as usual; Mattie was cross; and Baby Jim threw at him across the table great hunks of cornbread mixed with molasses; but he held little sister Betty on his knee a long time before he went back to work.

"Is you feelin' well, Lias?" asked Mandy, his mother, whose face had somehow never looked so careworn.

"Yes, I'm feelin' all right," replied Lias, with a twinge of conscience, avoiding Mandy's glance.

But for him night was long in coming. He knew where to find the old brown satchel that his father had sometimes used in his trips to town; that would more than hold all he had. If only that sun would go down! It had been in the same spot for more than two hours.

In the dead of night he was still awake. Just across the hall, however, his father was emitting sounds that told that he at least was far away in the land of dreams.

It was hard to leave Ma; and he had never known that he loved Betty and Jim so tenderly. Even Andy, who seemed born but to meddle with his things and get in the way, was dear to him after all.

But it was useless for them all to stay there and die. Perhaps if he got away he might become a rich man and help them some day. He might even go to school!

He looked out of the window. Suddenly the shrill song of the cricket broke forth upon the quiet of the night.

He arose and put on the clothes he had worn all day. Then he threw into the satchel the suit he wore on Sundays, and his ties, and the little reader he had last used in school; and he went forth into the hall.

This was the only home he had ever known, and he was turning his back on it! He was doing so deliberately.

The front door creaked slightly on it hinges. Lias started, but quickly recovered himself.

Moonlight floating over bolls of cotton, the road that led on to the town, and the trees that were to him as friends, met his gaze as he looked forth into the summer night.

"Is you leavin' us, Lias?" asked Mandy, only three feet away from him.

The boy gave a deep sigh. His hand fell off the door knob.

"Yes, I'm goin'. I can't stand it no longer."

"Where you gwine, Lias?"

"To Columbia, I s'pose," continued the boy doggedly. "I'm tired o' this way o' livin'. I don't want to work for Cooper no more. Eve'ything you want, go to de white man. If I wants a house, go to de white man; if I wants to marry, go to de white man; want sumpun t' eat, go to de white man. I done had enough of it."

"That's so," said Mandy thoughtfully.

"There ain't nothin' in it for me," Lias went on. "There ain't nothin' in it for none of us. I said to myse'f, it'd be better if Pa managed better, but he ain't never is goin' to manage no better. He can't. An' las' night I asked de boys on de team for fifteen cents for a baseball, an' dey ain't had it. All of us is down. I don't want to leave you an' de child'en, but dere ain't no use for us all to stay here an' die."

"That's true," said Mandy slowly; "I guess you better go."

"You see," she continued, "it's always been a sort o'

uphill climb wid us. Your Pa never did manage well. I tol' him years ago dat dere wa'n't no use tryin' to make it wid Cooper, but he wouldn't hear to it. He's always gittin' mo' an' mo' behin'. I never was used to wo'kin' in de fiel's; my own mother tried to give me half-way decent raisin'. But after a while I took my row 'long wid de res'. I was always glad to see you comin' on ahead o' de other chillun. It seem to gi' me hope somehow. Den dere was dat time when your Pa got in dat fight down by de railroad an' hurt a man an' went to de gang for three months. Dat was de wors' of all, for Mattie came while he was away. The Lord he'ped me wid it all somehow. 'Some day Lias will be a man,' I said; but you's mos' grown now, an' as you say, dere ain't nothin' here for you. You better go."

Mandy paused a moment.

"I used to say to myse'f," she went on, "dat I wanted to see you make a fine man o' yourse'f, go off to school, an' all dat sort o' thing. But we don't seem to git nowhere. Perhaps you better go an' try to make it for yourse'f."

The boy's gaze was blurred now. A great tear stole down his cheek.

"No," he said, "I'm not goin'."

Then the big fellow leaned on the bosom of the little woman and cried like the baby he had been eighteen years before.

BUTTIN' BLOOD*

By PERNET PATTERSON

THE canvas-covered tobacco wagon had been jolting over the frozen track of Little North Road since before dawn. On the seat huddled two small figures, almost submerged in a welter of old quilts. Silent they sat, swaying instinctively to the pitch and roll of the wagon, as the steel tires climbed screechingly from rut to rut.

The larger, a white boy, held the reins loosely in one hand, allowing the mules their own way. His eyes were fixed abstractedly on the road ahead; his shoulders bowed, as if under weighty responsibilities.

The clink of the breast chains, in soft accompaniment to the *clack-clack* of the mules' shoes on the frozen ground, and the rumble and creak of the heavily loaded wagon came vaguely to him as homely, comforting sounds, in the deserted stillness of early morning. And the intimate mellow-peach fragrance of Virginia sun-cured tobacco, together with the every-day mule-and-harness smell, drifted over him comfortingly, too.

With a sigh he roused from his reverie and quickened the lagging team. Glancing at the small head resting on his shoulder, muffled in an old slouch hat brought down about the ears with a fragment of blanket, his face softened into a whimsical smile. He gave a vigorous shrug, and shouted:

"Wake up, Nubbin! Sun's up, nigger!"

The little form straightened with a start. An ashy-black hand came out from the chaos of covers and pulled off the headpiece. Slowly he rubbed his face, scratched his head, and rolled his big eyes at his companion.

* Reprinted by arrangement with *The Atlantic Monthly* and the author.

"Huccome you 'niggah' me?" he demanded, frowning. "I got big graveyard in de woods full o' white boys what call me 'niggah.' "

The white boy threw back his head and laughed; then, turning suddenly, with an explosive "Baa!" butted his coon-skin cap roundly against the black ear.

"Ba-a! Phut! Phut!" went the little darky, jumping from the seat; and bridling like an angry goat, sent his bullet head thump against the white boy's ribs.

"Ouch! I give up! I give up!" capitulated the latter.

"You ain' gwine call me 'niggah' no mo'?"

"No! No!" acceded the white boy, shrinking into his corner. "Cross my heart—and double cross," and his mittened hand made youth's inviolable sign of the double cross.

"Dat's mo' like hit—an' you member hit too, Luther Patten," grinned the Negro. With a final admonitory "Baa!" and a half-dancing shuffle of his big-shod feet on the wagon bottom, he dived to the seat and snatched the quilts about him.

"Huccome you don' git col' like me? Huccome don' no white folks git col' lik niggah?" he asked querulously.

Luther smiled at the forbidden word; but of course it carried a vastly different meaning when used by Nubbin's race—an intangible, shadowy difference to the white mind, but to the black a difference as clear cut as a cameo.

He answered with an imitative question:

"Huccome nig—colored folks' heads harder than white folks'?" Wrinkling his brow, he pondered, 'I rully do wonder what makes yo' head so tough. Don't it hurt you, Nub, buttin' ol' calves and things? Just buttin' a pile of bags hurts me somep'n awful. I don't reckon," he continued resignedly, "I ever will be a butter. But," he added, brightening, "I can drive tobacco to Richmond —that's more'n you can do."

"Hunh!" disparaged Nubbin. "Drivin' ol' 'bacca down ain' nothin', but buttin' is buttin'."

Pausing, he continued as if in soliloquy: "But I ain' no buttah a-tall. You des oughter seen my gran'pa. He war de buttin'es' one in de county—in de whole worl', I reckon. He kill hese'f buttin'—

"Yeah. A white man offer 'im two dollah ef he butt de sto' do'. Well, de wo'd wan't more'n outen he mouf 'fo' gran'pa had back hese'f back, an' wid a shake er he haid, 'way he went, buckin' an' jumpin', scerse touchin' de groun'; and when putty nigh de do' he give a 'Baa!' an' des nachully sailed th'u' de air, an'—blam! He hit it, an' went clear th'u' it, mon, up to he shoulders."

"Dey had a hard time gittin' 'im out, an' de man put de two dollah in he han', an' say he war de buttin'es' niggah in de county; but gran'pa des give one puny 'Baa' an' pass out, right dar. De hole stay in de do' fo' fifty-fo' hund'ed year; an' 't would be dar yit ef de sto' hadn't bu'ned. I reckon I got buttin' blood."

Luther sat musing, without comment.

After a silence Nubbin continued prophetically, "One dese days I gwina be de buttin'es' niggah in Louisa County —maybe in de whole worl'."

He added the last words softly, as if almost afraid to disclose such an overpowering vision. Sighing, he pulled the quilts to his chin, squirmed closer to Luther, and drifted into reverie. No word broke the silence as the wagon rocked on down Little North Road.

Suddenly Nubbin exclaimed, "Dar Jesus! Look who heah!"

Abreast of the wagon, just out of sight, trotted a diminutive black-and-white beagle. With his mouth lolling in a satisfied grin he jogged placidly along, seemingly intent on his own affairs.

"Git! Git home, you ol' sneaker, 'fore I tan you!" yelled Luther, hurrying to dismount.

But the short stubby legs of the hound had suddenly developed surprising speed. Before either boy could find a loose clod in the roadway, the dog was facing his enemies well out of range. Slowly he sank to his haunches, head cocked to one side questioningly. A barrage of frozen clods forced him to dive into the thick woods, where he vanished.

The victors meandered back toward the wagon. They skipped, galloped, and pushed each other into ruts. Nubbin, in his cracked man's shoes that seemed merely to dangle on his small splay feet, half shuffled, half waltzed, a big sack coat flopping grotesquely about his knees, the long sleeves completely hiding his hands.

Suddenly he became a buzzard. Holding his arms out rigidly the sleeve ends dangling like broken pinions, he sailed and circled, swooped and banked down the road. Another, less natural buzzard materialized behind the first, following its track, reproducing its every movement. The buzzards came up to the wagon with such a grandiose sweep that the drooping mules were startled from their dozing.

Jolting along again, the boys chuckled and giggled. They certainly had scared 'at ol' Spot dog. Guess he was home by now. But wa'n't he some kind of a rabbit dog, though! And didn't he have sense? And he was a nice ol' dog. A hundred dollars—no, ten hundred dollars—wouldn't buy 'at ol' Spot. No sir-re-e!

* * *

As THE MORNING wore on, Nubbin's imagination began to picture the contents of the big lunch basket under the seat.

He wiped his lips frequently, but they would not stay dry. Feeling that he had reached the limit of all human endurance, he leaned far over the dashboard and carefully scrutinized the sun.

"Unhu-n-h! Gittin' close tow'ds dinnah time," he asserted. Luther cut a mischievous eye at him: "You're crazy! 'Tain' 'leven yet. Don' guess we'll eat till we get to Coleman's store."

Nubbin frowned: "*You* nevah could tell time by de sun—an' you know hit."

The argument was waxing vehement when a man on horseback drew up to inquire after Mr. Patten. Luther was much obliged to Mr. Thorpe: Yes, his father was a lot better, but a broken leg was a tedious thing. Yes, sir, they were taking the tobacco down. Yes, Luther knew the roads—he'd been down before with his father. Anyway, they hoped to pick up other wagons after they turned into the Big Road—at least to find them about sundown at the Deep Run Camping Ground.

"Well, you're a pretty spunky boy, taking the tobacco down with just that little nigger. Yo' pa ought to be proud of you," praised the man.

Luther flushed, but belittled the undertaking. Nubbin rolled his eyes at the white man.

Thorpe asked if Luther wasn't afraid he'd lose his dog in the big town.

"Dog?" asked the boy in surprise. "What dog?"

"Ain't that yo' li'l hound under the wagon?"

With a flurry of quilts the boys were out on the ground. Slowly wagging his drooping tail, Spot looked up beseechingly from under his lids, and, rolling gently over on his back, held up his front paws, crooked at the joints like little hands.

"Now ain't dat de beatin'es'!" Nubbin exclaimed,

mouth spreading in a wide grin. "'Tain' no use to whup 'im now," he interposed hastily, as Luther flourished the whip. "He too fur fo' drive 'im home."

"The nigger is right, Luther; you'll have to take him along," chuckled Thorpe.

"Oh, darn the ol' dog!" exclaimed Luther. He sprang to the seat and started the team so abruptly that the little Negro was caught with one leg over the dash-board. Scrambling in, glaring white eyed at his partner, he tucked the covers about himself in silence.

Finally Luther drew in the team beside a small brook and ordered Nubbin to unhitch and water while he built a fire. With the coffee pot steaming away and the heaping lunch basket before him, Luther's irritation melted. Nubbin, happy at his friend's softening mood, and utterly unable to watch quietly the arrangement of the mouth-watering biscuits, sausage, and apple puffs, shuffle-stepped in circles and, patting his hands, eyes half closed, sang softly in jig tempo:

"Sif' de meal an' gi' me de hus',
Bake de bread an' gi' me de crus',
Ho mart de Juba, Juba.
Juba dis an' Juba dat,
Eat de lean an' leave de fat,
Ho mart de Juba."

Spot was in the near background, keeping one eye on the basket, the other alert for any wild thing he might nose out of the brush piles. Suddenly a rabbit jumped from under his very feet! The basket was forgotten, the boy's yelling commands unheeded. Fainter and fainter grew the dog's yaps as the rabbit lured him on into the tangles of the deep woods.

With intermittent discussion of rabbit dogs in general —but particularly of ol' Spot and his qualities—biscuits, sausage, and puffs disappeared with alarming rapidity. Nubbin's jaws stopped working only after Luther had tied tight the basket cover.

The boys' prolonged calls and shrill whistles brought no Spot. Though thoroughly anxious, they could wait no longer. As it was, the sun would be low before they reached Deep Run Camp.

Both were silent as the wagon rolled down the long hill behind the trotting mules. Time must be made up on every down grade now.

At the foot of the hill a small black-and-white animal slipped out of the woods ahead of the team and, giving one self-assuring glance toward the wagon, trotted unconcernedly down the middle of the road toward Richmond.

"Look!" exclaimed Luther.

Nubbin chuckled. "Dat ol' dog!" he said admiringly. "Ain't he de beatin'es'?"

The other boy chuckled, too: "Ain't he some kinda smart ol' dog, though!"

The wagon lurched on and finally turned into the Big Road. Surely there should be other wagons now! But none were in sight. Perhaps they'd come up with one at the Forks. Gazing down the long deserted road, Luther's thoughts insistently turned to depressing possibilities. Suppose there were no wagons at the camp? His back crept. Deep Run was so ha'nty in late evening—with its black creek, winding like a monstrous snake into the blacker depths of the slash. And Nubbin wasn't much comfort—he was too scary. They must hurry on.

Evening approached, and still no wagons. Of all the tobacco that must be going down, why couldn't they pick up one single wagon? Both boys tried valiantly to keep the talk going, but after each fresh effort the periods of silence grew longer.

The sun was down before they became aware of it. The world went suddenly all dusky and fearsome. Luther was glad to feel Nubbin snuggling close to him again. He thought they should be close to Deep Run, but wasn't sure. He whipped up the jaded mules.

The way grew unfamiliar as dark settled over the road. The wagon seemed only to creep.

Nubbin shuddered: "'Tis gittin' so dark! Le's stop heah 'fo' we git in any mo' ol' black woods."

"Oh, we pretty near there now!" encouraged Luther. "'Twon' be no time 'fore we see a fire," but his voice trembled slightly.

He was tired—so tired with responsibility—and the mules were tired. Was it maybe three, or four miles yet to Deep Run Hill? Persistently he beat away the thought that the camp ground might be vacant. The thing was to reach it!

Then, pulling up a grade that seemed interminable, the off mule fell to his knees.

"Oh, Jesus!" whimpered Nubbin. "Ol' Rock down! We can't go no fudder." He began to sob.

But Rock regained his feet and the wagon strained on again.

"You shut up, you ol' cry-baby!" admonished Luther scathingly. "I bet I won't bring any more ol' cry-babies with me!"

"Oh, I's so skeered! Hit all—so dark—an' skeery. . . . Oh, please! Le's stop an' buil' a fiah, Luther, please. . . ." The little black head went suddenly under the quilts and down on Luther's lap, the little arms grasped Luther's leg.

Suddenly the team quickened its pace, the wagon rolled more easily. The seat slanted forward, and the mules broke into a tired jog-trot.

"Man, we're here! We're on the big hill!" Luther shouted.

They tossed down the slope, Nubbin holding fast to Luther. Then Rock nickered, and a flickering light showed ahead.

Big Buck Smith, the boys' idea of a veritable paragon of a tobacco man, welcomed Luther, and the roaring fire welcomed Nubbin. Buck's frank, bluff praise embarrassed Luther almost to speechlessness:

"So you an' the little nigger jus' set out to carry the Ol' Man's 'bacca down, did you? Well, now, ain't that the beatin'es'!" and he slapped Luther so bearishly on the back that the boy swallowed his breath. "Well, you jus' foller ol' Buck; he'll p'int you down—a-rollin'," and he bellowed such a loud, assured guffaw that Luther felt the devil himself couldn't scare him now. Nubbin's white teeth glistened bravely across the fire.

Luther was treated almost as a man; and he swaggered a little as he spoke knowingly of the roads, the weather, and the color of this year's crop "up our way." Nubbin swaggered too—silently, in reflected glory, as he struttingly ordered Spot hither and yon, to the little hound's great discomfort. Buck even passed his plug of tobacco over to Luther.

"Don't believe I'll chew right now," he declined casually. "Maybe I'll take a bite later on."

Nubbin gave him so searching a stare that his eyes fell.

After the cheering supper about the big fire, his last bone sucked, Nubbin rubbed his face well over with the pork grease on his hands and, rinsing them thoroughly in the residue, cocked his old hat more assuredly and drew forth a small battered harmonica. Softly, tentatively, he sounded a chord or two. Buck looked up: Could the nigger play?

"Play!" bristled Luther. "Why, he can make a ol' harp fairly talk, man. Play 'im 'Nelly Gray,' Nub."

Lovingly the little darky's hands wrapped themselves about the harmonica; slowly his eyes closed; gently his big shoes began patting a subdued accompaniment. The strains of the old ballad rose softly, then swelled into the double-tonguing roll of the born master. Through "Minstick Town," "The Bob-tailed Nag," through ballad and reel, breakdown and jig, moaned and laughed the battered harmonica.

Without pause it swept into the finale, the time-honored air of the tobacco trains, the men humming the chorus:

"Car' my 'bacca down,
Car' my 'bacca down,
Car'y it down Richmon' town,
Car' my 'bacca down."

"Nigger, you sho' can play!" exclaimed Buck, as they rose to go to their wagons. "But a player like you oughter have a good harp—a big one. Maybe," and his eyes twinkled, "Santa Claus will bring you a new one." Then, turning to Luther, he laughingly added, "I'll bet that nigger is no 'count for nothin' else."

Luther seemed puzzled for a moment, then burst forth proudly: "He can butt."

The men roared with laughter. Buck gave him another of his bear slaps.

"That's all right," bridled the embarrassed boy, climbing into his wagon. "You jus' wait'll you see him butt sometime! He's *full* o' buttin' blood."

Cuddled together, wrapped and rewrapped in old quilts, the boys nested upon the soft tobacco in the space under the canvas top and soon droned themselves to sleep.

LUTHER'S WAGON was second in the little train that crawled slowly into the Big Road next morning as the sun began lightening the shadows of Deep Run Hollow.

First was Buck Smith's big four-mule team: rugged, powerful animals that could, hour by hour, eat up the miles with four thousand pounds of sun-cured behind them in the scow-shaped wagon of hickory and white oak. The canvas top, in natural accord with the rising bow and stern of the body, was more sway-backed, more rakish than the others. Big bundles of fodder bulged under the rope on the rumble behind; buckets swung underneath; a smutty fry pan and coffee pot and a bright ax and lantern rested in their slots and hooks. Red, brass-mounted cow-tail tassels swayed and sparkled from the headstalls of the big mules, who, even under heavy strain, tossed their heads proudly. A small bronze bell tinkled comfortingly from the hames of each leader—leaders who by mere word of command, even mere inflection of tone, would steer the ponderous wagon as easily and surely as a fur-gloved horseman could guide his pair of trotters.

"Some kind er ol' team!" murmured Nubbin, overpowered by admiration.

Awaking sharp echoes from the woods and hollows, the little train rumbled down the Big Road. Gradually other wagons joined the file: one dawdling at a country store; another waiting at a crossroad; another, warned by the tinkling bells, hurrying in a trot down a deep-cut side road. Wagons of all shapes and sizes, carrying the tobacco down! Wagons mud-red from tire to top, from the limit of the sun-cured belt; others yellow with the mud from Green Spring country; one blackened with the loam of Locust Creek—even a pariah of a produce wagon, with its butter and eggs. A giant serpent of wagons slowly winding its way down the road to Richmond.

And men! Black, and yellow, and white men! Old and young men, who yelled one to another above the rumble of the wagons. And a sprinkling of boys, a favored few, bound on a glorious sight-seeing orgy. Many would be the Munchausen tales carried back to their less fortunate brothers. Log schools, churchyards, and tobacco barns would be stirred to their amazed depths ere spring plowing began.

Luther's team held its place by dint of both boys walking. Sometimes, on the long steep hills, they became fearful as the gap widened between them and the big team; but Buck would wait at the top to blow his heavy mules.

Hours of plodding; then dinner by Great Stony Creek! Coffee pots clattered and axes rung. A line of little fires soon puffed their smoke aloft, like signals. Luther and Nubbin toasted biscuits and sausage; absorbed tobacco talk; made friends with new boys who came up in diffident admiration to see these young paladins who could take the 'bacca down. The boys were sorry when Buck called, "Hook up, men, I'm a-goin'!"

By midafternoon the men were fagged from miles of walking to ease their jaded teams. Luther would long ago have ridden but for his pride; Nubbin would have brazenly mounted, pride or no pride, but for Luther.

At one of his halts on a hilltop Buck called Luther. Nubbin followed closely as his partner joined the big man in front of the team. Pointing to a smoky haze in the east, Buck grinned delightedly: "Thar she is, boys! Richmond! We'll be in 'fore sundown."

The road grew smoother—Nubbin marveled at its smoothness. He marveled, too, at the sudden change in the men. Their plodding steps had become youthful; their seats in the saddle or on the wagon more jaunty; their voices brighter. Even the teams were infected with the change. Their step quickened. Occasionally they broke into a trot.

Soon the men mounted. Nubbin was relieved beyond words as he limped to the wagon. Luther resented his not entering into the spirit of their approach to Richmond, but perhaps he was just tired out.

Presently Nubbin asked, "Ain't hit tur'ble skeery, wid all dat ol' smoke an' all dem ol' big houses, an' folks, an' things? What do hit look like—'zactly?"

Luther couldn't explain exactly what it was like; but it was powerful big, and everybody was hustling, and big policemen in funny hats watched you. Nubbin shuddered and, inching nearer the white boy, relapsed into silence.

At last the city! The first outlying saloon!—planted there to catch the wagon trade. Most of the men pulled to the side and stopped—a dram at Reily's was almost a ritual. The wagons strung out like a fleet of rusty ships at anchor. The few people on the cinder sidewalks stared with interest. Tobacco was sure coming down!

"Is dis de great Richmon'?" inquired Nubbin, with a vague mixture of relief and disappointment.

Luther sniffed. Pshaw! The unpaved streets and sparse buildings of this outlying section were nothing! Just let Nubbin wait! The sights downtown would pop his eyes out. Why, they scared even Luther—at first.

Nubbin wished they were safely in Captain John's high-walled yard, of which he had heard so much—a yard full of wagons and men, but country wagons and country men.

The laughing drivers yelled or slapped one another good-by, for here the train split into sections—some for Captain John Hundson's, some for Shockoe, some for Shelburn's—for any one of a half-dozen sales warehouses.

On the way downtown Nubbin made not a single comment at the sights Luther pointed out, nor a single reply to his banter. He kept his head over the side of the wagon, occasionally catching his breath audibly. As they turned into Governor Street the electric lights went on. Nubbin flinched and looked at Luther questioningly. Why, the light was almost as bright as the sun—you couldn't look straight at it!

The wagons rolled in a clatter down the ancient cobbled hill of Governor Street, back of the Governor's Mansion, the men lolling jauntily in their saddles or sitting in the wagons with knees acock, hats turned back. The mules were almost in a gallop.

Buck Smith gave a loud whoop, and in his deep voice imitated a fox horn's *Toot-te-toot-to-to-o-ot!* A door slammed in a house on the corner, a window went up; women were on the porch, at the windows, waving. Luther heard a shrill voice cry, "O you 'bacca boys! T'night!" He wondered why Buck acted so foolishly, made so much noise; why the women came out in the cold, half dressed.

With utter nonchalance Buck swung the four big mules and the heavy wagon downhill, around corners, through narrow streets, as calmly and with as little effort as a woman takes a stitch. Lounging in the saddle, he ordered his chariot by easy word or slight check of the leader line.

Luther was frightened. His arms were cramped, his teeth set. Nubbin huddled in the foot of the wagon, openly sobbing and praying. Spot, jolted off the seat, yelped in abject terror.

At last, with a swoop and a swing, Buck's long wagon rolled accurately through the big gate of Captain John Hundson's wagon yard. Luther, breathing relief, guided his team through after Buck.

Darkness came quickly down upon the night camp in the wagon yard. Red fires grew; vague forms, like misty giants, loomed and vanished again. Nubbin felt an eerie strangeness in it all. Even Luther was glad to join Buck Smith by his fire. But the cheerful champ of teams and laughter of men, the flash of bright tin cups and the aroma of boiling coffee and sizzling spareribs, soon lifted them and thrilled them with the all-pervasive, buoyant spirit of the occasion. Wasn't tomorrow the long-thought-of day of sight-seeing, of swaggering about the lower town with a pocketful of money, and of reunion, with toddies and gossip? Wasn't the 'bacca down?

After supper, with the pipe smoke rising in the frosty night air, the *plunk-plunk* of a banjo came from the far side of the yard, where the Negro drivers had instinctively herded together. Buck Smith yelled over that there were three fingers of rye to swap for a song.

The banjo awoke, and quickened to a run of chords. Then a smooth black baritone began:

"Road it mighty muddy,
Way it mighty long,
But a-soon I'll git my toddy,
Fo' de mule he mighty strong.

"Wo'kin' all de summah,
Like niggah in de fiel',
Jes' to git some money
Fo' city folks to steal.

"Car' my 'ba-ac-ca down,
Car' my 'ba-ac-ca down,
Car'y it down Richmon' town,
Car' my 'bacca down."

* * *

Next morning, after their tobacco had been unloaded, the boys strolled through the warehouse. With shoulders bent and hands clasped behind them, with jaws working, they passed up and down the long aisles between the piled flat baskets; two of a long line of men, walking and acting one like another; pulling out bundles to bury their noses deep in the peachy smell; spreading open the mahogany and chocolate leaves to note their color and feel; pinching off a piece here and there to roll it on their tongues.

The Negro boy aped Luther's every action—even to pretending to taste samples. Both frequently spat brown licorice juice, like amber. Spot walked bow-leggedly behind, sniffing at the baskets and sneezing often.

Wandering into a storage wing, they were accosted by a thick-chested black hogshead roller, his pig eyes taking in the small hound. "White boy?" he said threateningly, "ef you wants dat pocket-size dog evah see home ag'in, you bettah lock him in de Cap'n's safe."

Spot growled.

"Oh, you're a fighter, is you? You wait, I gi'e you somep'n t' fight."

Laughing nastily, the big Negro slouched away.

"What de mattah wid him?" questioned Nubbin apprehensively.

"I don' know," replied Luther, his face flushed, "but he better not be tryin' to bully men around here. I'll—I'll—I bet he'd be sorry if Cap'n John heard 'bout it."

Just then there was a flurry at the end of the warehouse—Captain John had come!

Captain John, red of face, debonair, military, the idol of his customers, and their best friend!

His arm about Luther's proud shoulder, one of his new dimes in Nubbin's pocket, he ambled beamingly down the aisles, shaking friendly hands, slapping friendly backs.

Luther's tobacco would be sold first! Yes, sir! The

son of the Captain's old friend should get his check first and be free to enjoy the day. And the Captain wanted the buyers to bid the limit on this boy's tobacco; he'd brought it down, alone, with only a little nigger—and there was no better tobacco grown in Virginia.

Captain John had a way with him, and when Luther's tobacco had been sold the boys were jubilant. The top price for sun-cured, the auctioneer had said! Wouldn't the home folks be tickled!

Did any fellers ever have such a trip—such a time! Chattering, whistling, they skipped arm in arm across the cobbled yard to feed the mules.

Luther must go over his mother's list before the exploration of Main Street began. They perched themselves in the sun on the edge of a platform projecting from the far door in the wing of the warehouse, while Luther sedulously checked the items with a smudgy pencil stub. Nubbin was swinging his heels impatiently against the timbers. Spot was sniffing about in front, looking for stray bones.

Softly, very softly, unheard by the boys, the door behind them slid back. The small-eyed, ugly black face of the hogshead roller leered out for a moment, then furtively drew back. A peculiar sound, like animal claws, on a wood floor came from within. Spot suddenly froze, head cocked aside, one forefoot raised. Nubbin half whirled about and looked over his shoulder.

A huge brindle dog, filled the open doorway. Slowly his powerful head swung, his vicious red eyes shifted from the boys to the poised figure of the little hound just beyond. A bullying growl issued from his throat.

With a terrified yell Nubbin rolled desperately over backward to the far corner of the platform. Spot squealed and darted for Luther's feet! The brindle snarled and charged!

Luther felt the heavy weight of the grotesque body as it struck him a slanting blow. Bowled over, he lay a moment confused and terrified. But the distressed muffled yelps of the little hound electrified him.

"Get a stick! Hit 'im, Nub—kill 'im!" he screamed. Running and dodging fruitlessly about the entangled dogs, he looked for a board, a stone, any weapon with which to drive off the bully, while he yelled boyish oaths and sobbed with fear and rage. He pawed at a protruding cobblestone which would not come free. Then a choking gurgle from Spot sent a shiver of fury through him.

Frenzied, he leaped at the brindle and swung his heavy-soled brogan into the dog's ribs. Once, twice, he kicked with all the power of his reckless fury, sobbing, mouthing: "Le' 'im go! Le' 'im go! You ol' heller! I'll kill you! I'll kick yo' ol' heart. . . ."

The mongrel whirled from the little dog with a snarl and struck at Luther's leg. Before the boy could move, quick as a snake, the brute recovered and sprang for his throat.

Instinctively Luther stiffened and threw up a guarding arm, but he was staggered by the heavy dog's impact. Stumbling, borne backward, trying in vain to keep his feet, he screamed in terror as the beast's hot breath came in his face and he felt himself going down under those terrible fangs.

The little darky had been dancing up and down as if stung with hornets, his clenched fists beating the air. His lips stretched from his teeth in a tear-streaked grimace of horror, his shrill voice screamed:

"He'p! He'p! Run heah, somebody! Run heah! . . ."

When he saw the brindle bring down his partner he made a spring as if starting to his assistance. But the prospect of facing those savage fangs was too much for him. Holding up his ragged arms in supplication, he shrieked: "O Gawd! O Jesus! Have mercy! He killin' 'im. . . ."

A cry from Luther of "Help, Nub, hel-l-p!" reached a new spring in his consciousness. Fear, dreadful fear, had bound him; but the appeal in extremity from his friend, his own Luther, snapped the leash. The blood of the Congo, the spirit of lion-hunting forbears—and a butting grandsire—seethed within his little body, quickened within his soul. He went berserk.

With a sobbing snarl he threw his hat viciously to the floor, and sprang jumping, bouncing down the platform. Bleating an instinctive sharp "Baa!" his slim body left the edge of the platform, and, like a tattered arrow, shot through the ten feet of space—straight for the brindle's head. Against that head struck the crown of a Negro of buttin' blood—small, but of famous lineage; the grandson, indeed, of the buttin'es' niggah in de county.

* * *

When Nubbin came up out of the blackness of long oblivion, he thought he must be in heaven. Before his tired eyelids could lift, he seemed to hear a voice in the far distance say: "He's th'—buttin'es'—nigger—in—th' —world."

It must be heaven! On opening his eyes he was sure of it: a long-white-whiskered, white-haired old gentleman was pressing his head.

"Gabr'el!" he thought. "Rammin' home de golden crown!" But the crowning hurt terribly.

"Hit's too tight! Too tight!" he moaned, closing his eyes.

"Lie still, son! I'll soon be through."

He felt a sharp prick in his arm. Gabriel was trying to hurt him.

Dimly, amid much talk, he heard a tearful young voice, a voice that sounded like that of his beloved earthly partner. Luther was in heaven with him? That was good!

"Doctor, is he dyin'?"

"Dying nothing! When the hypodermic takes effect I'll finish stitching his head and strap up that shoulder. . . ."

What funny talk for angels! But of course heaven *was* a funny place. Anyway, he could take a nap—Luther was there.

Later, when his eyes opened to full consciousness, they glanced about the walls. Big railroad calendars, a long black stovepipe, an an old buggy harness did not seem appropriate decorations for the walls of heaven. Trying to turn over, he cried out.

"Does it hurt so bad, Nub?" asked an entirely earthly voice.

"Who dat?" he questioned feebly.

"It's me—Luther."

The white boy leaned solicitously over the figure mummied in shoulder and head bandages. "You feelin' better?" he asked, stroking the black paw.

"You talks natchul," Nubbin remarked doubtingly.

Why shouldn't I? That ol' dog jus' chewed my overcoat collar. He hardly scratched my throat. But if it hadn't been for you," his voice broke, "I reckon—I'd been —mos' killed."

Nubbin's eyes were drawn back to the old harness.

"Den dis heah ain' . . ." he began, but his question was interrupted by a hot, black nose against his cheek.

With an effort he looked into the face of what resembled a blear-eyed, disreputable old man with a soiled stock about his neck.

Smiling faintly, he asked, "He hu't much?"

No, Spot wasn't dangerously hurt, but there was a bad gash in his neck, which Luther had bandaged.

Captain John, Buck Smith, and a dozen others came admiringly into the room.

Buck Smith stood beside the boy's cot and, leaning over, closed the slender black fingers about a narrow red-and-gold box from whose elaborate decorations stood out the words: "Full-Concert Harmonica."

Turning from the pinched face to the crowd, he said:

"Men, thar lays the buttin'es' little nigger in the world."

Slowly Nubbin seemed to awaken to the reality of his own familiar world, to the actual significance of those precious words. His eyes opened wide; they rolled from Buck Smith to the nodding men, then back to Buck.

He moistened his lips; his hand squeezed tight on the new harp. Then, slowly, like sunrise, a beatific smile lighted his ashy face. He sighed, as if unloading a great burden, and, closing his eyes, murmured:

"Yas, suh, I got buttin' blood."

CLOUD-CAPP'D TOWERS*

By EMILY CLARK

BROWN and still the garden lay in its mild October interlude. The second blooming of a few stubborn rose-bushes occasionally interrupted the monochromatic scene, but the October violets, lost under their thick leaves, gave no hint that they too were lingering to receive the late frost that comes to Southern Virginia. A charming wide house of white-columned buff stucco shone through the opening between two tall columns of box forming a half arch at one of the four entrances to the garden. On a wooden bench of a damp, dark-grey, unwholesome tint on the inner side of the arch Doctor Vesey sat, smoking one of his slim, brown Porto Rican cigarettes. Doctor Vesey, unlike other men of his generation, never smoked cigars, and his cigarette was a component part of an attitude always entirely debonair. Actually Doctor Vesey, who had been born many years after the War, and was by profession a schoolmaster, held intact in the flawless amber of his personality the authentic beau sabreur of a much earlier period. His thin, grey face, his thorough-bred nose, his shadowed dark eyes, tormenting a close observer with the hazy memory of a portrait seen somewhere of a Tuscan nobleman of the seventeenth century, his thick grey hair, and his close-clipped grey moustache made him easily the most picturesque figure in a community still sufficiently provincial for picturesque figures to occur with reasonable frequency.

Doctor Vesey was not only a schoolmaster, but a schoolmaster of girls rather than boys, further proof of an attitude perfectly achieved, an attitude eternally trium-

* Reprinted from *Stuffed Peacocks* by Emily Clark by and with permission of and special arrangement with Alfred A. Knopf, Inc., authorized publishers.

phant over the trivial realities of life. When, as a young man, he had turned his grandfather's amiably rambling house into a school for young ladies, even his friends and kinsmen, members, like himself, of the tribe which is assuredly the most casual of all this earth's inhabitants, a tribe which, temperamentally, knows not skepticism, were vaguely, spasmodically uneasy as to the outcome of Doctor Vesey's venture. Capital was not a plentiful commodity, but he had somehow managed to enlarge the building. He did not, true enough, enlarge it to an extent where entirely sanitary conditions could prevail. Doctor Vesey could remember the day when it was taken for granted that two people could exist comfortably in one room, more often than otherwise in one bed. He could also remember when bathing was an almost military duty rather than a sybaritic relaxation. And he saw no reason why young women—even young ladies—whose appearance was, as a rule, an accomplishment far less perfect than his own, should not live happily in conditions which had never proved detrimental to himself.

Into the matter of the financial support which every institution must have no one had inquired too closely. Whether those early debts for the foundation of the school had ever been paid no one knew, and to all public appearances no one cared. The school went on somehow. It had even managed—and this is no legend of the Old Southland, but prosaic fact—until six years ago to retain the two words "female seminary" in its five-word title, without obviously frightening away too many patrons. For the school derived both its pupils and its teachers from the lower section of the most ancient commonwealth—the half-mythical, partly preposterous, and wholly insidious section of the State that lies lazily, hushed, soothed, and caressingly blanketed in gloriously red mud, on the

Southern side of the yellow river. Doctor Vesey's son, now a physician on the Pacific coast, had murmured dreamily, on his last visit home, as he opened the gate where a crimson-stained Ford had deposited him: "Nothing could be better! It comes off in my hands just as it used to. How many other gates around here, I wonder, are coming off their hinges at exactly this moment?"

On each of these visits, however, the condition of the box borders in the gardens varied enough to contrast interestingly with the static air of the other attributes of the house and grounds. The box had, in the past—the past that Doctor Vesey ruled, not the nearly fabulous past of his ancestors—grown with such appalling luxuriance that access to a flower-bed had become almost as difficult as to the Sleeping Beauty's palace, with the piquant difference that what slept within was often not beauty, but weeds. During more recent years the borders were not only clipped, but startlingly scant at times, seasons when the roads from the North were especially crowded. Since even fragments of box were desirable, the Doctor and his wife at intervals parted with them for a price. Enterprising travellers returned North or West carrying bits of the academic hedge with which to refresh other less fortunate and cultivated regions, thereby proving the accuracy of a locally celebrated poem used periodically in the school catalogue.

In his locality Dr. Vesey glittered, an oriflamme for the gentle poverty of the little town and surrounding counties. He held his degree from a college of ancient and aristocratic if limited fame, and he still taught Latin himself. His teachers, both men and women, were chosen in friendly fashion for reasons known to the Doctor and trusted by the Doctor's patrons. They were not, for the most part, the owners of degrees from universities, great or small, but they were impeccably gentlefolk. They imparted, moreover, what learning was essential to the future careers of the young ladies—careers which alternated between a local marriage and a position as teacher in a local school.

Hard and fast academic standards did not prick the peace of the Doctor, his faculty, or his young ladies. Nor did athletic standards, for sports as part of a young woman's equipment were irrelevant, if indeed not definitely injurious. And the surface which Doctor Vesey preserved untarnished through years by no means luxurious was a testimonial in itself of the efficacy of the Vesey method, the integrity of the Vesey ideal. Even his clothes, semi-rural product as they were, assumed the grand manner when Doctor Vesey assumed them. The military cape of his overcoat, the gloves, the cane which he never forgot, and the wide, soft grey hat which remained with him through the seasons except in unendurable midsummer heat were the final contributions to the exterior of a truly distinguished gentleman. Whether or not this gentleman was also a scholar and a disciplinarian only a person cruder and more insensitive than the appreciative neighbours of Doctor Vesey would inquire.

The slow, soft march of the years brought the Doctor into gradual State-wide prominence. A leisurely honourable political post was assigned him by a governor always cheerfully ready to oblige such creditable and—it was becoming year by year more painfully apparent—temporary figures as the erect grey gentleman who so gracefully transmuted his meditative moments into smoke wreaths for his garden. More than one post in the commonwealth offered ample time for the consummation of the work it required, and Doctor Vesey's reputation was of such quality that when the completion of the job remained unaccomplished at the end of one administration, his appointment at the hands of the succeeding executive was secure.

The commingling of academic and political duties brought increasing alien contacts to Doctor Vesey. The methods and scope of other schools ceased to remain outside his consciousness. Even in his own State there were institutions for female learning where matters superbly ignored by Doctor Vesey were indispensable elements in catalogues and in fact. Golf courses, swimming-pools, gymnasia, saddle-horses, quite aside from purely academic features, threatened to fill the portion of the local horizon where Doctor Vesey had long shimmered, a conspicuous constellation. Now and again a girl from the North or West had been sent to him to acquire what, it was rightly believed from his appearance and manner, combined with the not less admirable impression invariably produced by his wife, was to be had in his academy. These, as a rule, were girls who would not be obliged to work, but who could not afford the expensive last touches supplied by other more celebrated schools in this State and others. The voice and manner which represented the most ancient commonwealth in what was once known to its orators as its perfect flower were considered, in certain quarters, surprisingly desirable. And for a life of modest indolence no special preparation was necessary.

As the State, however, became more and more widely known for its hunt clubs, as the revival of the noble English sport whose American birth occurred here was featured with interesting frequency in the many forms of State advertising which now raged through the land, as efficiency in swimming and games became important even in lives of modest indolence, Doctor Vesey realized that chamber-of-commerce methods no longer merited a gentleman's scorn.

In his garden he pondered on the matter and manner of his forthcoming catalogue. And his pondering proved not futile. The catalogue issued the following spring by Doctor Vesey contained not only the customary enticing photograph of the old cream and white house, with its driveway, its garden, and its printed promises of the atmosphere, environment, and example which had made the womanhood of the State what it was known everywhere throughout the world to be. There was more. A bracing picture of a sweep of golf links decorated the top of one page. At the bottom was visible a tiled swimming-pool. On another a young woman on horseback twirled her crop, with breeches, boots, and every flawless detail receiving full justice. There were paragraphs to explain and extol the illustrations, paragraphs which offered every benefit of the commonwealth's country life in addition to its well-known and long-established home atmosphere. That atmosphere, the catalogue, as of old, made clear, had produced and nurtured the loveliest women alive, they who in the words of a well-beloved poem had created historic gardens out of the wilderness, gardens

> whose fragrance lives in many lands,
> Whose beauty stars the earth,
> And lights the hearths of happy homes
> With loveliness and mirth.

It had, of course, been traditional with the gentlewomen, as well as with the gentlemen of the State, to love horses and to follow the hounds. And now, without sacrificing any particle of their feminine birthright, the most utterly feminine birthright in the universe, out-of-door activities in other forms would be added to the advantages already accruing to a period of a few years in the Vesey school. The catalogues were sent broadcast in greater numbers than usual, and the alert eyes of one capable Mid-Western mother were caught and held by the glory and the grandeur of the special sort that is not known west of the Alleghanies. Glory and grandeur too, at a singularly reasonable price. "Why not," she thought, "let my daughter grasp this extraordinary opportunity? An old culture with new facilities." And indeed, what more could be hoped for? Lofty standards, but of a simplicity which would make no girl dissatisfied with the limitations of her future life at home. A correspondence followed, in which Doctor Vesey surpassed his catalogue. For the art of letter-writing in the State still survived in amazing vigour.

Gladys Speed arrived from Illinois in late September, unaccompanied except by the faith and hope of her maternal parent. Gladys was of a taciturn disposition, and disinclined, it seemed to Doctor Vesey, to any comment, favourable or otherwise, on her surroundings. He was in ignorance of her reactions, but disposed to take the best for granted, as no complaints were made.

At Christmas, like the other girls, she went home for the holidays. In early January she returned to school, accompanied this time by her mother, whose faith and hope, it became instantly apparent, had been left behind. Mrs. Speed, who did not stay in the school, made no effort to see Doctor Vesey alone, being plainly engaged with effort along other lines. The school and its surroundings were thoroughly inspected without delay. Within the week Dr. Vesey received an invitation to attend a meeting of the Chamber of Commerce of the town near by. This was not a surprise, for the Doctor had figured at almost every variety of meeting, of either literary or community nature, throughout the State.

The meeting, however, failed in no element of the unexpected which the invitation lacked, for Doctor Vesey found confronting him the members of the familiar organization, with the astounding addition of Mrs. Speed and her daughter. Gladys, as always untemperamental, remained mute. Never a victim of the Doctor's notable personality, she seemed equally unmoved by the Doctor's turpitude. But Mrs. Speed lost no time in explaining her presence. She rose to make formal complaint against the Doctor and his academy. She had, she stated, received a catalogue setting forth the advantages, not only of a celebrated and time-honoured atmosphere, but of a swimming-pool, a golf course, and a stable full of saddle-horses. She had found the atmosphere as described in the catalogue; an atmosphere, it was true, a bit thick and stale, but none the less definite for that. But of the photographed facilities for out-of-door life she found not one.

She urged the Chamber of Commerce to bear witness to this, as a blot upon the town which the Chamber represented. Such a person should not be permitted to operate fraudulently in a community where the honour of men was held second only to the chastity of women. Public disgrace, alone, was a suitable reward for deception practiced with such brazen disregard for public opinion, such shameless carelessness of consequences to the victims of this deception. Mrs. Speed felt sure that so flagrant an outrage would not be condoned by a right-thinking, forward-looking institution. She left the matter in the hands of this institution with no qualms concerning the manner in which it would be dealt with.

The Chamber invited Doctor Vesey to reply. He did. He bowed first to Mrs. Speed, then to Miss Gladys, then to his fellow-citizens. He replied that the very golf course which ornamented his catalogue existed actually at the Country Club near by, and could be freely used by any pupils who joined that club, always in need of new members. The swimming-pool could be not only seen but used at the Y. W. C. A. Horses could be hired always at a few moments' notice from a convenient livery stable, with the undeniable advantage that, if not sufficiently spirited to be feared, they were at least sufficiently safe to be trusted, and by the most inexperienced young lady.

No prerogative of the pupils of Doctor Vesey's school had been in any way exaggerated or over-estimated in his catalogue. Should not all these features of a progressive town be utilized by a school which was only another embellishment of that town? Did not the Chamber of Commerce employ this same allurement in its own pamphlets urging outsiders to settle here? Was it not legitimate that the assets of the town should be at the disposal of the school, which brought a greater number of visitors here than any of its other institutions? Was it not absolutely logical that the young ladies should avail themselves of opportunities so close at hand? He desired no unpleasantness with, or for, Mrs. Speed. She seemed to him a little tired and over-wrought, in her tendency to find melodrama in a situation so simple. He retained, however, only the friendliest attitude to both of the ladies, and would do everything in his power to make the remainder of Mrs. Speed's sojourn in their midst as agreeable as possible.

Doctor Vesey was quite at his best. The association agreed with him cordially. More, it gloried in him. Doctor Vesey bowed again, to Mrs. Speed, to Miss Speed, to the gentlemen. With their permission, he said, he would now leave. The permission was his. He left. Mrs. Speed was unable immediately to speak. With blank eyes she watched his lean, distinguished back departing with no implication of haste through the nearest door. She gazed at the gentlemen assembled. She found in their collected countenances no trace of anything amiss. Opening her mouth and closing it again, she gathered up her wrap, bag, and daughter, vanishing through the same door. That night the Speeds left for Illinois.

The next day's noon recess, the air being mild, found Doctor Vesey on his garden bench, a Napoleonic figure with his cape overcoat gathered around him. He was making smoke wreaths to melt into the softly sympathetic air with which the Southside occasionally blesses her children, even in January.

DOWN BAYOU DUBAC*

By BARRY BENEFIELD

I RECKON I'll never get entirely through answering questions about that Deeves-Mendoza affair, though my conscience is clear and calm. I was of course in bed that midnight when Ed Deeves tapped at my window. Crebillion is a little town, and bed-time here is nine o'clock for children and grown-ups. Youth is about its own thrilling business from eight until any time at all. It was late May, and in Louisiana it is already good summer then. My wire screens were in place, my bedroom windows wide open. I had not been down Bayou Dubac since the summer before, and I was wondering when I'd get a good chance to go again. Of course I was already fishing a bit in Dubac up here near town, below the railroad tank, but there is nothing this far up except catfish, little perch, and those devilish terrapins that eat your bait and snag your line on a stump. But down the bayou! Lord save us, it's a debauch if you have a fisherman's passions.

Well, there I was respectably in bed only day-dreaming about real fishing and never expecting any good chance until June, July, and August when the parties of young people would be going down Dubac for four-day picnics and of course taking me along as the chaperon.

The white moon had come up, and I was lying there staring out at the big pine-tree across the street in Mr. Pelletier's back yard, and it looking like a great purple plume set against a silver screen. The wind was cutting up a bit, washing waves of moist air in over me, wind that had but lately kissed a million blooming magnolias. The old clock on the mantel had slowly pounded twelve times

* Reprinted from *Short Turns* by Barry Benefield with the courteous permission of the publishers, The Century Company.

on its throbbing coil of wire. Outside the katydids were swinging their tense monotonous rhythm back and forth, back and forth, when suddenly I heard a tapping on my window-sill.

"Who is that?" I called; which was a foolish question, because I was in the shadow, he was in the moonlight, and I could see Ed Deeves' square head, even the color of his brown eyes, as plain as day.

"It's me—Ed Deeves. Mis' Lyd, come on, let's go fishin'."

"Tomorrow, Ed?"

"Nome, right now. Could you be down at the wharf by two o'clock, Mis' Lyd? We'll be down Dubac several days anyhow. I'll go get the boat ready an' the supplies in."

It was a short enough trip from my house down to the wharf, goodness knows, and I was afraid he might change his mind if I tried to postpone anything. More than once a fine trip with a strong and willing boy who can pull a boat and cut fire-wood and get fish-bait has been lost to me through postponement, though seldom do I do the postponing.

"All right, Ed. I'll be there. You wait for me."

"If you don't see me right away when you get there, Mis' Lyd, just whistle like a whippoorwill."

I might have known some mischief was in the air when he said that. When a Southern boy makes a rendezvous and tells somebody to whistle like a whippoorwill he is up to devilment, or thinks he is. "No, Ed, I will not whistle like that weepy bird, because I can't, but if I fail to find you I'll raise my voice to high heaven."

I travel light through this vale of tears because I never know when I might get a good chance to go down the bayou for a few days. I have no cats, chickens, birds, or flowers except some hardy things that can get along by themselves in a pinch. By 1:30 I was footing it through a back street to Crebillion's broken-down old wharf. The infernal railroads killed off our steamboats and well nigh killed poor Crebillion; it's like a little old dried-up man wearing a suit made for him when he was fat and forty. We've enough brick buildings here for a city of thirty thousand—and have three, no more. And the wharf's going to pieces.

It was easy enough to find that Deeves boy. I just walked along by the old black piles until I heard a low buzzing of talk. "Hallo!" I shouted. Strangely enough I heard the cautious call of a whippoorwill. Ed was already in the boat, and he maneuvered the stern of it around so that I could step in. I am a plump person, but I am *not* a mountain of flesh, and I can handle myself in a boat without a lot of fuss and nonsense. I laid my poles in place, stowed my luggage with Ed's, and felt for the rudder-cords.

"Let's go, Ed," I said briskly. "Who's your friend up there in the seat ahead of you?"

"It's me, Mis' Lyd. I was just waitin' to see if you would recognize me when we got out of the shadow into the middle of the bayou where the moon is."

"Ruth Mendoza! Who'd have thought it—you and Ed Deeves together."

"I've got something to tell you, Mis' Lyd, when we get down to Ed's secret campin' place."

"All right, Ruth; I'll wait. Don't tell me now; I've got to pay strict attention to this rudder. Let's go, Ed." At times there is such a thing as knowing too much. I already knew, as did everybody in town, that after having been Ruth's standard escort since her pigtail days to all the many juvenile gaities of jolly little Crebillion,

Ed had been deliberately frozen out of the Mendoza home. Not that it had been much trouble to freeze Ed out: the Deeveses and all their connections have pride and to spare, especially Ed's mother, who was Fanny Crandall and went to school with me. We all had thought the reason was the Mendoza money, he being a banker, and the Deeves's comparative lack of it, Sam Deeves being a merchant who will give credit to anybody and was never known to foreclose a mortgage on a farmer in his life. And now here were Ed and Ruth going off down the bayou on a grand skylark. No, I did not want to hear too much; I wanted nothing to interfere with this trip down Bayou Dubac.

Well, Ed got his oars in place and laid down to his job. He was then only nineteen and an inch or so short of six feet. When he's forty-five he'll be fat; I know because I was like him. But, saints alive, he was *a* boy. His sleeves were rolled above his elbows, his thick upstanding tangled sandy hair was uncovered; and his soft-collared shirt wide open in front. The sharp prow of the boat was hissing through the water. He was feathering his oars on the back stroke, but that decorative stuff was for Ruth's benefit; I said nothing, he'd soon stop that. A heavy lot of luggage, one solid young man, and one entirely ample old widow-woman, not counting a seventeen-year-old 120-pounder, were load enough to discourage any fancy feather-edging on the surface of the water with the oars, which should come clean and clear.

Pretty soon he stopped that foolishness and got down to business. For four hours he pulled steadily on, and when the sun was pinking the east, the pale spent moon being still with us, we turned into the wide mouth of the slough that branched off from the bayou and ran back a mile or so into the deep dark-green woods. Ed pointed to a spot in what seemed to be the shore of the slough where the low-hanging limbs of some sweet-gum trees were dabbling their dainty fingers in the clear water. "Steer to that place, Mis' Lyd," he said. And when we got there, which I thought was the bank behind the limbs, he lifted them and pulled the boat past a lot of trees neck-deep in the slough, and we were out in a smaller lagoon that nobody could see from the big one when the leaves were on the trees.

At the far end of it the bank rose a hundred feet to level ground, on which were those miraculous tall yellow-pine trees that shoot away up into the air without putting out a limb and then suddenly spread out until their tops touch each other.

"A spring's on the other side of the hill," Ed announced.

"No one ever *could* find us here," breathed Ruth, clasping her hands and looking around with a wicked gleam in her eyes.

"Some fishermen and hunters know it, but not many town people, I reckon. This is where I was goin' to build my log cabin, Mis' Lyd, when I was about to adopt the profession of fishin'." Ed grinned as at the folly of silly youth long past; it had been about three years since he was in that fix.

Within thirty minutes that admirable boy had our stuff up on the hill under the pines, which would keep us dry unless there was a deluge. While Ed was making a fire, and we women were sitting against a copper-colored pine-bole as big around as a hogshead, Ruth leaned over and said, "Mis' Lyd, I want to tell you—"

"No, no, not now, child; I've got to get the things ready to cook; I'll bet that boy is famished, and I know

I am. You get the bucket and bring some water from the spring."

I scrambled to my feet and began pottering around in the grub-box. I was afraid she might—I say it may be that I was afraid she might—tell something that would make it necessary to demand that Ed take us right back to town. I knew he would if I told him to; he's that kind of a boy.

Here we were, a boy and a girl and the standard outdoor chaperon of Crebillion; all very proper indeed; and the weather and the water looked prime for fishing, and I hadn't had a good round with real fish since the year before. It hadn't rained in two weeks, so the fish should be hungry. The mist was curling up from the slough like incense. Red birds flashed among the dark-green bushes down near the water, their voices as clear and liquid as it was. The old pines away up there above us were whispering, "Hush, hush, hush!" No, it is possible that I did not want that handsome minx to do any inconvenient confessing.

If loss of appetite is a certain symptom of being, as they say, in love, then that Deeves boy and Ruth Mendoza were as cold to each other as if they had been hostile neighbors all their lives.

"If this keeps up," Ed moaned, "we'll be out of baker's bread in two days an' have to cook corn-bread or biscuit for every meal."

"That's all right, boy," I spoke up comfortingly; "you eat on; we'll want a change of bread, anyway, in two days, and Old Lady Pilduff will cook it. But whatever happens, we can't run out of meat because I feel the fish down there all lined up ready to be mine."

"This place was just waitin' for us," said Ruth in a rapturous whisper. "We'll remember this place an' this time as long as we live, won't we, Ed?" And leaping to her feet, she gave me a prodigious hug, which was of course meant for that big scalawag who was still eating.

"Go on, you two," I said, "and take a walk, while I do the dishes. And, Ed, you look for a dead pine-tree with sawyer grubs under the bark. Don't you dare bring back those brown dried-up ones; get fat white ones that a fish with some pride can eat."

They went away into the woods holding hands and swinging them up and down and touching their shoulders, elbows, and hips as they walked. The place was full of that pair.

Well, it was gorgeous that day, the fishing. We pulled out into the larger slough. Ed knew the sunken tree-tops that were the picnic-grounds of white perch, and I had such an orgy of delight as I had never had before or ever expected to have. A nibble at the hook deep down in the water, a little running, a sweet heavy weight on the line coming nearer and nearer the top—and then smack into the boat. White and black striped jewels of a pound or two, and, oh, so delicately flavored and firm and tender in the mouth! We caught enough to last us two days, and Ed resurrected a big old fish-box into which we put all we didn't want for supper and sunk it in a cool part of the little slough.

At five o'clock, with the hunger of wolves, we laid off and pulled for the camp. From 6 to 7:30 we ate, and by 8:30 this old coon was lying twenty feet away from the camp-fire on a deep bed of brown pine straw and covered with a mosquito-bar which Ed had rigged up on strings from trees. I was as full as a tick, dead tired, and my body shouted for sleep; but I lay there going over the thrilling details of that heavenly catch of fish. It was already cool, and the wind of the night was rich with smells of old earth, little green leaves, aromatic resin, old smoke, and young flowers. The pine-tops made almost a solid screen far above our heads, but through a crevice here and there in the dark foliage I could glimpse a faintly winking star. When I'd see one I'd wink back at it, like a sottish old fool.

Ruth and Ed sat before the fire with their backs against a log talking, she with a flaming buckeye blossom in her black hair. I had said to myself when I lay down that if that boy wished to kiss that girl no cry of horror would issue from my lips, even if I were awake to see or hear it. Once I looked in their direction and saw that his arm was around her shoulder, as if she were an old pal of his, as indeed she was; and he was just leaning over and taking something from her lips with an ease and grace that proved practice. I turned my back and looked out into the woods where a thousand fire-flies were spangling the blackness with soft golden sparks that melted in a moment. Ed and Ruth buzzed and laughed, their voices sweet and intimate, loaded with precious secrets that only they knew, sounding subtle overtones and undertones that somehow made music of their muted chatter.

Once I heard Ed say "Ssh," and Ruth answered, "Oh, she's asleep, an' anyway I've tried to tell her all about it twice."

Well, they went on talking, and the whole thing came out. They went back over their doings of the night before with proud particularity like a pair of enormously successful criminals. Now it came clear, over there by the camp-fire, that money had not been the reason for the freezing out of Ed from the Mendoza home.

"Honey, I don't want to hurt your feelin's, but I reckon I ought to tell you something before I go to New York. Even if you go away to school an' stay a hundred years an' come back the greatest doctor that ever was, papa will never willin'ly give me to you. You see, we aren't just Jews, we're Spanish Jews, an' they turn up their noses at everybody else in the world except other Spanish Jews.

"When I heard papa an' mama talkin' last night an' found out they were goin' to rush me away to-day, a whole week ahead of time, they said that when I went to New York to school I'd be sure to meet some Spanish Jews at my uncle's house—there aren't any others here, you know—an' I'd marry one in time. That's what they *said*. Puppy love they called ours, but, anyhow, I reckon they were afraid of it, because they were so anxious to push me away ahead of the time they had set themselves. First, they persuade me to go in May so I'd be acclimated by fall, and then they try to take my last week away."

As I say, everybody knew that Ed had been politely shooed away from the Mendoza home, but no one except him and Ruth remembered the time, when he was fifteen, that he had, during one of many and varied ambitious moments, decided to be a telegraph operator and had run a wire from his bedroom across his father's garden and on across an alley to the tall Mendoza stable that sits away back from the big house. After the freezing out, it now developed, Ruth would go often to the loft at night, give the old telegraph-key a click or two that let him know she was there and the way was clear.

They had reconciled themselves to the plan of Ruth's going away for four years, although of course she was always to wait for him and never marry the most fascinating New Yorker; and as for Ed, he was to put in ten years making himself a doctor—four years academic, four years medical, two years in a hospital. Ten years, mind you! Yes, they had agreed on that heroic schedule, bless their strong and gallant hearts; but before entering upon it they had planned to meet every night in the Mendoza stable, which was to be a sort of feast to fortify them for the desolate time ahead.

And then the night that Ed tapped at my window, after Ruth had slipped back into her room, she had heard her parents talking and so had discovered that steps had been taken to rush her away at once; whereupon she had gone again to the loft, summoned Ed, and they had cooked up the plan to steal away down the bayou, she leaving a note saying they had run away to New Orleans on the train. Ed, who clerked in his father's store, had a key to it and got supplies and his camping outfit without having to answer questions. As for my presence, it was due to a thought of his; a large sop to respectability.

"Just think, Ed, if we hadn't done this I'd be on the train a hundred miles away from you this very minute. It takes so little to make us happy, doesn't it—just to be together? Nobody ought to begrudge us that." I heard Ruth, with her head lying in the hollow of his shoulder as if it were made to hold her head and nothing else, murmuring that, "When you are away from me, Ed, I feel an ache—no, not like that exactly: it's as if I were terribly hungry an' thirsty an' weak, an' when you come it's as if I'd had food an' drink an' was whole an' strong again. My blood sings when you're near me, Ed. Do you ever feel like that?"

"Yes, Ruth, an' you make me feel like a string band does an' it on a boat going down the bayou almost out of hearin', an' like rain on the roof when it's hot weather an' the night is all dark outside, an' like moonlight on the water, an' flowers on the wind, an' like I used to feel a long time ago in Sunday-school when I sang hymns an' the organ played an' all the other voices caught me an' lifted me up an' up—oh, Ruth, if you marry a Spanish Jew up there, or anybody at all but me, I don't know what I'll do. I'll be ruined, I know I will."

Lord save us, I had never known that big hulk of a boy could talk like that. I'd known he had sense—Fanny Crandall's son would have—but I'd had an idea he was dumb at talking.

Well, I lay there, invisible under my mosquito-bar, listening to the wind whispering away up among the pine-tops and hoping that nothing would smash the plans of that perfect pair sitting behind the yellow flames of the camp-fire. But ten years! Great Cæsar, what a gallant and dangerous schedule! Ed would be a doctor all right if he set out to be, even if he did partly have to work his way through college, but ten years is a *long* time to youth. Loose-mouthed old sinner though I am, I said in my mind, "Please, God, give that boy his sweetheart, and be quick about it."

The next morning we lay late; it was so cool and dim under the pines that the sun did not wake us, so it was eight o'clock when a raging hunger dragged us to our feet. Again that boy and girl ate like cannibals after a ten-day fast, and Lydia Pilduff was not far behind, if any. Ed didn't much want to go out fishing again in the big slough; he said we had enough fish to do us for two days. But I bedeviled him so that he pulled out to sunken tree-tops that we had not visited the day before. Our luck holding, I was again drunk with the black and white beauties we hauled into the boat. If Ed opened his mouth to speak to Ruth I glowered at him. Fish fly from conversation.

After a while Ed said he was tired of fishing, in which sentiment he was strangely joined by Ruth, and would I mind if he put himself and her ashore, so that they could walk over to the bayou and get some boards from an old half-sunk house-boat with which to build a table for the camp? From motives partly of mercy and partly of self-interest, I agreed to his proposal, paddling back to my watery hunting-grounds after they had set out for Dubac. At our midday dinner they told me that Pink Beddo, a negro fisherman on the way up to town with a load of fish, had seen them working on the house-boat.

In the afternoon I paddled out to catch still more fish, leaving that blessed pair alone to piddle around building their table and to be together. Their precious moments were slipping away fast. At the most they had but a few days, and their Eden might come to an end at any time now.

That night, lying on my pine-straw, I heard them once more talking over by the fire, their backs against their favorite log.

"That fisherman will give us away, Ed; yes, he will, I just know it. There will be such a hullabaloo in town about us that he will hear of it, and he will then say that he saw us down here. Ed, I want you to take a long look at me, so when you come back an' meet me on the street you'll know who I am. Ten years! You'll be twenty-nine an' I'll be twenty-seven. Then you won't look at me unless I pretend to be sick an' send for you, an' then you'll just look at my *tongue!* Look at me now, Ed, an' tell me what you see."

"I see black hair—"

"Oh, fine; he knows my hair is black."

"I see black hair that lies against a forehead as white an' smooth as marble."

"And as solid, honey?"

"All right, I won't say any more."

He searched with much ado through four or five pockets, found his pipe, knocked it and scraped it and filled it; and Ruth waiting patiently with her head down, looking at him no doubt out of the corner of her eye, until his pipe was thoroughly lit.

"Now, Ed, go on; tell me some more."

He made no answer, but sat staring out across the slough, where the little waves were running after the white moon.

"Ed, we won't have each other long down here, will we? An' now you're mad at me."

"And your eyes, Ruth, are like deep black pools, but away down in them are little bonfires that beckon at me. Sometimes when you are quiet your eyes look so sad it's like a stab to me; your father's are like that too. But then they dance when you are happy. And there's your jolly straight little nose, like a Greek's in my history-book, that runs so much further up between your eyes than mine does. And there's your mouth that crinkles at the corners; I think smiles hide there so they can come out quick. And your impudent proud chin that says, 'I'm not afraid of anybody.' An' I'll remember your face always so tense as if you were forever *terribly* interested in something; an' your walk, swaggerin' like a boy an' takin' *enormous* steps for a girl of five-foot-three. All mine, mine; an' if when I'm ready to support you Mr. Mendoza will not give you to me, then I'll take you, an' it'll make no difference where you are, either—Crebillion, New York, anywhere."

"Oh, pull me tight against you, Ed, an' kiss me a thousand times. Oh, there, there, no more; I'm a litle drunk, I think, with them. But all the stars that ever were are singing inside of me, an' I can feel that the world really is only a little ball flyin' round, with me on the very edge of it almost fallin' off. Be still, honey, an' hold me just this way, an' let's hear what the night is sayin'."

"I hear your heart beatin', Ruth."

"I hear the woods breathin', Ed."

"I hear a sleepy bird singin', Ruth, away over yonder by the bayou, like he was afraid he would go to sleep before he finished his song."

"I hear the pines talkin' in little voices away up there above us."

"Listen, Ruth, there's somethin' small an' afraid stealin' about in the leaves over there among the buckeye bushes; maybe it's a red fox-squirrel, or a little molly cotton-tail rabbit, or maybe an old mother possum with four babies sittin' on her back an' holdin' to her tail."

"Be quiet, Ed; you might scare her, bless her old heart. Oh, honey, on such a night as this, with you against my heart, I love everything that is on this earth. I reckon, on such a night as this is, a thousand thousand other people are lovin' each other, but no two of them are so happy as we, Ed, are they?"

"No, Ruth."

After a deep round-eyed silence she went on: "Ed, wouldn't it just be fine if we could go to college *together?* We'd board the first four years, because I'd be as busy as you with classes; but later while you were in the medical school and in the hospital I'd keep house, and every night you could come back *home* even if it were only two rooms an' a kitchen. Oh, I know what you are thinkin', that maybe I'd have a baby before I got out of college. Well, if I did I'd quit school in a minute. One baby could teach me more, more that I want to know anyway, than ten professors could in a year; not because he would know more but because I'd pay more attention to what he said."

"Oh, Ruth, you do talk like a glorious fairy-tale!

Gee, I could work my head off with you near-by. But it's no use at all goin' on this way. I just naturally can't support you now; Mr. Mendoza will have to do that for ten years yet. My dad never promised to do anything except to help me if I'd help myself with summer jobs an' outside work while in college—and now maybe he won't help me at all. He'll try to beat me up when he first sees me, but he never stays mad long."

"If he won't help you, then I'll be the cause of it, because I put it in your head to come down here. Oh, dear, maybe it would have been better if you'd never known me at all, Ed."

"Don't you worry, Ruth; I'll work it through—and I'll come for you when I'm an M.D. Do you have any faith in me, Ruth?"

"Why, all my faith is in you, Ed. I'd as soon expect the sun to drop straight down out of the sky, like an old black burned-out sky-rocket, as you to fail."

And so they sat still, her head on his shoulder, staring with great eyes into the red heart of the fire. And after a while I felt Ruth's soft body against mine.

The next morning came marching up the eastern sky trailing white banners ten miles long. The air was still, the water smooth, and I saw a third sinful day ahead of me; so much mortal delight must be sinful, I felt. But though Ed and Ruth went out and got me a huge supply of bait they asked if they could not stay in camp and "tidy things up a bit"; and at eleven o'clock Ed was going to start cooking corn-bread, which takes a long time in a baking-skillet. I paddled out into the little slough and set out my lines with trembling hands, not knowing how soon our fishing would be over. When the sun stood straight above me I made camp with thirteen fat brem and a soft-shelled turtle, having a mind for turtle soup that night. Ed was stooping by the fire piling hot coals on top of the baking-skillet, Ruth by his side giving directions. I was out behind a pine-tree washing my hands when I heard row-locks out in the big slough.

"There they are, drat their hides," I grumbled, suddenly hot and cold as if I were terribly mad. Standing on a stump, I could see two boats headed for the hidden mouth of our little slough, and in the rear boat I recognized black Pink Beddo—confound him, I hate him yet—and fat Mr. Flagger, the Methodist minister, who is a poor preacher but a grand fisherman. Mr. Deeves seemed to be saying something to him, and then the second boat stopped outside, the first one coming on.

I called to Ruth and Ed, who had just woke up to the sound of the rowlocks: "I'm going to disappear. If they come, and they will, don't speak about me unless I tell you to. Don't say much of anything if you can help it, especially you, Ed; let *them* do the talking." So saying, I scuttled into a near-by thicket of buckeye bushes and sat down out of sight but within easy hearing distance of the camp fire.

It was in plain sight of the little slough, and presently I heard a boat-chain rattling as it was pulled up on the bank. Parting the bushes, I looked out: Ed and Ruth had not tried to run, they stood side by side awaiting their visitors. Then I saw Mr. Deeves, who is a fiery little man that takes quick, firm, short steps like a goat, rush up to Ed and draw back his fist. But the big boy just looked at him, and nothing happened.

"You've disgraced this girl, yourself, an' your family, you whelp, you. I ought to shoot you, an' I think I would if I'd had sense enough to bring my gun."

"Never mind, Mr. Deeves," put in Mr. Mendoza,

laying a hand on his shoulder. "That wouldn't help anybody, would it? Let's sit down."

He let himself down on the log in front of the fire. Ed, his sunburned face sort of ashy and set, stooped down over his baking-skillet, lifted the top off with a stick, gazed long and solemnly at his bread, saw that it was good and brown, and pulled the skillet off its bed of coals. Then he calmly dumped the coals off the top of the skillet, put it back over the bread, and sat down on the log, six feet away from Mr. Mendoza. Sam Deeves was charging around in a circle—which was a good thing because he was working off a lot of steam that wasn't needed—stamping the earth with his tiny feet and glaring now at Ed and now at Ruth. The other little father—Mr. Mendoza was no bigger than Sam—turned his black eyes on Ruth, who had taken her stand behind Ed, her hands on his shoulders.

"Well, Ruth, you've made a mess of it, haven't you?"

Ruth's chin was in the air, and she stared out across the slough and offered no answer to the question put to her.

"Yes," broke in Sam, stopping and pointing a dramatically accusing finger at her, "an'*you've* got to marry. You've both disgraced yourselves, but you've got to do that anyway. Down here together alone for two nights!"

"Three nights," said Ruth calmly.

I had known what was coming when I saw that second boat with the preacher in it. I trembled at the thought of what Ed might do. If he began excusing himself and telling about me he would be playing his cards like a washerwoman. I rattled the bushes around me, and I could see him lift his head.

"Why, Mr. Deeves, we just *couldn't* marry now," said Ruth, her voice sweet and poisonous, but those men didn't notice the poison. Any woman would have suspected something wrong at once. "Ed's goin' to be a doctor, as you know, sir, an' that will take ten years. We'd agreed to wait, an' I was goin' to New York to get ready for school, an' we only ran away because I heard mama and papa sayin' Monday night that they had prepared to send me away the very next day. We'd been meetin', secretly because we had to meet that way, an' we were lookin' forward to seein' each other all through this last week; an' when I heard that we were likely to lose even that if we didn't do something we came off down here so as not to lose it. But we agreed all the time that I should go to New York next Monday, which was the time first set."

"Maybe Mr. Mendoza will not now choose to send you to New York, young lady," Sam shot at her.

"Oh, fine! I was just goin' to please him. I'd rather wait for Ed at home."

"And maybe I'll not choose to help that young pup get through college either."

"He'll make his own way then, Mr. Deeves. Ed wants to be a doctor, an' he's goin' to be. There's no doubt about *that*."

"Is that so?"

"It is, sir; and if you weren't Ed's father I'd—"

"Now, now, Ruth, be still," put in Mr. Mendoza soothingly. "Of course you an' Ed had better marry, an' this afternoon probably. We've got a license, an' Mr. Flagger's out yonder in a boat behind the trees."

"Really, daddy, I don't think I ought to do it now," and I saw Ruth dig her fingers into Ed's shoulders. "I couldn't stand to have him go off an' leave me right after marryin' me. I'd rather wait if we couldn't go together."

"Bosh!" snorted Sam. "You don't know what's good for you."

"We've thought of that," went on Mr. Mendoza quietly. "Ruth, we're goin' to put together the money I'd have spent on you within the next ten years and what Mr. Deeves meant to give Ed, and you two can go as far on that as you can; go together if you like; or you, Ruth, may stay at home part or all of the time."

She went tearing around the end of the log and flung herself on her father's neck. "Oh, daddy, we'll go together; we'd talked of that, but we thought it wasn't any more possible than a fairy-tale."

And then she flew down to the edge of the water, and I heard her shouting in a voice that was a song, "Mr. Flagger, oh, Mr. Flagger, come on, come on, quick."

Well, they did it there in the cathedral quietness and dimness of the pine forest; and when it was done, and they were making a lot of noise, I crawled out of the farther side of the thicket from them, walked out into the woods, circled around, and came sauntering back into camp, humming a merry little housewife's tune. When I hove in sight of the party I shouted: "Hello, hello; we didn't expect visitors. Welcome, friends; you come just in time for dinner, therefore thrice welcome of course. Ed, I couldn't find any fish-bait, so you'll have to look for it yourself after dinner. Let's have a grand feast. Sam, you all bring up all those nice things I know you brought along. We've got the fish, a hundred pounds of them."

Before I had come up to the party Ruth ran out to me and buried her head in my bosom. Tip-toeing, she whispered in my ear, "Mis' Lyd, you're a wizard. You've caught me a whale, an' I love every pound of him an' you too."

"Have you been here all the time?" Sam asked sourly when I walked in among them and began shaking hands with Ed, who was dry-grinning like a possum, as if I'd just heard from Ruth the news. "If we'd only known you were here—"

Well, that blessed pair decided to stay out their week in the woods, especially as they wouldn't be going away to college until the fall. They begged me to remain with them, but I said, "No, I'm kind of tired of fishing; I'm crazy to get home." As we pulled away from the camp late that afternoon, leaving behind that heavenly fishing-place and that miraculously lucky time, my heart was like to break. "But they fill the woods themselves," I whispered to myself, "and now you'd be in their way."

"Next summer we'll do it again, Mis' Lyd, won't we?" shouted Ruth, waving her hat, her hair full of flowers. "And *every* summer after this."

I had no voice to shout back at her, but I daintily fluttered a four-inch handkerchief like a silly old fool. "Next summer," I moaned in my soul, "I may be dead; and, anyway, never in a thousand years will the fish bite like this again for me." And they haven't.

PIONEERS*

By WILBUR DANIEL STEELE

ARCHIE CABOT had no idea but that he loved New York. Tamman Krokaw loved New York. Two of Archie Cabot's great-uncles went west in the wagons of the Fifties, one to Nebraska, the other to California, pioneering; they loved New England but they wanted elbow-room. Elbow-room has moved in seventy years. When Archie Cabot started out to "digge after gold & trayde with the inhabitants" he packed a kit bag with clothing, a golf-bag with clubs, and a dispatch-case with his new pet South Carolina Canal and Power Development paper, taxied to the Grand Central, and got up into a Dixie-bound Pullman; for, though he was as young as the uncles had been, his race was older in the land.

Tamman Krokaw's was not so old. He loved New York but he wanted to be "in on the ground floor" somewhere. On the running boards of the superannuated Cadillac taxi he had bought from his cousin Felix Poululos, all his goods and gods were tied in bundles; inside of it he had Rachel, his wife, and little Tamman, little Rachel, little Greta Garbo, little Henry Ford, and little Al, and still one other little somebody, for Rachel was big. And in his wallet, in his pocket, Tamman had a draft for ten thousand dollars.

They would much rather have turned back. They were homesick. Hive-dwellers, the open spaces frightened them. But now they couldn't turn back. The covered wagon had them.

Archie Cabot would have been amazed to be told that he did not altogether love New York. Where one does

* Reprinted from *Harpers Magazine* with the courteous permission of the publishers and the author.

well one is naturally happy. In the eleven years since his graduation from Carnegie Tech, which had been twenty-three years after his birth in Nantucket, Massachusetts, he had forgotten Carnegie, and he had forgotten Nantucket Island, and he had done as well as the next young man in the financial district; the evidence of the trust the Firm put in him was in the semi-independent "flyer" in the shiny, fat cowhide dispatch-case.

The case was no fuller of it than Cabot himself was. One with his age, "bull-minded," shrewd salesman, yet it was good to know that this was not a thing that had to be "put over" on anyone. Obvious destiny was his selling-point. South Carolina, Power, Development—mathematical. No, there would be no call for anything but a straight eye in saying his say to the people down there in Charleston and the Sea Island country, "Finest harbor on the South Atlantic Coast . . . logical, inevitable outlet of the industrializing Piedmont . . . Not that this wouldn't be underwritten in a day in the New York market; but we feel that the bigger the block that's covered here in Charleston locally, the bigger your stake in your own power-development, the solider a proposition it's going to be for our subscribers from Maine to California. By that much, it's up to you. That a man can't lift himself by his own bootstraps, that's un-American and it's bosh. There's no other way *up*."

Cabot's young enthusiasm was puissant precisely because it was pure. Though he hadn't been south, he could see the thing ahead of him vividly. Fallow fields and sleeping money, sleeping men. Then of a sudden, harnessed water, channelled lightning, fields astir, chimneys rearing, smoking, men and money awake and working. . . .

It was still daylight through New Jersey. Forests

of chimneys. It came daylight again in the Piedmont of North Carolina. Chimneys. Hives of glass and steel and concrete against the sky-line; trunk-lines of copper walking from horizon to horizon on cantilever legs. In the washroom Cabot apostrophized a fellow-shaver, "You know, by Jingo, this state pays the second biggest internal revenue in the Union. Yes, it does."

But where were the sleeping fields, the dreaming men?

The land lost altitude. Red clay, blue hills and black smoke-towers gave way to dunner hues, browns and grays, the only brightness left, the brightness of the green. The swift cathedral chill of a cypress swamp; sudden lowering of the pulse-beat: accolade.

And here they began at last, the sleeping fields, half-planted squares, half-whitewashed cabins, sun-drugged negroes blinking after the train. Or wider clearings, wraiths of clearings, regrown in briar and dogwood, mounds of centenary live-oak avenues leading in to scars of brick-dust and fallen pillars. Or still again, penumbral on the edges of slow yellow rivers, memories of laborious rice-squares forgotten under the reconquering reeds, mile on mile, thousand-tinted, giving up marsh fowl in staccato flight.

Cabot felt strange: the hollow at his midriff was like a kind of sickness.

The road that kept a wiggling pace alongside gave him the blue devils with its emptiness. Sometimes a mule, a nodding black man, a wagon with wobbly wheels; once in a while a car, but nearly always at a standstill, having a tire changed. Cabot would have liked to laugh, but he couldn't. It wasn't simply the depression; it was the internal queerness, the feeling that something mysterious was about to grab hold of Archie Coffin Cabot of Nantucket, Pittsburgh, and Broadway, and do something funny to him, and he didn't know what it was. He tried to lay it on the livid moss that wept from all the trees. "It gives me the willies!" He thought it was the idiot meandering of that sun-white road. "Look there now; still another fellow with a flat tire. Can you beat it!"

Nevertheless, that one came nearer to giving him the relief of a guffaw than anything else had, because the stalled car, its running-boards swollen with belongings and its insides stuffed with frowzy heads, looked so like a superannuated New York taxi gone pioneering, lost in the wilderness.

* * *

WHEN TAMMAN KROKAW had got the tire changed he was too worn out even to scrape the grease from his hands. He had changed so many. Climbing in, he put his foot on the starter. A dying gasp, and the battery was dead. He sat there deaf to the sixfold despair of the family, resting desperately a moment. Then he got out and cranked.

The next two or three miles it was easy going, one of those breathing-spaces without which Tamman would never have got so far. At a crossroad, always fearful of going wrong, he hailed a black man, who, with another, basked in sun-soaked idleness, "Whatcha say, boss, would I be going right yet for Charleston this way, yes?"

The negro, white eyes for incredulity and white teeth for mirth, could only give him half a nod. "Do-Jedus, hear dat t'ing de white man do call dis-yuh nigguh, he call me 'boss,' he done do."

Tamman, as he rattled on, wrung sweet water of hope out of that episode in the desert. It went like that; the minute the dream of the pioneer was nearly done with weariness, some little fillip, and it glowed a dream again. To another the sight of those able bodies loafing the good day away while earth lay fallow would have augured but drearily for the Promised Land ahead. To Tamman, who, with his rounded shoulders, greenish temples, and skinny chest, asked no more of Heaven than to be let work the eight hours the world worked, and eight more while it played, and then the third eight, even in his sleep dreaming how to save—and to Rachel, horn-of-plenty of a woman, indefatigably fruiting, her handsome, dark, insect-mother eyes wanting nothing of the future but room on earth, room for her egglings to grow in, batten on, and in their hour fruit a dozenfold—to these two the sloth of the Philistines was milk and honey for their busier, hungrier hands to take.

That was the trouble with New York. It seemed as though teeming ten thousands were as bent on it, eight hours and eight and eight, sweating, scheming, fecundating as industriously as they, weazening the profits, narrowing a man's room as fast as his elbows could make it. When Tamman had got a little fruit-drink stand, then a second to go with it, then four in a chain, what good? A big chain of a hundred began to reach his way. He might have fought, might have just survived. So might his parents have done before him, and just survived in north Hungary, if they had been content to. They too had loved their town.

One reason Tamman loved New York was that he knew it. He knew the streets, the ways, the peculiar chances and perils. He was a timid fellow and he felt safe there. So did Rachel, and so did little Tamman, and little Rachel, little Greta Garbo, Henry Ford, and Al. Out here there wasn't a mile that might not be the end of them, and no end of miles. The swamps were the worst.

They came into that big swamp a little while after

Tamman had hailed the negroes. Where there had been sun on the road dust, now there fell a shadow on ruts with threads of glimmer in them, like glimmers of cold sweat. It wasn't simply the shadow of the sun shut out, it was more a Thing; it got into the throat and started to say "Ooooo!"—then stopped and was very quiet. At first Rachel and the children held so, very quiet, watching Papa. He had to keep those wheels turning in the slippery ruts, keep them going somehow, or else—"Good night!" He had to do it all with his two weedy wrists and the two greeny-white cords at the back of his neck, or else. . . . There was nothing but a lake of water as black as black ink and as still as black glass, mirroring the innumerable gray boles of cypress trees, and the "knees" they breathed with, and the pale, long windless hangings of the moss. "Good night!"

When the car did stall, even yet for a few seconds the children kept still. The only one that moved was the one without a name, and Rachel felt that one bumping against her heart. And catching at herself in panic, in all weak, wicked mutiny the woman thought, "This is a swell business, this is! Why for God-sake should it have Tamman, that fool, such a dumb head we should give up a good enough home and ride around nowheres like a lot of bums like this? *Now* we gone and done it! Oh, my God! Oh! my God!" But she only thought it, and kept her mouth shut and, when Greta got a breath for yelling, she gave the girl a good one on the side of the head to hush her. Hush? With that, front seat, back seat, the whole kit of them let it out with all their lungs.

Well, then. Tamman Krokaw could yell a little himself. He laid about him with the strength of his completed terror. "Shut up the mouths! Take that! I'll give you! With this here wrench I'll give you. Such a cry-babies! *Mama!* You got it a stomach-ache, you got? What would *I* got it, you think? Henry, if you wouldn't stop crying, Papa going to give you a —aw, listen, give Papa a minute he could get out of here and fix it."

Tamman started to open the door beside him, so weak it took all his strength. Then he quit and sat. He had never seen a snake alive in his life. Thirty yards ahead a five-foot moccasin flowed in a soft, slow wave across the drowned ruts and entered the water on the farther side without a ripple.

But there was a ripple, by and by. One ripple. It came from somewhere beyond sight. Here the pediment of one cypress took a piece out of it, there another took another. But in a queer way the undulant black water mended itself; wider and wider the ripple ran.

One of the children began to yell.

* * *

A MAN has to be alive these days to sell anything. Archie Cabot had the names of a few Broad Street men. At the full tide of three that afternoon he started out to establish his Charleston connections and, because he had not yet got rid of his mysterious "willies," he took care to make his feet ring sharply on the pavement of the wide, low-built, harmoniously colored place of affairs. It would have been better to walk gently and raise no echoes, for the echoes from the soft old walls of the "sea-drinking city" came back and got into a lump in his stomach, like cold milk on a hot day, swallowed too fast.

Seeing him so headlong, the genius of the Low Country smiled a little, withdrew, and took him in ambush. The first and the second of the offices on his list he found as dead as dead, save for the negro factotum, whose "More bettuh you come back tomorruh, suh; he done jes' now gone home foh he dinnuh," where it should have exasperated him, only confused and depressed him, at the same time that it so strangely excited him, the more.

"Dinner! Three o'clock in the afternoon! And *this* is in *America?*"

The third, and set down as one of the best, of his prospects was a lawyer, Tradd St. Julien. When Cabot had climbed one steep flight of hollowed stairs through the half-night of a building perfumed by the legal ruminations of a hundred years, it came to him, "Why, no, it's not within a thousand miles of America." When he had climbed a second flight, knocked on a dim door, and found St. Julien actually in he was almost sorry for the anticlimax.

St. Julien, sensing it, apologized with a twinkle. "We dine at two-thirty at home; ordinarily I try to be there by three. But we law fellows are as bad as doctors. I've some rather important clients coming here, supposedly at two o'clock, and so I. . . ."

At the word "clients," Cabot was up quickly to go, but St. Julien would have none of it.

"Sit down, sir, and tell me how you like our Charleston. We've hours of time."

He was about of an age with the Northerner, yet in a way he seemed twice the years. Cabot had known two or three old, admired men in the Street who had made so much money that they could afford the luxury at last of a clear-eyed, mellow-minded pessimism. This fellow, St. Julien, still half in his youth, had amazingly the look of that. Surrounded by the gracious, grimy panelling, the high brown shadows, the gray-brown, green-brown books of this office that was like no law office in Cabot's experience, as fit in the hollow of his leather chair as if in truth it had taken himself two hundred years to shape it, his long young face was not so much lined as deeply bitten, cordial, cynical, museful, balanced, and in a glint of a way to puzzle the other, devil-may-care. For whatever he had, it was not in any sense a negation of living. In the regret he expressed that Cabot could not have come to the Low Country at an earlier season, when the ducks were flying, and the snipe and partridges, and the deer running, and the 'coons and 'possums climbing and shining in the chill red torchlight, and toddies and Hoppin'-John a-steam in the sylvan halls, and beauties dancing, there was betrayed a simple gusto of living as exciting as is the measured sipping of an old, strong, mellow wine.

"But you are just in time for the gardens," he said, and there was a gusto in that too. And he went on, "I'm glad you've come to Charleston, sir. You were born in Nantucket, you tell me. Well, Nantucket and Charleston were as different as two places could be, I imagine. And yet, in a way, sir—well, they were alike in this: they knew how to live with a certain comeliness. They could walk without running, talk without shouting, take without grabbing. And they built their houses roomy and strong and beautiful, to last them a long, long while. I'll bet, sir, you've lived in yours there for half a dozen generations; there's that in—how do you whalers say it?—the cut of your jib. There are a good many 'Americans' through here, nowadays, in a hurry to get to Florida. Charleston, to them, is quaint, it's slow, it's amusing, it's 'not America.' But I'd like to lay a wager, sir, that to you coming to Charleston will be like coming home."

Cabot felt his face getting hot. Ridiculous, but what could he say? He couldn't break out guffawing. "Nantucket! Good Lord! I left there when I was hardly more than a kid; there was the old house, to be sure, but I've hardly thought of it in years; we in our business haven't time for that sort of thing." He got hold of his dispatch-case with a grab, like the drowning man, his straw. Desperately he tried to marshal his talking-points. Power! "The finest harbor . . . inevitable outlet . . . Piedmont . . . untapped resources. . . ." Harnessed water, channelled lightning, fields astir, chimneys rearing, smoking. . . .

It wasn't St. Julien's fault that it didn't seem to go quite as it had gone in rehearsal. He listened with an impeccable interest, his eyes, slightly wrinkled at the corners, fixed on the talker's. It was apparently with regret that he said then, "I'm sorry, but I think I hear my clients coming at last. No, please don't go, if I may ask a favor of you."

The clients were in, an old, very black, dried-up woman, hugging a basket of eggs, and a strong black man, her son, she turbaned with a towel and a hat with a feather on top of it, he in overalls and a starched shirt, a miscellany of root-vegetables and live fowls clutched in one hand, a soiled, folded paper in the other, and the dust of all the way from John Island on everything but his shoes, which were painful and obviously just now put on.

What a hullabaloo! What volleys of perfectly incomprehensible words, and what a gamut of grins and tears! "Important clients"! Cabot was human, he didn't like to be had.

By this and by that, the much-folded paper was signed at last, and Cabot, asked to witness the two crosses, did so, a little hot, but not so hot as he was sick with the mysterious lump of swallowed echoes that seemed to be growing bigger and bigger all the while in the hollow pit of him. Old Venus Gaylord and her son departed then, vociferous in joy, ferocious in a last-minute squabble with St. Julien, who would *not* have their grateful turnips and squawking hens left on him, confound them! but compromised finally by accepting the eggs. When they were gone he explained to Cabot.

"A Chicago man, an Italian, was by way of getting some acres away from them. That spikes his guns, I think. But I must keep track of it. They've always been our people."

St. Julien took up his hat and the basket of eggs.

"If you'd be good enough to drop in some other time, Mr. Cabot, about the Power—"

"To-morrow morning?"

"I'm sorry, to-morrow I must go to Castle River Plantation; it's Grandmother Tradd's birthday. The day after is Saturday; then there's Sunday. But if, some time early in the week. . . . I'm walking toward the Battery, sir, if you happen to be going that way."

Cabot was not used to walking around town for nothing, and especially he was not used to walking so with an impeccably dressed young gentleman carrying on his arm a country basket of Adam-naked eggs. St. Julien himself did not seem aware of anything incongruous, however, nor did any of the few friends to whom he nodded or spoke in passing, queer fellows. Why "queer"? Cabot undertook to analyze it. Then he perceived it was because it was like the last refinement in stage armies, always the same man, doubling around in front again, so much these Carolinian Americans were all alike in conformation and speech and bearing, and so strangely, to the eyes of Manhattan, they were American.

For a man already an hour late to his dinner, St. Julien kept to a grave pace. At the corner of Meeting Street, turning south under the pillared shade of St. Michael's, he found time to put back the iron lace of a gate and step inside the high-walled yard. Bright as it was outside, the sunshine seemed brighter here, asleep on the grass and the ranked white headstones. He stood there so careless of the sliding minutes that the great, time-soft bells in the tower were chiming four when he spoke.

"Didn't I tell you, Cabot, it would be like coming home? For I've no doubt that in Nantucket, too, you've a church-yard where, wandering, reading the names on the stones, you wonder why they sound so familiar, and wake up to discover that you've been reading pure pages in American history. Eh?"

It made Cabot miserable and it made him mad. Had it been St. Julien with whom he was angry, the two might have conversed politely for weeks without its ever showing. It was precisely because it was not against St. Julien, but because, with a sudden intuitive flair, he saw himself and St. Julien, himself and this yard full of dead men who had known how to live in a certain way, himself and this worn, defiant, contained, and beautiful city that stood at bay between its colonial rivers on the shore of an English sea—it was precisely because he saw himself with them, all in the same boat, that he could turn so fiercely.

"What about it? What the devil has this got to do with my trying to sell you Power?"

It was amazing. Something had clicked. Now it was as if they had known each other, not for their years, but for their generations. St. Julien grinned belligerently, sadly.

"What's it got to do? For the life of me, I can't say. Can you, Cabot?"

"No, I can't. Just because some of us keep up with the parade and some of us—"

"Well, well, perhaps you're right. Come on along."

They went out and down Meeting, St. Julien less than ever in a hurry. Cabot had had to do with many kinds of "boosters"; he had been shown some towns. He had never been shown like this. Little said. Here, "The Lucas wisteria is flowering heavily this season, isn't it?" —so much, and no more, for a garden like no other town garden on earth, glimpsed through an iron tapestry of gate in a yellow wall, a garden of blossoming wood breaking up in one great, caught, breathless wave against the tiered, slenderly-pillared galleries of Berkley House. And there, for the wind-worn heights of Laurel Court, despair of living architects, "The wild gobblers are gobbling this month, I see! Cousin Will Pinckney's blinds are shut, and they've all gone up to the turkey woods on the Santee." And as little, with a machiavellian wisdom, for twenty others. And nothing at all for the green of trees and blue of water filling the bottom of the warmly noble vista.

Once, before another gate to another garden, St. Julien paused and lifted an aimless, unintelligible hail. When an old and ragamuffin darky had come slipper-flapping out of nowhere he put the egg-basket in his hands. "See here, Mingo, take that in to Cousin Lou Rutley. Tell her they're no good and she can throw them away if she wants to; certainly *I'm* not going to lug them around any more. . . . And now, Cabot, if you don't mind just stepping over into Legare Street, there's a gate I'd like to have you see. I'm curious to know if you-all in Nantucket have got a finer one."

"St. Julien, look here, I left Nantucket when I was fifteen. I don't know one thing about it and care a damned sight less. And I thought you were late to your dinner."

"Well, I've decided I'm not very hungry yet."

"But that doesn't alter the fact that it's waiting for you all this while."

St. Julien appeared to wonder at him. "What of that? It's a great deal easier for *it* to *wait* than for *me* to *hurry*, isn't it? I eat my dinner; my dinner doesn't eat *me*." But then a fine, satirical line went down around his lip. "I see what you mean. When all this is gone—" he waved a hand over the spacious, gracious edifice— "when we've bought your bonds and you've built our chimneys, strung our wires, deepened our rivers, and torn all this wreckage down, then it will be my dinner that eats me."

He began to laugh as he walked westward, as if at a great joke. "Do you remember when Marion jumped out of the window, Cabot, when the Britishers were after him?" He pointed with a shoulder. "That is the window."

"Yes, but I still think you ought to be at dinner."

"And now, getting down into Legare Street—"

South of Broad, east of Orange, north of the Ashley's sea-turn, and west of the Cooper's tide—Legare, King, Meeting, Church, East Bay, East Battery, Atlantic and Lamboll and Water, the streets of the peninsula lie in a maze and a dream. Not asleep, not altogether quiet. Negro children dance in the sunny mouths of areaways, and white children with hair as blond as Swedes, and long, long knees like French children, tow their enormous-bosomed black "dahs" toward the pleasance of the Battery. There is a melodious laughter of older young girls behind a garden wall. There is a small, unhurrying come-and-go of straight, lean people, punctilious in the amenities, sensuously alert, preoccupied not with yesterday, in this town of yesterday, nor with to-morrow, but with to-day's half-past-four and its errands, melancholy or pleasurable, its drifting scents of tree-flowers, and its slanting rays of sunshine that lengthen the arabesque shadows of high, slim balconies on warm old plasters bearing scars of wars.

Cabot had entered this maze with the trouble already in him. He came out with it established, a nostalgia no logic could account for, a sickness, not of a man, but of a race.

For logic protested, "My stock and their stock, my New England and their Carolina, manners, aspirations, anything—what the devil had they in common?" He remembered the white villages of his hard-mouthed, hard-handed coast; here, wherever his eye went, it found only conflict of colors harmonized by sun and time, terracottas and faded beryls, ivory and primrose and rain-streaked pink. Once he spoke his puzzlement aloud.

"It isn't, either, that they didn't like to make money. You did, and so did we."

St. Julien nodded gravely. "I've thought about that a lot, too. Maybe it's like the dinner-eating; maybe it's simply they didn't like the money to make *them*."

"I don't know. I don't even know if the older thing was actually better, but damn it—"

"Come in here, and ask." St. Julien had stopped before a tall, pink-washed East Battery mansion, slender handrails leading up in perfect congruity to a massive door. "My Great-aunt Elinore Rutley will be serving benne-cakes and rice wine just now; she and Great-uncle Edward will love to see you. Great-uncle ought to know about the money-making, for he's never made any. He would have loved a little money if he could have loved it enough. The trouble is, he loved too much to fight—he was the handsome aide to handsome Beauregard—and next to fighting he loved fair women, and he loved camellia japonicas, and most of any, perhaps, he loved chemistry, and he taught it seven bad years for nothing at the College."

"Wait!" Cabot grabbed his arm. "That reminds me. I had a grandfather. He was a whaler. He never made the money he would have liked to make, and partly it was because he loved ocean currents more than he loved the sperm. What he should do was to chase the whale; what he *had* to do was to discover a lot of little coral specks and map upwards of a million square miles in the South Pacific that had never been honestly mapped before, and the whales wouldn't always go with the currents where the new islands were. I remember him in the big house on Orange Street, a quiet-voiced, red-cheeked, sitting man in broadcloth and hard linen, in a big, quiet room with ivory-white panels to the ceiling, and his neighbors and relatives around him—an aristocrat, St. Julien, if ever there was one. . . . And I remember my grandmother there, in silk, because she was a fine lady, and gray silk because she was a Quaker, serving vanilla wafers and elderberry wine. And discussing—Lord! how long since I've thought of it—Emerson and Whitman and free love."

St. Julien grinned and opened the door, "Ask Great-uncle Edward. And then if you want the truth of it all, ask Great-aunt Elinore."

Cabot gazed about him at the sumptuous austerity of the Georgian hall. "This house is not anything like that old house in Orange Street. And yet, damn it, St. Julien, there's something—Say! I didn't know it was a *party!*

"It's not. They just drop in."

Figures a little shadowy at this hour that got on toward dusk in the vastness of drawing-rooms, fiercely gentle old people and people in middle-age, bowing with a cordiality enriched by reserve when his name was given, and among them, as if to confound him the more in his nameless nostalgia, not a few youngsters, boys of college years, and pretty girls, and merry ones, showing by no sign that they were not content to waste their priceless, irretrievable moments in such staid amusement.

Oh, but it was a bad place for Archie Cabot, cog in a polyglot wheel, to find himself.

"Why, these, damn it! *these are my people!*"

Now that Edward Rutley, who had loved fighting, women, camellias, and chemistry, was an old man, he sat in a chair. But when his young kinsman, speaking with a glint of mischief for his Yankee friend, wondered why the living in other days should have seemed handsomer than the living now—no matter if it was bad for the old gentleman—spleen had him up. Erect, gaunt, transfigured, "the handsome aide to handsome Beauregard," he stood and struck out, not bludgeoningly, but in passionate quiet, like the swordsman of an old, pure race wielding a thin blade. And Archie Cabot was thrilled, and the more fiercely thrilled when he perceived that the argument was little better than invective, and the blade was blind.

Let it be blind! Who cared! Hit 'em! Slit 'em! The go-getters, the boosters, the hundred-percenters, the melting-potters, the high-gear fellows, the efficiency boys.

Caught in the grip of an amazing atavistic loyalty, Archie Cabot of Nantucket saw red.

"And then, if you want the truth of it all, ask Great-aunt Elinore."

Of a patrician poise, a tranquil humor, a beauty still arresting at eighty-odd, Elinore Rutley had perhaps done more fighting than her lord, and loved it less.

"Who knows whether it was handsomer or happier or better? I'm only a little over eighty. When I'm a thousand I may dare say." She put an arm around St. Julien. "It's not that it was better, or worse, but that it was ours." She had been studying Cabot with her shrewd eyes. She laid her other hand on his shoulder of a sudden, making them three. "And we are growing old," she said.

"*I!*" Cabot protested to himself, rebellious. "I am

not growing old!" He could understand the alarm in it; what he couldn't fathom was the melancholy sweetness, the tragic thrill.

"You should have opened up your Power in there," St. Julien mused, when they were out of doors again. "For doing your business in a lump, that was your God-sent chance."

"That house! Those people! No, by God! sooner than tamper with that priceless—"

"Wait a second. Let me see the names you have." When St. Julien had read the list of prospects in Cabot's notebook, his malign grin deepened. "They were there, nearly every one of them, and nearly all my kin."

For a moment Cabot felt really scared, really sick.

"Damn old man Morganthaler, why did he let me come here? I hate this town."

It was only a step to the battery. On the quiet walks under the trees, or on the pavement at the water's edge, hundreds of people loitered to watch the changing sky. The ray of the sun, on top of the St. Andrews woods, came down the sea-turn of the Ashley and emptied into the broad room of the harbor. As it cooled, as it withdrew the heart of its fire from the water level and swept it higher and higher up the sky, it left only the islands out there burning, jewel-size and jewel-bright.

"That one," St. Julien pointed, elbows on the seawall, "you ought to know. Sumter."

"*Fort* Sumter?"

"Fort Sumter."

"Lord! Is Fort Sumter *real?* Somehow I always thought of Fort Sumter, well, like Washington Crossing the Delaware and the Pilgrims Landing—a picture in a book, in black and white, with shells bursting—"

"Didn't they, though! We licked you there."

"Licked us! Say, if you want to talk of *lickings*, what happened at—"

"Of course, with all your factories, and your money. But we were in the right."

"Right, nothing! You ought to know by this time. Listen, Johnnie Reb. . . ."

Old men in the twilight. No heat, no bitterness, only a divinity of fraternal raillery, old children playing with old lead toys turned gold.

"You couldn't hold it as a fort, you Yanks, so you'll hold it as a Sight-to-See. You couldn't take it with gunboats, so you'll take it with excursion-steamers, like a Coney Island, lugging your lunches with you, and your brats, by your thousands—"

There was an interruption, amazing.

"Please to excuse me, gents."

A face with greenish temples and narrow-set, excited eyes came up beside them.

"Please to excuse me, but I heard what you said already. Please, you should tell me, they got it a concession already out by that island you talk about?"

"A—what?"

"Con*cession*. You don't know? Like you should be a licensed vendor you should sell ice-cold drinks and nut-bars and gum and magazines. Didn't I hear you, you says it was excursioners? . . . Excuse me."

When he had left they eyed each other and snorted. The sun was gone with its fire; the peace of dusk lay over the water and the town.

* * *

WHEN TAMMAN KROKAW left them he went back to what was left of the taxi-cab, parked by the sea-walk, spewing out its freight. Little Tamman, little Rachel, Greta, Henry, all out on the concrete of the Land of Promise under the fabulous sky of Journey's End; big Rachel and Little Al, in arms, half through a window, gaping.

There was something strange about the way Papa walked. It wasn't that he walked like a tired man, for they had grown used to seeing him do that in the days of the migration whose beginning began already to be dim—a very glutton, Papa, for weariness and fright. No, it was that he did *not* walk like a tired man, dull-eyed, but shiny-eyed like a man who has taken a drink of whiskey on an empty stomach, his feet stepping high.

"Look it, Rachel! What a dumb-heads, they don't know even what it is a concession. They got it an island already for excursioners like Coney Island with steamers, and is it so much as one news-stand or soda-fountain on that whole island? Not!"

"Oh, Tamman! Oh, Tamman, we got here. Could you believed it yesterday?"

"Got here!" Papa had shoulders and a chest between them. "Why wouldn't we?" Papa had biceps. "Who would stop us, please you would tell me, Mrs. Krokaw!"

Mama looked out the other way. "My, it's a lot of people at that, but so funny; they got nothing to do with themself, only loaf around; no amusements. It reminds me of my mother, the town she was born before she come over, and that one wouldn't have so much as five hundred inhabitants in the town."

"Wait!" Papa looked momentous, mysterious. "You would be a little bit thirsty, eh? Wait a minute I should go there where it's the people I should buy a pineapple drink and maybe a bag peanuts by the refreshment stand. You'd like?"

CHORUS: "I'd like." "I'm hungry." "I want a piece apple pie."

"Yi! What a joking! You find for Papa a place he

could spend a nickel in this here park, he would spend you a dollar, each and every one."

"And it's such a nice park here too, Tamman; for the ocean breezes and the lovely foliage the Battery could be no better."

"The Battery! You talking about New York, are you yet, Mrs. Krokaw? If you would not be so ignorant —wait a minute—give a look." His fingers all thumbs with eagerness, Tamman unfolded the map of Charleston he had got at a gas-station. "Give a look."

"I never could see much from a map."

"What it got here printed, eh? *'Battery'!* Give a look the shape the city—squint up careless the eyes. Suppose now, listen, where it says printed 'Cooper River' I should print it 'East River,' and where it stands 'Ashley River' it would stand 'North River'—wait a minute—and look it this street it runs down through to the Battery—what it says? 'Meeting Street,' eh? If I would take it and print it 'Broadway'—so? Eh?"

"Could you believe it! 'King Street' it would be Sixth Avenue, and—I would write Miriam Shuber she should come here she should live cheap in the Bush Terminal Building."

"I would write Alex, and yet his brother Steffin, they should come right away down here they should rent for nothing an entire building on Broadway, they would have the market to themselves in Misses' Outing Creations. . . . Rachel, you don't got it the stomach-ache no more now; you look better in the face."

Why shouldn't she look better? No more worry about Tamman's worry, no more road-bumps to look forward to with the bitten lip of terror. All the lines as fine as hair were erased from her face and the color brought back again, like the rich color of the fruits pouring out of a picture of the Horn of Plenty. Supper? A roof and a bed? Yes, of course, presently. But just for now, like Tamman, so drunk with weariness she forgot she was weary, she wanted nothing but to roam, weave fantasies, and build castles.

Just so, on the night in the Fifties when Cabot's Great-uncle Bancroft reached San Francisco overland, he was so dead-beat he could have slept in a gutter, it seemed. Yet all that night long he went roaming through the golden camp, laying out kingdoms and dreaming palaces. And so, on the night when Bancroft's Cousin Adam outspanned on the Nebraska prairie, he could not rest his racked bones beneath the wagon canvas, but had to be out in the star-light, shooting at coyotes' shadows, peering here, there, and everywhere, at the way his dominions folded down to the winding river, feeling with his soles the firm softness of the womb of the wheat. And so, probably, their fathers before them, room-hungry, land-hungry men, rolling up their axe-arm sleeves against the morrow in the beauty of the dark New England forest, pioneers.

But if the primeval forest was beautiful to those pioneers, how doubly beautiful was this wood of Charleston to these, Tamman and Rachel and their young, where the great, cluttering trees stood already girdled and sap-dried for them, so easy to the axe!

"What a out-of-daters! You wouldn't lose it a lot, you would give a foot and push all this old, homely-looking, over-grown shacks of houses down, so then you could put up some modern lofts and apartments, with the unemployment it looks here, cheap. A man would be a go-getter in this town, he would be willing to work hard and look ahead, he would own it. Don't let me forget, Rachel, I should write it a letter to my brother and Felix

Poululos, they should sell out and come down here quick to get in on the ground floor."

"Look it . . . look it!"

This wasn't Meeting Street they drove up; it was a Broadway for the making.

"Look it!"

"Look it where that window has got some boards over, a man would put a tailor shop in there for day-and-night valet service, and no competition. I would maybe put your cousin Berg in there, Rachel, he should make his fortune and bring us in some profit."

"What a loafers, Rachel! Can you imagine, that grocer store there, a fine residential corner, shut up for business at here seven-thirty P. M.! He should sell out cheap, the money he would lose, such a loafer. I would go in there, I would put in a nice line delicatessen for the evening trade. . . . Look it, the engine it's gone and stopped again. . . . No, I *got* my foot on it, I tell you. Out of gas; a leak maybe in the feed-line. What to do?"

"You would go in this apartments, inquire where it is the nearest gas-station."

"Apartments!"

"Well, it wouldn't be a loft building, or yet a theatre, would it, so it could be only apartments, so big. Because it is dark in front? Go then by the rear, in the gate there, Ignorant, you would find maybe somebody home in the rear."

When Tamman had been gone for some minutes, they heard his voice coming back through the huge old gate. "Rachel, come right away in here."

"I should come in there, I can move hardly? . . . Wait now, you children, if one of you would so much as put it one foot from this car, I'll give you. . . . Yes, I'm coming."

Wonder smote Rachel as she entered the garden, an immensity of vine and blossom silhouetted against the beginning stars to open her eyes, a fragrance to dilate her nostrils. She almost forgot Tamman. The Promised Land? No, something ran back farther. The Garden of Eden, the very Garden, and she walking, dreaming, possessing, the regnant, pregnant Eve, got back somehow or other past the flaming sword, and into it again.

But there was an Eve already. She was to be seen as no more than a slip of gray in the shadow cut by lamplight from a kitchen window at the rear of the pillared gallery.

Tamman loomed at Rachel's shoulder.

"She would be maybe bashful or maybe scared a little to talk with a man. So ask her." "Mrs., excuse me, but the car it's out of gas, we should want to know simply—"

The interruption from the gallery was as colorless and quiet as the figure there.

"I have no car myself, so I really *can't* say where the nearest gas-station is."

"I know, but wouldn't it some other family in the building could tell us maybe?"

"Other family? There's no other. It is my house, and I live in it alone."

"You live, excuse me, you mean to tell me—but look it, my gracious, Mrs., you must got it twenty rooms at the very least."

"I believe I have just ten."

"*Just* ten. Just simply a mere ten, Tamman, you listening? We would have this house, we would have not only a living room with a separate dining room, we would have for each one a separate bedroom so big it would be a house for an ordinary family, one for us, one for Tamman, one for Rachel, one for little Ai even, and this lovely garden—Mrs., listen—Tamman, you would wait a second—Mrs., would you rent to us one or maybe two rooms, we would make you no trouble?"

"I'm sorry, I don't rent rooms. You might ask about the gas-station next door if you—"

"Wait, but *listen!*" Here was passion. "What a wastefulness; even for yourself it ain't right, lady. Even you would have money already to burn, you would be foolish—"

"Money to burn!" A sound of queer mirth in the shadows. But then quickly, half imploring, half sharp, "Please! Oh, do, whoever you are—they may pick a few of the flowers if they want them—but do please don't let them break the vines!"

Invasion. Stealthy patterings. Whoopings under the breath. Lootings in the fabulous half-lights. Vandals. Scandals.

"Tamman! Look it your children, you stand there, be ashamed. . . . Children! Out! The idea! Is this your property already? Greta, you would say excuse me to the lady. Rachel! *Rachel,* you would let it be the vine and you would give it the flower into Mama's hand. Such a shame! . . . Give a look, now you done it, in the gate there, the policemen maybe."

In the gateway, beyond which a street-lamp had come on, two men stood silhouetted, their voices, as they communed, clear in the sudden hush of guilt.

"Cheer up, Cabot; to-morrow you'll be your rational, practical, hard-boiled self again."

"Not here, I won't. Not if there's a train out for the north. If I stayed here, I'd have to—why, I couldn't even make a living as a street-sweeper, because I don't want even the dust on the streets disturbed. If Charleston had a neck, I'd wring it, for what it's gone and done to me, St. Julien. No, if anybody's going to re-pep and re-prosper your good-for-nothing burg, it's got to be somebody else but the idiot I am. Damn it all!"

The woman in the gallery called, "Cousin Tradd."

Tradd St. Julien turned an ear. "Cousin Lou? Get the eggs? What's wrong?"

When he perceived the serried Krokaws, he roughened it, "What's wrong? What are you doing here, you people? Tell me at once. Or else, get out."

Tamman Krokaw was a timid man. But he had his bigging mate there, and his young.

"You should talk so to us, what we done? We ask simply, of the lady, where it is a gas-station. You look at me, you think I am a bum, but I am no bum, I am an American citizen, I come here to settle with my family, do some business, and I got a good deal money I would invest it in this town. So, that begins to make a difference, yes?"

St. Julien's eyes went to Cabot's. He laughed, a wry, malign, satiric merriment.

"Come, clear out," he bade Krokaw, "out here, and I'll show you where the gas—yes, all you little tikes, out here—but where's the woman gone? She started with us."

They went back into the dark and found Rachel at a corner of the fair old house of many rooms, looking up at it with a light of covetous patience in the darkness of her insect-mother eyes.

A TEMPERED FELLOW*

By PAUL GREEN

ALL DAY long he hoed among his cotton. Row by row, and round by round he travelled, the rhythmic hanh, hanh, of his hoe keeping time to the turmoil of hurt and anger within him. It was near night, with the sun hanging low in the tops of the pines by Little Bethel Church. When he reached the fence he stopped and surveyed his handiwork behind him.

"Aih!" he said with grim exultation, "three acres chopped and a hour to go yit."

Turning sharply, he spat upon his hands and fell to thinning another row.

Ah, but he was a worker. Let it be rolling logs, splitting rails, or cutting with a cradle, he stood above them all. And many a hot August day when "the monkey was riding" old man McLaughlin's hands in the bottom, Eddie's loud halloo could be heard among them, urging them on to their fodder-pulling.—But he had a bad temper. —Three hundred bundles a day was easy for him. Yea, he could pull five stacks in a week; had done it all right. And to-day he had set a new mark. Three acres of grassy cotton chopped out by one man was a record. He thought about it. Who could equal it? But on this day he was mad, mad to the bottom. Mad and hurt. And his hurt and anger drove him, beat on him like a flail. He had quarreled with Ola. Aih, worse than that, he had slapped her. A little slap, not much—he glanced at his heavy hands.

But he had stood enough to make any man mad. What had got into her nohow? Here he was with the

* Reprinted from *Wide Fields* by Paul Green through arrangement with the publishers, Robert M. McBride & Company.

grass eating his cotton up and he hoeing his liver out trying to save it. So much rainy weather. And she. —Lying up in the house down there in the field, doing nothing—ready to spend every cent she could get, buying lace and jewelry from the peddlers who passed in the lane. "Says she's done working in the fields, she does," he muttered wrathfully. "Yea, but I'll see!" And his hoe flew over the ground. He had had no dinner, his stomach was empty. Evening was coming on. Everything looked gray, lonesome, it shore did. And now he'd have to go on home. The mule and cow had to be fed and there were the shoats too. "Dang, I didn't never plan on things like this!"

He loved Ola, always had. —Temper it was. Too much temper. His mother used to say it would bring him trouble. He'd ought to be patient. Still, she had tried him—worried him nigh to death it seemed. And now he remembered that in their courting days old man McLaughlin had warned him of Ola's dressing and finery. Her pappy and mammy couldn't satisfy her. They were too poor. Take a bank to hold her, he had said. That's right, she didn't treat him decent, and he slaving day in and day out to get ready and buy a piece of land of their own. They were both the children of tenant farmers, the grandchildren of tenant farmers, the great-grandchildren, and on back. But he'd change it for himself. He'd pay taxes on his own land before he died, he would. Aih, she knew it when she married him and seemed glad. He stamped and spat upon the ground.

He tore through a dozen more rows before the dusk came down. And when the moon had begun to shine up in the middle of the sky, he laid his hoe down and stood gazing over the wide rich fields. He would make big cotton here, a bale and a half to the acre and more maybe.

And over there towards the hollow was his corn, popping with strength and as green as poison. He was a farmer and this was his, the earth was his. It was fine, aye it was, bless God. This level forty acres would be his in a year or two. McLaughlin had promised it as soon as he could pay a thousand down. Money. Ola would have to quit spending his money. Not another cent to waste, not another damn red. It was foolish. It was foolish for her always to be looking through Sears-Roebuck's catalogue, picking out lace curtains and tablecloths and window-shades. He'd told her a thousand times. And then this morning—yea, God! —With a muttered oath, he turned and went off through the darkness home.

He fed the mule and cow and the clamorous pigs. As he came up the walk to the house where Ola had wasted a lot of good guano planting a border of cannas, he saw her sitting on the porch in a cool white dress. His heart softened towards her and he could have taken her in his arms. She was sweet. She was always clean and cool and sweet. He stopped before the steps embarrassed, trying to think of something to say. The lamp was lighted on the table in the room, and he saw the waiting supper spread out on a new white tablecloth. Aih, that was it—finery! She would ruin him yet. His heart hardened again.

"Supper's ready," she said. "I got tired of waiting and had mine."

He went on into the kitchen, soused his face and arms in a pan of water and dried them hurriedly on a fresh towel, then seated himself to his meal.

"Don't you want nothing more, Ola?" he called.

"I've et," she answered.

He leaned over the table eating in huge mouthfuls. He fed his hunger with beans, side-meat, corn-bread, preserves, and a few pieces of fried chicken, washing it all down with great gulps of black coffee. His sweaty arms made streaks on the new cloth, but what did he care, consumed as he was by hunger and the thoughts within?

When he had finished, he sat picking bits of meat from his teeth with his finger-nails. Now and then he could hear Ola stirring in her chair on the porch. He was tired and sleepy, and if all was right he might go happily to bed against the next day's labor. But now—No, he was too worried to sleep. She was out there thinking things. He would go out and talk to her.

Sitting down on the steps, he took off his shoes and stretched his feet in the soft sand of the walk. He waited, hoping she would say something for he could find no words. But she held her peace. Time went by and drowsiness began to steal over him. Like a dream he heard the frogs creaking down near the mill-pond, and an owl screaming further in the swamp beyond.

"You're sweaty. The tub's by the well there." Her words startled him. He fumbled with his shoes and made no answer. Presently she went into the house and brought him some soap and a rag. As she came near him the odor of sweet cologne entered his nostrils. She was sweet enough to eat—sweet—

"Peddler been by to-day?" he asked quietly, choking down his anger.

"No," she answered, coldly, "no."

"Looks like a new tablecloth. Thought maybe you'd been a-buying."

"Your money didn't buy it. It was brung to me." She turned sharply and sat again in her chair.

"Who brung it?"

"Ella and her friend from Raleigh. They et dinner here."

"A high-collared dude, riding round this busy time of the year. He'd better stay away from here. I could take him in my two hands and break him like a dead dog-fennel." Ola laughed softly. "Now what do you mean by that?"

"I'm going to Raleigh to-morrow with him to visit Ella awhile."

"And the grass eating up our crop!" he cried incredulously.

"Yes."

"By God, you won't," he roared wrathfully, as he got up and began walking back and forth in the yard.

"I'm going, I tell you," and her voice quavered. "I'm gonna get a rest from your slaving and sweating and your dirt and all."

"Well, for God's sakes, listen at her!"

"I won't be run to death. Pa didn't run me to death."

"And look at him. He's gonna die in the pore-house. And I ain't, I tell you." He slumped down on the steps, hugging his knees in anger.

"And this morning you hit me. If Pa knowed it, he'd come over here with his gun and shoot you down like a dog." Now she began sobbing.

"Dry up, dry up I tell you.—Hanh!" He snorted scornfully, "I'd grab him up and bust his brains out ag'in the ground." He got to his feet and slammed his way into the house. "All right," he called back. "Go on if you wish. You'll be back in a week." And he went to bed.

All night she sat on the porch, listening to his heavy snores coming from the little back room. When the dawn broke beyond the old mill and chickens flew out of the china tree with a clatter, she got up and started breakfast.

While the biscuits were baking she went out and milked the cow for the last time.

Ed rose and ate his meal in silence. When he'd filed his hoe and started into the fields he stopped and called. "Going, are you?"

"I am," she said.

"Well go and be damned," he shouted, and off he went up the path, kicking the dust before him.

Again a second day he hoed from morn till evening. The fiery sun burned down upon his back, drying up the sweat and leaving splotches of salt upon his shirt. When night came he had another three acres hoed clean and standing up for the siding plough. Again he went home under the moon, devoured by hunger and thoughts within.

The house was closed and there was no light. He found a note stuck in the door. "I am gone. Don't look for me till you see me coming," it said. He could read the clear letters in the moonlight. Tearing the paper into bits, he made his way to the lot to feed. When he had cooked his supper, he gorged himself and lay down in his clothes on the bed. Soon again his snores echoed through the house.

The next morning he awoke and called her. And then he remembered that she had left him. It seemed as if his head flew all to pieces, for he began cursing in loud oaths, cursing her curtains, cursing her trimmings, and he even seized one of her flower-pots and hurled it into the yard. The calendars and magazine covers shook on the wall with the violence of his voice. He cooked his breakfast in the same unwashed pans and ate out of the same dirty plate of the night before. Why should he clean up now? Let the house rot down. Let the maggots work in the dishes. God knows, he didn't care.

All that week he did mountains of work. He hoed and

ploughed and ploughed and hoed, driving his mule up and down the windy fields like one possessed. Old McLaughlin came and tried to commiserate with him, but grief and anger were eating in his heart like lye. He said, "Please let me alone." The loneliness of the house, aih, that harried him to death. He became restless and unable to sleep at night. And on Sunday morning when he had shaved himself and sat alone on the porch staring across the wide burning fields, he gave in. Fishing out a stub of a pencil, he wrote, "Deer Ola," he said, "Won't you come back? i speck i done you wrong. Ill do better, honest i will. the crop is in good shape. and there ain't so much to do. there aint nobody to churn and theys a pile of eggs i caint eat. Im well and hope the same.—Ed." He set off up the road, dropped it in the mail-box and waited.

The next week he worked, worked and waited. The grass was killed, the cotton sided, and all looked fine. Then came a note from Ola saying, "I am having a good time. Please look in the top bureau drawer and send me my white slippers.—Ola." He was stupified with rage. All that afternoon he sat on the porch unmindful of his crops and the world about him. Near night he rushed into the house and began putting on his store-bought suit. "I'll go get her, I'll go get her," he kept shouting to himself. Hurrying to the barn, he hitched the mule to the buggy and went driving away in a cloud of dust to the north.

Late that night he drove up the shining main street of the capital city. The bright lights astonished, even frightened him. But he held his way. Turning to the right near the middle of the town, he went several blocks eastward and stopped before a small frame house. There was a stir inside and a light came on as he hammered on the door. "Who's that, who's that?" Ella's sleepy voice called.

"It's me," he cried, pushing his way into the hall. "And I want Ola."

A door opened in the hall and Ola came out.

"Ola, Ola," he said, "come home."

"Maybe next year," she said, and gave a little laugh. Ella went away and left them alone.

"Git your things, I tell you," he almost whispered.

"I ain't going. Good night. You're crazy as a fool, Ed."

—Temper, temper, that was it. For he couldn't keep his hands off her—hands that could lift a bale of cotton. —She couldn't make a whisper, not a sound.

Then he stumbled down the walk to his buggy. He'd done it all right. He'd killed her all right. He knew all the time, every long mile to Raleigh, that's the way it 'd be. He'd choke her to death. —Temper, temper. With a clatter of blows, he urged his mule towards the south. A big star was shining above the road he travelled. It caught his eye as he drove, and he rocked his head in grief, "I wisht I was where that star is, clean away. Oh, I do!—" And he sobbed as he passed the moonlit hedges.

When the sheriff came for him in his little house, he was quiet and dignified. Poor fool, he was sitting on the porch dressed in his Sunday best with his head bent over in his hands. The dishes were washed, the floor swept, the flowers watered, and all in order. He went away like a child and stayed so till the last day.

BIOGRAPHICAL NOTES ON THE AUTHORS

BENEFIELD, (JOHN) BARRY. Born in Jefferson, Texas, and a graduate of the University of Texas. For several years Mr. Benefield engaged in newspaper work in Dallas, New York, and Brooklyn. More recently he has been in the publishing business. Three of his books are: *The Chicken-Wagon Family* (1925); *Short Turns* (1926); and *Bugles in the Night* (1927). His present address is Peekskill, New York.

BRAWLEY, BENJAMIN. Born at Columbia, South Carolina, in 1882. He is the author of several books, perhaps the most important being: *A Short History of the American Negro; The Negro in Literature and Art; A Short History of the English Drama; A New Survey of English Literature.* Educated at Morehouse College, the University of Chicago and Harvard, Brawley has been, since 1923, professor of English at Shaw University, a Negro institution at Raleigh, North Carolina. Most of the Negro literary figures have written from New York or Washington; Benjamin Brawley is one of the few who have consistently maintained their residence in the South.

CABLE, GEORGE WASHINGTON. Born in New Orleans, October 12, 1844. His best known volumes are: *Old Creole Days* (1879); *The Grandissimes* (1880); *Madame Delphine* (1881); *Dr. Sevier* (1884); *Bonaventure* (1889); *Bylow Hill* (1902); *Gideon's Band* (1914); and *Lovers of Louisiana* 1918). Cable was a member of the Fourth Mississippi Cavalry. At different times in his life he had worked as a surveyor and in the cotton business and as a reporter on the *Picayune.* After 1884 he lived in Simsbury, Connecticut, and in Northampton, Massachusetts. He died February 8, 1925. Cable's writing reputation springs particularly from his colorful and romantic portrayal of Creole life in Louisiana. (*George W. Cable, His Life and Letters* by Lucy Biklé, a daughter, is the standard biography.)

CHESNUTT, CHARLES WADDELL. Born at Cleveland, Ohio, in 1856. His chief books are: *The Conjure Woman; The House Behind the Cedars;* and *The Colonel's Dream.* Chesnutt, a Negro, spent considerable time in North Carolina where he was a teacher and, for several years, the principal of the State Normal School at Fayetteville. Chesnutt's stories are written more definitely from the point of view of his race than are those of Paul Laurence Dunbar, another Ohio-born Negro who wrote much of his people in the South.

CLARK, EMILY (Mrs. Edwin Swift Balch). Though born in Raleigh, North Carolina, Miss Clark is most frequently associated with Richmond, Virginia, where besides being one of the founders of *The Reviewer* she also served as its editor over a period of years. She has written frequent essays and stories. Her book is *Stuffed Peacocks*.

COBB, IRVIN SHREWSBURY. Born in Paducah, Kentucky, June 23, 1876. Cobb is the author of many books; some of the best known are: *Back Home* (1912); *The Escape of Mr. Trim* (1913); *Old Judge Priest* (1915); *Speaking of Operations* (1916); *Local Color* (1916); *Thunders of Silence* (1918); *Snake Doctor* (1923); and *Goin' on Fourteen* (1924). Irvin S. Cobb was educated in public and private schools and began his reporting on Paducah papers at a very early age. At nineteen he was editor of the *Paducah News*. For several years he has worked for various New York papers and magazines as special writer and humor editor. During 1914-15 he was European war correspondent for the *Saturday Evening Post*. His present home is in New York City.

CRADDOCK, CHARLES EGBERT (Mary Noalles Murfree). Born at Murfreesboro, Tennessee, in 1850. Her best book was her first, a collection of short stories called *In the Tennessee Mountains* (1884). Though Miss Murfree wrote six novels or more, all deeply characterized by her interest in local color, she was never able to repeat the success she attained with her stories,—probably because she persisted in writing novels when her forte was something shorter, more compact than the novel. After a childhood in Murfreesboro and Nashville, Miss Murfree lived in St. Louis for some years, later returning to her native community which she portrayed so frequently in her writing.

DARGAN, OLIVE TILFORD. Born in Grayson County, Kentucky. Educated at the University of Nashville and at Radcliffe. Before her marriage Mrs. Dargan taught school in various Southern states and in Canada. For the past few years she has lived in Western North Carolina, her present residence being in West Asheville. Her first books were poetic drama: *Semiramis and Other Plays* (1904); *Lords and Lovers* (1906); *The Mortal Gods* (1912). Volumes of her poems are: *Path Flower* (1914); *The Cycle's Rim* (1916), and *Lute and Furrow* (1922). Her one collection of stories and sketches is *Highland Annals* (1925).

DUNBAR, PAUL LAURENCE. Born in Dayton, Ohio, June 27, 1872. His first volume of poems was *Lyrics of Lowly Life* which appeared in 1896. He published many volumes of short stories, novels, and poems. The best idea of his poetry will be secured from a reading of *Complete Poems* (1913). His best volumes of short stories are: *Folks From Dixie* and *Strength of Gideon.* Dunbar died February 9, 1906. Most readers of Dunbar's stories will, probably, be impressed by the similarity of his treatment of the Negro with that accorded the race by the white writers of his time, Thomas Nelson Page, Joel Chandler Harris and the rest. There is little of the attitude of the modern Negro toward his people in Dunbar's stories; an Ohioan by birth he writes of the Southern Negro more from without than from within.

FURMAN, LUCY. Born in Henderson, Kentucky. Educated in private schools at Henderson, at Sayre Institute, and at the University of Cincinnati. For many years she was associated with the Hindman (Kentucky) Settlement School of which work she has written in several of her volumes. Some of her books are: *Mothering on Perilous* (1913); *Sight to the Blind* (1915); *The Quare Women* (1923); *The Glass Window* (1925); and *The Lonesome Road* (1927).

GONZALES, AMBROSE ELLIOTT. Born, May 29, 1857, on a plantation in Colleton County, South Carolina. Gonzales contributed to his native state and to the South two literary and cultural gifts—his building up of the *Columbia State,* a newspaper always eager to further literary and artistic intelligence, and four books which speak for the lore and legendry of the Gullah Negro. The books are: *The Black Border; With Æsop Along the Black Border; The Captain;* and *Laguerre.* Here are kept alive the dialect and folk-ways of a people.

GREEN, PAUL. Born near Lillington, North Carolina, March 17, 1894. Some of Mr. Green's books are: *Lonesome Road*

(1926); *In Abraham's Bosom* (1927); *The Field God* (1927); *Wide Fields* (1928); and *In the Valley and Other Carolina Plays* (1928). Green was educated at Buie's Creek Academy, the University of North Carolina, and at Cornell. He is now a professor of philosophy at the University of North Carolina. Primarily a dramatist, Paul Green has published and had acted many plays, one of which, *In Abraham's Bosom*, won the Pulitzer Prize. (For further biographical fact and critical comment see: *Paul Green* by Barrett H. Clark, a pamphlet published by Robert M. McBride).

HARRIS, JOEL CHANDLER. Born in the neighborhood of Eatonton, Georgia, December 9, 1848. Early newspaper work brought him in 1877 the recognition of the Atlanta *Constitution* on the staff of which he served many years. His first Uncle Remus sketch was published in this paper on November 28, 1876. His first Uncle Remus volume was *Uncle Remus, His Songs and Sayings* (1880). This was followed by many others, some of the better known being: *Nights With Uncle Remus* (1883); *Uncle Remus and His Friends* (1892); *Told by Uncle Remus* (1905); and *Uncle Remus and the Little Boy* (1910). Harris wrote various books besides the Remus volumes. Some of these are: *Free Joe and Other Sketches* (1887); *Sister Jane* (1896); and *Gabriel Tolliver* (1902). Toward the end of his career, Harris edited the *Uncle Remus Magazine*. He died July 3, 1908. The standard biography is that of Julia Collier Harris: *The Life of Joel Chandler Harris*. In addition to the reputation he holds for the charm and grace of his Negro stories, Harris has taken high rank as a student of the folk-lore of the American Negro.

HEARN, LAFCADIO. Born on a Greek island in 1850 and educated in Ireland, England, and France, Hearn belongs to American literature only through the fact that he began his writing career here before going to Japan. For ten years (1877-1887) Hearn contributed essays, sketches, and editorials to New Orleans' journals, papers which have since his death been collected by editors into three or more volumes: *Fantastics and Other Fancies* (1914); *Creole Sketches* (1924); and *An American Miscellany* (1924). Hearn's life, one of the most fascinating in all modern literature, may be read either in Elizabeth Bisland's *Life and Letters of Lafcadio Hearn* or E. L.

Tinker's *Lafcadio Hearn's American Days.* Hearn died in Tokyo, Japan, in 1904.

HENRY, O. (William Sydney Porter). Born in Greensboro, North Carolina, September 11, 1862. A few of his many short collections are: *Cabbages and Kings* (1904); *Heart of the West* (1907); *Voice of the City* (1908); *The Four Million* (1909); *Options* (1909); *Roads of Destiny* (1909); *Strictly Business* (1910); *Whirligigs* (1910). A good one volume selection of his stories is that edited by C. Alphonso Smith. Porter was educated by his aunt in a private school at Greensboro. He had a varied experience with life, working as a drug clerk, as draftsman, living on a Texas ranch, as teller in an Austin, Texas, bank. Upon the failure of the bank and his being charged with embezzlement, Porter, who insisted on his innocence, escaped to Central America, returning to Austin in 1897 upon learning of his wife's serious illness. After his return he was convicted and served from 1898 to 1901 as a druggist's assistant in the Ohio penitentiary. He had published before taking up his life in prison, but with the beginning of his Columbus experience he turned his attention seriously to the writing of short stories. The "O. Henry" appears to have been first used as a pseudonym in 1901. After release from Columbus, Porter went to New York where recognition came rapidly to him. (The standard biography of Porter is by C. Alphonso Smith: *O. Henry Biography.*)

HEYWARD, DUBOSE. Born in Charleston, South Carolina, August 31, 1885. Educated in the public schools of Charleston and engaging in business there, he has done much of his writing about that city. As organizer, along with John Bennett and Hervey Allen, of the Poetry Society of his state, Mr. Heyward's influence on the poetic development of the South has been great. Heyward has published two volumes of poetry, *Carolina Chansons* (1922) with Hervey Allen and *Skylines and Horizons* (1924). Since 1924 Heyward has turned his attention chiefly to prose writing. His first novel, *Porgy* (1925) is a story of Charleston; his second, *Angel* (1926) portrays the life of mountain people in North Carolina; his third, *Mamba's Daughters* (1929) returns to Charleston for its background. *The Half Pint Flask* used in this collection is one of few short stories which Mr. Heyward has published.

JOHNSTON, RICHARD MALCOLM. Born on the family plantation "Oak Grove," in Hancock County, Georgia, March 8, 1822. His early education was in an old "field school" near home; this was followed by study at Mercer University. Later he prepared himself for the law by studying while he was teaching. He was, for a while, professor of literature at the University of Georgia giving up this work to start a private school for boys which he later moved from Georgia to Maryland. By all odds his most famous book is *Dukesborough Tales* (1871) though he also wrote other stories and several volumes of essays, biography, and school texts. Other worthwhile books are: *Old Mark Langston* (1883) and *Mr. Absalom Billingslea and Other Georgia Folk* (1888). Johnston died in Baltimore, Maryland, September 23, 1898.

KING, GRACE ELIZABETH. Born in New Orleans, Louisiana, 1852. Miss King's long list of books and serious interest in the city and state of her birth have won her a recognized position as an authoritative interpreter of her region. Some of her many books are: *Monsieur Motte; Tales of Time and Place; New Orleans the Place and the People; Balcony Stories; History of Louisiana; Pleasant Ways of St. Médard;* and *La Dame de Sainte Hermine.* Miss King resides at 1749 Coliseum Place, New Orleans.

LONGSTREET, AUGUSTUS BALDWIN. Born at Augusta, Georgia, September 22, 1790. He was educated privately and at Richmond Academy going later to the Yale Law School. He practiced law in his native state and, in 1822, was made Judge of the Superior Court in Georgia. Later Longstreet gave up the law for the ministry, became president of Emory University, and, in turn, president of Centenary College, the University of Mississippi, and South Carolina College. He died at Oxford, Mississippi, September 9, 1870. He wrote much on politics, religion, and related questions, but his literary reputation rests firmly on one volume: *Georgia Scenes.* The standard Longstreet biography is that by John Donald Wade: *Augustus Baldwin Longstreet.*

MARTIN, GEORGE MADDEN (Mrs. Attwood R. Martin). Born in Louisville, Kentucky, May 3, 1866. Some of her best known books are: *Emmy Lou—Her Book and Heart* (1902); *House of Fulfillment; Abbie Ann* (1907); *War-*

wickshire Lad (1916); *Children of the Mist* (1920); and *March On* (1921). Educated in the public schools of Louisville, Mrs. Martin still maintains her residence in that city.

PAGE, THOMAS NELSON. Born at Oakland, Virginia, April 23, 1853. His first collection of short stories was *In Ole Virginia* (1887). Page was educated at Washington and Lee and was graduated from the law school of the University of Virginia in 1874. His greatest contribution is as a romancer writing about the South at the time of the War Between the States. From 1913 to 1919, Page was United States Ambassador to Italy. (The standard biography is *Thomas Nelson Page, a Memoir of a Virginia Gentleman,* by Rosewell Page, a brother).

PATTERSON, PERNET. Born in Henrico County, near Richmond, Virginia, in 1882, of French-Scotch-English ancestors who settled in Virginia in 1700. He was educated privately before attending the public schools, the Virginia Military Institute, and the Stevens Institute of Technology. Denied the companionship of white boys by the nature of his plantation environment, Patterson early grew to know the Negro. Their beliefs and superstitions became nearly his own. This familiarity with the plantation Negro it is which gives particular distinction to Mr. Patterson's stories.

PETERKIN, JULIA. Born October 31, 1880, in Laurens, South Carolina, and a graduate at sixteen from Converse College. Her rise to literary prominence has been very sudden, her earlier work appearing only a few years ago in *The Reviewer* (Richmond). She is the author of three books: *Green Thursday, Black April,* and *Scarlet Sister Mary*. Her home is the Lang Syne Plantation, Fort Motte, South Carolina.

ROBERTS, ELIZABETH MADOX. Born near Springfield, Kentucky. Her first published work was a volume of verse: *Under the Tree* (1922). Since then Miss Roberts has won a fine reputation for herself as a writer of novels. Her other books are: *The Time of Man* (1926); *My Heart and My Flesh* (1927); *Jingling in the Wind* (1928); and *The Great Meadow* (1930). Miss Roberts' forebears settled in Kentucky in 1803, having moved over from Virginia. She has attended the University of Chicago, and lived in the Colorado

Rockies and in California, but always she has been a Kentuckian writing and thinking of her native state. Essentially a novelist famed for the grace and subtlety of her prose, Miss Roberts has written few short stories. *On the Mountain-Side,* her story included in this volume, somewhat misrepresents Miss Roberts' usual background, since she is not so much a writer of the Kentucky mountains as of the region between Harrodsburg and Louisville. (For a further biographical fact and critical comment see: *Elizabeth Madox Roberts,* a brochure including brief papers about Miss Roberts by seven writers. Issued by the Viking Press).

SAXON, LYLE. Born in Louisiana, September 4, 1891. Educated at Louisiana State University and worked for ten years as a newspaperman in various places, but his longest service was on *the Times-Picayune* of New Orleans. Saxon has contributed to various magazines and newspapers and had short stories included in various collections. His books are: *Father Mississippi* (1927); *Fabulous New Orleans* (1928); and *Old Louisiana* (1929). Saxon now lives in Baton Rouge, Louisiana.

SIMMS, WILLIAM GILMORE. Born in Charleston, South Carolina, April 17, 1806. The author of a long list of volumes, most of them concerned with the Revolution and frontier life in South Carolina, Simms has come to be associated always with Cooper as the chief romancer of frontier and Indian life in America. Particularly is he the exponent of South Carolina history. He wrote several biographies (of such figures as Marion, Captain John Smith, and General Greene) and a host of novels, the most popular titles being, perhaps: *Martin Faber* (1833); *Guy Rivers* (1834); *The Yemasee* (1835); *Woodcraft* (1852); *Eutaw* (1856); and *The Cassique of Kiawah* (1859). Simms received only a meagre schooling as his father had lost his fortune when Simms was a boy. He served as an apprentice to a druggist at one period. Later on he visited his father on a plantation in Mississippi, a visit important to his later writing since it brought him considerable familiarity with frontier life in the South. Prolific in his writing, a born story teller (though not always artistically restrained) he became the center of the South Carolina literary group at his home, Woodlands, until the house there was destroyed in 1865 by Sherman. Simms died in 1870 never fully recognized for the merit which has been since accorded him.

STEELE, WILBUR DANIEL. Born in Greensboro, North Carolina, March 17, 1886. Mr. Steele has written various volumes: plays, novels, and collections of short stories. Among the novels are: *The Isles of the Blest* (1924); *Taboo* (1925); and *Meat* (1928). Collections of short stories are: *Land's End* (1918); *Urkey Island* (1926); *The Man Who Saw Through Heaven* (1927); *The Tower of Sand* (1929). *The Terrible Woman* (1925) is a collection of plays. Steele was graduated from the University of Denver in 1907. Later he studied art in Boston, Paris, and New York. His stories are drawn from an extensive familiarity with many lands and people and are frequently marked by an atmosphere of the supernatural. Mr. Steele has been conceded by many critics the first position among contemporary story writers of America.

A SUGGESTED BIBLIOGRAPHY OF SINGLE STORIES RELATED TO THE SOUTH

Author	Story	Source
Adams, Ned	Nigger to Nigger	*Scribner's Mag.*, July 1928
Alexander, Sandra	The Gift	*The Reviewer*, April 1925
Bradford, Roark	Child of God	*Harpers Mag.*, April 1927
	River Witch	*The Forum*, Nov. 1927
	Cold Death	*Harpers Mag.*, July 1928
	The Final Run of Hopper Joe Wiley	*Saturday Eve. Post.*, Jan. 5, 1929
Burt, Struthers	Beauty and the Blantons, in *They Could Not Sleep*	Scribner's
Carver, Ada Jack	Cotton Dolly	*Harpers Mag.*, December 1927
	Redbone	*Harpers Mag.*, February 1925
	Treeshy	*Harpers Mag.*, February 1926
	Singing Woman	*Harpers Mag.*, May 1927
	The Old One	*Harpers Mag.*, October 1926
Chapman, Maristan	Treat You Clever	*Saturday Eve. Post*, March 30, 1929
	Sib to We'uns	*Century*, Nov. 1928
Cobb, Irvin S.	Romantic River	*Cosmopolitan*, July, August, September, November, December, 1927: January, April, June, September 1928
	Snake Doctor	O. Henry Memorial Prize Stories of 1922
	Boys Will be Boys	O'Brien Best Short Stories of 1917
	No Dam' Yankee	*Cosmopolitan*, November 1927
	Blacker Than Sin, in *Local Color*	George H. Doran
Connolly, J. B.	Down River, in *Head Winds*	Scribner's
Daniels, Roger	Bulldog	*Saturday Eve. Post*, Nov. 13, 1926
Dickson, Harris	Black Sheep's Wool	*Saturday Eve. Post*, Oct. 12, 1929

	The Fishhook Lawyer	*Saturday Eve. Post*, Oct. 20, 1928
	The Tail Puller	*Saturday Eve. Post*, July 24, 1926
Edwards, Harry Stillwell	The Blue Hen's Chicken	*Scribner's Mag.*, October 1923
Fauset, Arthur Huff	Symphonesque	O. Henry Memorial Award Prize Stories of 1926
French, Alice	Half a Curse, Whitsun Harp, Regulator, The Bishop's Vagabond, and Ma' Bowlin'—all in *Knitters in the Sun*	Houghton Mifflin
Gordon, Armistead C.	Panjorum Bucket	*Scribner's Mag.*, February 1920
	The Silent Infare	*Scribner's Mag.*, March 1916
Haardt, Sara	Mendelian Dominant	*American Mercury*, March 1926
Hergesheimer, Joseph	Charleston	*Saturday Eve. Post*, July 9, 1927
Heyward, DuBose	Crown's Bess	*Forum*, August 1925
	The Storm	*Bookman*, Oct. 1925
Johnston, Mary	Nemesis	*Century*, May 1923
Lane, Rose Wilder	Yarbwoman	*Harpers Mag.*, July 1927
Niles, John J.	Hill Billies	*Scribner's Mag.*, November 1927
Patterson, Pernet	Conjur	*The Atlantic Monthly*, December 1928
Peterkin, Julia	The Sorcerer	*American Mercury*, April 1925
	Maum Lou	*The Reviewer*, April 1925
	Heart Leaves	*Saturday Eve. Post*, Oct. 5, 1929
Ravenel, Beatrice	Something to Remember	*Harpers Mag.*, January 1920
Risley, Eleanor	Mountaineers and Mill Folks	*Atlantic Monthly*, November 1928
Roberts, Elizabeth M.	Death at Bearwallow	*American Caravan*, 1927
	Buried Treasure	*Harpers Mag.*, Dec. 1929 and Jan. 1930
	Children of the Earth	*Harpers Mag.*, November 1928

Robinson, Robert	The Ill Wind	*Collier's Weekly*, Aug. 29, 1925
Saxon, Lyle	The Long Furrow	*Century*, October 1927
	Cane River	*Dial*, March 1926
Smith, Edgar Valentine	Freed	*Scribner's Mag.*, June 1929
	Pardoned	*Harpers Mag.*, July 1925
	Cameo	*Harpers Mag.*, December 1924
	Prelude	*Harpers Mag.*, May 1923
	'Lijah	*Harpers Mag.*, August 1924
	Substance of Things Hoped For	*Harpers Mag.*, August 1923
Steele, Wilbur Daniel	Satan Am A Snake	*Harpers Mag.*, August 1928
Stimson, F. J.	By Due Process of Law	*Scribners' Mag.*, April 1923
Stribling, T. S.	The Return of the Sledger	*Everybody's*, Dec. 1923
Tarleton, Fiswoode	Curtains	*Golden Book*, November 1928
Toomer, Jean	Blood-Burning Moon	*Prairie* March-April 1923
Weeks, Raymond	The Hound-Tuner of Callaway	Columbia University Press
Young, Stark	Grandfather McGehee's Wedding, in *Heaven Trees*	Scribner's
	The Poorhouse Goes to the Circus	*Scribner's Mag.*, December 1929

A SUGGESTED BIBLIOGRAPHY OF VOLUMES PRESENTING SHORT STORIES RELATED TO THE SOUTH

Author	Title	Publisher
Adams, Andy	Cattle Brands	Houghton Mifflin
Allen, James Lane	Flute and Violin and Other Kentucky Tales	Macmillan
	Landmark	Macmillan
	The Doctor's Christmas Eve' and Other Stories	Macmillan
Baldwin, Joseph G.	The Flush Times of Alabama and Mississippi	American Book Company
Benefield, Barry	Short Turns	Century
Bradford, Roark	Ol' Man Adam an' His Chillun	Harper
Cable, George W.	Strange True Stories of Louisiana	Scribner's
	Old Creole Days	Scribner's
Cabell, James Branch	Gallantry	McBride
	Line of Love	McBride
	Certain Hour	McBride
	Chivalry	McBride
Catherwood, Mary H.	The Queen of the Swamp and Other Plain Americans	Houghton Mifflin
Chesnutt, Charles W.	The Conjure Woman	Houghton Mifflin
Chopin, Kate	Bayou Folk	Houghton Mifflin
	A Night in Acadie	Way and William
Clark, Emily	Stuffed Peacocks	Knopf
Cobb, Irvin S.	Back Home	George H. Doran
	Old Judge Priest	George H. Doran
	The Escape of Mr. Trimm	George H. Doran
Cooke, John Esten	Stories of the Old Dominion	American Book Company
Craddock, Charles Egbert	The Young Mountaineers	Houghton Mifflin
	In the Tennessee Mountains	Houghton Mifflin
Dargan, Olive	Highland Annals	Scribner's

Author	Title	Publisher
DEVEREUX, MARGARET	Plantation Sketches	Privately Printed by Riverside Press
DOBIE, J. FRANK	A Vaquero of the Brush Country	Southwest Press
DUNBAR, PAUL LAURENCE	Folks from Dixie	Dodd, Mead
	Strength of Gideon	Dodd, Mead
EDWARDS, HARRY STILLWELL	Eneas Africanus and Other Stories	J. W. Burke
	His Defense and Other Stories	Century
	Marbeau Cousins	Century
	Two Runaways and Other Stories	Century
EGGLESTON, G. C.	Southern Soldier Stories	Macmillan
	The Warrens of Virginia	Dillingham
FOX, JOHN JR.	Hell fer Sartain and Other Stories	Scribner's
	Christmas Eve' on Lonesome	Scribner's
	In Happy Valley	Scribner's
	A Cumberland Vendetta and Other Stories	Scribner's
FURMAN, LUCY	The Quare Women	Little, Brown
	The Glass Window	Little, Brown
GREER, HILTON R. (Ed.)	Best Short Stories from the Southwest	Southwest Press
GONZALES, AMBROSE E.	Black Border; Gullah Stories of the Carolina Coast	State Company
	Captain; Stories of the Black Border	State Company
	Laguerre; a Gascon of the Black Border	State Company
GREEN, PAUL	Wide Fields	McBride
HARLAND, MARION	In Our County, Stories of Old Virginia Life	Putnam
HARRIS, JOEL CHANDLER	Mingo and Other Sketches in Black and White	Houghton Mifflin
	Free Joe; and other Georgia Sketches	Houghton Mifflin
	On the Wing of Occasions	Doubleday, Page
	Tales of the Home Folks in Peace and War	Houghton Mifflin

	Uncle Remus, His Songs and His Sayings	Appleton
	Nights with Uncle Remus	Houghton Mifflin
	Balaam and His Master, and Other Sketches and Stories	Houghton Mifflin
	Uncle Remus and his Friends	Houghton Mifflin
HEARN, LAFCADIO	An American Miscellany	Dodd, Mead
	Occidental Gleanings	Dodd, Mead
	Fantastics and Other Fancies	Houghton Mifflin
	Chita	Harper & Bros.
HENRY, O.	Selected Stories from O. Henry, Edited by C. Alphonso Smith	Doubleday, Page
HEYWARD, DUBOSE	The Half Pint Flask	Farrar & Rinehart
JOHNSTON, RICHARD MALCOLM	Old Times in Middle Georgia	Macmillan
	Dukesborough Tales	Appleton
KENNEDY, R. EMMET	Black Cameos	A. & C. Boni
	Gritny People	Dodd, Mead
KING, GRACE	Balcony Stories	Macmillan
	Tales of a Time and Place	Harper & Bros.
LONGSTREET, AUGUSTUS BALDWIN	Georgia Scenes	Harper & Bros.
MACKAYE, PERCY	Tall Tales of the Kentucky Mountains	George H. Doran
MARTIN, GEORGE MADDEN	Children of the Mist	Appleton
PAGE, THOMAS NELSON	In Ole Virginia	Scribner's
	The Burial of the Guns and Other Stories	Scribner's
PETERKIN, JULIA	Green Thursday	Knopf
RUTLEDGE, ARCHIBALD	Days Off in Dixie	Doubleday, Page
	Heart of the South	State Company
SALE, JOHN B.	The Tree Named John	University of North Carolina Press
SASS, HERBERT RAVENEL	Way of the Wild	Minton, Balch
SAXON, LYLE	Old Louisiana	Century

SMITH, F. HOPKINSON	Colonel Carter of Cartersville	Houghton Mifflin
STUART, RUTH MCENERY	Napoleon Jackson, the Gentleman of the Plush Rocker	Century
	In Simpkinville	Harper & Bros.
	Moriah's Mourning	Harper & Bros.
	The Golden Wedding and Other Tales	Harper & Bros.
WISTER, OWEN	When West was West	Macmillan
WOOLSON, CONSTANCE F.	Rodman the Keeper	Harper & Bros.